Just A Matter Of Time

Until the End of Time

Arnold Kropp

Acknowledgments

Appreciation goes to the Novel Idea group at the senior center: to Mary for her leadership, to Rita, and her steadfast editing and critique work sentence by sentence from the beginning to the end. And to all the others for comments and edits. They've been a blessing in encouragement and helpfulness. Thanks to all of you.

This is a work of fiction. Names, characters, businesses, places, events, locales, and incidents are either the products of the author's imagination or used in a fictitious manner. Any resemblance to actual persons, living or dead, or actual events is purely coincidental.

Copyright © 2019 by Arnold Kropp.

Cover design Copyright © 2010 by the Author.

Author picture by Glenna Watkins Renflo.

All Rights reserved.

Published through IngramSpark.

ISBN 978-0-578-60371-1

Tic-Toc,

Tic-Toc.

The clock is ticking, so let's start.

ONE

Janice Amwestson carefully steps between the rows of vegetables in her backyard garden alongside the greenhouse. She looks over the roof of the greenhouse, her ears tuned for a whirling noise. She directs her gaze over the house, into the blanket of treetops, as the rising sun illuminates the scattered white fluffy clouds. *Another beautiful day.*

Her husband, Robert, hollers out the back door, "Honey, I'm leaving. I may be a bit later at the office. I'm taking the bike. Got that meeting tomorrow evening."

"Be careful," Janice replies as the screen door squeaks.

Janice has a wicker basket over her left forearm that holds a few of the selectively chosen first ripened tomatoes, an immature head of iceberg lettuce, and a few cucumbers. She methodically bites into a tomato concentrating on the taste. Looking at the other half, she wonders at the complexity of the intricate design. *How magnificent this is.*

Arlene's voice from the other side of the picket fence interrupts her thoughts. "Hey, Jan. How's it going? Are those the first?"

"Oh, good morning Arlene," Janice answers, looking to her neighbor standing near the vine-topped gazebo.

"Didn't disturb you, did I?" Arlene asks.

"No, no," Janice replies. "What's going on with you guys? Anything new?" Smiling, Janice gently steps over the row of lettuce and onto the double railroad tie border. "Here, try one of these." Janice picks a cherry tomato out of the basket and hands it over the wood fence to Arlene. "They're terrific, but you'll have to get your salt."

Until the End of Time

"Thanks." Arlene slowly bites the tomato in half.

"How many of those white seeds are in there?" Janice shares her thoughts. "It's amazing whenever I take the time to look at the details of these things we thoughtlessly bite into. We enjoy the flavor while thinking of something else, never pondering the nature of a simple tomato. How did it grow up from one of those white seeds? What enables it to do that?"

"Huh?"

"You weren't listening?"

"My mind was wandering again," Arlene replies. "You guys still having that meeting?"

"Yes, you're coming, aren't you?"

"No, Charlie changed his mind. And I agree. It's too much."

"What do you mean, too much?"

"Well, come on, Jan, don't you think you're getting into dangerous territory? You're crossing the line."

Janice interrupts. "We've heard that before, and we'll handle that if it comes. But I wish you would. After what happened to the Smiths, you're going to drop it? You guys were all for it. Why the change?"

"We've got to protect ourselves now that our retirements are so close. We could lose everything Charlie's worked so hard for, and mine too. Now the kids, they need our help."

"Why? What happened? Are they all right?" Janice responds.

"Not that well. It's falling apart. We learned last night that Bruce might lose his job, and Maycie is experiencing excruciating pains from that recent back surgery. He told us that the doctor couldn't increase the medications."

"I'm sorry." Janice reaches across the fence to touch Arlene's hand.

"She tries to sleep through it, has even thought of putting the girls in the developmental center. Bruce is beside himself. He called 911 the other night, but they told him that unless she was in imminent danger, they couldn't dispense an ambulance."

"That sounds about right."

"Bruce would have to take her to the ER and bring the kids along too. But the insurance wouldn't pay for it if his doctor would not allow the additional dosage. He is blaming himself for her accident. He's been to confession a dozen times. He took time off work to stay with her through the first couple weeks, and now he's about to be fired. Something about insurance."

"You're still going to take that trip to Alaska?" Janice asks.

"Nah, that's been put on hold. You guys pray. Remember us, will you?"

"Sure, Arlene. I'll mention it at the meeting."

"Thanks, we're packing to head over there to see . . . Well, to comfort them, see the kids, and engage Maycie a bit. Try to get her mind sidetracked from her body discomfort. And, ah, to give Bruce a break too."

"Good for you. Tell Maycie that we'll be praying for her. Here, she may enjoy some fresh fruit." Janice hands Arlene the basket.

"Thanks."

"Keep me informed."

"I may stay a week or so. You may not hear from me until I get back."

Arlene looks to the sky around the homes and leans in close to the fence, whispering, "You have any OxyContin left over from Robert's surgery?"

"Huh?"

"Yes, that pain medicine Robert had."

"Even if we did, you know I can't give you any."

"Oh, come on. Nobody will know."

"I'll know."

"I'm not going to tell anyone. Maycie is suffering."

"Arlene, it's wrong and against the law."

"Come now! It's for Maycie. She needs something."

"I can't. You know that."

Arlene's demeanor turns sour. "Yeah, you and all your self-righteous bunch. You go out helping the homeless and won't help a neighbor."

Until the End of Time

"Arlene. I can't. You know that."

"Yeah, you do it all the time on those trips you take."

"No, I don't."

"Yeah, you do." Arlene looks up and loudly says into the air. "There's a meeting here tomorrow."

"Arlene, stop it," Janice yells, trying to reach across the fence for her neighbor's hand. "I know you're up against a wall. We'd both be in trouble. You're a good friend, and I'd do anything for you, but this, you know I can't."

"Oh, forget it." Arlene turns away, stomps back toward the house, muttering, "Go ahead have that meeting of yours. Get back into that closet. Damn hypocrites!"

"Arlene, wait! Arlene!" Janice shouts as her friend slams the door. Janice freezes, dumbfounded. She stares at the screen door. *Is this a nightmare? A dream? What happened? What? What? Why?* Forgetting the veggies, Janice slowly walks back to the house, pausing every few steps to look toward Arlene's back door. "Why, Lord? Why?" She steps up on the deck and takes one last look at Arlene's back door.

Janice was studying to become a hospitality nurse, while Robert concentrated his time in construction and engineering at the second-tier academy outside Boulder, Colorado. A few months after graduating, they got permission to marry and moved to this area of northeast Oregon twenty-two years ago. Robert had accepted a position with a local construction company. Their house sits on a cul-de-sac of four homes backing up to a forest. It was the acre of an open backyard that enticed Janice and her love of gardening.

Entering the kitchen, Janice hears Jimmy coming down the tiled floor hallway.

"Boys, come on, let's go," Janice hollers.

"Mom, Franko is picking us up this morning," Jimmy says.

"Where's your brother?"

"He left his tab in the basement."

Hearing the soft whirl outside, Janice opens the door to the basement, "Johnathon, Franko is here."

"I'm coming! I'm coming!"

Just a Matter of Time

Janice turns to Jimmy. Leaning forward on her tiptoes, she whispers in his ear, "Love you." Relaxing the embrace, she looks into Jimmy's eyes. "Now, I want to see that diploma when you get home." Johnathon approaches with a soft black briefcase and steps into his mother's arms.

"This is it, guys. Your last day at the Academy."

The twins had accepted the appointment to study and to acquire the skills in the art of sculptured cabinetry and stone masonry in the Arts and Crafts Academy. Today, they will graduate. In the fall, they will assume their assignments to a works apprenticeship program. According to their birth records, Jimmy is the oldest by three minutes. He will receive the gifts of inheritance and enjoy life in one of the portable dwellings. Johnathon, the second-born, will live in the dormitory until he finishes the one-year apprenticeship.

The boys have always wanted to stay together. All the fun they've had messing with others as to who is who. "You Jim? No, you're John. Dang it, guys stop it."

Now, it's time to relax and have fun. They've applied for a summer exploring the Grand Canyon but have not yet received permission.

From the steps of the front door, Janice watches them board the school copter. It hovers over the yard, and away it goes skimming over the treetops to deliver the twins to the Academy.

Going back into the house, Janice pauses in front of the mirror, brushes her hair back, smooths the rouge on her cheeks, and freshens her lips. With her purse strapped over her shoulder, she exits the kitchen. She presses the screen to open the car and garage door.

Relaxed and belted in the back seat, the charging cord releases. Pushing a button on the dashboard screen, Janice speaks to the screen, "Office."

A response announces, "Arrival time seven-twenty-two."

The car backs into the cul-de-sac. The garage door closes. The three-passenger vehicle pulls forward and slows at the corner yield sign. Following the stripes, the car slowly approaches the boulevard traffic light that changes to green. And off it goes taking her to the office, while she reviews her schedule for the day.

TWO

In his office, Robert has been talking on the phone with the crew chief of the re-habilitation government project the company is working on in the Reno Nevada Hills. The agency appointed Bilko Construction Company the contract to revamp an abandoned retail strip mall into public housing units. It was the sixth federal grant the company had worked on, this one the most frustrating, but the most financially rewarding.

Peter Bilko, the assigned owner of the company, bursts into Robert's office. "I got another call from that idiotic federal lawyer."

Seeing the hassled look on Peters' face, Robert tells the tablet screen, "Dale, keep me apprised. We've got to get this thing wrapped up."

Peter leans over in front of the screen, saying, "Now Dale! Not tomorrow, not the end of the week. It must be capped, and the entire crew must be out by this evening."

"Okay boss," Dale replies. "But we'll be leaving a few unfinished items. We need a few more days. Clean up stuff."

"I've got a flight to catch. You talk it over with Robert but get us outta there. Quick!" Peter responds. He reclines in the leather chair, angled in front of Robert's desk. He waves his hand, signaling Robert to take the security precautions. Robert pushes the button to turn the screen black and puts it in the aluminum sack.

"What's happened? I thought we had till the end of the week," Robert says.

"Robert," Peter starts, "The newspaper got wind of the find. Now the Ag Department wants a voice added to the mix. And, our buddies told the media they knew nothing about it until a local reporter stumbled upon it. That damn Reno Daily Bit! The Ag lawyer read about it and called me first thing. They're gathering signatures for a class-action lawsuit against us."

Just a Matter of Time

"What? Okay, I got it, Peter. They don't have a thing against us that would stand up in court. Calm down. I'll take care of it. But, please, don't get us into any more of these contracts."

"You know how they spin the news . . . Damn reporters. I must go. The car is waiting for me. Call when you finish this deal."

"They're all bark but no bite, Peter. It's scare tactics. That's all."

"You always say that," Peter retorts. "And, that's not all. Lawyers are coming over about noon to discuss it, bringing an idiotic city reporter along. You're going to have to entertain them. I've got to catch that flight." He pauses. "I'm about to jump ship. Get out! Going go to an island somewhere."

"No, you're not. And remember, I'm taking that vacation."

"Not if you don't get me out of this mess."

"I'll take care of it, boss. Take a deep breath, okay? I'll use the van and take them to that biker barbeque for lunch, and everything will work out fine."

"Don't you dare."

"Kidding. We didn't do anything wrong, and I'll stand by that until the end. Go! You'll miss that flight to Denver."

Peter slams the door behind him.

Robert exits the office to give the secretary a scribbled note, "Sandy, I need your help."

Reading the note, Sandy says, "Sure, no problem."

"Thanks. Oh, one other thing. I'll be taking the van out for lunch since I rode my bike today. I told Peter I'll take the feds out to the biker barbeque for lunch, and he didn't think that was a good idea."

Sandy chuckles, "He's right about that."

Back in the office, Robert pauses a moment beside his desk. He looks out the window at the beautiful blue sky framed with billows of white streaming clouds surrounding the sun. "Lord, I need your help."

He hears Sandy's voice, "Dale is on line one."

Until the End of Time

Robert opens the tablet in the sack, pushes the button on the screen. "Dale, I need it all, what, when, how, why? Everything about this strange find. Peter is on his way to a meeting in Denver."

"Okay. But let me get over to the trailer where all my notes are. I'll call you right back. Five minutes at most," Dale says.

Robert signals Sandy on the intercom. "When Dale calls back, I'll get it. And hold all calls until I get off the air with Dale. I'm going to have him 2Fax some material. When it comes in, signal my tab."

"Okay, got it. I've found a few things you asked for."

"Good. Bring it in."

Robert's tablet rings. He pushes the button, "Hey, Dale, I'm ready."

"First of all, that meeting in Denver," Dale says.

"What about it? Hang on a bit," Robert says as he carefully places the screen inside the aluminum sack, leaving an opening to see Dale. "Okay, go ahead."

"The guy from Urban Development informed me that the agency is holding an auction in Denver the rest of the week to solicit bids on vacant federal property. The agency wants to make homesteads on that land. Our company was one of those selected contractors invited to bid, and he wondered if Peter planned to attend the meeting."

"Huh?" Robert answers. "Not another project. Eh, gads, when will he learn? Well, anyway, what was it that stirred up all this trouble?"

"It was a spider that one of the local men said he found crawling around outside the rear of the building. He collected it for his son to bring to a show and tell in school. I think the kid's in fifth grade. The teacher never saw one like that. She called in an expert from the University, who knew right away what was in that jar—a protected spider that makes its habitat somewhere else. And that's how it escalated," Dale pauses.

"That's it? There's something else here. Peter said something about an article on the local net."

"Yes. A few of those who have already signed up to rent these units complained about having to move into areas that have spiders. They implied that we hadn't done our jobs to make the place safe for their innocent children who could get bit and die from the poison. That's the way the news spun it."

Just a Matter of Time

"Hang on a moment, Dale," Robert pushes the intercom button. "Sandy, concentrate on projects that have found endangered species while under construction."

"Okay, Dale. 2Fax me whatever you have, okay? Tell me everything about the guy who says he found it."

"He's a local guy the agency sent over. The University biologist was here digging around looking for a nest or something. I watched it all. It was kind of silly to see this grown man wearing plastic gloves and a pair of those plastic shoe covers, while he carefully moved dirt with a teaspoon. He demanded that we remain ten-feet away and keep silent during his half hour inspection."

"Did you document it all? Pictures?"

"No, it didn't occur to me," Dale answers.

"Do that now. Write down everything timewise: who was in attendance, what was said by whom, and what happened next. Take a picture of the spot and send it all as soon as you can. Thanks."

"Sure will, I'm on it already. But, Rob, we need a couple more days. The end of the week should do it. I'm ready to come home."

"Anything else?" Robert asks.

"Oh, yeah. We were also informed not to spray the area."

"What? They don't want to ensure the new residents will be safe? Get it to me quick. The fed lawyers are coming in a few hours."

"It'll be ready in twenty to thirty minutes," Dale replies.

"We'll see you on Monday unless you hear from me before."

THREE

The swirling, whispering wing rotors of the academy mini-copter hovers over the treetops of the neighborhood as it approaches the interstate. It banks left, follows vehicle traffic to the outskirts of town, and toward the edge of the rising forest. It slowly descends circling the three-story flat-roofed Academy, landing on the marked spot. A uniformed officer escorts the twins off the copter after the rotors stop.

"Good morning, Jim, John," the Director of the Academy greets them. "In room 102, you'll find your garb for the ceremony. But first, I must ask for your signed agreement. You've done that, right?"

"Yes, we have," the twins recite together.

Jimmy punches a few times on the tablet and says: "Send Agreement." The Director checks his tablet to acknowledge receiving the four-page document with the required initials and signatures. The Director looks to Johnathon and hears Johnathon say: "Send Agreement."

"Thanks, boys. Go on in."

In the hallway, a fellow graduate gives the twins high fives. They each lower their arms to their knees and raise the arms making circular motions. They drop their arms to their side again and up to shoulder height, where they press their thumbs together and shout, "Yahoo!"

"This is it. Finally, we'll be out of here," Jackie says. He lowers his voice, "Out from under the Director."

"Yeah," Jimmy replies, "And that nurse."

Johnathan interjects, "Yeah, here we are in the Academy being harpooned by a nurse named Acamady."

"Well, this is it. We'll be outta here," Jimmy says. "I'm ready to get the Museum going. You'll be there too, right?"

"Yep, assigned to the same as you. Jimmy. Sorry, Johnathon."

Johnathon replies with a smile, "Hey, I'll be celebrating in the dorm, and be away from Jim. Sounds great." Jimmy pokes Johnathon in the belly and is then grabbed around the neck by his brother. Jimmy forces Johnathon to the floor, and they fun wrestle.

"Break it up!" A lady dressed in all white and a hijab hiding her brown hair. She hollers at them. "Get in there. Now! The end of that stuff. Get going!"

"Ms. Acamady, is that you?" Jackie asks, recognizing her as the chief nurse of studies, a lady of medium height framed like a barrel of wine. A pair of glasses hanging from her neck.

"Get in there, Now!" she roughly tells them.

Inside the room, the other seven graduates silently get ready for the ceremony. They open their numbered locker, pull the neatly folded drapery fabric off the shelf, and rub their hands over the soft black cotton. They throw one end over the right shoulder, the other end around the waist and over the left shoulder, the two ends dropping below their knees. Looking in the mirror, Jimmy hums: *'Okie dokie, time for pokie.'* He turns and sees Jonathon looking in the mirror and placing the ribbon draping off the cap. "Let's go, bro," Jimmy grabs his brother's arm, and they follow three classmates.

On the way to the first classroom down the hall, the ten students chat back and forth, enjoying the knowledge of making it this far and the new freedom.

The nurse, Ms. Acamady, enters the room. The door bangs as it closes behind her.

"Good morning, everyone. You've made it, and congratulations! Before the ceremony officially gets started, we have a movie for you to watch, one that will get us in the right frame of mind. It's short. It's brilliant. Our concentration must always be in the future as we work here in the present. She reaches behind to pull down a screen. She touches a button on her tablet, and the lights in the room go off.

The title displays on the screen.

The Graduation Gift Of Unity

Until the End of Time

Presented by The Department. of Academic Studies.

The movie starts with a panoramic view of the Academy. Then, it scans out, showing the ascending hills up to the snow-covered mountain tops. The view changes to sloping forested hills. To streams feeding a lake, and slowly backs up through the clouds to a night-time view of the cosmos where it pauses. Back to mountaintops, to close-up views of the valleys meeting together, forming steams flowing through the forested slopes. It focuses on telescopic sights of individual trees and their branches mingling together. It shows a panoramic view of the forest to a close-up view of ten vertical white clouds.   One word appears on each cloud: **"One tall with others one body one but not alone."**

Suddenly the screen turns black and slowly transitions to soft greys and into bright white, where one big letter at a time appears from right to left:

      ONE   PEOPLE   TOGETHER   AS   ONE

The screen goes blank.

Ms. Acamady approaches the center of the room. She's now adorned in a floor-length green dress, her long brown hair flowing over her shoulders. Green low heels replace her black boots. "Okay," she says. "Time is now. Line up! Let's go!"

They get in position next to the wall with the smallest in height leading the way. "Ready, let's go. One, two, one, two, the left, the right, the left, one, two, one, two," she continually counts. She leads the students down the hallway, around a corner, and through a double door opening. They continue to march to the entrance.

"Stop!" The nurse commands, reaching the doorway covered in black curtains to the floor. Ten candles are above the drapery illuminating the scene.

The nurse stands stiffly in front of the ten students. "Now, today is your day. I congratulate each of you. We've restricted you from this area since you arrived a few years ago. The time has arrived for you to be permitted to advance. The significance of this doorway has much to do with your future life. Those candles represent the dim beginning light into the brilliance ahead."

She slowly steps to each student to shake their hands. After the last in line, she turns and raises her arms, yelling, "Let's hear it! You're one!"

Just a Matter of Time

All ten raise their arms reaching high shouting as previously instructed, "It's done. We're one. Yes, just one."

Jimmy hums to himself, *Me and me is one*.

The sound of a musical thump, thump, thump, increases in volume and speed when the curtains slowly open to a wide pictograph of a dense forest stretched in front of the snow-covered mountains beneath a clear blue sky. One eagle highlights the center. The sun shines through the trees, leaving shadowed steps to a lake.

"Now, my ones, line up facing this scene," the nurse states. "When I give the signal, you are to run together in unison with your arms forward, your fingers pointing out like this. Keep your head down as you hit the scene. When you do it in unison, you will break through, entering another element. When I say go, run hard!" She moves back a few steps to look at the students and corrects their line-up: arm's length apart, each with their right toe on the taped line on the floor.

"Ready . . . Go!"

The students plunge forward, their arms outstretched, their heads down for the ten-yard sprint. Together they burst through the paper scene, ripping it loose from the rafters. The narrow strips of paper are now hanging over their caps, their shoulders, and to the floor. They come to an abrupt stop before running into the crowd, which yells at their entrance. "You're tall with others, one body, one, but not alone."

"Yahoo!" the graduates shout as they stare into the crowd of hundreds. Slowly the crowd quietly separates, leaving an open area for them to walk to the front. All goes quiet, everyone standing still.

Ms. Acamady leads them single file down the steps, one step after another. She loudly counts each descending step until they reach the front of the stage. "Twenty!" she shouts. She finishes and turns toward them. They stop. The nurse starts singing,

"Twenty becoming One.

Body and soul as One.

Ten bodies, ten souls, now One.

Twenty steps done as One.

It's done. All together as One."

Until the End of Time

The crowd goes wild, yelling with arms and hands raised shouting: "Now we're One. Working . . . Living . . . as One." The crowd repeats the phrase over and over.

On the stage, ten girls outfitted in long, white, loose skirts draped to the floor parade back and forth in front of the curtain. They kick their legs high in unison with each word of *One*. Back and forth, the girls go across the stage, kicking their legs high with each '*One.*' The music stops, and the girls disappear behind the curtain. The nurse points at the first in line to go to the left to step up to the stage. A light blinks on each step. She instructs the next student to the right. Alternately each graduate ascends the four steps up the stage and sits behind the Super standing at the podium.

The crowd goes quiet.

The Super starts, "Yes, Good morning Every . . . **ONE**! Here we are today celebrating another graduation from our esteemed Academy of the best there is. These students were chosen to be the best as one. They have worked and studied hard over the past three years, proving themselves while desiring this promotion above everything else. One with us, one with the pests, the flies, the snakes, and the ants, one with the cows, with the horses and the butterfly, the camel and the eagles. Yes, one with the moon, the sun, the galaxies, the entire universe, as one with each other, together as one tree, we make the forest to enjoy its cohesiveness. Your future is now with us as **ONE**!"

"Over the past centuries, backward men learned the hard way. History has had absolute leaders who concentrated their power by controlling the masses. Trial and error have produced many mistakes in judgment. Stupidity is trying the same expecting different results. We have learned. We have advanced. We are on the path as one, one people, one unit, one earth."

"Welcome now to this day when peace prevails, love prevails, and our unity is secured by becoming one. And that my fellow people, that is where we go from this day forward, working together as one giant **ONE**!"

He pauses, looking from side to side of the auditorium. He turns to look at the ten graduates now kneeling.

"So, let's hear it!" he shouts out.

The crowd of earlier graduates stands to their feet, raising their arms high as the ten girls rush onto the stage, jumping and kicking their heels

Just a Matter of Time

high in unison. Up and down they kick, with their arms reaching high with each kick as the auditorium shouts into the air,

"We're One. We're One, done, and One.

You're done. Now working as One.

We're One. You're One, done, and One.

You're done. Now with us as ONE!"

"Congratulations to these students," the Super shouts. "You're now One with us."

The students stand to attention, click their heels, and fold their arms across their chests. The ten girls separate to kneel beside each student. Ms. Acamady rushes onto the stage to assist the Super. He hands each student their personal framed diploma. She slides the celebratory ring on each student's middle finger of their left hand, and shouts, "You're One." Each of the girls throws their arms around, hugging the student.

Releasing the hug, the graduates throw their caps in the air, yelling, "Yippee! It's over! Yahoo!" Jimmy, Johnathon, and Jackie high five and thumb twist. Jimmy softly sings, "two legs as one, dittily do da, dittily one," as he chest bumps Jackie.

After the commotion ceases, the nurse directs them back to the classroom. "One more assignment for you. I have your tablets, so here." She places the tablets into the hands of each student. "We want you to pen an essay about your three years here. Do you feel you've learned your craft well enough to put it to use? What other plans do you have for the future? Marriage? Children? Hobbies? It must be no less than 200 words. It may affect your bonus." She pauses to look at each student. "Okay, go. Quiet down. No talking. It must be your own, in your own words. When you finish, send it to my heart page. No talking! All right, go!" She sits behind the oak sculptured desk watching.

FOUR

"Mr. Amwestson, the gentlemen from Washington, are here," Sandy announces.

"Good afternoon, Mr. Amwestson. I'm Hosea Hernandez from the Department of Agriculture, and this is Ralph Carmichael, also from the department. Ralph is our legal counsel."

"Thank you, Sandy. It's good to meet you guys. Mr. Bilko sends apologies for his absence." Robert shakes their hands. Mr. Carmichael, an older man, appears like a balloon about to burst, a head without a neck and arms that barely extend beyond his belt. Hosea looks like he could have been an NFL wide-receiver, tall and slim. "Have a seat. No reporter? Mr. Bilko indicated a reporter was coming."

"No, she couldn't make it," Hosea announces as they pull the chairs slightly away from the desk. "Anyway. Robert, we've been informed that the contract you've been working on in Nevada was compromised."

"Compromised?" Robert asks as he leans forward on the desk, moving one hand across the desktop to push a button on the tablet to record the conversation.

"You've not followed the procedures the contract calls for, according to the specifications laid out." Hosea states. "You were to notify UD if you found any foreign substance or such during the reconstruction. The onsite inspector said the spider was discovered at one of the rear doors, and removed from the site. Thus, your company has violated the contract. We've been sent to notify you of that neglect and breach."

"What? Breach of Contract?" Robert says. "The Urban Development inspector has been watching and approving the details as it progressed."

Ralph, the attorney, adds in his legal monotone, "The contract calls for you to halt construction when any nonresidential item is found. They were supposed to contact the field agent immediately and stop the work. He did not do that but continued working."

"The inspector did not witness it?" Robert asks.

"No, he was in another area at the time the spider was found and removed."

"So was my foreman. It was one of the agency men who *said* he found it. He's not on our payroll. And he removed it without telling anyone."

"He was working on the project under the authority of your supervisor."

"But he's not one of ours," Robert states again, flipping a pencil between his fingers.

"Yes, but the project was yours, and your foreman oversaw the work and did not stop."

"Why would he stop without reason?" Robert asks. "My foreman was not told about it. The guy from UD must have put the spider there. Interrogate him. Did they find fingerprints on the spider?"

"Funny, huh? This is a serious situation. The possible renters are upset. You've put them in a precarious situation. They've already put forth the down payment. They're demanding a release," Mr. Carmichael adds.

"Is there real proof he found the spider on the property?"

"Yes, your worker said he found it."

"That agent guy was not hired nor insured by us. He is not on our payroll. People can say anything, but that doesn't mean it's true," Robert replies. "He was a local guy on a temporary assignment by the agency. What do you know about him?"

"We've got a man on the way to find out."

"Gentlemen, again. Our insurance does not cover his work. He was put there by the agency," Robert adds as he continues flipping the pencil.

"Yes, we know that. But you're still responsible for the project."

"I was informed that he excused himself to use the restroom. Then he must have placed the spider. And that reporter," Robert says. "He needs questioning too. What he wrote on the net sounded horrible. Yeah, I'd want a refund too."

"Bilko construction is still responsible," Ralph Carmichael informs.

"Well, take the reporter down. Make him report the whole truth," Robert says.

"Well, uh . . ." Ralph pauses a bit and continues. "We are here to inform you of the company's breach of contract. That's all."

"We did not plant nor remove that spider. The agency man said he found it, claimed it for his own so his boy could bring it to school for a show and tell. His son took it to school in one of those glass jars so all the kids could see it. Check the fingerprints on the jar. That'll tell you who did it."

"That species of spider," Hosea adds. "does not make the Nevada Hills its home. It was removed from its natural habitat and relocated to the construction site. To make matters worse, that specific spider has been on the endangered list for five years. You're not just guilty of breach of contract, Mr. Amwestson. You're also interfering with the natural well-being of an endangered species. That spider is protected by law."

"Not one of my paid or insured men found or removed the spider. The man assigned to the site by UD had . . ." Robert stops, gathers his thoughts. He asks, "Was there a marking on the spider indicating that it was protected by law?"

"Well, no. Don't make light of the situation," Ralph interjects.

"I'm only pointing out a few facts. How would one know the spider is on the endangered list?" Robert leans forward on the desk, looking directly at the agency men. He pushes the button on the tablet saying, "Sandy, get our attorney on the line."

"I don't think you need to get your attorney," Mr. Carmichael, the legal counsel, admonishes. "We are only interested in informing you at this point. Here is the copy of the complaint and the compliance requirements you must follow."

Robert briefly looks at the head of the paper reading, "Department of Agriculture." Scanning the first page, he notices the phrase: Official Notice of Non-Compliance. "Okay, you've informed me that the company does not need an attorney. Not right now, but later we will. So, what do we do now to protect ourselves, to comply with your insinuations?"

Just a Matter of Time

"This is serious, and we expect you to treat it with the same respect," Hosea states.

"Okay, so where do we go from here?" Robert asks.

"Well, first, your company must address the concerns of the public. The residents are concerned that one of those spiders could bite their child."

"We don't know who the residents are, so how can we quell their fears? I'd contact the reporter, but he'd probably not listen to me. But to you, he may. Tell that reporter to print the whole truth. Your next item?" Robert asks. "And, get that agency guy who found it. He's the one responsible. Make him confess. Report that to the news."

"There's the criminal aspect of this law," the attorney, Mr. Carmichael says. "Your foreman could be charged with neglect and possibly with aiding and abetting the relocation of an endangered species. He could go to jail for a very long time, and the company could be a coconspirator."

"My foreman? The company?"

"It's possible the law could go that far. That's pretty much up to you and how your cooperative efforts are effective in correcting the perceptions of the public."

"Oh, I'll be texting that reporter for sure. And, yes. How you guys will look to the public should be your concern too. And next, there must be a next."

"Let's not get off-topic."

"Gentlemen, it was not one of our employees insured by us who found that spider, and purposely removed it from its natural habitat hundreds of miles away and placed it next to the building. All that, so his son could take it to class for an exercise in show and tell."

"We are gathering that information as we speak. His son indicated that the family visited the natural habitat a few months earlier," Hosea answers.

"You interrogated the kid? Was an adult present during that interrogation? Have you interrogated the guy who said he found it?"

"We can't share those details," Mr. Carmichael answers.

Until the End of Time

"No, of course not. Are you telling the people that there may be more spiders lurking around the site, lying in wait till their kids go out to play? Has the guy relocated other endangered spiders to the site? Come on, guys, this is ridiculous. Shouldn't you assure the rest of the lessees that the likelihood of additional endangered spiders making their way to this spot, hundreds of miles away from their natural habitat? Huh? That's about nil! And get the news to post it right."

"Well, that's all. We've informed you of the status of the project. Bilko construction is being held responsible."

"And another point gentleman, we don't have the names of the people who've already signed leases, so we can't contact them. That's your job, not ours." Agitated, Robert leans back in his chair.

"Okay, gentlemen. If I may, I'd like to summarize this meeting, what has happened at the construction site, and what our responsibility from this point on might be. We were awarded the contract by UD to rebuild and to re-furnish the existing structure into many family units. And, to add a central community and playground center. The department had inspectors onsite since the beginning, approving each phase of the process as it materialized. Everything was going fine until last week. None of our employees live in the area or send their kids to the local schools."

Robert pauses, "Does that about sum it up?"

Mr. Hernandez, getting a nod of approval, says, "yes, that's about it."

"Well, good. You'll be able to take my response back to your superiors in white on black." Robert turns to speak into his watch, "Sandy, post this summary to their in-box, please."

"Gentlemen, this meeting is over. Thank you. It's your project. We are the contractors. I would hope you contact the renters and tell them that there's no concern about additional spiders. I'd do it myself, but you don't release their names to us, so I can't. And gads, we were also told not to spray the area. There's more focus on the spider than on the safety of the renters."

Robert escorts the gentlemen out of the office.

"Thank you for your time today," Mr. Hernandez says, as he reaches out to shake Roberts' hand. Mr. Carmichael tells Robert, "If you need more clarification, give me a call."

"Good day," Robert says and watches the two suited men leave the office.

"Sandy, get Dale on the tab for me," Robert tells her and returns to his office.

FIVE

Johnathon and Jimmy burst into the house and head to their bedrooms. Janice notices the noisy interruption. "Hey! Come back here!"

The twins stop, turn around and step toward the kitchen, meeting mom in the hallway. "Mom!" Jimmy exclaims. "We made it through that ceremony. Here." Jimmy hands her the framed diploma.

"Why it's beautiful. And that ring. It's huge."

"Johnathon?"

"Yeah. Here."

"Okay, out with it. What happened? You've graduated, had the ceremony, and ready to get to work in the fall. But why do you seem so upset? Something. Tell me."

Janice watches Johnathon reach into the refrigerator for a Pepsi and sits at the counter. Jimmy grabs a Bud LightFree.

"Out with it," Janice demands.

"I didn't recognize the nurse, *that* Ms. Acamady, at first." Jimmy says, "She was dressed like a Muslim with a turban and herded us into the locker room. She showed us a movie about a graduation ceremony sometime in the future. All singing and shouting the same phrase over and over, 'We're One, we're One, done and One.' Mom, it was way out there, like Martians greeting us into their world."

"The real ceremony was not much different," Johnathon tells her. "Dad would've had a fit."

"What else? Did you get into a fight again?"

Just a Matter of Time

"No, mom." Jimmy quickly describes the entrance to the auditorium and the chants of the audience of previous graduates. "All that crap of being One with everything."

"Did you capture it on video?" Janice asks.

"No, we had to leave our tabs in the locker."

"Well, anyway. . . Congratulations! It's over, and in September, you'll be working fulltime doing what you enjoy." Janice tries to appease their displeasure. "I'm proud of you guys. Remember, we're taking you out for dinner tonight. I'm sure this will blow over, and when you're working, it'll be put away as one of those days. The ceremony was out of your control, so leave it at that. You graduated, and that's all that counts." She looks again at the diploma. As she goes to place the frame on the counter, she sees the ten by twelve picture taped to the rear, "What's this?"

"Ah, that's the cabinet I made," Johnathon replies.

"You made it? John, it's beautiful. Why haven't you told me about this before?"

"It was just a project I was assigned."

"No, not *just* a project. Wait till your dad sees this. He'll want one for the office."

"Jim?" She turns his frame over.

"Was that made of stone?" Janice asks, seeing a snapping turtle with his head out-stretched, mouth open, tongue hanging to one side ready to snap something to eat.

"Yes."

"How big is it?"

"Six feet in diameter. They'll put it outside the entrance to the Museum."

"Come here." She pulls them in for a hug. "I'm so proud of you guys."

"Thanks, mom. But, I'm not so sure about this assignment at the new Museum." Jimmy states, slipping away from the hug.

"Why?"

Until the End of Time

"It's all this one-nunce stuff we've heard for the past months. As individuals, we're damned. Gotta be one-nunce with them."

"One-nunce? Well, what we imagine is not always what is, so we've got to take one day at a time and usually things work out when we patiently do our jobs as assigned." Janice tries to console them.

"Dad's not going to like it. Not even the sound of it," Johnathon adds.

"Yeah, he gets fired up. Well. Maybe, you shouldn't tell him," Janice adds. "But that's your choice."

Robert abruptly enters the kitchen from the garage, "What shouldn't I know?"

"It's nothing, dad. Here, our diplomas." Jimmy hands the two framed documents to his dad, along with two envelopes from his other hand. "We got bonus checks."

"Come here, you two, and let me congratulate you properly!" Robert gives them high-fives and pulls them in close. He whispers in their ears.

Janice points toward the back door.

Robert and Janice follow them onto the deck, as the twins excitedly pull on the sheets draped over the large boxes. They see pictures of personal drones.

Johnathon mumbles, "Oh, my God. Wow! My own?"

Jimmy intently looks at the picture and scans the words describing the machine. He tears into the cardboard box. "I don't believe it! Oh! My!" He looks back at his mom and dad. He pulls the flaps open, and softly sings, "I'll fly away, oh Lordie, I'll fly away."

"Your license is on the way . . . should be here any day," Robert informs them.

Johnathon bends over to read the fine print on the side of the six-foot square box. "Thank you! Thanks! Oh, wow!" He gets up and hugs his mom and dad.

Jimmy, standing on his tiptoes, has already torn into the cover. He holds back the edges and peers inside at the wrapping and pieces of foam.

"Oh, my head is spinning," Johnathon mumbles as he stares at the contents.

Just a Matter of Time

"Go ahead, read the instructions. We're going out to eat," Robert says. "Are you ready, dear?"

"Ready," Janice answers, wiping the drips from her cheeks. "You did get permission to dine at the Steak House, right?"

"Yes, I did. Two weeks ago. So, let's go. It'll still be here when we get back. Let's go celebrate." The twins grab the instructions to digest on the ten-minute ride.

*****

Sitting in a circular booth in the corner of the nearly full restaurant, Robert carefully looks around the surface of the table. He feels the band of the edges. He picks up the menu holder. He examines the piece holding the individual condiment dispensers. He runs his fingers over the ruts of the antique wooden boards that decorate the booth. He carefully looks at the framed landscape picture on the wall. He reaches again for the condiment display and removes the plastic advertisement from its top. Upon careful examination, he feels the bubble. He crumbles the piece and puts it in his back pocket. "We're okay," he says.

Robert holds up his glass of wine. "I propose a toast." The three of them reach for their drinks. "To your future. You guys have made us proud. The best is yet to come." The glasses clink together, and they each take a sip.

Janice, with her eyes open and looking across the table, prays. "Lord, we thank you for your blessings, your guidance, and oh, Lord, your grace and mercy with us. Now open our ears and hearts to understand the ways and means. Thank You. Amen."

Sitting next to her, Johnathon softly says, "Thank you for the way you led me through these years. Thank You. Amen." With his eyes looking at the table, Jimmy offers a quick, "Amen."

Robert turns his head toward Janice, his eyes concentrated on her sweet brown eyes. He mutters his thirty-second recitation and ends with "Amen."

They lean back and relax. Janice says, "Rob, you suggested we each have the same kind of steak, right?"

"Yeah, a thick filet to celebrate this tremendous achievement of our boys. Okay?" Robert raises his arm.

Until the End of Time

The waitress approaches the table with her tablet ready. "Mrs. Amwestson, you can order anything from the menu, and considering the muscular boys, they can too. But sir, your BMI is a bit high, so here is your menu. I'll give you a few minutes to look it over."

"Wait a moment, there. We're celebrating, and celebrations mean food and lots of it. We eat and eat, and go back for seconds, and there are desserts too. Yes, what's a celebration without lots of sweet desserts? So, take that BMI thing and ..."

"Rob!" Janice interrupts.

"What a bunch of bull! Oh, if I could get my hands on . . ."

Robert leans back, breathes deeply with a long sigh, "Okay. Okay, but."

"No buts, Rob. Come on. Relax. We're here for the boys."

The waitress returns, and Robert orders, "One of those thick eight-ounce filets for each of us. Mine medium rare with the side *salad*, no topping."

"How'd you like yours? Mrs. Amwestson."

"Well done for me, a baked potato with sour cream and bacon bits."

Johnathon says, "medium rare, and I'll take the onion rings."

"Same here," Jimmy says.

She enters the orders into her tablet. Looking at the twins, she says, "I wish to congratulate you two for finishing the Academy." She turns to look at Robert, "a refill on the wine?"

"No, we're fine," Robert answers. "You could bring me a cup of coffee with the meal. Thanks. *No sugar!*"

"Sure." She places the tablet in front of Robert, who presses his first two fingertips on the screen. Seeing 'Approved,' she replies, "Thank you." She moves to another family a few booths away.

Robert starts, "Your tabs are off, right? So. Ah . . . Hang on." He points to the rings on the boy's fingers. The boys slide the graduation rings off their fingers and hand them to him. He carefully exams Jimmy's ceremony ring. Robert points to his ears and puts the rings in an aluminon sack in his pocket. "Another one of those," Robert tells them. "Okay, remember when they appointed you to the Academy, you expressed a little doubt that that was what you wanted. Has it turned out like you hoped, or

Just a Matter of Time

do you wish you'd have gone a different way? We've discussed this before, but how do you feel, now that it's over?"

Johnathon is the first to reply, saying that he's ready to apply the skills he's learned. "I'm glad to get on with it. It's been a long three years."

Jimmy says, "Yes. Glad it's over. But, yet sometimes, well, I keep in touch with Nortan. They assigned him as one of the assistant rugby coaching positions at Wendell High."

"Didn't they win the state championship?" Robert asks.

"Yes, they did, the last two years," Jimmy answers. "The head coach thinks he may be upgraded to the University level if they have another good year."

"So," Robert says. "Nortan will start as the second assistant under this very successful coach, and he may have the chance of moving up."

"Yep, that's the way he sees it."

"Good for him. And you still think about it?" Robert questions.

"Yeah."

"So, what don't you like about the stonework you've been doing? The picture of that turtle was fantastic. I want to see it, feel it, and rub my hand over it for real."

Janice adds, "Yes, and now I think I'd like to put one in our front yard."

Jimmy glances at Johnathon and back to his mom and dad.

"Well, out with it. Jim," Robert insists.

"Oh, I don't know."

"Sure, you do. Share it with us."

"Well, it's lonely working with materials all the time. I'd rather be more involved with people, to have someone to talk with, to be around, to fellowship with."

Janice says, "I thought so. You do have that burning, don't you? Would you like to go to the seminary and become a pastor, a counselor?"

"No, coaching is it. Even baseball would be better than working alone, making objects for others to admire."

Until the End of Time

"Why haven't you told us about this before?" Janice asks.

"Well," Jimmy says, "you were excited that I got selected for the Academy, and I thought I was too. But now, I know deep down I wasn't. I didn't say anything because I thought it was one of those negative ideas coming against me."

"Oh, we disappointed you, didn't we?" Janice answers. "I'm sorry."

"Sorry, Jim, that we didn't pick up any of that," Robert says. "We should have. I should have. If I had only concentrated more on your senses, rather than what I thought would be a good experience for you. Yes, it may have worked out differently." Robert pauses. "You do know that winning coaches get lots of admiration."

"John, did you know about this?" Janice asks.

"No, this is the first I heard about it."

"I didn't tell anyone." Jimmy interjects, "I thought I imagined it because Nortan was going, and I didn't want to disappoint you."

"Son, there's nothing you would do that could cause us not to love you," Robert says.

"Amen to that," Janice adds. "Don't ever forget that. You too, John."

"We're very proud of you that you stuck with it. And we wouldn't think of trading you in." Robert pauses. "But there have been times . . ."

Janice playfully elbows him in the ribs.

"How about you, John? Do you have any misgivings about your academy work assignment?" Robert asks.

"No, I like the idea of creating things, working with wood."

"You're sure?" Janice asks.

"Yes, Mom. Positive."

"Okay, now it's out," Janice says. "Let's remember this and in the future share with us any misgivings. That's what the Lord wants us to do. Seek, and you will find. Look into the deepest part of your soul, and you'll find what is there for you to implement."

"Yeah, and after you start this project, you may begin to enjoy it," Robert interjects. "You won't know till you start that you may have co-workers."

Just a Matter of Time

"Rob and I do this all the time," Janice adds. "We talk things over. And sometimes I must draw it out of him, to face the facts, to listen, quiet that judgmental attitude."

"She's a master of that," Robert answers, lightly poking her forearm. "And sometimes she pouts for a day or two when I don't readily submit. Boy, can she pout." He leans into the aisle to get away from the expected elbow punch.

Janice asks Robert, "Is there's anything we could do now to help Jim change his appointed field?"

"I'm not sure we can. He'd have to start all over."

Jimmy says, "I did ask the Super about it, and he said that. I would have to submit to another questionnaire and State exam. Wait for answers and open positions, which might take a couple of years. So, I forgot about it."

"Sorry, son," Robert says. Looking at Janice, and back to Jimmy, he adds, "I'm sorry. We should have delved into this sooner, like before you accepted the Arts and Crafts Academy."

"We got the appointment after that exam," Jimmy states. "We didn't think there were alternatives."

Robert chews the last piece of steak. "Ah . . . That's not the way it used to be. It's crazy."

Janice tells the twins, "I received and read your essays. Were you guys coerced into thinking along these lines?"

"They asked us to think about our future and describe it," Johnathon answers.

"Jimmy, in your essay, you said that you wanted a big family, possibly four, five, or more kids. Whenever you do get married, your wife will have a lot to say about that. She may only want one or two, or none, and that marriage coach will have input, too. You also said you wanted a home with acreage so that you could have chickens, a few pigs, and horses, too. Where are you going to find something like that around here, and be able to afford it?"

"I've already put in a bid on five acres that one of the local farmers is partitioning off from his hundreds."

Until the End of Time

"You put a bid on it?" Robert asks.

"Yes, I did, and John did too. If we get it, it'd be paid off in three years. Heck, I can live in a shack that long."

Robert and Janice exchange looks, hearing this from their twenty-year-old son who, a few years ago, was electric skateboarding after school with his buddies. Their eyes turn to Johnathon.

"John, you indicated you also wanted a piece of land to set up a kennel for stray cats and dogs," Janice says.

"Yes, we should know by the end of the summer."

"Oh, my," Janice mumbles. "Well, I won't have to keep knocking on your door to wake you up in the morning!" she pauses and changes the subject. "So, Rob, when are we leaving?"

Leaning over to her side, Robert asks, "Um? Are you ready for this? You're sure now?"

"You know I am," Janice says. "Why do you ask again? Rob, what happened? Something at the office?"

"Well . . . No . . . Yes, we're going. Leaving next week, on the twelfth."

"That's ten days," Jimmy says.

"Good math," Robert replies. "Now, tell me more about that secret ceremony."

Silence.

"Jim. What happened?" Robert asks again. "Tell me about it."

A glance at his mother, Jimmy starts, "It went fine. We walked the aisle to the stage where the Super was, and he gave us the diploma. We all threw our caps in the air. Like the pictures of your graduation."

Janice adds, "You saw the pictures of their work. They will be on display in the Museum. Perhaps John could make one of those cabinets for you. It'd look terrific in your office."

"It would. So, you have ten days to do it."

"Dad, that took me months," Johnathon answers.

"I still don't understand why parents were not allowed to attend," Robert states.

Just a Matter of Time

"You couldn't have gone anyway with what's going on at the office. Sandy called me today." Janice tells him, hoping to take his mind off the ceremony.

"She did?"

"Told me you needed prayers as the feds were coming."

"Yes, they did, and we'll have to wait and see. Did she say anything else?"

"Not really. Will this interrupt our trip?" Janice asks.

"No, it's settled with Peter. We're going. It's been on the books for months," Robert says. "Guys, remember back to last summer, you wondered about the possibility of that Canyon project? Your mom and I thought about it too, realizing it would be great for you, and us too. But upon investigating, we were told that permission would have to be granted by those folks in Washington who control those visits."

"Have they been approved?" Jimmy asks.

"They informed us that it would be doubtful, as they would not review your application until they had investigated the others. Only ten can go each year and no relatives. You didn't like the idea of visiting uncle David in Boulder. Like I said before, we'll be leaving on the twelfth. Have you decided to go with us, or have you made other plans? Has the Super any ideas for your summertime?"

"No, the summer is off," Johnathon replies.

"What are you going to do?" Robert asks.

Jimmy answers, looking at his brother, "Well, now that we got the drones . . ."

Johnathon interrupts. "Yeah, playing around the area, exploring the forest, and looking at the land available. That kind of stuff."

Janice interjects, "We'll be away for two weeks on our trip, so you understand what that means."

"Yeah, one of those nannies takes over if we stay home," Jimmy answers.

"You're sure you want to stay here?" Janice asks.

Until the End of Time

"We know the rules, mom. We discussed it and have agreed that we'd behave," Johnathon answers. "And, there'd be nothing for us to do there."

"Yeah," Jimmy says. "We'll lock the nanny up and have parties in the basement."

"We'll be fine, Mom," Johnathon adds.

The waitress arrives, setting the deserts down. "Thank you. Enjoy! Will there be anything else?"

"Looks great, thanks," Janice replies.

Robert slices his pear in half, and about to eat it, when he says, "Okay, you guys would rather stay here. Then I'll discard the permission slips we received."

The boys look at each, back to dad, a glance at mom. Together, with raised voices, they ask, "You got the okay?"

"Yes, it came. Your applications were approved. You're going to be part of that Canyon Project!"

"Yahoo! Yippee!" they shout above all the chatter in the restaurant, high fiving and smiling, as Robert and Janice sit back watching their glee.

"Can we take the drones?" Jimmy asks.

"You sure can. That aided your priority status. I've got the tickets and the permission slips. You guys are going." Robert assures them. Looking at Janice, he says, "And, we'll be seeing the Canyon for our first time."

"So, when?" Johnathon asks.

"You weren't listening. We're leaving on the twelfth."

Robert and Janice review the trip they've been planning for months, as the twins scope out the net for further information about the summer project. At the Grand Canyon, they will drop the boys off, then continue through to the Denver and Boulder area. A two-week vacation for them, and ten weeks for the boys. Janice's brother, David, is now the pastor of a large church near Boulder. Janice and David's wife Ruth were on the Sports Academy girls' golf team.

SIX

Janice is preparing the appetizers for the meeting, deviled eggs, and well-garnished fresh vegetables picked from the garden. Assembled, cooked, and ready, are the Swedish meatballs and steamed cabbage.

Raising her head, Janice hears Robert's footsteps coming down the hallway. "Honey, is there anything I can do?"

"Thanks, I'm fine. Have you finished your notes for the meeting?"

"Yep, I'm ready," Robert answers, as he pours himself a cup of coffee. "The table looks fantastic."

"Thanks. Tom and Linda should be arriving any minute now. I'm going to freshen up, Listen for the doorbell, okay?"

"Sure."

Robert hollers out. "They're here." He sets the coffee cup down and walks to the front entrance.

"Tom and Linda, greetings. Glad you could make it."

Janice approaches from behind, "Linda, wow, that's gorgeous."

"Jan, what have you done with your hair? It's lovely," Linda says.

"Oh, well, Robert likes it. What more can I say?"

The four of them step into the kitchen, where Janice fills four cups with coffee. Taking their seats in the adjoining living room, Tom and Linda lean back on the sofa. Robert reclines in his leather chair and Janice in a cushioned armchair next to them.

Until the End of Time

Tom points his finger at the ceiling.

"It's okay, Tom. All taken care of."

"Good. Tell me more about this meeting," Tom requests.

"Besides you, the Emerasens and the Jacksons are coming," Robert answers. "You heard of the Smiths and the problems they had over there in Portland. It's getting out of hand. What happened there is settling in here at home, too."

Linda adds, "The Smiths are recovering. It wasn't as bad as it sounded at first."

"Yes, it was. They lost almost everything," Robert replies.

"Come on, it was one of those isolated incidents," Tom says. "We talked with them a week ago, and they're doing fine. It could happen to any missionaries. Anyway, Rob, do you think the Giants have a chance of making it to the series?"

"If Concernerie and Wabbcom continue pitching the way they have, they could go all the way," Robert answers.

"Yeah, did you see the game last night?"

"No, I didn't."

"Last night was a disaster. An umpire decision declared the catcher missed the tag allowing the run. The fans went wild, throwing trash all over the field."

"The fans did what?"

"Threw their drinks, everything. Even with all the security people around, they went crazy. The umps suspended the game, the police took over, but the trash kept coming. A multitude of them jumped on the field, running like crazy."

"Can't you guys talk about anything but sports?" Linda speaks up.

"Wow! The one exciting game, and I miss it." Robert responds. "The instant replay called him safe?"

"They still got it wrong," Tom continues. "Everyone could see it on the screen replay. The media jumped to commercials . . ."

"Come on! Let's eat!" Janice interrupts.

"Yeah. I'm hungry for your meatballs," Linda adds.

Just a Matter of Time

The four of them sit at the dining table, enjoying the meal and conversations. Janice shares about the boys and their excitement over the engagement at the bottom of the Canyon. Linda tells about their upcoming summer vacation plans to camp in the hills of Washington State. Tom informs them about his difficulty in running the plumbing company and keeping up with the rules.

The doorbell rings.

Robert opens the front door, "Marie and Will, good to see you. Gladis, you're looking great. You've recovered." He reaches out to shake her husband Mark's hand.

The eight of them are comfortably seated in the living room in front of the stone fireplace. A six-foot square picture window opens a view of the side yard. The wood fence displays a circular outdoor thermometer, a similar sized clock, a small birdhouse, and two big planters showing ribbons of colorful flowers. A metal sculpture of a young girl holding a flute that spurts rhythmical water into an oval pool. On the street side wall next to the fireplace are three ceiling height mahogany cases with sparsely placed treasured family pictures spaced along the shelves. The numerous TV games the twin's play are lined up on the bottom shelf. The seventy-two-inch TV hangs on the wall separating the dining room from the living room.

"I'm glad you could make it tonight," Robert starts. "Let's take a moment by holding hands, each of us silently praying, acknowledging our Creator. I'll end it."

Each of the guests reaches for the hand of the one beside them, lower their heads and close their eyes in respect. Robert mumbles his prayer softly, "Thank you, Father God, for this meeting of friends. Now guide our discussions and thoughts. We desire to spread righteousness among each other and to this nation of ours, oh, yes to this country, and . . ." A loud knocking on the front door interrupts his meditation. Robert ends it. "Amen." He looks at Janice. "Are we expecting someone else?"

"Not that I know of," Janice replies. "Well, perhaps it's Arlene and Charlie. I'll get it." She heads to the door, and the guests return to their chatter. Mark reaches out for a snack and takes another sip of his drink.

Janice opens the door and sees a policeman dressed in riot gear, a large German Shepherd with its tail wagging and his tongue dripping foam.

Until the End of Time

Three other officers are close behind with their arms around rifles pointing toward the ground. The men are in standard riot gear. Looking to the side, Janice sees four guards disappearing around the house. Blocking all traffic are four squad cars with emergency lights striking the evening darkness.

"Do you have a license, permission to hold this meeting?" the Lieutenant asks.

"We don't need permission to invite friends over."

"Yes, you do, ma'am," he states and forces his way past Janice. An officer holds Janice's forearms and pushes her against the brick wall.

"What's going on. Wait a minute! You can't!" Janice says in a loud voice. The officer holds her.

Two officers, the dog, and the Lieutenant enter the living room. He announces in a loud voice, "Everyone, remain seated! Don't move!" He assumes a defensive stance, his rifle pointing at the ceiling. "Sit down, sir!" he emphatically tells Robert. He gestures to the other officers to fan out. One goes down the hallway, the other into the kitchen and dining area, and the basement.

"What the . . ." Robert exclaims. "What's this all about?"

"Mr. Amwestson. Keep quiet while we satisfy our purpose."

"Hey, we're just having a few friends over."

"Shut up! Raise your arms!" the Lieutenant states. He begins to rotate a slender rod from the armpits, down along the outside of Robert's body, past his hips and to the floor. His left-hand moves the search wand up and down the inner legs, while his right-hand presses against the rear pockets. Satisfied, he tells Robert, "Okay, sit down!"

"Everyone, keep your hands free where we can see them. Now!"

Two officers lift and move the long coffee table to allow the dog room to move between the knees of the guests and the table. The big shepherd's tongue locks in. It sniffs and moves its head from the shoes up to Will's knees, to the arms of the cushioned chair, and back to the floor and around his feet. The dog's nose moves up the other leg. Finished with Will, the officer pulls on the leash directing the dog to the sofa where Marie appears terrified. The tail is waving back and forth, showing forth its enjoyment of the game. The officer leads the dog with a tug on the leash from one person to the next, each of them intimidated and stiffening themselves against the intrusive sniffs.

Just a Matter of Time

The officer who inspected the basement shouts, "Clear!" as he brings the twins into the living room. "Take a seat and keep your hands out."

The lieutenant tells his officers. "Okay. Start the individual search. Everyone, as we get to you, stand and empty your pockets. We'll need your fingerprints."

An officer approaches the lieutenant and whispers in his ear.

"Come with me, sir," he says, looking at Robert. "The rest of you, sit still, keep your hands out and you'll be okay. The officer holding the dog's leash commands it to sit.

Robert follows the lieutenant. Passing the front entrance, Robert sees Janice detained outside. Stopping there, Robert looks directly into the lieutenant's shaded helmet shielding his eyes. "Lieutenant, I demand to know what is going on here. I need to see the warrant."

"You don't demand anything here! I'm in charge, and you'll do as I say, so shut up! Now take me to where you hide your guns." He pushes Robert into the office and to the closet, where a full-sized armored safe with the words Red Head emblazed on the front.

"Open it," the officer says.

"No. What's in there is my business. Where's the warrant?"

"Open it," the officer demands, raising the rifle into Robert's chest.

Robert's stance stiffens. His face flushes. "Go ahead, shoot."

*****

Arlene and Charlie are about to start the trip to visit son Bruce and his family. They've packed the car for the trip to Denver. Charlie takes the last sip, sets the cup down, when Arlene tells him, "Janice told me they're still going to have the meeting."

"So?" Charlie answers.

"You told me that it's against the law."

"Any neighborhood meeting over seven adults is. We've been in these meetings before, and nothing happened. You didn't call it in, did you?"

Until the End of Time

"Yes," she answers.

Agitated, Charlie asks, "Why? What'd they say?"

"They already heard about it, and said they'd look into it, that's all. Forget it. Let's go. I did what I had to do."

"Ugggg," Charlie mutters, shaking his head. He breathes deeply and slowly sighs. "Gads Arlene. Sometimes . . ." He mumbles. Shuffling his feet against the floor, he gets up from the table and starts the walk toward the garage. "Damn it all, I was looking forward to a peaceful trip, and now all I'll be thinking about is this." He reaches into his shirt pocket for the tablet phone.

"Don't. Forget it. Charlie, all they said was they'd look into it."

"Dammit, when we get back, you got to make this right with them."

Arlene brushes his side as he swipes his fingers across the remote to open the car door. Charlie takes a deep breath watching her settle back in her seat. As the garage door opens, the sight of the police cars comes into view.

"Oh, my God, Arlene, why?" Charlie says.

Janice turns her head toward the sound of the garage door opening, then Charlie's car backing down the driveway. Charlie waves his arm out the window, as the car backs into the street and out of the cul-de-sac. She turns to look back at the officer. "Sergeant, you don't need to hold me so tight," Janice softly tells him. "I'm not going anywhere, okay?"

The officer relaxes his grip on her arm.

An officer quickly exits the house, goes to a police van and returns with a piece of paper.

"Do you have any kids?" Janice asks.

"Yes. Three. Two boys and the last is a girl."

"Your wife, does she work?"

"She teaches mid-school grammar."

Seeing a smile creep on his face, Janice says, "Sounds like a lovely family. Sergeant Newscom, would you mind contacting me – us – sometime after this fiasco is over? I'd love to meet your wife and family. You could come for a backyard barbeque. We've got a pool table in our basement your kids could use, and our twins would be happy to entertain them."

"Ma'am, I think . . ." he begins.

"She can come in now." An officer notifies him, and he then leads Janice into the living room.

An officer enters the office and gives the warrant to the lieutenant. He looks at it briefly and hands it to Robert, who slowly reads the official document.

"Unbelievable," Robert states. He presses the code to open the safe door.

"Okay, guys, you know what to do," The lieutenant says.

They remove each weapon and read the serial number into a tablet. They put the guns back in the safe and carefully record the inventory of the ammunition. Robert intently watches the technology used. A beep, beep, and a voice announces, "Weapons registered. Ammunition legal. None fired since last November."

Robert locks the door and announces to the lieutenant, "There." He tries to sidestep around the officers.

"We're not done here yet," the lieutenant tells Robert. Your gathering exceeds the personal limit on the number of guests allowed to gather in one home at one time according to code number 714-NV-205BB."

"Hmm, we came together tonight simply as a group of friends for fellowship, and I guess that's against the law now. What's next?"

The lieutenant says, "Here's the citation and a ticket."

Looking at the paper, Robert sees the fine at $1,500. "Huh? What's this?"

"You had three over the limit."

"No. One, that's all. Three couples. That's it, a total of eight."

"Duh, the boys are of legal age. The fine is payable at the county courthouse. You have five days. Okay, guys, we've done our job."

Robert and Janice, stand hand in hand on the front porch and solemnly watch the officers leave the house one by one.

Until the End of Time

"Good evening," the Lieutenant says, as he passes by.

"Hey, where are you going with that?" Robert asks.

"You're not allowed anything of this kind," he sternly replies.

"But that's my father's High School yearbook. It's a treasure, full of memories."

"You said it yourself. No books. Period!"

Lowering his head and away from the officer, Robert mumbles, "get outta here." Janice grabs Robert for an embrace. They silently watch the squad vans drive out of the neighborhood.

The twins return to the basement. Will and Marie, Mark, and Gladis rise from the couch to prepare to leave.

Robert announces to them all, "I'm sorry. I should have known about the code, but who'd have thought. I'm sorry . . ."

"We should have known," Tom says.

"I didn't think it'd reach this area so soon," Robert says as the couples extend their condolences. "Sorry, but we should go."

He watches the two couples walk the brick pavement to their cars. Curious neighbors, watching the commotion, try to get explanations from Will and Mark as they silently approach their vehicles.

Janice and Linda quietly carry the cups and salad bar to the kitchen, leaving Robert and Tom in the hallway.

"What are you going to do?" Tom asks.

Closing and locking the front door, Robert says, "not sure. But now, I need a good drink."

Entering the kitchen, they see the ladies silently putting away the salad bar and loading the cups and saucers in the dish washer. Seeing Robert and Tom, Janice hugs Robert's neck, "I'm sorry." She whispers.

Tom and Linda embrace.

Robert breaks the silence, "Honey, get my dad's bottle of Jack Daniels, and let's sit and relax. You know where it is, right?"

"Thanks," Tom says, as Janice hands him a one-inch shot glass.

After taking a sip, Robert says, "I feel like John Wayne, in the mood to shoot up that town hall of ours. These tribulating times. Yak!"

Just a Matter of Time

"All of that, because we violated a code limiting the number in a private gathering," Tom says.

"How did they come up with the number seven anyway?" Robert surmises, having taken another sip. "Shouldn't it be an even number?"

"How did they find out about it?" Linda asks.

"That could have been Arlene," Janice says.

"What are we going to do?" Linda asks. "They've got our ID's. Are we going to get a ticket or a summons to appear before a judge?"

"I don't know," Robert says. "But I'm glad you didn't leave. Thank You."

"Yes, thanks for staying," Janice says. "I'd be hearing Rob rant and rave the rest of the night if you had left us alone. Thanks. Okay, anybody for a piece of pie?"

"She's right. I would be," Robert answers. "So, thanks again. Yesterday at work, I had to endure the feds threatening the company for supposedly violating a spider's habitat. And tonight, this encounter with the Gestapo."

"What happened at work?" Tom asks.

Robert briefly tells of the endangered spider and the following ruckus.

"Wow," Tom responds. "What's the company going to do?"

"Oh . . . I don't know. The owner was out of town, and I think he's got a scheme already cooked up for the company," Robert says. "I guess I'll find out Monday. I did post a comment on the reporter's page, stating the facts he left out. It had better get the attention of the public. Anyway, one thing after another in these stupid times."

"This one tonight is not your fight alone. I'm with you, and if you need me, I'll go with you to see the mayor," Tom says. "And I'll help with that fine."

"Thanks, but I'll handle it."

Tom opens his tablet, slides his finger across the screen, pushes an icon, slowly touches it again, and again. "Next Tuesday afternoon at three, there's a town hall meeting. We should go."

Until the End of Time

"We'll be on vacation," Robert says.

"The following month?" Tom replies. 'We've got a month to collect our thoughts."

Tom looks at the tablet again, "All we need is to submit a request to comment. We would have three minutes."

Robert says, "Three-minutes? Oh, I could yack in their faces for hours." Jan reaches to squeeze his hand.

SEVEN

It's the morning of the twelfth. The family is prepared for the drive to the Canyon Headquarters and on to Boulder. "Honey, we're ready, let's go."

Janice tells Robert, her purse hanging off her left shoulder. "The boys are in the camper waiting on us."

"Good," Robert replies.

Janice asks, "Are you okay?"

"Yeah, yeah, I'm fine," Robert replies.

"Something's bothering you!" she states.

"No, no . . . I'm ready. All is taken care of, right?"

"Yes, let's go."

Robert grabs her, bringing her in close for a hug and whispers in her left ear, "Thank you. I was pondering, well, ah, dropping the kids off, the uncertainties, the possibilities of that Canyon adventure of theirs."

"Yeah, I know it's been bugging you. But we've prayed about it." She pulls her head back and pushes her lips up to his. She whispers, "Everything will be fine."

Robert opens the front door for Janice. He presses his forefingers in front of the sensor above the doorknob to double lock it. He takes a few steps down the brick path, stops, looks up at the camera. The twins, with their tablets, sit at the dining table behind the driver's side of their great-grandfather's antique converted Winnebago. It's hooked up to a trailer carrying the partially assembled drones which are covered by a tarp.

Until the End of Time

Robert slides his forefinger over the screen to start the engine. Looking at Janice, then in the rear-view mirror to the twins, he bows his head, "Thank you, Lord, for this trip, for our safety, for paving the way Lord. We thank you for your blessings upon us." He finishes and rattles softly on in an indistinctive foreign monotone as he steers the vehicle into the street.

When he goes quiet, Janice says, "I have great plans for you that you know not. I am with you always."

Janice reaches over to the dashboard pressing the screen a few times to bring up Maps and uploads the destination. She pushes another button for classical music and adjusts the seat to a reclining position. She leans to the left, and directs her voice to the twins, "What are you guys playing back there. Turn the volume down."

A shadow suddenly appears and disappears in Robert's left side mirror. "We're being followed," he comments.

"You did get permission to leave, right?" Janice asks.

"Sure did. Also, to drive this antique. The forms are there in the glove box."

Janice turns her head toward Robert. "I love you," and places the earphones over her ears and leans back.

After a few hours, they stop to show permits, identification papers, and pay the fee to enter Idaho. They've now passed through Boise and are back into the open plains. Robert announces, "Anyone ready for a bite to eat?"

"Ready," Johnathon answers, followed by a 'yes' from Jimmy.

"There's something up here a bit," Robert says. A billboard advertising a campground looms high along the highway. The blue signs indicate the names of lodging available, names of restaurants, names of rest, and re-gen stations. Robert follows a delivery truck into the rear parking area of Travel Stop.

Entering the building, Robert points to the restroom sign, "Get a table. I'll be there in a minute."

Greeted and sitting at a booth next to a wall, Johnathon begins the search of the table, the placeholders, and decorations. He finally finds the hidden mike and hands it to his dad, who has just joined them.

"You found it already?" Robert says.

Just a Matter of Time

The young waitress, beautifully adorned in a floor-length green gown with a portrait of a forest, approaches the booth with the menus and places the plastic wrapped glass of water in front of each announcing, "Greetings, Mr. and Mrs. Amwestson, we're glad you stopped here on your trip to Boulder. All our meals meet the best BMI standards. The special this afternoon is the double-sliced chicken breast with lettuce on a toasted bun. Total of 120 calories, all natural, non-GMO, oven cooked. What'll you have to drink?"

"Hot tea." Janice answers.

Robert says, "Coffee, black."

Jimmy orders a Lemonade, and Johnathon asks for a Pepsi.

"Sorry, we don't have soda pop," The waitress replies.

"Water then, with a slice or two of lemon," Johnathon says.

"Swell," she says. Looking directly at the twins, she says, "I was at the Canyon project last summer and had a marvelous time. You're going to enjoy it." Reaching in to shake their hands, she adds, "I'm Andrea." Surprised at the waitress and her directness brings a smile from the boys watching her leave the table.

"Very cute, isn't she," Janice says.

"Mom, the girl's camp is miles away from where we'll be," Jimmy says.

"Yeah, I guess there's no reason to worry as you'll be in God's hands and under Him in all you do."

"Amen to that," Robert says. He looks at the menu and informs them that he's going to have the grilled cheese. "Janice?"

"The cheeseburger, oops, here she comes."

Andrea places the drinks on the table, and asks, "What'd it be for the Amwestsons?"

She enters the orders into her tablet. "So, guys, is this your first summer in the Canyon?"

Jimmy replies, "Yes, it is."

Andrea turns, looks around the area, pulls a chair from a nearby table over to the booth. "I was there last summer. What'd you like to know?"

Until the End of Time

"Won't you get in trouble?" Robert asks.

"Nah, the boss encourages it, that customer-first-thingy. So, what do you want to know?" Andrea says, focusing on the twins.

Jimmy leans in on the table and asks, "Would you go back again?"

"Oh, you betcha. It was great. I met my boyfriend there. It was at the mid-summer get together when we played games, canoed, had a campfire, and a dance. Ethan and I hit it off from the start."

Janice asks, "So, what kind of work was the group doing? The work assignments and supervisors. How were they?"

"Okay," she answers. "Well, the first few days were hard. It reminded me of what I'd heard about military boot camps. A bugle woke us up before sunrise and had exercises before breakfast. It was a tough first few days. We tried a walkout, protesting to the supervisors."

"How did they respond to that?" Robert asks.

"Called us all together and explained the greatness of being chosen for the summer. That it was only a select few from thousands of girls our age given the opportunity. She told us we were the best, and how much we would benefit from the hardships." Andrea pauses. "They said, that yes, we could excuse ourselves, but it would be on our permanent record hindering future employment."

Janice asks, "If finishing that would help your employment opportunities, then why are you working here? Why not something more beneficial?"

"Well, I'm . . . Ah, well, as you can see." She rubs her swollen stomach. "I'm five months pregnant. So, I'm filling in time. We plan the marriage ceremony to be in the delivery room as the baby is born." The tablet buzzes. "Your orders are ready," she announces, pushing the chair back to the table, and walks off to the kitchen.

Janice leans into Robert, watching her leave. She reaches for his hand. "Getting married as the baby is born. Huh? The hospital will allow that?"

"I guess so. Hmm? What do you guys make of the boot camp part?"

Jimmy responds, "We heard some of that through the grapevine."

Just a Matter of Time

Johnathon adds, "The guys I talked with had some of the same thoughts. The Director indicated a bit about the physically challenging aspect of it."

"Imagine that hon, our sons are two of thousands," Janice says.

Robert replies, "Well, we've heard her side of the story, but let's not get carried away here. Our research into this adventure of yours was quite different than what Andrea indicated. It may be somewhat similar or may not be. There is one part of her story I tend to believe."

"What's that?" Jimmy asks.

"The supervisors telling them that if they quit and left, it would be on their record and would damage future employment. The feds do that. They can, and they have. They're trying to do that to Bilko."

"They are? How?" Janice asks.

"Peter told me yesterday as I was about to leave."

"Oh. Will this affect your job?"

"It might. Peter's looking into other possibilities, even overseas jobs. Told me not to worry about it." Robert lightly squeezes Janice's hand. "We'll be fine. Now back to this adventure of yours. What do you think, now that you've heard a supposed eyewitness account of the summer?"

Johnathon answers first, "I'm ready. Yeah, we can handle that boot camp stuff. We survived three years of that nurse and the head honcho, so this may seem like a vacation."

"Yeah, we'll be fine," Jimmy says. "Let them throw the book at us. Wow, and now that we've got the drones."

"Yeah, and flying off to the girl's camp," Janice responds.

"I'm sure they will monitor the operation of the drones," Robert says. "Now remember that a little skepticism beforehand is always beneficial when undertaking something new and different. To me, the bottom line is the spiritual aspect to be open to receive or reject, based on that inner spirit. What she said gives you guys something to be prepared for and think about."

Andrea approaches, balancing a platter high above her head. A portable stand slides out from between the booths. She lowers the tray onto

Until the End of Time

the stand. She places the first dinner in front of Janice, and removes the cover, then Roberts meal and finally the twins.

"It's been my pleasure to serve you today," Andrea says.

Janice leans in to smell the two-inch thick cheeseburger and the side of roasted fries, "Looks great."

"Okay, enjoy your meal," Andrea says. Looking at Johnathon and to Jimmy, "The girls will be after you guys! Enjoy the ride!"

"Andrea!" Janice exclaims.

"Oops, sorry about that, but I'd be wanting to catch their attention," Andrea says and leaves the booth.

Robert reaches for Janice's hand and across the table for Johnathon completing the circle of hands. Robert softly speaks, "Lord, we thank you for this food put before us, this trip, and now for our boys, as they're about to enter unknown territory. Protect and guide them, Lord. And Lord, bless Andrea, open her heart, provide her with an easy birth, and secure her future in your loving forgiveness. Thank You. Amen."

"Okay. Eat up, and let's get out of here. Hopefully, we'll spend the night somewhere around Salt Lake City," Robert says as he picks up the grilled cheese.

Janice looks across the table at her sons enjoying their sandwiches, and starts in her motherly voice, "Guys, I've told you along the way of my childhood and school years. My parents were very strict about everything. My clothes, the words I used, the way I walked, the chores that I had to enjoy doing. Not a thing could take the place of attending Mass. Nothing. No sports, nothing! I think I also shared how, that in Middle Eight, I knew some girls going to public schools, and they would share their experiences with boys. I was embarrassed hearing about it, thinking that it was shameful to even think about what they had done. But I also wondered. I tried to put that wonderment, that curiosity aside. I knew that, wow, would I ever get in trouble if I had done anything those girls said they had done. A sense of shame was connected with all that, and we had to go to confession for thinking about it. All that is gone now, and that's not good." Janice pauses, wondering how to phrase the next comments.

"Andrea, although she says she is getting married, doesn't feel any conviction for having gotten pregnant before marriage vows. Looking back now, I appreciate how my brother and I were instilled with that. And when you get our age and have kids of your own, I hope you'll look back thanking us for our strictness."

"Yes, your mother is right on," Robert says. He looks deeply into her eyes. "From that first day we met, I knew you were one in a million."

"Thank you," Janice tells him.

There's a period of silence as they concentrate on finishing the sandwiches. Robert briefs them on the coming attractions: the Great Salt Lake, the Grand Canyon, the Rocky Mountain forests, the Denver and Boulder areas, and spending time with Janice's brother.

Inside the Winnebago, Robert announces, "We should be at Salt Lake City for dinner."

EIGHT

"Well, here we go, a roadblock ahead," Robert states, as traffic slows to a crawl, watching the bicycles pass.

Peering ahead, he notices that many cars continue on the highway, while other vehicles pull into the rest area for inspections. Finally, the Winnebago reaches the first of several officers standing on the side of the road holding bold signs: STOP. Applying the breaks, shifting to park, he opens his window to ask the officer, "What's going on?"

"You're about to enter Utah. That's a beautiful camper, Mr. Amwestson. Amazing update. Love it. Pull into the rest area, please," the officer says. He steps away from the window and points toward the entrance. Jimmy and Johnathon stand in the aisle, watching the commotion.

An officer tells them to exit the camper and bring all documents, licenses, registration papers, and permits. They quietly submit to the requests. Robert reaches up to the ceiling between the driver's seat and the dining area. He detaches the covering of the bubble and places it in the glove box, presses a button on the wall, and follows Johnathon out of the Winnebago.

As the police dog enters the Winnebago, another officer walks up from the rear. He asks about the contents of the large boxes on the trailer. "Those are two personal drones that my sons will be using at that UN summer camp in the Canyon. We'll be dropping them off, and my wife and I will continue to Boulder for a week to visit her brother." Robert reaches into his shirt pocket to retrieve a document. He hands it to the officer, who scans it and gives it to the officer in charge. He reads it and looks back toward Janice and the boys standing about twenty feet away under elm trees. The officer with the dog exits the camper and gives a thumbs up.

Just a Matter of Time

"Thank You for stopping. You can continue into Utah," the Sergeant informs Robert. He returns all the documents to Robert. Janice and the twins enter the Winnebago. "That's quite a camper. My grandfather had one like it. Have a safe trip, Mr. Amwestson."

"Can I ask you a question?" Robert asks. "Why was this stop necessary?"

"It's required by law for the control of unauthorized shipping of items across state lines."

"We didn't have this much of a problem entering Idaho," Robert says.

"Each State has its limitations. Wait till you get to Colorado."

"But I did notice that many personal cars are not stopped and searched. Why is that?"

"Mr. Amwestson, the newer ones, are equipped with sensors that would disable the vehicle if any narcotic or illegal substance was inside."

"I just wanted to hear someone say it. Thanks."

"Go!" the inspector asserts.

"Well, next stop is Salt Lake City," Robert states.

Janice puts the earphones on to listen to music, which the muffled sound reaches Robert, who starts thumping his palm on the steering wheel.

Sitting at the table, Jimmy points to an area on the tablet showing a half-dozen small tents encircling a large canvased tent. "There it is, John,"

"Which is it? Ours or the girls?"

Jimmy pens a name into the search box, and the home screen of the agency appears, showing a view of the entire Grand Canyon. Jimmy touches "About" and slowly reads the text. He touches, "Who this year" and sees his and Johnathon's names in bold, along with 18 other names listed alphabetically. Pressing on his name, Jimmy looks at a photo of himself and text beneath it, which includes his height, weight, his hometown, education, special interests, and his specialty of stone carving. "Look at this, John."

Until the End of Time

Johnathon reads his biography. Jimmy ponders the information available to anyone. John selects "Purpose" and reads the text appearing in a shaded box. He presses, "Experiencing the Beginnings," and reads on. "We'll be searching for remnants of past settlers, even in caves," Johnathon tells Jimmy.

"Why couldn't we see this months ago?" Jimmy asks.

"There, on top. The date posted was last week."

Jimmy softly tells Johnathon, "Let's read about the girls."

Johnathon presses on the name Julia Swensen, and the words appear: "You do not have permission to read this."

"Huh?" Jimmy says. "Can't read about the girls?"

Janice leans over, "Aha! It comes out; the girls are what got you interested in the project. Is that it?"

Robert beams a smile, "Well, that probably would've caught my attention too. I remember how you gave me a look over through that fence. And why do you think I was there to practice at that particular time?"

Janice falls quiet, remembering back to that day they met, what her golf friends had said about the boys playing tennis. "You guys be careful, that's all. And, keep your pants on," she commands, watching the expressions on her sons' faces. She raises her motherly voice and says, "There, I said it."

"Amen to that," Robert agrees.

Conversation lulls inside the Winnie as they watch the scenery. Soon Robert hollers back to the twins, "Hey, guys look to your right. It's that Salt Lake."

Janice points to a sign announcing a viewpoint to the Lake. "Turn up there, and we'll get a close-up view." He slows the camper, turns right and follows a narrow road a few blocks to the parking lot.

Riding a Segway, a man cuts in front of the Winnebago. "Mr. Amwestson, this area is for personal cars only," The man shouts to Robert through the open window.

"I see that now," Robert answers.

"There's another visible area about a mile up the road."

"Thanks."

Just a Matter of Time

"Have a safe trip to Boulder."

Robert nods his head and slowly continues along the highway. "Hey guys," raising his voice to get their attention, "Look over there. That's a drone like yours." The twins rise to see the drone flying like a roller coaster over the shore of the great lake.

"We'll be doing that soon," Jimmy replies.

Robert turns the Winnie into the asphalt road spotted with yellow knee-high posts. He finds a parking spot. "Okay," he says, "let's go see."

The twins step barefooted onto the hot asphalt, jumping and running toward the grassy area in front of the Visitor Center.

"Like two-year-old's being let out," Janice remarks.

Robert and Janice join other tourists peering into the expanse of the calm lake. A somber wonderment overtakes them. Soon, a young man sporting a red ball cap and thick horned-rim glasses interrupt Robert's thoughts, "This your first visit, Mr. Amwestson?"

Robert turns his head and acknowledges, "Well . . . yes, it is."

"It's something else, isn't it? Imagine all that salt locked away here a thousand miles from the ocean."

"Yes," Robert replies. "It is amazing, and I suppose we ought to thank the people of Noah's time for it."

"Huh?" the man questions.

"That's what I was thinking. Noah in the book of Genesis, where it says, 'the fountains of the deep broke up, and the waters prevailed for 150 days.' Can I ask you something?"

"Sure."

"How'd you know my name?"

"My glasses are recon. I just got them." The stranger responded. "They're terrific. Keeps me from approaching a dangerous person. Oh, well, you live in the country. So yeah, you need to get out more often." He pauses, looking at Robert and adds, "Hey, have a nice trip to Boulder." The stranger walks off in a hurry.

Robert looks at Janice. "When we get home, I might get me a pair of those."

Until the End of Time

Further on the road, Robert stops in front of the Guardian Visitor Motel, allowing Janice and the twins to enter the lobby with the luggage. He drives the vehicle to the rear parking lot. The twins, with their backpacks strapped over their shoulders, pull two suitcases to the front desk.

"Good afternoon to the Amwestson's. Your rooms are ready. How was your trip?" the young lady asks. She rings a bell, smiling as she looks at the twins.

"Where do you recommend for a nice, quiet evening meal?" Janice asks.

Susan, the clerk says, "Right here, of course. Home cooked meals all prepared according to the most recent health updates." She leans over to rest her elbows and forearms on the countertop. Her shirt, barely covering her nipples, reveals a deep cleavage. She speaks directly to the twins darting her brown eyes from Jimmy to Johnathon, "You guys may like to take a dip in the pool after dinner. I get off at eight."

"Susan!" Janice exclaims.

An electric cart enters the area. The suitcases are placed on the back. Janice and the boys sit on the open seats. "Rooms 120 and 121," Susan announces to the cart.

When Robert enters the lobby, the clerk points to the hallway, "Room 120. Mr. Amwestson."

While unpacking and freshening up in their room, Janice tells Rob about the clerk. He leans over lightly, caressing her shoulder as she combs through her long hair. He brushes aside a few hairs and plants a soft kiss on her neck. "I'll go talk to the manager."

"Let's find a different place to have dinner," Janice suggests.

"While parking the Winnie, I saw one down the block a bit. A local cafe."

"When you're ready, collect the boys, and I'll meet you in the lobby," Robert says.

"Time to go, guys," She loudly announces through the door. Walking the hallway to enter the main lobby, Janice tells them, "Your dad went to talk to the manager. We're going to eat somewhere else." Janice purposely chooses chairs faced away from the desk.

"So, how did that go?" Janice asks Robert as he approaches them.

"We're leaving. I'll tell you more in the Winnie," Robert answers. He pulls her up from the comfortable chair. "Come on, guys, we're leaving."

"What happened, dad?" Jimmy asks.

"I'll tell you later," Robert says. They quickly pack the suitcases.

Robert tells them, "Out the back exit to the Winnie."

Settled in the camper, Janice says, "Okay, the suspense is killing me. What happened in there?"

"Well," Robert starts, "the manager is a she, and she was upset, not with the clerk, but with how we understood the gesture. We must have misunderstood, she told me, as she has never yet had a complaint in the two years this great employee has been at the desk. All she gets is compliments. She even said that if it offended us, we ought to find another place. Said, she would never again let us book a reservation, naming us as easily offended people."

"Dad, that's unbelievable," Jimmy says.

"What'd you tell her?" Janice asks.

"Good, we're outta here," Robert answers. "Jim, what did you think? How did you perceive her actions? John?"

"Well, like she was offering herself to us. Nothing unusual. But here in a motel with our mother right there?" Jimmy answers.

Johnathon adds, "Yeah, she gets the most tips. Mom, you were offended, but Jim and, well, it's . . ."

"Yeah, normal part of life," Jimmy interjects.

"Normal?" Janice repeats. "What would you think if you saw me doing that to a prospective real estate client?"

Robert cuts in, "There's a campsite on the other side of the city."

Until the End of Time

Following the highway through the city. Robert asks Janice, "How much further?"

"It's near Pleasant Grove. On Utah Lake, another 30 miles."

They find the camping area on the shore of the lake. Settling in, they sit outside under the warmth of the evening sky, enjoying the burgers and salad Janice put together. The conversation was mostly about the ten-week adventure for the boys, what they expect based on the information they've received from the Department of Advanced Studies.

Robert and Janice heard about the program two years ago through Janice's brother. Reading about the summer activities of exploring the Canyon, Robert was impressed as a way of advancing their skills and abilities, plus having a fun time after graduation. They submitted applications for the twins as potential candidates for the summer adventure of discovering and journaling the history of the Canyons in its microevolution. Initially, the twins did not like the idea because of the heat, and the tedious work of scraping away dirt. The part they liked was the thoughts of camping and canoeing the river, enjoying the atmosphere, exploration of caves, and the possibility of visiting the girls camp.

NINE

"Okay, guys, here we are. Finally," Janice says, looking back to see the twins slouching. "Hey, wake up back there. We're here."

Robert inches the Winnebago toward the gates as it approaches the Canyon National Park Entrance.

A neatly uniformed gentleman holds a tablet focused on Robert. "Good afternoon, Mr. Amwestson. Pull ahead to the next gate, please."

At the gate, the guard asks for the permits and identification of the students. "Thank you, Mr. Amwestson. Follow the blue signs on your right to the registration office." Two personal cars ahead of him turn to the left following red signs pointing to Girls Camp. He follows the narrow one-way dirt road, around the curves through the sandy wasteland of sage brush. He slowly maneuvers the Winnie and trailer around the bends, finally seeing a billboard in large print, 'Canyon Headquarters, Men's Camp.' Below in smaller type, '*A UN project of exploration into the history of these Canyons.*' Below that is another bold statement, 'The Best of America.'

He is directed to park the Winnie and the trailer in the lot in front of a mobile home office.

Two middle-aged gentlemen dressed in state ranger uniforms meet them. "Greetings and welcome. Now, these two must be Jimmy and Johnathon." He reaches out to shake the twins' hands. "I am the Director of the male program, and this is Kenneth Smithy of the historical society. Guys, you are about to have the summer of a dream come true. Thank you, Mr. and Mrs. Amwestson, for arriving on time. I see you have the drones. Thank you for that contribution to this project. Now, we'd like to get the drones unloaded and set aside. Then Kenneth will lead Jimmy and

Until the End of Time

Johnathon to the tent to meet the other boys already here, and those yet to arrive."

They set the drones alongside the office. Janice intently watches the twins with their sleeping bags and backpacks following Kenneth. She crosses her forearms across her chest, beaming with pride, sadness, and tears, her lips smiling and drooping. Her focus stays on the twins as they disappear behind the office.

"Now, Mr. and Mrs. Amwestson, please go into the office to sign the required documents, and then we'll direct you to the Canyon overlook area near the stadium where we'll have our meeting."

The documents signed, they start the trek on the gradual declining red sandy clay path edged with various rocks.

"Look over there," Robert nudges Janice, and points to his left. An area is shaped in a half circle of ten ascending layers of rectangular blocks of stone, rising to the top where ten columns frame the auditorium. "Wow!" Janice says, "It reminds me of a Roman Coliseum."

"Yes, I was thinking the same."

Reaching the peninsular overlook of the vast Canyon, Robert inhales, followed by deep sighs and gasps of air, as he peers down the Canyon wall. A propeller-driven volleyball with two-eyes flicking left and right, two lips dancing up and down, appears before them announcing, "Please step back. Do not lean over the railing."

"What?" Robert hollers at the thing and turns to look back to the office.

More parents, relatives, and friends meet at the lookout point, introduce themselves, chatting and somberly gape at the view of the Canyon. The volleyball returns to warn the new arrivals. Robert and Janice start conversing with a couple from the Seattle area.

Janice tells them how excited the twins are anticipating canoeing the river, campfires, exploring caves. "It sounded like a great summer for the kids, and here they are. And this is our first time to see the canyon."

Robert says, "The information in the packets we received only touches the surface of the program."

The Seattle gentleman informs them about the mid-summer get-together the boys and girls will have. "Junior met his wife there, and soon we'll be grandparents. Your boys will have a great time. Junior wanted to come back, so he applied for the counselor position right after the summer ended. And, now two-years later, here he is."

A whistle blows, and a voice announces over the loudspeakers. "All right, everyone. It's almost time for the celebration to begin. Please proceed to the amphitheater. Thank you."

At the iron gate to the arena, the visitors get their faces and fingerprints scanned and given a pamphlet. An usher carefully escorts Janice and Robert down the steps toward the half-circle elevated stage. Reaching the area, Robert rubs his fingers over the smooth granite blocks forming the platform. His fingers softly touch the front paw of a sculptured lion, poised with mouth open exposing upper teeth, tongue extended, ears back with long tail draping to the granite. They follow the guide up the six steps to the third level. The guide stops and points to his left. "Seats five and six."

Slowly the theatre fills with parents, extended families, and friends of the ten students and five counselors.

Janice grabs Robert's hand. "Our boys are leaving."

"Yes. Jan, we should be proud, not forlorn."

"Twins, but different, aren't they," Janice says. "Johnathon and his fascination with nature, the trees, and the various wood grains that he chisels and rubs. And Jim, wow, I love to hear him humming and singing when he's creating something,"

"Jan, you've done it. You've made me proud to be their dad," Robert whispers, squeezing her hand.

"Greetings." A voice says from the rear of the arena. Looking up toward the sound, Robert points to a column left of center, "There's Jim," he says. "And John, two columns to the left."

"Greetings and welcome." The voice announces again over the sounds of families saluting their sons.

A respectful stillness envelopes the audience.

"Thank you."

The Director of the project rushes onto the stage. "We will now get started. Remain standing, and let's welcome our select group of students

Until the End of Time

to this Canyon Project. But, please hold your applause to the end. Over the past few years, these ten brave young men have expressed their desire to enhance their strengths to meet their higher abilities. The authorities have recognized them as worthy of participation in this summer project. You parents are thus proud, and we thank you for your continuous faithful, diligent fortitude in guiding your child along this road of reaching maturity. Again, please hold your applause until the end. Thank you."

The Director announces a name. A student standing at the far-right column walks to the center, turns, and slowly descends the ten-foot-wide steps to the front of the stage. He sits in one of the chairs on the stage, facing away from the audience. One by one, the Director introduces the students. All ten now have their backs toward the audience.

Drums roll, a bugle blasts, and the Director of the project shouts out, "Let's hear it." The boys stand, shaking and raising their arms high and waving toward their relatives. The audience erupts in applause, cheering, and waving.

Slowly the audience quiets down as the Director, middle aged well-structured with hints of gray streaks of hair combed over his ears, takes center stage. He's dressed in a navy-blue tee-shirt that pictures the Canyon walls descending to the belt buckle of his knee-length navy blue shorts.

"Thank you, and greetings to all. Welcome to this celebration of the best of the best. Now let me introduce the five counselors who have completed the project over past years."

He announces a name, and the counselor appears from behind the curtain to stand between two students. Five counselors position themselves between a pair of students. The relatives of the counselors start the applause, which explodes through the crowd.

A scene slowly appears on the curtain behind the students. The crowd sees a satellite picture of the revolving Earth continents separated by the Atlantic Ocean. White cloud formations move north and east, mingling with grays swirling around a black hole.

The satellite scene advances to an outline map of the 48 states appearing on the numerous ripples of the curtains. As the curtains lose their ripples, the words **United Country** are stretched from the West coast to the East coast. The scenery turns into a rotating view of the Statute of Liberty and a close-up on the torch's flame. A scene of the Lincoln Memorial on a snowy day comes into focus and slowly dissolves. Next, is

Just a Matter of Time

one Jet flying high over rural land, hills, forests, farmland, and a large lake, where another jet accompanies the Navy plane.

On and on, they fly over farmlands coming upon a forested area. The jets descend and turn slightly to the left, as a rainbow touches the faces on Mount Rushmore. They wave their wings at the tourists below.

The voice of a pilot announces, "I started as one. We're now two joined together as one for one purpose."

Behind the students, the scenery disappears, the curtains rise, and the Director steps to the podium, "Ladies and gentlemen, let us all rise and wave our appreciation," One Army and a Navy plane zoom over the auditorium. The crowd goes wild.

"Amazing, was it not?" the Director asks. "Thank you. We have the support and direction of three phenomenal organizations in this summer project: The UN, the EPA, and the World Health Organization. They initiated it years ago. Now, let me give you a brief tour of their duties and responsibilities during these ten weeks. First, in the morning at daybreak, they will start the journey down that narrow, safe, but strenuous path to the bottom of the Canyon to their homestead for the summer. They'll arrive at the campsite in the greenery alongside the river. In past years, when I reached the bottom, all I wanted to do was look up, take a deep breath, sigh, and be grateful for the experience. It's an exciting time of internalizing the grandeur of the Canyon formation over eons of time as the waters carved out the area.

"That is the first of many hard-earned satisfactions these ten will endure during this project.

"I shall not go into the many details of their daily activities, as that diminishes the anticipation of parents and relatives to hear their stories when they return. At the top of the list will be exploration. During the day, these strong boys will explore the crevices, the mounds, scraping, and cutting, looking for whatever may be there. They will explore the caves, the recesses of the Canyon sides to collect samples of the various layers of rock for scientific studies.

"Next will be knowledge and understanding, followed by sharing. Evenings will be around campfires, enjoying games, meditation, and the comradery of being One with each other. As the sun descends, they will view through telescopes the wonders in the far reaches of the Universe.

Until the End of Time

Scientists call this the power of the magnitude of ten. Ten students observing the various steps of ten.

"Over the past projects, we have discovered more marvels to share with the scientists in their confined labs. One of the most important has been the recognition and acceptance of an outpouring of waters devastating this area. When the rains stopped, and the clouds dispersed, the sun started the drying process. The waters receded, forming lakes, streams, and rivers. The force of running waters cutting through the layers, pushing and shoving the mud, the dirt, the small rocks, and boulders without foundations. Nature is continuously changing. We desire to observe those changes.

"A bit up stream is another summer camp project for highly motivated girls. They will be performing similar tasks but centered more on how nature feeds itself, nourishing through that circle of life. In the middle of the event, there will be a gathering time when those girls and these boys will celebrate together for a couple of days of fun and a pairing.

"That's it, folks, and thank you again."

The audience erupts in applause.

The Director turns toward the boys and counselors to quietly talk to them, as the parents greet each other and start conversations. When Robert and Janice reach the stage, the Director approaches, "I wish to thank you again for that great contribution of those personal drones."

"How will they be used?" Robert asks.

"For any necessary trip to the top, for any unanticipated necessity, shortage of supplies or medical help. The drones will make that easier. Thank you, and they'll be well supervised. One of the counselors is a licensed technician."

Janice asks, "Near the end, you said the word pairing. What is meant by that?"

"What I mean by that is what the authorities have discovered. Do your boys already have a steady girlfriend at home? If not, they may find one here. You should be excited as they meet one of the talented girls trying to navigate this difficult period of entering maturity. We try to aid this process by bringing the best of America together for a few days of enjoyment. Again, thank you for those drones." He turns and heads off to chat with other parents.

Just a Matter of Time

Janice looks at Robert, and in a soft voice, says, "Oh, Rob, I don't know if I'm ready for this."

Robert grabs her around the shoulders to bring her in close. "Yeah, they've been our little boys, and now, they're leaving. But they'll be fine."

TEN

It's now close to six, as Robert and Janice, after the brief opportunity to pray for and wish the twins well, slowly walk to the Winnie. They are about to open the door when they hear a voice off to the left, "Mr. Amwestson."

Looking toward the voice, they see the parents they had met and chatted with while peering into the Canyon. "Larry, and Renee, you heading back to Seattle?" Robert asks.

"Yes, we want to wish you a safe trip to Colorado," Larry says. I wanted to give you my card, so if you'd like to get together sometime over the summer, we'd be delighted. Just give us a call." He pauses and looks up at the top of the Winnebago."That's a fantastic rennovation. Wow! Mind if I snap a few pictures?"

"No, not at all. It meets all requirements," Robert answers.

Larry steps back and points the tablet at the sides, the tops from various angles. Robert reaches for his wallet for his business card. "Eh, here's mine, and thanks." Robert glances at the name on the metallic card.

"Janice, I couldn't help but notice the concerned look of yours," Renee says.

"It was that evident?" Janice answers.

"The boys will be fine. Junior will be with the boys the entire time."

"Oh, Renee," Janice says. "It's that our boys have never been away from us for more than weekends, and those were to church camp-outs. This is far from it. I suppose I shouldn't be, but yes, I am, whatever."

"They can't take their tablets. We can't call," Robert says.

"They'll be fine. Junior made it, so your boys should do quite well."

Just a Matter of Time

"We'd better be going," Larry says. He presses a button on the remote hanging from his belt. Their vehicle slowly approaches, stops, and two doors open. "Enjoy your trip," Renee waves.

Inside the camper, Robert looks at the business card in his hand. "He works for the New Leaf department."

"Rob, I'm going to lay down," Janice informs him while rubbing her hand over his right shoulder. "I don't even feel like eating."

Unhooked from the trailer, Robert steers the Winnie out the narrow winding dirt road toward the main highway. Several hours later, ten that evening, he sees a rest area sign ahead and turns into the area to park alongside a few trucks. He pulls down the windshield shade. Locked and secure, he steps into the small restroom before sliding into bed next to Janice.

Early the next day, they cross the state line to enter Colorado, where they waited hours to get approval to enter the state. They had to present the previously secured permits. They got their fingers swiped, and the inside of their wrists stamped. They were forced to wait in the office, as the inspectors surveyed the Winnie from the solar panels on top to under the axles. They searched inside the cabinets, the refrigerator, the drawers disrupting Janice's organized packing. They pay the large vehicle fee and are permitted to continue their trip to Boulder.

"We'll never, ever, ever again return to Colorado after this trip. That's the last straw. What is happening in this country?" Robert mumbles after boarding the Winne.

"Rob, if you'd like to bang your head against the wall, I could drive," Janice suggests. He looks at Janice. Her sweet demeanor, her soft eyes, her smiling forehead, and her dimples soften his irritability.

"You know how. You're an angel. Thanks. I'm okay."

Back on the interstate, they enjoy the scenery of the Rockies. Five hours later, they're nearing metropolitan Denver. Robert follows I-70 through Wheat Ridge, catching the road through Arvada, and on to Broomfield and northwest to Boulder.

"Rob, honey, on the screen, there it is. David's house up the road a bit." She points out the location and pushes #5 on the dashboard, hearing it ring, ring, ring. "Ah, they're not answering." She pulls out the tablet to send a text message.

Several minutes later, the tablet vibrates and rings. "Hell-O. David. Yes, we're around the corner." Janice tells her brother smiling at her on the screen.

"Hey, I'm in Oklahoma. I thought it was next week that you'd be here. I'm helping out here for a few days."

"David," Janice says. "I texted you several messages about our expected arrival. Did you not receive it?"

"Ruth was taking care of that. Sorry, but this trip had been in the works for months. If I had known, I'd – I'm sorry, Jan. Forgive me. But I won't get home till Monday. Ruth is in the hospital for pneumonia, and possibly something else, so that's probably the cause of the mishap. Sorry, Jan," David pauses. "But hey, it's about a five-hour drive here. I'm in the very western part of the state. Come on down. Join me."

"What hospital? We could go spend time with her," Robert says.

"That's the problem; she's in a secure unit. No visitors allowed," David answers.

"It must be serious. What are her chances?" Janice asks.

"Oh, she'll be fine. Ten days they said. It's the procedure now, you know, the safety thing. So, come on down."

Janice sees Rob nodding his head. "Well, okay. Sorry about Ruth. You're sure we can't see her before we head south?" Janice asks.

"Nobody can. I can't either. She's locked in. It's a hell of a mess."

Robert speaks into the tablet, "Google us your location."

"Great, I can't wait. Jan, it's been years. How are you? You're looking good."

"I'm fine. Dave, when did you start the beard?"

"She's more than good, Dave," Robert says. "She's the live one keeping me in-line, and she looks better now than that first view through the fence."

"Well, see ya in a few hours."

"Dave, it's four-thirty. It'll be about ten when we get there," Robert says.

Just a Matter of Time

"The roads are good. I'll be up and waiting." David signs off.

Robert maneuvers the Winnie through the neighborhood, around a circle, and back to enter the highway again.

"Oh, I was looking forward to spending time with Ruth. Now, this will take days away from that." Janice says.

"Let's get through Denver, and . . . oh, no, another state crossing," Robert mumbles.

His eyes briefly scan the map displayed on the dashboard, David's location shows up as a red dot, a few miles inside the border. "Jan, see what you can find about the Boise City area in Oklahoma."

Finally making it into rural land, he turns onto I-25 heading to Colorado Springs. He turns his eyes on Janice, who's raising her seat back to its upright position. She removes the neck pillow with headphones and says. "Let's stop soon so I can stretch these legs, and I'll fix a sandwich."

Entering Oklahoma was a breeze. They pull into a campground on the outskirts of Boise City, met by a lowered gate at the office. Through the window, the manager tells Robert, "Sorry, we're full." Robert backs the camper into a turn-around, and Janice sends a text to her brother.

Janice pushes the 'voice over' button, so Robert can hear David. "Rob, drive through town. You'll see a steepled church on the left. You can park it there. You can't miss it. I'll be waiting for you."

The Winnie approaches the tall spires of the ancient stone church visible over the sparse single-family units along the two-lane road. "Jan, look up at the tower. Built in 1877."

"Jan, you're looking fantastic," David emphasizes, as he pulls her in for a hug.

"Oh, Dave, it's been too long," Janice softly says.

He greets Robert with the same embrace. "How you doing, man?" David says. "God, this is great. Sorry about the mishap." David looks up at the Winnebago, "Wow, that's ancient. How did you get that updated to standards?"

Until the End of Time

"It took several years and about twenty inspections," Robert answers. "Go ahead, look it over."

David steps onto the out positioned two-step and into the dining area behind the driver. He leans to his right to look closely at the dashboard area, the screen, the buttons below, and two cup-holders. Turning around, David internalizes the dining booth, the stove, refrigerator, and the four-drawer cabinet supporting the tabletop. He glances toward the rear at the opened door of the bedroom. "Man, this is something else. The workmanship is fantastic."

"The boys helped a great deal."

"But what drives it . . . the power source?"

"The solar panel on top is part of the energy re-gen. The belts of those wind turbines keep the axles turning. It'll do sixty all day long without reducing the battery."

Looking around the interior, David points at an oak frame prominently displayed above the dining table. "Rob," he states, "that's a museum piece!"

"I put that together years ago."

David leans forward to inspect the display of a one-dollar bill, a two, a five, a ten, a twenty, a fifty and a one-hundred dollar bill, horizontally spaced around a red panel of coins: a copper penny, silver nickel, dime, quarter, half-dollar and a silver dollar in the middle.

Scratching his ear, David says, "Wow! I may still have a few of those somewhere."

Janice interrupts. "What about Ruth? When will we be able to see her?"

"I was talking with her after your call. She's excited about seeing you and wanting to get the hell out of that damm hospital. She's fine. But she needs prayers too."

"Where are you staying?" Janice asks, ignoring her concern about his use of a vulgar term for a Christian to use, especially as a pastor. "Here, made a fresh pot." She hands him a cup of coffee.

"Right here in the church with the pastor and his family," David answers, "He's part of the national Re-Group that reaches out to the victims of disasters. A tornado hit this area a month ago. Thanks, Jan," as he adds a spoon full of sugar and takes a sip.

Just a Matter of Time

"David, I want to thank you again for leading me to embrace the truth," Robert tells him. "That awakening experience has been on my mind ever since, and now I'm pleased to have the opportunity to get to thank you in person," Robert pauses. "Thank You."

"Eh, I was only a messenger. You were easy."

Janice suggests that they pause and pray for Ruth. Lowering their heads, Jan starts. David comments, "Yes, Lord, we ask for her complete and quick recovery. Minister to the hospital staff all that they need, wisdom and righteousness. Amen."

"What are your plans, your schedule?" Robert asks, sipping his coffee.

"Hey, you're welcome to join us. We're roofing a house. The group meets here at seven for breakfast, and a short devotional before we head to the homes."

"Rob, you go ahead. I'll rest here in the Winnie," Janice tells him. "Sorry, David, but the boys are on my mind."

Janice shares her concerns for the well-being of the twins over the summer, her fears about the chances of them returning with girlfriends, and moving out of the house. David explains his role as senior pastor of the church on the outskirts of Boulder, how the church has grown, how the youth group has expanded, how the vacated store was revitalized to accommodate the larger attendance, which requires two services Sunday morning.

"As the senior pastor, I am free to go on trips like this," David says. He breathes deeply, sighs, takes a sip of coffee, and says, "Oh, Jan, I got a confession. You should know." He takes another deep breath. "It's been bugging me all these years that you did not know the truth. You've always wondered why we did not have children." David pauses, exhales another deep breath, and continues. "It was during my teenage years." He pauses and breathes deeply. With a solemn expression, he brings out more about those days when society had welcomed homosexuality. He tells them about how a teacher first befriended him and slowly led him into a sodomizing relationship. "After a year, the teacher broke off the relationship finding another student he liked more. That devastated me. I realized I was being used. Oh, Jan, the guilt, the shame hit me so hard and deep. It ruined my ability to function."

Until the End of Time

"Oh, my!" Janice says, wiping a tear away.

David adds, "Jan, I'm sorry. You were the apple of the eye for mom and dad. I was supposed to have been a girl."

"Oh, Dave. What I remember is that you kept to yourself and hardly ever associated or played with me."

"It was our seven-year difference in age," David says.

"I thought something was wrong with me. I didn't think you liked me. Did you ever tell mom and dad?"

"No, I couldn't. You were a youngster when I was going through that. It happened even though we were immersed in the Catholic Church growing up." David sips coffee. "Yet, all that outward show of tradition was nothing more than that to me. Just something we should do. Sure, I pretended to embrace it all." David goes into the details of his conversion in college. "The roommate assigned to me in that freshman year dormitory was a deeply committed Christian, and Catholic too. He continually shared the gospel with me in such a way that it slowly caught my attention. I listened to him expound on the truths in the Bible, and the astounding nature we have around us testifying to those truths. Months later, I was alone in a nearby park, meditating, sadly looking around. I fell on my knees and with tears flowing out. I screamed to the sky, 'Take me, God,'" David sighs. "And, here I am, where God has brought me now."

Robert touches David's hand, "Yes, here you are, now teaching others. Your ability to reach people appears clear in the growth of the church."

Wiping tears off her cheeks, Janice says, "Dave, this has touched me deeply. I feel it. I'm now at peace about the boys. Thank You."

"Jan, you're welcome to join us tomorrow," David breaks the silence. "The ladies are working in another home, cleaning, and painting. Robert can come with me and you with the ladies. There's about eight of them. They'd be pleased to have you join them."

ELEVEN

"Ready to go, boys?" the Director asks the group of ten students and five counselors, about to start the trek to the bottom of the Canyon. "Before we go, let me clear up some questions. First, the girls will be taking a different path, so get all those thoughts out of your minds. Yep, no meetings with the girls until the middle of the project."

"Second, there is nothing easy about this long trek we'll be taking today, even though it's downhill. Keep to the middle of the path. There are several places along the way where you'll be able to see the destination camp and take in the majesties of the Canyon. Ready? Let's go!" A robotic camel carrying two large baskets of supplies follows the Director. Two similar camels with loads on their backs follow the last counselor.

He pulls sharply on the rope tied to the camel. The boys are lined up according to their tent assignments, with the experienced counselor following each pair. Sixteen of them, now carefully walk the narrow, hard, dirty, clay path along the walls of the Canyon. At first, there was little conversation along the way as they accustomed themselves to the hardship of the continual downhill walking.

Jimmy is paired off with Joseph Hamacka from western Pennsylvania, who could be the center guard of any basketball team. He's tall and lean, dark complected with black hair like a mop, thick eyebrows extending over sunken, confident eyes. Joseph informed Jimmy of his family's history when a long-ago grandfather was shipped to the States as a teen from Nigeria and slaved to the coal mines. "My grandfather is a professor at Yale. He likes to tell stories of his boyhood being schooled by a mama who would whip his knuckles red for missing a comma." Joseph continues telling how his parents pushed him into sports. "I starred in high

Until the End of Time

school, was about to get a scholarship, when I broke my shoulder on a stupid daredevil trick. My girlfriend Maria expects us to get married after the summer, and I start my assigned job of coaching."

"Basketball?" Jimmy asks.

"Yep, I've been assigned to Penn State."

"Good for you," Jimmy says. "I'm a stone carver, and I'll be working at a new Museum in our hometown. I wanted to get into coaching but was assigned stonework."

Johnathon is with Albertaldo, a kid from Arizona, who is fascinated with wildlife photography. He's got a position with the Fish and Wildlife Department after the summer. "John, I love traveling to those remote spots and document the habits of hard to find species. My great-grandfather was brought up in the jungles of Brazil. My dad's parents fought hard to immigrate to the U.S. when dad was only three. John, I was homeschooled until the sixth grade when I entered the public-school system. It was a breeze without wind."

"You got a girlfriend back home?" Johnathon asks.

"Nope, with all the traveling I'll be doing, who needs someone at home, perhaps hooking up while I'm gone. How about you?" Albertaldo asks.

"Nothing serious."

The trail opens to an indented rest area. They remove the backpacks and boots to massage their legs and feet. From there, they can look hundreds of feet down to the river.

"Sometime in the past," the Director gets the boys' attention. "Our natives were probably fishing, and their kids swimming in waters of only a few feet deep, at this level we're at now. Look over there." he points across the Canyon. "That is the remains of an elevator built to transport tourists up and down. It was poorly constructed and was torn apart by the wind and the shifting of the walls. Four people died in the collapse. That ended the desire to make it easier on everyone to get to the bottom by mechanical means."

Jimmy interrupts, "Why couldn't John and I use our drones?"

The director ignores the question. "All right, let's bust our butts!" The Director jerks the camel's rope. Lights flash from its eyes as it rises on its hind legs and off the front knees. The students tie their bootstraps, throw their backpacks over their shoulders, and get back into formation. "We won't get to another rest area for several hours. Ready?" he shouts.

The group stops at the next rest area for a half-hour break and a light lunch. "Okay, guys, the next stop will be the bottom," the Director says, as he fastens the straps to his backpack. An hour or so later, the Director stops and raises his right hand to eye level to look at his medical watch. He speaks a word to the camel. Its eyes blink, and it stops. He walks back through the line of students. He stops in front of Henry, "How you feeling?" the Director asks.

"I'm fine. Tired, that's all. How much farther is it?" Henry asks through a faint breath.

"Your heart rate is very high, Henry. Hey!" he announces loudly. "We're going to take ten."

Everyone focuses on the Director kneeling alongside Henry. The Director helps him remove the backpack and holds a water bottle to his lips. "Take slow sips."

One of the students, a twenty-year-old from West Virginia named Waldo Jackabsum, kneels close to Henry, rubbing his shoulders. "Henry, it's okay. We'll get you there." Waldo helps the Director reposition the backpack to allow the sleeping bag to be a pillow.

The Director reaches into his backpack. He grabs a towel and an ice pack from the insulated first-aid kit. He places the damp cold cloth around the back of Henry's neck. Henry closes his eyes, breathes deeply and exhales softly.

Looking at his watch, the Director calculates how much farther it is to the plateau. He stands, looking over the rest of the crew. Raising his voice, he announces, "Henry is suffering from heat exhaustion. Anyone else feeling weak or possibly dizzy?" He pauses, focusing on each student. Relieved that no one answers, he says, "Good. As a caution, sit, rest, and drink that water. We may be here awhile."

Twenty minutes pass, allowing Henry time to regain composure. The Director announces, "Ok, guys, let's proceed, about an hour to go, that's all."

Until the End of Time

The trail soon flattens out to everyone's relief. The Director continues treading ahead to a turn shaded by dozens of trees. There, the students see him diving into the river.

The boys unbuckle the backpacks, throw their boots into the air, remove their shirts, and dive into the refreshing waters.

"Ah," Jimmy announces to the air, and grabs Johnathon around the waist and pulls him under the water.

The Director watches the group enjoying the refreshed atmosphere of the river. Ten minutes later, he blows a whistle, waits and blows it again, and yells to the subdued ruckus, "Okay, guys, it's time. Come on out and let the sun dry you off."

They pick a spot to sit, to lie on the grass. Jimmy leans back against his arms and hums: *"When peace like a river . . ."*

The Director rises and steps into his shorts, he throws the UNGCP embellished tee-shirt over his head, puts on his boots, and slowly ties the strings. "Okay! About a ten-minute walk from here," he announces.

Reaching the edge of the campsite, they stop, inhale, and view six white canvassed tents half-circled around a large square tent. There's an arrow on top pointing into the air. Fifty yards away from the individual tents are a half-dozen outhouses with open shower stalls nearby. On the other side of the large canvas tent is a volleyball court, and next to that are tree-trunk benches circling a campfire pit. There are eight upside-down aluminum canoes near the river.

The Director starts to read three names and points them to their assigned numbered tent. Johnathon, Albertaldo, and Youmentis, the counselor in tent two. Jimmy, Joseph, and their counselor Junior go to tent number four. Upon entering the tent, Jimmy throws his backpack and sleeping bag onto the cot to his right. Junior is along the rear wall and Joseph on the left of the Outfitter ten-foot-square tent with screen windows on each side, allowing air to flow through. The floor is simply ole, dry, hard, tan dirt.

Jimmy flattens out the sleeping bag. He reaches into the backpack, removes his pillow and places it at the open end of the thick, cushiony sleeping bag. He lies back and breathes deeply.

Just a Matter of Time

Junior, slightly less than six-feet tall, is a broad-shouldered, mid twentyish guy, his skin tone matching his light brown hair. "Well, guys, it's time to eat, and then, well, the Director talks on and on."

Jimmy catches his brother on the way to the large tent. "Have you seen our drones?"

"No!" Johnathon replies. He turns to Youmentis. "We thought our drones would be here. Where are they?"

"They're coming," Youmentis answers.

At the cafeteria-style food line, they take a tray, a large plastic plate, a small one, and tan-tissue-wrapped silverware. Junior starts spooning out the main course of noodles. Next was a pan of steamed rice and fried green tomatoes, which he skipped. He covers the noodles with the thick tomato chili sauce. Next was mixed vegetables, desserts of small vanilla cakes, red Jell-O, or a half-slice of a soft pear. Last along the line were small rolls smeared in butter. Standing behind the long table of the food pans was a mid-fortyish gentleman sporting a white chef's cap and white apron with the red letters GCP across it. In broken English, he greets each student by name as they continue along the line.

The Director is at the end, looking closely at the contents of each tray as the students pass on the way to choose a table.

"When will our drones arrive, and who will bring them," Jimmy asks the Director.

"That's all being taken care of," the Director replies.

The sun descends behind the ridges of the Canyon and covers the campsite in deep shadows. The Director presses a hand-held remote to light the interior of the central tent. He blows a whistle, pauses, and blows an extended blast to get everyone's attention.

"Students and counselors. Congratulations on walking that trail today. We began as individuals and knit together in one group. Our goal here is the same: ten students from various locations coming together to form one group, working and united together in unity to complete the tasks as One.

Until the End of Time

"Tomorrow, we'll start with an early wake-up call. We'll do stretches to get the blood moving and give you time to visit the latrines. A quick breakfast, a period of calisthenics, and a few sprints. After a relaxed lunch, we begin the work. Each of you has a specialty you've been learning. I hope to use that to our advantage, to boost our understandings, and learn more about this Canyon. We hope to do that without endangering the natural beauty and wildlife that freely use our surroundings.

"Every year, I get the same questions a day or so after arriving. Like, what about recreation time. Yes, you will have time to enjoy games and activities. But first and foremost, our purpose is to meet the desire of the agencies who've arranged for this summer project. In the past, we've uncovered clues to the antiquities of past civilizations occupying this land. It's exciting to scientific minds, as we help in unraveling the unknown past. We want to know who was here, what they ate, what they had to fight off to survive. What was their average day like? Were their features the same as ours? We've seen their carvings, their paintings on the walls of caves, but how did they communicate during a typical day? Nothing to write on but the walls of these caves, or the skins of animals. Did they cooperatively form personal relationships, or were they coaxed? Was there always a need for kings to lead them as a group, to help them manage their daily lives? How did the ancients agree on rules to live by?

"How did they move from one area to another? By camel? By horseback? By walking like we did today. Did they get exhausted, and how did they handle physical needs like that? How did they cook their meals, and where did that food come from? When did someone pull leaves out of the ground, discovering carrots? How did they learn the various methods of cooking? They created pots and pans, and vases to drink from. How and when did that start? Who was the first to discover that a fire would make the raw meat of an antelope taste so much better? We, in our modern industrialized society, think of the ancients as barbarians grunting at each other over a piece of raw fish. But, think back. They found ways to survive against the forces of nature. They learned how to build walls, damming creeks, and leaving us with musical instruments.

"Now, we run inside an air-conditioned home to escape a thunderstorm or the summer's heat. What did they do? Did they moan and groan because the rain prevented a beautiful day at the beach?

"Every religion says they have the answers. But scientists are discovering that much of the ancient writings are contradictory, refuting past manuscripts. Through our use of microscopes and the Giant Magellan

Just a Matter of Time

Telescope, we are finding astounding answers from that technology. They can see light years into the vast universe. Does the universe operate on the same time scale we have, or is it timeless? On dusted off remnants in unusual locations across the planet, they've uncovered the varieties of DNA, enabling them to date the age of a bone, a skull, or when a manuscript was written.

"We want answers to so many questions. It's our job as onsite inspectors to find and collect remnants of the past. That is our mission. You will be shoveling and dusting. You will be digging in the mud. You will be constructing ladders to the caves and crevices of the Canyon walls. You will be exploring those caves. Sometimes we discover artifacts in the most unsuspected areas."

One of the students raises his hand. "Yes. What's on your mind, Harold?"

"Will we be coming at this from the standpoint of standard evolutionary development or the mystery of creative intelligence?"

"Hmm," the Director says. "I see from your biography that your specialty is archeology. On student visas, you've already been to active sites in foreign lands learning the methods of discovery. You worked at the ancient Inca city in Peru. That's wonderful. Your talents have the utmost respect here. I've read that after this summer project, your assignment is still uncertain. What have you heard about that negligence?"

Harold responds. "I will find out more when the summer is over."

"I'm sure you will. It takes time for the authorities to carefully review every applicant to make sure, as the old saying goes, if the shoe fits, you'll get it. Your successful completion of this project will benefit that assignment."

Turning back to address all the students, the Director says, "I'm noticing that many of you are showing signs of fatigue, so let me close with a final thought. Three-quarters of the way down the trail this afternoon, you saw how exhaustion hit Henry. I was surprised. That's why we will have our calisthenics exercises every morning. It's the weak, dying fish that float downstream, but to go against the stream requires strength.

"There's another aspect of our wellness that we will do every evening before we hit the sack. This is the mental aspect of our training.

Until the End of Time

"Now, I want you to move over to the open section of this tent where we'll sit in a circle. We've already placed cushioned rug mats on the ground with your name stapled on them. Okay, push your chair in and find your mat."

The Director takes his place in the center of the circle. "This will be our time of meditation and reflection. Sit, cross your legs, and let your arms rest on your thighs. Sit up straight, no slouching. Keep your head up. Close your eyes. Tonight, we'll concentrate on your body. To begin, let your mind wander. Do not direct your thoughts. Sit, relax, and feel your heart beating, your lungs expanding. Listen to your body. Let your mind wander as it relieves mental stress."

"Whoever is humming, stop it. Now!" He looks around the room, "Jimmy, was that you?"

"Yes, sir, ah . . . it's something I unconsciously do."

"Not during this meditation period. Okay?"

"Listen to your breathing, to your exhaling. Are you breathing fast or slow? Is it deep or shallow? Do you feel the air going in through your mouth or your nose? What do you hear? Yes, your ears will pick up the faint noise of the fan, but do you hear other sounds off in the distance?" The Director pauses to look at each student and how they're positioned on the mats.

"Ready? Let's start. I'll ring a bell when the time completes. Keep your eyes closed and let your mind and body repair itself."

The Director pushes a button, the lights dim, and the gentle breeze from the ceiling fan blows upon the students. He positions himself on the square mat, starting his own time of meditation.

TWELVE

"How did you sleep?" Jimmy asks his twin, meeting him on the way to the outhouses after the two-minute exercise session.

"All right, I guess."

Standing in line for breakfast behind Joseph, Jimmy picks a tray, sets it on the counter rails, grabs a plate, and the silverware. The chef scoops scrambled eggs mixed with chopped tomatoes and green peppers onto his plate. There's a sign on the next pan boldly declaring, '**No more than TWO sausage links.**' Next is a sign saying, '**One muffin.**'

"That's it for breakfast?" Jimmy mumbles as he joins Johnathon, Albertaldo, and Joseph.

The Director has been wandering between the tables, watching, and listening to the conversations. He stops at a nearby table and tells the students, "Stop the yakking about the breakfast. You don't want a full stomach before the exercises."

A bell rings. The Director takes his place facing the students and counselors. "All right, time to go! Leave your plates on the tables. Let's go! Now!" He leads them out of the tent to the open area. He instructs them to line up on the yellow line painted on the ground. "Counselor Junior will lead this morning's calisthenics," the Director says. He returns to the tent, as Junior takes his position.

"Ready guys? Let's go." Junior starts the exercises with jumping jacks, "A-one, a-two, a-three," he counts while watching each student following along. "Twenty," Junior stops and lies flat on the ground. "Next, push-ups. On your toes and fingertips. A-one, a-two." He keeps counting each up and down, showing how their nose must breeze the dirt. "Ten," he

Until the End of Time

shouts and stands to shake his arms and legs. "Next. Sit ups. Ready. Ten of these. One, two, keep your legs flat, knees, and the muscle of the calf always on the ground, your elbows out as you rise. Three, four, five. Five more."

"Good going. And now we'll run in place."

"Come on, lift the knees high. Feel them clicking. Feel the toes hit the ground."

"Not too bad," Junior says after two minutes. "Now, down to one push-up, up to one jumping-jack. Down and up, one after another, same pace. Let's do it." They drop down for the push-up, and up for the jumping-jack trying to keep pace with all eyes are focused on Junior.

Junior stops repeatably breathes in deeply, with long sighs of relief. "Very good. Relax."

Soon the Director walks out to stand next to Junior. "Well done," he says. "I'm proud of the way you followed along, and it appeared to me you carried on as One. Ten becoming One. Sit and relax a bit before we do the sprints. Competition has always been a motivating factor in societal development. It's inbred as part of nature to survive, to compete, to be better than the next guy. Sometimes it leads to disagreements, fights, wars, and deaths. So, we've learned to set rules and initiated referees – judges of ten, judges of hundreds and those of thousands." The Director pauses, looking from student to student. "Okay, take a break."

The kids move into the grassy area, sitting with legs crossed, a few reclined, and looking up at the clear blue sky. Jimmy looks at his brother and says, "John, I was wondering about what Andrea said. Were their exercises the same as ours?"

"I doubt it, Jim. But the way things are now, who knows."

"Yeah. Hey, at our get-together, let's ask them."

The Director returns to the area. He's got a can of yellow spray paint, a pistol, and four red-flags. He paints the starting line, paces off ten yards, and sprays a dozen dots. At each ten-yard space, he paints the number alongside the solid yellow line dividing the two lanes. He sticks two flags at the starting line and two more at the fifty-yard finish line.

Junior calls the guys together. "This is a barefoot race between you and your tent partner. The winner will take on the tent counselor. That's it. Let's go. Tent number one, you're first." Junior scampers to the finish line.

Just a Matter of Time

The two students of tent one line up on the yellow line.

Pop! The director fires the pistol. The two students take off running barefoot on the dirt path. They pass the ten-yard mark, the thirty, and across the finish line where Junior is standing to record the times into the tab. "Good one. Time: 6.72." He gives Victor a narrow red ribbon.

Next in line is tent two. "Johnathon and Albertaldo. Ready guys?" The Director questions as they take their positions and checks their lineup.

Jimmy yells from the sideline, "Get it, John. Pour it on!"

Pop goes the gun, and off they go. Johnathon takes a quick lead at the ten-yard line. Albertaldo catches John at the thirty and slowly moves a pace ahead. Jimmy yells at his twin at the forty, "Turn it on, now!" Johnathon stretches his legs out, forcing his body into high gear, and passes Albertaldo, beating him by a foot.

"That a way, bro! You did it!" Jimmy taps his brother on his butt. Johnathon is informed of his time of 6.79 seconds and is given a red ribbon.

"Good race, John," Albertaldo shakes Johnathon's hand.

Harold, of tent three whips Henry. Now it's Jimmy against Joseph. Jimmy looks at him, taking his position on the starting line. "Joe, take it easy on me."

Pop! The pistol fires a blast of smoke, and Joseph takes off, leaving Jim inhaling dust at the thirty. Joeseph easily beats Jimmy. After recovering from the exhaustive sprint, Jimmy asks Junior what his time was. 6.81. Johnathon yells to Jimmy, "I beat you, bro!"

Waldo wins tent five by 0.60 seconds.

The Director calls them together, congratulating the winners and announces the times. "First place goes to Joseph at 5.81 seconds. Very good." Everyone applauds as he gives Joseph a red ribbon.

"And now, the winners against the counselors. Tent one, you're up."

The counselor is in the right lane. The Director is on the counselor's right aiming the pistol straight up. "Ready? Get set!" Pop! And off they go running hard as the nine students loudly cheer for Victor. The counselors urge their fellow counselor. Victor beats him by half a second.

"Tent two, your turn." The Director points to Johnathon, ready to go on the left, and Youmentis on the right. During last summer's project,

Until the End of Time

Youmentis had exhibited his physical ability in all aspects by winning the sprints, the canoe race, archery, and rock climbing. His achievements enabled his acceptance as a counselor this year.

The other counselors start cheering and repeating the phrase, "Get 'em You. Get 'em You," as he takes the running position. To cheer his brother on to let it all out, Jimmy has moved to the thirty-yard mark.

"Ready? Get set!" the gun pops.

The two push hard, nose to nose at the twenty, at the thirty Youmentis slowly advances. Jimmy is on the sidelines. Youmentis is still slightly ahead when Jimmy waves his arms, yelling, "Now, John, now!" At the forty, the two are even. Youmentis is gaining ground when he stumbles, falls, and rolls over in the dirt, grabbing his right foot yelling "*I-yi-y!!!!!*"

They all rush to his side.

"Youmentis, lean back and let me have a look," the Director says. He pulls Youmentis's hand away from his foot, puts a little pressure on the heel of his foot, raises it, and turns the foot left and right. "Doesn't seem to be anything broken," he says, as Youmentis grimaces. The Director lowers his head to see the bottom of his foot. "Hmm. Here it is, some blood. You stepped on something."

Arriving with the large first-aid kit, Junior asks, "how is it?"

"I need the scanner," the Director sharply says. Junior presses the button of the kit, watching it slowly open. Junior pulls out a four by eight, two-inch thick box marked by a red cross. The Director slides his hand under the rear strap, pulling the Velcro end to meet Velcro. He presses a button on the right side of the black box and watches until it blinks a soft yellow light. The Director starts above the ankle bone and slowly moves it to the bottom of his heel. A click and a flash. Another flash as it reaches the sole and his toes. The scanner beeps. "Got it," the Director says. He pushes a button and sees the words *working* next to a rotating green circle imaging the insides of Youmentis's ankle and foot.

Victor, kneeling and watching the procedure, says, "Director, I'm trained as a surgical nurse. Let me get a close-up view."

Recognizing Victor and his biography, he says, "Yeah, sure."

"You got a tweezer?" Victor asks.

Just a Matter of Time

With a damp cloth, he cleans the spot and starts swiping with the tips of the tweezer across the half-inch puncture mark. He focuses on the puncture, and with the tip of the tweezer, he digs a bit into the hole. "I feel something there, but it's too deep. Can't get a grip on it," he announces as he wipes away the blood.

"Thanks, Victor," The Director says. "There's something there, right?"

"Yes, I could feel the resistance."

"Let's get him to the tent."

Victor softly places a gauze pad on the area, and wraps the two-inch bandage around the foot, taping the end.

Two counselors grab Youmentis and pull him up. He holds his right foot slightly off the ground.

The Director addresses the students. "I want you to inspect the path in the area where Youmentis stumbled. Look for anything unusual. You will need to search every inch of that area slowly. Be careful. Thanks."

Junior closes the first-aid kit and straps it over his shoulder. Giving the scanner time to complete the sending process, the Director turns to watch the students scour the small area. He tells Henry to go inside the tent and get scrapers.

"There must be something under the surface. Scrape it slowly."

"Alright, EMC has it. We should find out within the hour."

The Director bends down next to Johnathon, "Feeling anything?" he asks.

"Nothing here, but Albert said he felt something next to the line."

"Show me."

"Right here. Rub your fingers over it."

"Hmm, yes," the Director agrees. "Junior, give me the scanner."

The Director straps on the scanning tab, turns on the energy, waits for the yellow light, and starts moving it across the spot, hearing it beep, beep, beep. "Yes, there is a metallic object in there," he declares.

Henry arrives with the scrappers and kneels next to the Director.

Until the End of Time

"We found something here." The Director points to the spot. He takes a three-inch scraper and begins pulling dirt from the area around the spot when the scanner beeped. Carefully, he goes lower and lower, leaving the area untouched. With a pocketknife, he starts scrapping the hard dirt hiding the object. He begins to see it and removes more dirt. "Wow!" The Director softly and reflectively exclaims, looking at the find. Turning the scanner on, he presses two-buttons and takes a picture of the object.

Jimmy, squatting nearby, says, "It's nothing but an old ink pen."

"You've seen one of those?" The Director asks. "Yes, Jimmy, these were used before ball-point pens were invented in the late 1800s. Why is it here, who left it, and how long ago? Perhaps there's more. This is fantastic! What a discovery we made already. Unbelievable."

Jimmy surmises, "The tip appears broken in half, so the rest of the tip may be what's inside Youmentis's foot."

"You could be right, Jimmy. And if that's the case, he'll need a surgeon to remove it."

"I could do it," Victor says. "It'll take an incision, and a local anesthetic."

"Hmm? Perhaps. Let's go check on Youmentis." To Junior, the Director says, "Rope the area off, and you and Mohab can continue the races."

Jimmy takes his brother off to the side. "John, I don't know about all this. The whole thing, it's driving me nuts. Whoopie, we found a fountain pen. What are we doing here?"

"Huh? What you talking about?"

"Ah, the Director. Did you see him last night after the meditation period?"

"No."

"Well, right before I entered the tent, I looked back, and I saw him and the chef . . ."

Junior calls out, interrupting Jimmy. "Hey guys, get over here. We're going to finish these races before lunch," Junior announces. "So, back to the starting line. Let's go."

"Tent three is up," Junior announces. "Harold and Mohab."

"Ready, get set . . . Pop! The pistol fires.

Just a Matter of Time

Counselors are cheering, students yelling as Harold takes off in a rush wanting to beat the counselor Mohab, and to spoil his chances for a return next summer. "Go, Haro, go, go, go," the students yell. At the forty, they're nose to nose. "Go, Haro, turn it on!"

Junior announces: "Mohab wins by a nose."

"No! It was too close to tell," Albertaldo tells Junior. They all gather around Junior as he presses a button on the timer, and peers in for a close-up view of the two as they crossed the line.

"There," Albertaldo points to the student's nose. "See, he got it. His hand crossed the line first."

"No," Junior states, "see the red dot on his nose. Mohab won it. It's the nose that counts."

"I object," Albert says. "They should race again."

"No. Harold lost by a nose."

"Next up, would be Joseph and me," Junior announces. "I forfeit the race to Joseph."

"Tent five, you're up. Waldo and, Oops, Kenneth is helping Youmentis."

Inside the tent, Victor removed the item from Youmentis's foot and is now bandaging the area. The pictures the Director took of the broken pen tip are sent to EMC, the Canyon Project leadership, the historical society, the EPA, the ecological society, and the archeology group.

"I've been directed to remove the rest of the pen, and to scrape further, expanding the search site in hopes of finding more artifacts," the Director tells Junior.

The students have been relaxing in the sun. Jimmy, Johnathon, and Albertaldo found a spot at the river to dip their feet into the cool waters.

"John, doesn't the Director have a name?" Jimmy asks. "I asked Junior, and he told me to forget it."

"Jim," Johnathon says. "Remember, our Director in the academy was known only as the Director."

"But how do they get around that? Everybody has a name."

THIRTEEN

The students devour their evening dinner of noodles covered in, well, whatever the chef had left over from lunch, plus the every meal salad and one roll. The Director paces back and forth, hearing them complain about the lack of the plentiful food choices they had back home.

"Okay, students, before we get into our meditation period, I've got a few things I'd like to congratulate you on. Today was an exceptional day. You're progressing quite well, and I thank you for your cooperation. Take some additional time to relax. In the morning, we will investigate a few sites in the area. And, the next day, we will canoe to visit an old Indian homestead. Thank you." He walks out of the tent.

Ten minutes later, the Director is back. "Okay, students, it's time to revitalize. Tonight, we will hold our meditation outside under the clear skies. During this evening's meditation, I'd like you to concentrate on the blessings of being here. Push any negative thoughts away. Concentrate on the pleasant weather, the nourishing food, and the camaraderie. You've all done well, adapting to each other and working together as a team. Ten becoming One in unity. Thank You."

*****

The morning arrives.

They've gulped the light breakfast, finished the exercises. They are now involved in the digging, scrubbing, and brushing away plots of dirt near and under the spot where they discovered the fountain pen. So far, they found what appears to be a diary scribbled on an animal skin. The notes, buried in the hardened moist clay for that length of time, were barely discernable. There were also bone fragments alongside the diary.

Just a Matter of Time

Halfway through the morning, the Director splits the students into three groups. Johnathon, Albertaldo, and the counselor Youmentis are sent off to explore a cave. Jimmy, Joseph, Harold, Henry, and Junior are exploring a region on the other side of the river where the crevices of Canyon walls formed an open tunnel. The rest of them continue to look further into yesterday's find.

Following behind Joseph, Jimmy wisecracks as Joseph ducks his head to enter the tunnel corridor, "Careful Joe." Jimmy kneels, to rub his fingers over the smooth granite that form the walls. "Joe, this is the kind of stone I used to build my turtle. Look at it. Feel its timelessness."

"Timelessness?"

"Think, Joe." Jimmy starts his dialogue learned at the Academy. "Future generations will explore these same granite walls a hundred, a thousand years from now. Constantly moving waters can't erode these walls. No way. It takes dynamite, a massive blow, a sudden shifting of the earth plates to split these walls apart."

"Not so, Jim. Raging rivers of eons ago carved these walls. Fast moving waters for millions of years whittling away . . ."

"Hey, you guys, whatcha doing?" Junior asks, as he, Henry and Harold, duck their heads as they enter the twenty-foot long tunnel.

Jimmy answers, "Sorry for going ahead of you, but this was intriguing."

"Please, we must stay together as a group. The Director sent us over here to see if there might be writings or paintings on these walls. So, let's look. Split into pairs. Use your candles as you rub your fingers over the ridges. Look for anything unusual. If there are rough, dusty surfaces, there could be a treasure there. Settlers or original natives could have used this area as a protective shelter. Take your time. Jim and Joe, you two start working from the far opening, and these two will start here. I'll be in the middle."

As Jimmy and Joseph stroll toward the far entrance. Jimmy starts to sing, "'*I'll take the high road, and you'll take the low road.*'"

"Where did that come from?"

"It's an old Scottish song from back in the eighteenth century."

Until the End of Time

"But you're not Scottish?"

"No, a fearless Viking from Norway. But, Joe, could it be that taking the high road is more dangerous, like walking along the top edge of the Canyon? And us Viks are more prepared to take the high road, rather than those who took the safer low road here in the bottom of the Canyon."

"It sure would be safer for you to get out of my way when I'm rushing at you to dunk the ball," Joseph retorts.

"Joe, the meanings of the original Scottish song has changed over the years. Taking the high road indicates someone who does the right thing, walking the morally right road. Taking the low road is the route to revenge."

"Jim, I thought so. You're out for revenge because you lost the race."

Jimmy sings again, "*'I'll take the low road, and I'll be in Scotland a'fore ye.'* Think what you want, but because of your height, I'm forced to take the low road. So don't bang your head."

"Scrape the walls man," Joseph tells him. "You may find a picture of your last girlfriend since it's been many years ago since one looked at you twice."

"Girls are forced to look up to you because of your height, not your character."

"Shut your damn mouth, or I'll give you a piece of my character."

"Quiet down," Junior admonishes. "This is serious. Your full concentration is required, so keep it quiet."

"Ah," Jimmy says, "Joe is …"

"Jimmy, stop it now," Junior chastises.

Jimmy moves close to the wall. olding the candle steady in his left hand, he rubs inch by inch the smooth surface of the orange horizontally striped walls with his right hand. He reaches high, and in a dusty spot, he scribbles *dust me* with his licked fingertip. For the next half-hour, they quietly work opposite walls rubbing the dust covered granite, finding nothing but smooth surfaces with periodic ridges. Carefully holding the candle to shine on the wall, Jimmy starts softly singing: "*'This little light of mine, I'm gonna let it shine, let it shine, let it shine.'*"

Reaching into his pocket, Jimmy removes a toothpick out of the plastic holder, rubs it with dust, splits it. Looking around to see if anyone was watching, he reaches for dirt. He spits in the dirt, using that mud to hold the toothpick under a ridge near where Jimmy scribbled the two words. Raising his voice loud enough for Junior to hear, he says, "Oooh! That hurt! Hey, I found something here."

Junior takes the few steps to see. "What is it? Let me see." Junior shines his candle on the spot. Intrigued, Joseph turns from his position on the opposite wall to look over Jimmy's shoulder. The other two students also gather around to see the mystery.

"It looks like a toothpick," Jimmy tells Junior.

Looking at the item closer, Junior responds, "Why yes, it does. Hmm? Very unusual. Junior points to the words 'dust me, "Did you do that?"

"Yeah," Jimmy says, "and I was about to dust it when my finger caught the pick."

"Good work, Jim. It's our first find." He taps Jimmy on his back. Junior brings his pad up to eye level, and is about to snap a picture, when Jimmy says, "Gotcha."

They all look at Jimmy smiling. Joseph, Harold, and Henry start chuckling.

"Jimmy!" Junior rebukes. "Oh, I'd like to . . . Ah, come with me."

Out of hearing range, Junior stops, turns, and looks hard at Jimmy, "All right, what were you thinking? Why did you do it?"

Jimmy answers, "You know as well as I do, that we'll never find anything here. You're telling me that in previous years, no one has looked at these walls? Come on, Junior, they've been looked at and looked at over and over. It's something to keep us busy."

"Oh, you think so. What gives you that idea?"

Jimmy says, "Footprints on the floor? They weren't made a hundred years ago. If we're gonna find a relic, we'd better start digging, perhaps right there." Jimmy points his finger at an area near the river. "Yeah, we should start looking under those raised areas by the river. Couldn't they be burial grounds?"

"The Director has been doing this for six years now, and you think he sends a group here just to keep 'em busy?"

Until the End of Time

"Well, I'm not sure if it's only busyness or to teach us something, whatever that might be. And where's my drone?"

"Jim, let me give you a little advice if you want to complete this summer."

"I'm not sure about this so-called project," Jimmy responds.

"Well, tough. Get in line and do what you're told. If you want that job of building that Museum, you had better follow along with a happy face. Now, between us, I'm not going to tell the Director what you did today."

Junior turns, and walks back to the tunnel, leaving Jimmy to ponder his fate. "Okay, Jim did pull one on me, but we're going to leave it at that. Don't mention this again, ever! That's the end of foolishness, right?"

Joseph, looking down at Junior, says, "Come on, it was a joke. A good one too."

"Joe, we're supposed to follow along and diligently do our assigned tasks, nothing more, nothing less. All of you. Got it? Like I warned Jim. How you perform over this summer will affect those assignments you got."

"You're saying that having fun is dangerous to our future?" Joseph asks.

Junior responds, "There's having fun, and there's making fun."

Jimmy, about to say something is winked at by Joseph, who says, "Man, what a slippery slope that is. Who determines what having fun or making fun is?"

"I do, and the Director," Junior answers.

Jimmy speaks up, "Are you telling us that we must not question anything? Keep our mouths shut and obey orders. Is that it?"

Joseph adds, "Sounds like the army, without uniforms."

Harold and Henry have been silently watching and hearing it all. Harold speaks up, "Jimmy is right about this area. We should be digging and not rubbing walls. There's nothing but dust on these walls. All those structures found in Peru were because of years of intensive digging. I saw it with my own eyes."

"Guys, you don't understand. I'm here, and you're here because of our previous excellent accomplishments. We did not defy the authorities.

Just a Matter of Time

We worked with them. Don't you understand that? We cannot go against them. If the Director says jump, we jump."

"Even if what he says is nonsense or stupid, we jump. Huh? How high?" Jimmy asks.

"All right! I will keep this conversation between us, but guys, remember this: how you perform here can have a direct effect on your future work assignments," Junior emphasizes.

*****

Youmentis rests his foot on a log, watching Johnathon and Albertaldo construct the makeshift ladder from fallen trees and their branches. With his pocketknife and a chisel, Johnathon has carved notches at every one-foot mark of the two-inch thick long branches. He and Albertaldo have chopped tree limbs sixteen inches long. They carved notches two inches from each end. Albertaldo has placed the notch of the short piece into the cut-out areas of the long trunk and ties them together. He tests the tightness of the strings. The assembled ladder is leaned against the wall below the edge of the cave.

Albertaldo adjusts his full weight on the first step, the second and the third. Satisfied, he climbs to the top and pulls himself up, rolling onto the ledge of the small cave opening. He throws the rope down for John to tie on the sack of brushes, candles, and matches.

"Good start," Youmentis says. "Wish I could get up there."

Johnathon carefully climbs up the ladder. A lighted candle in hand, Albertaldo crawls through the low opening to a few feet inside the cave, holding the candle which has a curved piece of aluminum behind the flame to light the dark interior.

In an excited voice, he tells Johnathon, "Wow! Look! Hundreds of bats! Be careful. We don't want to disturb them."

"Bats? Not me! I'm getting out of here," Johnathon hurriedly backs out to the ledge.

"Oh, John, bats don't sting. They're hibernating." Albertaldo relates his experiences learning about bats on his trip to the sacred sites in Peru

Until the End of Time

vacated hundreds of years ago. "The bats have made a few of those caves their habitat over the years. It was astounding." He hands the candle to John, "here, take a look."

"Nope. Not me." Johnathon says. He yells to Youmentis, "There are bats in this cave, we can't go in there."

"Bats? All right! We've got to make a barrier at the entrance."

"Barriers? For who, what?" Johnathon asks.

"Take the measurements, and come on down," Youmentis says.

Johnathon and Albertaldo relax in front of their counselor, who is chatting with the Director on his pad. "Yes, sir, we'll start that part of it now. We can do that with what we have in the area."

Youmentis tells them the plan. "First, we need more branches and chop them according to the entrance dimensions. We'll tie them together, leaving narrow openings for the bats to fly through." Youmentis draws a picture in the dirt. "For now, we'll lean it against the cave."

They scour the area, collect and trim branches. They begin tying the pieces together using three vertical pieces as separators of the long branches to provide openings for the bats to fly through.

"That's looking good, and ought to do it guys. It's lunchtime." Youmentis continues to inform them that finishing the bat protection will require the entire crew to get slabs of stone to hold the wood in place. Youmentis starts to scrape an outline in the dirt, "there, something like that."

Johnathon asks, "and the weight of it, how do we get them up there?"

"How did the Egyptians build the pyramid?" Youmentis asks.

"Nobody knows?" Johnathon replies.

Albertaldo says, "I wondered the same thing when seeing the ruins on that mountaintop in China. It looked like they were cut with modern day saws using tee-squares, tape measures, and levels. Aha! This is part of our learning experience here, to understand or to reckon how the ancients did things without any of our modern-day equipment."

Johnathon says, "So that's why we're using candles! How come I got to keep my pocketknife? They certainly didn't have a Craftsman chisel, nor hatchets, did they?"

"There are exceptions to everything," Youmentis comments.

Just a Matter of Time

Johnathon says, "I want an exception from that bat cave."

Getting that intimidating look from Youmentis, Johnathon says, "Yeah, yeah."

"Time to head back," Youmentis says. He gets off the log, gets the crutch, and starts hobbling back to the tent a quarter mile away. "The Director is going to be pleased with the wooden barrier you built."

"Whoopie!" Johnathon snaps, as he bursts into a gallop toward the campsite.

FOURTEEN

David, Robert, and Janice have returned to Boulder and are now sitting on the deck behind David's home with a view of the Rocky Mountains. The fresh air of the elevated landscape envelops them.

"Minus the mountains," Robert says. "This reminds me of our backyard. We can sit out there and not say a word. We get so quiet we can hear our hearts beat while we watch the moon rise as the sun slowly disappears."

"Time for a drink," David says, and excuses himself to get a bottle of red wine to finish off the meal of charcoal-roasted ham steaks and corn on the cob.

Robert leans over to Janice. He brushes her hair back a bit to place a tender kiss on her left forehead. "Thank you for suggesting we make this trip. Sitting here has brought back good memories. But," he turns to look at the door. "Do you have questions about David and his . . . well, his use of words?"

"Yes, I was surprised."

"Here you go," David announces, as he slides the glass door behind him. "We'll drink a toast to Ruth's discharge in the morning,"

"To Ruth and her happiness," David announces.

"To Ruth," Robert and Janice echo.

"How's she doing physically?" Janice asks.

"The last few days, they've had her exercising, preparing her for the discharge."

Just a Matter of Time

"I'm still not clear as to the need for those extreme conditions," Robert says.

"I don't understand it either. It is what it is," David answers.

The next morning, Robert and Janice are relaxing under the canopy of the Winnebago, waiting for David to return with Ruth. Hearing the horn beep, beep, they see David's car turning the corner and into the cul-de-sac.

"Here, they come!" Janice exclaims.

They're at the side of the car as it comes to a stop. The rear doors open. "Janice!" Ruth shouts, as she gets out of the car and embraces Janice. "Oh, my, what a sight," she whispers in Janice's ear.

"You look great!" Janice tells Ruth.

With outstretched arms, Ruth tells Robert, "Come here, you mighty one."

"Ruth, we're thrilled. You're looking good," Robert says.

"Am I ever glad to get out of there. A nightmare. Wow!" Ruth says, looking at the Winnebago. "Mind if I look inside?"

"No, of course not."

"Ruthie," David says. "perhaps later. You need to come in and relax first."

"Phooey with that," she replies as she pulls Janice toward the Winnie. "I gotta see this. Show me." Robert walks ahead to open the door, and the two-step slides out. Janice reaches for Ruth's elbow.

"I don't need your help," Ruth says. She shoves Janice aside, and steps inside. "Wow, this is a dream." She gapes at the insides. The frame of bills hanging over the dining table catches her eyes, "Holy moly! I haven't seen any of those for years!" She turns and looks at the driver's area. "Oh, yeah, cup holders. Does that screen tell you where to go, and how did you ever get permission to use this?"

"That's a long story," Janice answers. "Ruthie, don't you think you ought to go in where you can sit back comfortably? Let's catch up on all the news. It's been years."

Until the End of Time

"Don't start that poor-ole-you stuff. I'm fine," Ruth answers.

"David said you caught pneumonia."

"I don't want to get into that crap now." Ruth snaps. David tenderly holds her fingers in his. "Hon, let's go in and have a cup coffee, shall we? Celebrate your homecoming."

"God, I'm ready for coffee," Ruth answers. "Dave, I'm fine. Don't need your damn help. Jan, let's do some gardening. I'm sure it needs it."

"We'll get to that."

"Gads, I missed you," Ruth replies. "You're going to get your nails dirty."

The four of them kick their shoes off in the foyer and make their way through the carpeted living room and into the kitchen. David reaches into the cabinet for coffee grounds as Robert and Janice pull two chairs out at the table. At the counter next to David, Ruth turns to ask Janice, "You did say tea, didn't you? Constant Brazil, right?"

"Sure, you remembered."

"Of course. I'm not senile."

David gently leans into the side of Ruth, "I got it. Tea for Jan, and coffee for the rest of us. Go sit with them while I get this?"

"Yeah, sis, come on over here. I got a payback for you from years ago," Janice says.

"You got a payback? I owe you four of them! Good ones, too," Ruth responds. She turns her stout body away from the counter to step over to the kitchen table. She moves the chair into position, stares at Janice as she places her elbow on the table.

"Come on," Ruth says, raising her right arm. "Rock, paper, scissors."

"Oh, my! How long has it been?"

"Ready?" Ruth loudly says. "Two out of three. One, two, three, go!"

Janice wins the first round, as she lowered her hand with an open palm while Ruth's hand was closed. "Ready . . . Go," Janice states. Their arms lower, Janice with two fingers extended, and Ruth's hand flat.

"I won. Eh, little sis beat the big sis," Janice gleefully shouts.

"You always got to bring my size into it, don't you?" Ruth mutters, abruptly getting up from the chair, stomping out and down the hallway.

Just a Matter of Time

Stunned to silence, Janice looks to Robert and over to David, each of them surprised by the sudden unexpected reaction. "Oh, my. What did I do?" Janice asks.

David leaves the kitchen to follow his wife.

"Rob?"

"Yes?" Robert answers. "Has she ever reacted to a comment like that before?"

"No, never. Her physical size never was an issue. She boasted to everyone, Anything you can do, I can do better."

Sensing that David is consoling Ruth, Robert and Janice discuss their past lives with Ruth and David. Ruth and Janice became friends by being on the girls' academy golf team. They enjoyed the competition and belittling the loser into doing better next time. "Ruth's success as a golfer was because she was more muscular and heavier than the rest of us girls. She was able to hit the ball much farther."

Janice continues. "David had enlisted in the Navy after a year of college. He served overseas for six years. After his discharge, he lived at home for the first two years while studying at the seminary. I was studying nursing when I pushed him to ask Ruth out, and it was love at first sight. They got married right after David graduated."

"To my recollection, Ruth has always been very congenial," Robert says. "Pneumonia is not known to cause . . ."

Robert is interrupted by David and Ruth's footsteps in the tiled hallway, and upon entering the kitchen, Ruth speaks first, "Hey, I'm sorry. I'm sorry, Jan." She pulls Janice into a hug. "I'm sorry."

Janice whispers, "Forgive me. I didn't mean to upset you. I'm sorry."

"It's the damn medicine!" Ruth exclaims. "I was having the same sort of reactions in the hospital."

"After Ruth settled down," David says. "I looked in her purse. I found something prescribed by the hospital. There was this very tiny, barely discernible note on the bottom: *Certification under consideration.* I gave her a sedative that she's used before."

"We suspected that it was the effects of medication," Janice says. "The Ruth I knew was always full of delight and enjoyable to be around. So, Ruthie, be of good comfort."

"Discard it," Robert suggests to David.

"I did," David replies. "She'll be her old self soon." He slides his arm around her shoulder. "She suggested that we go for a ride up the hills where the scenery is amazing, and there's a fantastic restaurant there."

"Sounds good to me," Robert replies.

"Ruthie, do you still play golf?" Janice asks.

"Not very often anymore."

"I brought my clubs," Janice adds. "Let's get out at least once. Okay?"

"Sure," she answers. "But, now, I'm feeling numb."

Entering the garage, David slides his forefingers over the sensor on the wall. The garage door opens. They fasten the seat belts, the cord releases, and the car starts. He pokes a button on the dashboard screen and slowly speaks their destination. He turns his seat inward to see Robert and Janice relaxed in the back. Ruth appears comfortable. The car maneuvers out of the cul-de-sac and through the neighborhood streets to the main highway. David nods his head and raises his eyes toward the ceiling while his index finger points to a light fixture in the center of the car.

"Ah, those bugs," Robert says, "I've found a method of ridding myself of those mosquitoes and other pests, too."

David starts the conversation about the status of the ministry. "Several years ago, the youth leader reached out to other churches which were having the same problems of attracting the youngsters. He finally got their cooperation to create combined services. It's grown to over a thousand youngsters and young adults. It's been an unbelievable ride for the last five to seven years."

On the way, David also points out different areas of interest as they pass through open vistas between the densely forested regions of the mountains. The car easily maneuvers the increasing elevation of the curving two-lane road. He leans over to Ruth touching her forearm. "Feeling better?"

Just a Matter of Time

"Yes, I am. Thanks. I'm ready to eat, though."

"We'll be there soon."

Feeling a vibration, Robert reaches for the tablet holder attached to his belt: "Yes, Peter, what's up?" Robert answers. After carefully listening to Mr. Bilko for a moment, Robert says, "I can't right now." After a pause, he speaks again, "Okay, I'll do it when I get back to the camper. Pete, I'll get to it later tonight or in the morning." Another pause as he listens to Peter. "Hey, I'm on vacation. Dale should be able to handle it. Sandy can upload all of that for Dale, and he could take care of it. I'm on vacation." Robert shakes the tablet and listens to more. "Bye." Robert slides the tab back into the leather pouch. "These things. Ugg! No peace!"

"What's up? This won't affect our time away, will it?" Janice quizzes.

"No way. But I'll be tied up for a while later this evening. Sorry, David. But my boss is one of those right now execs. Now, not later."

Ruth turns her head to Robert, "Want a pill?"

"I need more than a pill. I need a new boss."

Looking out the windshield, David says, "The lookout is around this bend. Let's eat first."

Entering the restaurant near the top of the mountain, a waitress greets them. Looking directly at David, she says, "Pastor Mathish, I'm sure Mr. and Mrs. Amwestson would prefer a booth next to the window. This way, please." She leads them to a half-circle booth with the seats facing a large window overlooking the scenery. Janice and Ruth sit next to each other. David and Robert at the ends. The young waitress places the single page menus in front of them.

Looking at the menu, Robert says, "Hey, this is Spanish."

She reaches in and turns the menu over. "I'll get your drink order shortly."

"What a view! This wasn't here when we were kids," Janice states.

"No," David responds. "It was built about ten years ago by the Department of Hospitality. They operate it, too."

The waitress approaches the booth and provides small glasses of water, straws, and slices of lemon. She places a twelve-inch tall open-folds plastic pictograph of the mountain and surrounding areas with descriptions on each inner fold marked with the initials A thru F. "I'll give you a few minutes."

"Take a close look at this," David tells Robert.

Robert checks the smoothness around the edges and finds a half-inch circular bump on an outer fold of the display. He points his finger to the bump and lays the item flat on the table close to the window. He pushes the pictograph between the table and the window to see it disappear to the floor. He leans over to look under the table. With his shoe, he brings the item in closer and carefully places his shoe on top. "Jan, have you decided yet."

"What do you recommend, Ruth?" Janice asks as the waitress nears the table.

"I've always liked the smothered roasted chicken breast and a salad," Ruth answers.

"What's it going to be? The waitress asks.

David orders the same as last time. Janice decides on the bacon wrapped cheeseburger, and Robert orders the soup of the day.

"Thanks, it won't take long. Enjoy the scenery."

"Because of the noise of the kids singing and shouting." David starts the conversation. "The neighborhood alliance came against us for disturbing their peace. They insisted that we get permits to hold our weekly concerts, And, they wanted the auditorium inspected for safety before every service. We've been forced to install facial recognition screens to protect the entrances."

"You got to be kidding," Robert states.

"No, It's true. We tried to resist. But Rob, that technology has become so helpful. We know who is there, and how often they come. It has also aided us with first-time visitors. The greeter at the front desk will hear a beep when a stranger enters, and we can immediately greet and welcome them. The software informs the greeters about them, and they can direct them to areas that satisfy their interests."

"Oh, my. Where are is this taking us?" Robert asks.

The waitress brings the meals along with the dessert special. "It's on the house."

Just a Matter of Time

"Okay," David says. "Let us bless this food, for our safety and well-being, and Ruth here."

"It's been an amazing journey," David says, after a few bites of his double-burger. "Now we're looking for a rural location to build a new stadium. We bid on one site, but denied."

Robert asks, "What authority do you have in the direction the church is taking?"

"The elders have superior authority under my guidance. I sit on the board and offer my opinions, and direct them on the spiritual aspect," David answers. "I deliver most of the sermons after the council approves."

"Council?" Robert asks, "Your sermons need approval?"

"Merely a formality."

Robert asks more questions about the authority of the council when a middle-aged gentleman approaches wearing a loosely fitted green Flagstaff Vista tee shirt. "How's the food?" He reaches in to place another pictograph on the table. "I guess she forgot to provide you with our special points of interest flyer for you. I'm sorry. I'll talk to her about it. You know how it is with young people."

Watching him replace the item, Robert says, "No, she did, but somehow it fell to the floor. It's there somewhere." He slides his foot off the item and pushes it closer to the wall. "Thanks, it's beautiful. Would you mind if we took it home with us?"

"We've got 'em at the check-in for you," he answers. "Thanks for coming, Mr. and Mrs. Amwestson. How was your tip from Oregon?"

"Very nice. Thank you."

"Have an enjoyable time." The gentleman says and leaves the table.

Robert starts to push the display off the table when Janice leans over and whispers in his ear.

"Rob," David says. "The elders have been searching for a construction manager for the new facility. Yeah, come and work for us."

"Ha," Robert responds, as Janice's expression brightens.

"Hey, that would be fantastic," Ruth says. "Oh, Jan, you'd be returning home. Wow!"

Until the End of Time

"No way." Robert answers. "I'm getting to the point of relaxing, taking it easy. I'm certainly not thinking of the trouble of selling the house and moving. That's the last thing I want to do."

"Rob, we'd be back home." Janice reminds him of their school years and where they met. Dave, is it still there?"

"The Academy has moved."

"We played hockey on that lake," Robert remembers. "We would bring shovels to remove the snow and used sticks to define the goals."

David adds, "Can't do that anymore. That building is now a Middle Academy. While you're here, we could visit the old homestead, the old school, that lake and all that. Would that entice you to move?"

Janice replies. "I would like to tour the area while we're here. But I agree with Rob, we'd be away from the boys. We'd never see them again. Sounds good, but no."

"Jan, you're right. Sorry, David. The job has been good to us. The twins have already put a bid on nearby land, so moving is out."

"Dave. I enjoy seeing new construction take shape," Robert says. "But moving is not a joy. Sorry."

"Well, think about it anyway."

FIFTEEN

Back home, David suggests they sit outside and relax before calling it a night. David and Robert start a fire in the raised fire pit. Ruth prepares a kettle of tea.

Janice asks, "Ruthie, how's your work with the Girl Scouts? What do you do with them?"

"If I were on that campout, I'd be enjoying the games and assisting the girls cooking over fires."

"Where did they go?"

"Over into Utah by the Flaming Gorge recreational area. They have another week. Oh, I wanted to go so bad, and this happened, locked up in a hospital when I could have been out camping and enjoying myself. Why God? Why?" Ruth says.

"Yeah, I know the feeling."

"She discovered a lump on my chest, so she wouldn't sign the release to go. Had to put me in the hospital for further investigation. Oh, I was madder than a hornet! When I finally got to call David, well, at first, he was stunned. He said the usual claptrap about God works in mysterious ways."

"Ruth, if you were camping, we couldn't visit. It'd be only David. Let's go join the boys."

"Come on out," David says, as the ladies exit through the glass door, carrying the tea and cans of BudweiserFree. "We were tinkering about driving around the old neighborhood tomorrow. What do you want to do the next day?"

Ruth is the first to answer. "As we said before, Jan and I are going to hit the ball around, so you can do whatever."

"Rob, did you bring your clubs?" David asks.

Robert's attention is on the whirling sound of a drone hovering above the two-by-eight wood beams covering the deck. It lowers itself to set on one of them.

"Rob, did you bring your clubs?" David asks again.

"Huh? Oh, clubs. No. I guess you didn't see it."

"See what?"

"That drone. It's up there," Robert answers, pointing to the four-propeller-driven machine on the deck canopy.

"No, I heard it, but try to ignore those things," David responds. "Kids in the neighborhood playing around."

"Ha. Kids in the area. No, Dave, not kids, it's the . . ."

"Rob, not now," Janice softly interrupts.

"Be careful." David slowly whispers, putting his forefinger across his lips.

"Well, ok, back to golf. I don't play much, and Jan does not like it when I join her."

"I do too," Jan says.

"Well, ok, I don't like playing with you," Robert answers. "She tries to remain calm and not giggle."

"Aha, now the real reason comes out. Can't be beaten by a woman, huh?" Janice quickly replies.

"What will you do when we're playing?" Ruth asks.

"We were kicking around the idea of going on the Ute trail, near Aspen," David answers.

Robert says, "But, that's a three-hour drive, so we decided we'd go along and watch you."

"No, you won't!" Ruth responds.

Just a Matter of Time

"Well, Dave, I guess you and I will go to the mall, shopping," Robert says.

"No, seriously," David says. "We are going to walk the Centennial Park trail. When I shared with the youth group that you guys were coming, they replied that if we did any hiking, they'd like to join us."

David looks at his watch. He picks up his tablet, presses a button, another, and presses #6. "Hi, Romero, we were discussing that Centennial Trail. We plan on it for Wednesday. Could you and Frank join us? And possibly some others?"

Romero answers, "Sounds good to me. I'll make the calls and get back to you. You'll need to leave early, no later than seven."

David speaks into the screen, "All right, good. We'd love to have the company."

"How many of the kids will make it?" Robert asks.

"When he first mentioned it, Romero said there were eight."

"Super!" Robert replies. "What do we need to bring?"

"Hiking boots? And water."

"No pants and a shirt?"

"If that's the way you wish to do it, the kids would probably join you. And there's always the possibility of meeting girls hiking the trail."

"Ruthie, I think we'd better go," Janice says.

"Nah, nothing to worry about for Dave," Ruth adds.

"Tell me more about this youth group," Robert asks.

"They're a bunch. Girls dominate it three to two. Mostly Second Academy kids. When the new youth Director came on board, the first thing he did was to regenerate the worship time to youth-oriented music. Romero had been in the Philippines on a missionary assignment for several years after seminary, and it was there that he fell in love with a native Philippina. They're young, attractive, energetic, and wow! What enthusiastic messages he delivers. His wife, Maria, oh, she can woo a tiger! When they started, we only had about fifty kids. Now it's getting close to 1600."

"You said he reached out to other churches," Robert asks.

Until the End of Time

"Yes, he did. He knew other churches were having the same problem we were having, getting teens to come to church. He visited other youth directors and pastors in the area, and they agreed. She is great at reaching right into the heart of the youngsters by telling her story of growing up in deprivation, poverty, and incest, and then receiving the good news."

Janice asks, "Any chance we could meet her while we're here?"

Ruth replies, "She's on the campout." Sighing loudly, Ruth breathes in and sighs again. "I'm tired. I'm going to bed." She rubs her hand around David's shoulder and neck and slowly walks into the house.

"Good night, dear," David tells her. "I won't be long myself."

There's a long pause in the conversation. Robert leans back to watch the moon peek through the clouds moving southeast.

Janice asks David, "What time should we get up?"

"I'll be up about six. I usually come out here for devotions and to watch the sunrise. Now, Ruth—how she'll feel in the morning is uncertain. Sometimes she joins me, and sometimes she sleeps in. I'm surprised she's stayed with us this long," David says.

"Dave, it's been a great evening, and day," Robert adds. Rolling his eyes toward the drone, he suggests that they say a few words of encouragement for Ruth to have a good night's rest and be herself in the morning. Robert softly offers the prayer for Ruth.

"Okay, Dave, we're going to retire ourselves," Janice says, getting up and standing beside David, showing she wants a hug. He throws his arms around her and whispers in her ear, "Oh, Thank you."

"Rob, you coming?" Janice asks.

"No, not yet, okay." Robert answers. "I'm enjoying this atmosphere too much."

Replying, she says, "well, good night, but don't stay out long, we've got a full day tomorrow." She bends over gently rubbing his cheeks, and plants a light kiss on his forehead.

Robert softly says, "I'll try not to wake you."

"That moon up there," David says as he gazes out into the sky. "Every time I look at it, I think of the first man who experienced walking on it and looking back at this earth. Too far away to see people doing what they do. But God sees the ants crawling back to their nest, and us sitting here and hears our discussions too."

"Yeah," Robert states. "Does God smell us too?"

"Smell us?" David replies.

"Dave, I'd like to know your thoughts on something. I was watching a ballgame one-day last week. The right fielder was running hard to his left to catch a fly ball. The movements of his legs caught my attention and my utter amazement. How does he do that? How does he tell his legs they must rotate like that, at that speed and in that direction?"

"Was he thinking along the way? There it is, I see the ball coming. Move legs, faster, faster, toes, grab the ground, and push hard." Robert continues detailing the movements of the body and the position of the glove. "Good work, body. Thank you. The coach, the teammates thank you. We won," Robert ends his three-minute recitation. "So, what'd you make of it?"

"How do you come up with such thoughts?"

"It . . . a word comes, and off the mind goes."

David emphasizes, "We don't have to think about how the body moves, it just does."

"But why? How?" Robert quizzes. "How about this. Nah, forget it, I'm boring you."

"Rob, it's all right to do it on your own."

"Well, hey, we'll read long articles on the tablet, but if I get long winded in speech, you get bored. Why? Yeah, if I fingered my thoughts on that tablet, you'd probably read it."

"There's a difference. If I don't like it, I can shut you out and go to another."

"Okay, I get it. So, from now on, push my button, and I'll stop. That's what Jan does. I enjoy sharing these ramblings I get. Sometimes, it will smite others, just as I was when that thought came."

"Okay, go! I'll try."

"Here's one I received while driving the Winnie through Idaho. This body is a physical combination of millions, perhaps billions of molecules forming our various components." Robert continues naming the numerous parts of the body. "The body of Adam was lying immobile on the ground when God liked what He saw and breathed life into it. It's that energy of life that causes the lungs to breathe and the heart to beat. It's the air we take in providing us the power to move our legs." Robert pauses. "Every time I inhale a breath of air, am I breathing in a breath from God?" Robert looks for a reaction from David, anything but that expressionless face looking through to the trees and beyond. "I didn't hear you push my button."

"But, did you have to list all the body parts to get to the conclusion?"

"I bet you do that in your sermons."

"Humm?"

"Dave, here's another question I've had. Intelligence, imagination? How does it operate within us?"

"Well . . . It seems you want to experience God with your five senses."

"Well, why not? Wouldn't we behave better if we could see God frowning as we were about to do something? God hears us and sees us, but we don't see or hear God. If I could hear God telling me, *Robert, don't do that,* wouldn't I act differently?"

"You do now. It's the Holy Spirit living within. It's that still quiet voice."

"Yes, but we don't always hear in this busy, noisy world of ours. Sometimes, I need a shout. Are you saying that someone like me, and I consider myself one of the millions who hasn't studied the scientific basis of things, should not even question why? Dave, there are so many questions I have along this line."

David says with finality, "Rob, let's call it a night. Yeah, I'm pushing your button." He grins, as he gets up from the chair and adds, "Get a good night's sleep, and we'll talk more in the morning,"

"Good night, Dave," Robert says. *Hmm? He did not want to hear my conclusion.*

SIXTEEN

Janice slides open the door and sees Ruth busy at the stove. "Good morning, Ruthie."

"Good morning," Ruth replies, seeing Jan approaching.

"Did you sleep all right?" Janice asks.

"Sure did. Yeah, finally. Dave had to go to the church already, something about the council. Hand me that platter up there," Ruth says, pointing to the cabinet to her right. "So, you wanna beat me. Ha, that'll be the day."

Ruth removes one of the six-inch pancakes and carefully places it on the plate. "How many do you want? Rob still sleeping?"

"Three should do it. Thanks. They look delicious. No, he's on the deck, doing his contemplations."

"Well, call him. Breakfast is ready."

Janice tenderly rubs her hand across Ruth's back. Opening the deck door, Janice calls out, "Rob, breakfast is ready."

"Ruth, this is scrumptious. Thanks," Robert says, after taking the first bite. Sliding the fork to cut another piece, he asks, "Why did Dave have to go to the church so early?"

"All he told me was something urgent with the council," Ruth answers. "He also wanted to discuss with the youth about your hike tomorrow."

Until the End of Time

"Have you done it?" Janice asks.

"Yes, we took the Scouts on it last year. It's beautiful but tough."

"Be aware. This is the year I beat you," Janice says.

"Oh, you think so. Ha!" Ruth replies, pushing Janice's hand to cause a piece of the pancake to fall to the table.

"What do you know about that council?" Robert asks.

"I'm not aware of the details, but, yes, he must submit the sermons. They normally reply within a day or two," Ruth answers. "Jan, when I heard you were coming, I cleaned the clubs, readied the grips, and went to the range. So, I'm ready."

"My clubs are always clean," Janice replies and begins to add another comment.

Ruth interrupts, "Yeah, because you never use them. Get your clubs, Jan. I'm gonna change."

Janice gets up and starts to grab the three plates and forks. Ruth pushes Jan's hand away, "leave it. Get your clubs."

"Come." Janice grabs Robert's elbow and leads him out the door toward the camper. "She's in good spirits this morning. Rob, I had a hard time getting to sleep last night. Thinking of the boys."

"Been wondering about them myself, but I thought you had come to peace with it."

"I had, but last night those worries came back."

"Jan, they'll be fine," Robert comforts.

Before stepping inside the Winnie, she tells Robert, "get my clubs out. I've got to change."

Now in her golfing outfit, Janice sits next to Robert at the dining table, interrupting his time on the net. "Rob, right before I was about to slide into bed last night, I got a call from Arlene. She is upset about what's happening and thinks the state is about to remove the girls. She rattled on and on about all their troubles. Finally, she asked if there was any way we could drive there today. She hung up after I told her we had plans for the next few days."

"Arlene called? Last I heard, she was madder than a hornet with you."

Just a Matter of Time

"I know, Rob. But. She's scared. One of the girls burnt her hand. Two ladies from the State implied that Maycie was negligent when she left the girls outside to play while the smoker was burning."

"Okay," Robert gives in. "Call her back, and we'll pray with her." Janice finds the number and presses, 'Talk.'

"Yes, hello," Arlene answers. "Ah, Janice, thanks for calling."

"Arlene, Robert is here with me, so if you don't mind, bring us up to date on what's going on, and we can pray about this together. I'm sorry about last night if I seemed short, or not concerned." Janice informs.

"No, Janice, it was me. I'm Sorry. Oh, Jan, I'm the one who called the cops on you. Sorry. I've regretted it ever since."

"Arlene, you're our neighbor, and we love you. So, bring us up to date on what's going on."

"Thanks. Here it is if I get the details right. Samantha and Elizabeth were running around the backyard, you know, playing that hide and seek thing. Samantha tripped over a chair on the porch and fell into the smoker, scorching her hand. Maycie had gone in for a minute to check something and then heard the scream. The burn was bad enough for her to check the Doctor app, which told her what to do. A few days later, two State reps came to the house. The one from that Protecting Children Agency told Maycie, she was not a responsible parent. And that's not all," Arlene is heard tearing up. "Oh, where was I? Jan, this is too much, it's disrupting our plans for that trip to Alaska. Can't you drive down?"

Robert speaks into the tablet. "Is Charlie there?"

"Yes, sitting here."

"Charlie, what's your take on this?" Robert asks as Charlie's face appears on the screen.

"Well, who knows. If something like this happens again, it'd be up to them, and the girls could be put in foster homes."

There's a loud knocking on the door to the camper. "Hey, Jan, are you coming?" Ruth asks loudly.

Janice opens the door and briefs Ruth about the call. "Sorry, this may take a few minutes."

Until the End of Time

"Charlie, Arlene," Robert speaks into the screen, "These agents use that fear factor to keep us in line. It's all about installing a sense of fear in us, so we don't cross their imposed line. That's why they make these appearances look so harsh. Now, I'm sure the girls have learned a valuable lesson to be more careful about their surroundings. Is your daughter-in-law there? What's her name? Maycie? How's she doing?"

"Yes, let me get her for you."

"Hi, Mr. Amwestson, thanks for calling," Maycie says. "It was all my fault for not watching them closer, not being there."

"Maycie, this is what these agencies do, scare the daylights out of you with their threats. The bigger the threat, the more we'll fall in line. I guarantee you, the girls will not do that again, and they'll be more careful in the future. It was not your fault. You could put a rope around the kids, and they'd find a way to learn a lesson."

"But what if they get hurt in another way?" Maycie asks.

"Yes, I know that fear. Every so often, remind the girls. That's how they learn. That hot stove acted as a rod of correction." Robert pauses. "And, I'd get rid of that Doctor app. Don't use it again. Phew, I've said too much."

"Thanks, Rob," Charlie says.

"Maycie, take care. The girls have learned from this," Robert emphasizes. "Oh, how's your pain from that fall?"

"Oh, that's subsided. Not like it has been," Maycie replies.

"Thanks for the call, Rob. We're heading to Alaska in a few days," Charlie says.

"Have a great trip. It's one place I've never been to and would love to see it."

Arlene leans over into view, "I'm sorry for calling the police about your meeting. I never should have. Sorry, forgive me. How did it end up?"

Janice answers, "Forget it! Robert yelled out to me about the meeting before he left that morning as a drone flew over. They did the usual, inspected everything. We're okay. Have a great time. Be safe, and God's blessings on all of you."

"Whew!" Robert mutters, and tells Janice, "Hey, go practice."

Just a Matter of Time

"Sorry, Ruthie. But our neighbors are having a bit of a problem." Janice says, getting up from the table and rubbing Robert's knee. She leans in for a kiss. "Blessings on your work Rob. I'm gonna show Ruthie how this game is played."

"Ha!" Ruth snorts.

Robert starts re-shuffling notes together in chronological order on the tablet and saves them to the Bilko Nevada Hills folder. Almost ready to fax them to Peter, he takes a second look. He points the arrow to one of his favorite sites. *No, that's not the one.* He starts the search again, scanning the saved names, the titles, re-checks the original folder, the second folder, the one under it, the folder connected to Bilko, the folder emphasizing safety regulations, everywhere. *What's going on?*

He leans back, scratches his head. Looking over the screen, he presses the shutdown button. He waits a minute before triggering the power switch. He watches the screen load to the screenshot of the forest behind his home. Showing up at the bottom of the screen is a single underlined word "password." He enters the password. He watches the green circle go round and round, getting larger with each rotation. A small line appears at the bottom of the screen: "Sorry, your password is incorrect. Try again."

The scene of the forest comes alive.

He slowly and carefully enters the password he's used the last two years. It happens again. He slowly repeats the process to ensure he gets it right. Satisfied, he presses the 'enter' button, and this time the screen goes black. A hideous snickering face appears and slowly dissolves fading away. "Dammit, I've been shut out." He slams it against the top of the table. He gets up and exits the Winnie slamming the door. A squirrel runs out from under the Winnie to the side of a tree twenty feet away, paws its way up to hug a branch, and looks back at Robert. "Yes, that's exactly how I feel."

Robert walks around the side of the house to the deck. He sits, leans back and looks up through the beams to the parting clouds while thinking about the disaster of losing the files Peter needs.

"Lord, now what?" he says, looking up at the passing clouds. He looks in the direction of the camera in the beams. "Oh. I'd kick your butt if you showed up."

Until the End of Time

"Huh?" David says as he opens the patio door.

Robert sees the look of David standing in the doorway. "Oh, not you, Dave. Sorry, you heard that. My tablet got hacked," he calmly states.

"Ouch, how?"

"It went kaput. I promised my boss I'd call at nine this morning. Somehow, all my files, everything is gone, the tab is useless, a piece of plastic."

"Use mine," David says and goes inside to get it. In a moment, he brings it out. He slides his finger across the screen, and pushes against a clip shot, and hands it to Robert.

"Thanks," Robert says. He rises out of the chair and walks to the Winnie. He grabs his three by five card holder and walks to the back of the yard and the beginning of the tree line. Robert sits on the grass and crosses his legs. He presses against the screen seven times. Peering into the screen, the face of Peter Bilko appears.

"You're late. Robert, you better have it all for me."

"Peter, I'm sorry, but my tab got hacked this morning."

"Bull. Where the hell are you?"

"I'm outside Boulder, Colorado. I was almost complete with the data you wanted when the screen went blank, and now I'm using my friend's tab. All those files you needed were there, and I was about to 2Fax them, and now, without my tab, I can't get them. I'm sorry."

"You know what this means. If I can't get that information to the feds, we'll be closed up immediately! I depended on you. Damn it. I should never have let you go on that vacation." Robert sees Peter look away from the tab for a moment. "What are we gonna do?"

"There's one final out," Robert says. He looks up and around the area. "You got a pen and paper ready. I'm going to read off a list of files and where you can find them. Ah, . . . Get Sandy. She could do it easier. Peter, I can't bring the files up on my friend's tab, as his is monitored. We need to be quick about it."

"Okay, hang on," Peter responds.

"Hi, Rob. You having a good time?" Sandy appears on the screen.

"Yes, I was until this happened. My tab got hacked and shut down, so all I have are the notes of where I saved my files on the alt-nets. It's a habit I formed long ago to keep lists on note cards for such a time. Are you ready to copy?"

"Rob, is there anything I can do to help?" David asks.

Robert raises his finger to his lips.

"Shoot," Sandy says. "Is someone there with you?"

"Yeah, my friend David. I'm using his tablet now."

"When you're ready, Rob, go."

Robert starts slowly reading the https addresses, the folder, subfolders, and file names he uses on the alt3net. He dictates one after another to the secretary. He reads seven different https locations and the names to the screen. Coming to the last one, Robert says, "Now the name of this one, I'm not sure of. It's the summary I had composed late last night. It merely summarizes the other files. Sandy, I'm sure you could do that yourself. And, Dale would be a great help. Is he there today?"

"No, he's out getting supplies," Sandy replies.

"Okay, here is what I have about this last one." Robert reads off a location and adds, "Sandy, It probably has only the date and time as its name. It's on the alt4net."

"Thanks, I got it," Sandy says.

"Peter, you need to give Sandy a good raise. She's terrific," Robert looks over to David. "Would you mind if they used your number if they need to call back?"

"No problem. Sure," David answers.

"Peter, good luck with the feds," Robert says. "My prayers are with you. Expect to see you on the twenty-ninth."

"Rob, you only got two weeks, not three. Yeah, you'll be here. I've got a new one lined up, a new lawyer too, so, you better be." Peter ends the conversation, and the screen goes blank.

"Thanks, David," Robert says as he rises off the grass and brushes off his shorts. "Whew, glad that's over. Thanks to you."

Reaching the deck, Robert sits and relaxes, his head leaned back against the support and exhaled a deep breath of air. His eyes focus back to the camouflaged camera pointed at him. Robert sticks his tongue out.

"David, let me use your tab again. I'd like to have a picture of this deck of yours. It's beautifully constructed." David hands it to Rob. He takes several pictures from various points around the deck. "Okay," he stops and adds, "that ought to do it. Now, I should be able to build me one."

"A few guys from the church built it for me several years ago."

"Let's go look at it from a distance," Robert suggests as he steps off the deck onto the grass, walking toward the trees. Reaching the open area, he stops and tells David, "The reason I took those pictures was so that I could put together a gizmo that would fuzz that camera over your deck. That spying eye wouldn't work. I use it at home and have not had a problem. I got one in the Winnie."

SEVENTEEN

"You ready, Rob?" David asks.

"Yeah, sure, been waiting for you to say the word," Robert answers. He gets up from the kitchen table. He takes one last sip of coffee and pours the rest in the drain. "Let's go."

Navigating into the rear parking lot of the church, the car goes to its assigned spot along the sidewalk. The doors open, and David whistles to the assistants.

"Good morning. Hey, guys, my brother-in-law, Robert Amwestson from Oregon. Rob, this is Michael Boomstead, the youth leader. This is Two A, taking the place of Jackolan. His name is Abel Abolfo."

Abel smiles, spouting off a bunch of indistinguishable words to Robert.

David introduces Robert to each of the teens. The oldest is a senior, one junior, and three freshmen students. One of them grabbed Robert's attention the moment David's car door opened. Robert's eyes stuck on that student wearing exceptionally thick-rimmed glasses and a baseball type cap.

"Mr. Amwestson, good to meet you," the sixteen-year-old boy tells Robert. "Yeah, you're wondering about these glasses I'm wearing. I was born deaf, so these glasses provide me the excitement of communicating as everyone else does naturally. Oh, by the way, call me CC."

"Amazing technology. Um, CC. There have been times in my life when I wished I could turn the noise of society off or on at will."

Until the End of Time

CC reaches up with his right fingers touching an outside section of his cap, announcing to everyone with a big grin, "I turned you off."

Robert smiles and gives the kid a thumbs-up. He watches the kid touch his cap and squeeze.

"But CC, where does the power come from?"

"My shoes," he says.

"Your shoes?"

"Yeah, specially made with micro-electric threads within the soles which generate electrical current as I walk. No wires. The glasses receive the signals and power the computer that translates voices to the glasses. When I'm sitting, say in class or at church, all I need to do is flex my toes to put pressure on the soles. I think the guy said it was nano-tech or something like that."

"Wow, that's amazing. CC. But, how did you learn to talk without the ability to hear your mother's words? From early on, that's how we all learn, by mimicking the sounds people make."

CC slowly answers, "Hmm, I did say I was born deaf. Well, almost. My first few years, I did hear enough to be able to copy the sounds. My mother worked with me, raising her voice, demanding I repeat what she said. I was about seven or eight when I was diagnosed as totally deaf."

"You were blessed with a wonderful mother."

"Thanks, Mr. Am-west-son. See, I can say your hard-to-pronounce name."

David and Abel quietly step away to chat off to the side. Robert turns his attention to the small group of five students gathered in a circle. He asks if any had walked the trail. Robert listens as one of the boys describes the route and what they might see.

"The scenery is fantastic," Michael says. "It's kind of tough on the legs and hips as we reach an elevation of over 6,800 feet."

Out of the corner of his eye, Robert notices David raising his arms as if to resist or push against what seemed like a shove from Abel. Abel trots away from David, slides into a car, and leaves.

Joining the group, David announces, "Abel will not be joining us today." He reaches into his pocket for the remote, and the doors of the bus open. The solar roof white bus, with the name of the church in bold blue along the side, has a seating capacity of twelve. A sliding door behind the front control panel opens, exposing an aisle separating two rows of six single seats leading to a chair lift at the rear. They fasten the seat belts to the rail, the charging cord releases, and David presses on the screen seeing a blue circle. A voice asks, "DESTINATION?" David touches the screen with the cushioned pen, sliding the felt tip to his right and down. He presses the minus sign to expand the view. With the tip, he pushes on the target destination. A red circle appears, "CENTENNIAL TRAILHEAD PARKING. SLOT SEVEN RESERVED. CONFIRM." David presses the screen, and a green line appears showing the assigned route. "CONFIRM." Another press and the voice announce, "YOUR TRIP IS SECURED." The bus quietly moves out of the parking lot, and into the streets.

Sitting across from each other, Robert leans over and asks David, "what happened back there with Abel?"

"I asked him what happened to Jackolan, who was supposed to be the assigned activity Director, when Abel asked why I did not want him," David replies. "Well . . ." His eyes roll back toward the students. "I'd rather not get into that now. Later. Michael can handle it."

The students occupy themselves with their tablets. CC, sitting in a row by himself, has removed the glasses and is peering out the side window.

A half hour after leaving the church, the bus turns into the parking lot, slows, and carefully drives to post seven. The bus stops, the post disappears, a bell rings, and the screen announces, "DESTINATION REACHED." The seat belts release and the door slides open. A metallic click indicates the bus is hooked up to the re-gen power station.

A Ranger steps inside, "Good morning. Pastor David Mathish, I assume you have the permits."

"Yes, we do, but there's one who couldn't make the trip today. Cancel Abel Abolfo."

"Mr. Amwestson, I hope you're enjoying our beauty here. Okay, let's debark, we'll get the requirements taken care of, and you can be on your way." Everyone is scanned, physically checked, and provided a bottle of water. The Ranger tells the group, "if there is a physical or medical problem on the way, I've provided Pastor Mathish with a locator button. Stay together and do not leave the trail. You'll be expected to return here between five and six. Enjoy our Centennial Trailhead." He tips his cap and walks toward a car waiting for clearance.

David addresses the group, "If you wish to stop and look over the landscape for a moment, say so, and we'll all stop to enjoy the view with you. The same goes for if you get tired. I'll stop at various times to point out interesting areas. Any questions?"

"Good. Let's go." David and Robert lead them across the road and onto the city-maintained trail. It starts as smooth asphalt wide enough for two or three to walk side-by-side. Michael is bringing up the rear alongside Edward, the junior.

Down the path aways, Robert turns, begins walking backward, and starts shouting, "The left, right, left, the left, right, left . . ." The three freshmen surprise Robert by mimicking the march, echoing the words while marching in step. The kids shift their legs, so the right foot hits the ground when Robert yells left.

"Hmm," Robert watches CC doing his own thing. His glasses and cap are now hanging around his neck as he looks unimpeded at the scenery. CC grabs the elbow of another student and points to an eagle circling in the sky.

"By not having normal functioning ears, CC is more attuned to nature," Robert tells David.

"Yes, he is, and is always ready to point something out."

"I'm gonna hang back and walk alongside CC," Robert informs David.

"Don't. It would make him feel that he must put the glasses on. Let him be. How the legs doing?"

"Okay. But telling me I need more exercise," Robert confesses. "You said this trail was an easy hike. How is that Ute trail?"

"Yeah, you seem to be forcing it," David replies. "One must be in excellent health, have good knees, hips, and legs to finish that one."

"Dave, the kids are lagging behind us. Why was Abel so upset?" Robert asks.

David turns his head to see how far back the kids are. "He does not get along with the group. As the church has grown, he's been after us to change some aspects of the services. He wants those old hymns reinstated into the services. But, that's not what drew these youngsters to our church. They want to feel the real, the here and now, expressed in explosive worship where they can let it all hang out."

"Why doesn't he leave and find a church more to his liking?"

"He grew up here, been part of the body from its beginning."

"Dave, I'm in that group. The words of those hymns are what's so great about them. Think of the authors and what they felt. Their heartfelt spiritual connection inspired those words. Sometimes when I'm alone in the car, perhaps after a stressful day, I'll start singing *'When peace like a river attendeth my way.'* I then visualize the burdens of the day flowing down the river. Dave, it brings a peace and that stress I felt leaves."

"I understand, but this is a different generation, and their affections are not with history, but to the here and now."

"Oh, they're missing so much."

"Here we are, we can take a break," David announces. "That path leads to outhouses."

Robert reclines on one of the benches to look out at the rolling hillside. CC sits next to Robert, his glasses resting on his chest. Robert watches as CC uses two fingers to point to his eyes and moves his arm to point out across the hills. His forefinger and third finger indicate something walking, and then his hand comes back to touch his heart.

Robert points to the glasses and his head. CC smiles and removes the glasses and cap and hands them to Robert. "Sure, see what I see." He watches Robert slip them on his head and adjusts them carefully. He looks at CC and the other kids standing nearby.

Michael raises his pocket tab snapping a picture while saying, "Now that's a sight."

Seeing those words projected a foot away from the glasses, Robert points to Michael and to the glasses. CC nods his head. David and one of the freshmen return to the group, seeing Robert with the glasses.

"What'd you think?" David asks.

Robert points to the edge of the glasses and says, "You're turned off," which brings a smile and faint laughter to CC. Robert removes them and hands them back to CC.

Until the End of Time

"Dave, they are fantastic." Robert looks at the students, "Guys, you don't understand how blessed you are. Think about it. When I was a kid, there was nothing like what CC has. And, those tablets you've been using to take pictures. When my father was a kid, there was none of this tablet stuff. They had books. There used to be libraries where one could check out a book, take it home, and leisurely read it for two weeks. Have you guys ever held a real book, one made of three hundred pages bound together?"

"Rob, you're at it again," David rebukes.

"No! Go ahead, it's interesting," Michael says.

"You are blessed with all this technology, but you're also missing a bunch. All that history recorded in those books has been deemed unnecessary relics. The tablet is a marvelous piece of equipment. But it has limitations placed within its design. There are no government limitations in those books. My grandfather said his father thought the Wright Brothers were out of their minds trying to fly like a bird, and now you can do it in your drone. What will technology bring us next?" Robert asks. "Huh? Robots walking this trail sending pictures to you, so you don't physically have to. You text your friends with pictures that you walked the trail today."

David speaks up, "We should be on our way. About two miles to go, and we'll stop at the Inn for a bite to eat."

Reaching a bend in the trail, David stops and points, "Over there on top of that hill is the new prison."

"Wow, it's like an old castle," Robert says. "No one will be escaping from there." The students have their pads out zooming in to snap pictures.

CC, with his glasses off, elaborates, "The granite walls are what looks like four by eight slabs. And wow, the top reminds me of that wall across China."

"Yes, it does," Robert adds. "That's huge, Dave. How long did it take to build?"

"Six years and the prisoners did the work. It will house over five-thousand. We paid for it in many of our permission fees and future bond taxes." David gives CC a thumbs up and says, "The first time I walked this trail, I missed it. Now, look into that valley. That fortress there alongside the river is an Army-Marine training camp. It opened two years ago. Well, let's move on. I'm getting hungry."

Entering the Inn, a greeter leads the group to a large circle table on the patio with a view of the snow tops peeking out above the forested hills. "Ah, we have the group from the Rockin Hillside Church with us today. Welcome." The young male greeter says as they arrange seating positions. He provides each with a single page menu. As his habit, Robert scans the ceiling area, the fan directly overhead, and around the table.

Michael asks, "what's so interesting about the fan?"

"Ah, it caught my eye, that's all," Robert replies. "Hey, everyone, the meal is on me."

"No, Rob. The church has provided funds for this," David informs.

Starting with David, the young man enters the menu selections into his pad and says, "I visited the church a while back, the videos and music were outstanding, very emotional and uplifting."

"Have you returned?"

"Nah, my partner, well, he wasn't turned on like I was."

"Sorry to hear that. Give us another try," David says. "We've increased the greeting staff to make everyone feel welcome from the moment they enter. Jesus welcomed all."

"Thank you." The young man says as he swipes David's forefingers with the pad.

During the meal, Robert learns a bit more about each of the teens, and they learn more about Robert, about his twins and their start in the Canyon Project.

"I read about that program," the junior student says. "I've been instructed to put my application in early. How long to be approved?"

"Ours was a fluke. They were near the top of the list within the first year, when they dismissed Jimmy. No twins. No relatives. When they found out the boys had personal drones, the permissions came out of nowhere. The boys were excited, so there they are."

Michael shares about his two-year military assignment before he entered the seminary. "I suspect that the way things are going, it will become mandatory soon. They'll draft everyone after they finish the Academies."

"I've had that same thought," Robert adds, and says, "we all need discipline when growing up. The military can do that."

"Well, sensitivity training seemed more important than anything else. Sure, we learned how to use a rifle and had physical workouts, you know, the usual stuff. But, as far as the goal of defeating the enemy and protecting the country. Hah! When you see the enemy, don't shoot, there might be civilians involved."

"Hmm," Robert mutters.

David announces, "Well, guys, we must get on the trail again. It's a different route on the way back."

An hour later, the trail narrows between the trees lining the path, they approach a lookout point when David stops. "If you look closely over there near the creek, you'll see an old log cabin. It's now a historical site."

"Let's go," Michael says.

"Nah, we better not," David says.

"I've done it before. It's not that bad. We can do it."

"No! You heard the Ranger. We're expected back at the lot."

"Ah, come on. We'll make it back in time."

"Michael, I said no!"

Looking at the others and Robert, Michael asks, "anyone wish to go with me? CC? Anyone?"

Raising his voice, David rebukes, "Michael, no! You're not! We started this together, and we're going to finish it together."

"Michael, I'd love to, but perhaps another time," Robert interjects.

"Ah," Michael gives in. "So close . . . Everything we do now is monitored. Time checks!"

Looking into the frowned eyebrows shading Michael's eyes, David tells him, "This is not the place for outbursts. Keep those to yourself. It brings division."

EIGHTEEN

"I'm still three up," Ruth tells Janice, as they're about to tee off on number 16, a short 135-yard par three, with two bunkers on the right, and a depression on the left of the green in front of the smiling sand trap.

"Go ahead, you're up," Ruth states, after dropping one to Janice on the 15th.

"Three to go," Janice replies. She grips the five-iron, lining up, her eyes on the pin location near the front of the green. She focuses on the front left, corrects her stance a bit, and adjusts her grip. She squares the clubhead behind the ball. She raises the shaft, wiggles it, and replaces the clubhead softly behind the ball. Staring at a dimple on the ball, she slowly starts the backswing and whoomph. They watch the ball heading to the left. It slowly fades right, bounces on the apron grass, bounces again, and slowly rolls softly hitting the flagstick and drops into the cup.

"Yahoo!" Janice screams, dropping the club on the ground and starts jumping.

"Unbelievable. Luck, pure luck," Ruth responds.

"If you bogey it, we'll be even," Janice says with a smile.

Pondering the club choice, Ruth grabs the seven-iron. She's lined up, has shortened the grip, and goes through her pre-swing routine. She hits the ball and watches it hit a high spot, which causes the ball to bounce back and into the deep depression on the left.

"Oooh."

"Oh, I love this game," Janice says. "I'll grab the pin."

"It's not over yet," Ruth replies.

Until the End of Time

Ruth ends up parring the hole with a terrific chip shot to within three feet and makes the putt. "I'm still one up."

Sitting in the cart on the way to the next tee, Janice asks, "Ruth, why didn't you pursue the game further. I always thought you could have made the tour."

"Remember, our coach was never around for encouragement. All she did was schedule our matches and arrange transportation. You were my encouragement. As an upcoming sophomore on the team, you were good. I watched you and thought, no way is she ever going to beat me."

"I wanted to beat you so bad, it drove me to the range," Janice says.

"Yeah, I was out partying, and I was still able to whip you," Ruth responds. "We've got two more."

"I think I'll let you win, Ruthie," Janice informs, as she grabs her driver for the 349-yard par four curving to the left. She puts one 190 yards on the right side where the green is straight ahead without hazards. Ruth steps to the tee and carefully places the ball with the blue line facing the center of the fairway. She swings and watches the ball draw toward the trees. It hits a branch and bounces into the pond.

"Oooh," Ruth mumbles.

"Tough luck," Janice softly says.

They don't speak a word on the ride to the 18th tee, a 470-yard straightaway par five. Janice is now one stroke ahead of Ruth.

On the eighteenth green, Janice calmly aligns the face of the putter, hits the ball, and it stops a foot away. She taps it in for a par and screams into the air, "I did it," and starts singing and dancing, "I beat Ruthie, I beat Ruthie. Oh, what a joy it is."

Ruth walks over to Janice and grabs the putter out of Jan's hand and throws it toward the golf cart.

"Let's go, I'm buying lunch," Janice says.

"Yes, you are," Ruth says. "If it weren't for the 16th, I'd have won."

Approaching the car in the lot, the trunk opens, and Jan puts Ruth's bag in first. After changing shoes, they ride back to the clubhouse to return the cart, when Janice says, "Wait till I tell Robert. Yeah, and David lost the bet. He owes me twenty."

"Stop it! Enough of that," Ruth vents.

Just a Matter of Time

"I give. Sorry," Janice says. "But, oh, how much I've wanted to beat you over the years. You were always the best and could have gone on. You still are, and always will be. The hole in one *was* luck. Because you would have won, you're buying."

Ruth chuckles and replies, "Ah, I've missed you. How long you staying? Could we do it again before you leave?"

"Where could we send the boys?" Janice asks.

Fastening the seat belts, Ruth tells the screen, "Rocky Mall, by way of Centennial Park."

As the car starts the ten-minute drive to the large shopping district, Janice asks, "Ruth, If I remember right, back in our high school days you wanted to have children, so how did you . . ."

Ruth puts her forefinger over her mouth and rolls her eyes up at the glass bubble protruding from the ceiling. "The weather has been fantastic. I'm glad you came this time of the year," Ruth says. She points out the window, "remember this?"

It's an open park area of small trees and shrubs surrounding the center playground of slides and swings where twenty-some small children are enjoying themselves. Sitting on benches, several ladies have their heads down, concentrating on tablets.

"Same as always," Ruth says. "Now, this next area opened eight years ago."

"Ruth, it's time for your medicine," the dashboard screen announces.

"Okay! Okay! One of these days. I'll . . . ."

The car slowly follows the curvature of the two-lane road. Janice peers through the tall pines, outside the fenced-in open area the size of two soccer fields. In the center, three uniformed adults watch a boy maneuver his small drone through circles, squares, triangles, and rectangles.

"Wow!" Janice exclaims. "Rob would want to see this."

"Spectators must get permission . . . Hold on. I think the church has permanent permission rights for open times," Ruth says. "I'll make the arrangements." She slides her finger across the tablet, presses a few flat keys, and the picture of Centennial Park appears. She selects a tab on the top, scrolls, and picks 'Credentials.' With her felt-tip pen, Ruth enters the name of the church. "Permission granted. Four adults, tomorrow at 10 a.m. Access code: 1248-9653,25."

"All set," Ruth announces, and presses 'Print.'

"That'll take part of the day, what'd we do tomorrow afternoon?" Ruth asks.

Janice replies, "Oh, hang out together somewhere. Yes, I'd like to see the church."

"Well, here we are, the car slows and turns into the parking lot, stopping in front of the clothing store. The right-side door slides open. Ruth presses the screen on the dashboard, announcing to the control '*Go Park.*' When Ruth shuts the door, the car takes off.

Janice announces, "Restroom first."

"Welcome." The robot greets them. "What's on your mind today?"

"The Restroom," Ruth says. They follow the robot adorned in fancy attire with a tag on its outfit indicating 'half-off today only.' It leads them through the aisle to the front of the store, where the head turns around. It raises an arm pointing left. "Thank You," it says. Janice follows Ruth through the door labeled, 'EVERYONE.'

Now in the open mall area, Ruth stops, and steps on a sign on the floor. Soon a rainbow-colored miniature bus stops alongside the ladies. "Grab a seat," Ruth tells Janice. She speaks to the screen: 'Food Court.' "Jan, we'll get something to eat, and then I wanted to get something from JJ's."

"JJ's?"

"Anything you want for the house, they got it. Stands for Jane and Jack."

Janice focuses on the various physical attributes along the way: the yellow and white lines down the middle of the open area, the beeps as it passes the entrances to the stores. The decorations adorning the walls gets her attention, along with the cameras. The bus stops in front of the enormous food court where people are lined up at the numerous restaurants.

"Well, Jan," Ruth says, stepping off the bus. "What would you like? Remember, you're paying. Chick-for-me?"

"Sounds good," Janice answers.

Just a Matter of Time

Ruth leads Janice to the eight-sided stand in the center of the court. She selects the menu from the display screen. They each press a tab, and the screen announces, "Your selections will be ready shortly. Thank you."

Janice presses her two-fingers on the screen. "Approved." Janice's face appears on the screen.

Backing away from the counter, they get in line between the ropes.

Carrying the trays, they select a table for four. Ruth says, "David checked it, and there are no hidden mikes around here. The usual cameras, that's it. So, what'd you want to know?"

Janice slowly chews, "Yes, it was about David not being active sexually, and you always wanting to have children."

"Well, when David confided in me about those years, he was so repentant and disgusted with what he had done. I felt sorry and ashamed with him. You know what I mean? His pain became my pain."

"He confessed that while you were dating?"

"Oh, yes. I'll never forget that evening. It was after dinner and a movie. During the dinner, I sensed something was bugging him. After the movie, sitting in front of my house, he interrupted our discussion about the actions in the movie.

"'I've got to confess something,' he started. 'It's about my past that you need to know.'

"I became all ears. He started to caress my hand and looking at his knuckles. He let it all out, all the details, all the wrongs he had done. He told me every bit of it while trying to be macho, keeping his tears back. I'll never forget it.

"It tore me up. Here I had been under the impression that he was Mr. Clean, a great guy who had never done anything wrong. I went straight to the bedroom and wept as I'd never done before. Yeah, I wanted my own family, two or three kids to nurture, and he tells me there's no way. I did not want to see him. It was over. Oh, how I cursed God, pounding my fists against the pillow," Ruth says, drying tears again.

"Oh, I'm so sorry," Janice says, as she reaches over to touch Ruth's hand.

Until the End of Time

"Jan," Ruth says, wiping her cheeks. "Thank you. It's been good to let this out." Ruth starts again. "It took me, ah, a month or more to come to terms with it, and finally, I found the courage to call Dave. We got together, talked about adoption, and I agreed to his marriage proposal."

"Why didn't you go through with the adoption plans?"

"We almost did, but the ministry took off, and we threw ourselves into that." Ruth pauses. "This has been a relief. Feels good to get it out. Thank You. Now, dag gone it, why don't you take the offer to move here?"

"Have some of the fruit," Janice offers and reaches for a couple of her fries. "These are good. Now, after the summer, well, who knows what happens next. There could be wedding plans."

"Huh? I thought you had said they did not have anyone they were serious about."

"They don't. But the talk about the project has me thinking. The boys could come home and announce to us that they've met someone and will be getting married."

"How can they meet someone at the bottom of a Canyon?"

"There's a girl's camp a few miles away, and they get together, partying, dancing and all. The Director called it a time for pairing."

"Uh-oh, I've heard that term before. It's being done here in the Boulder advanced school system," Ruth says, and then explains more of what she's heard about it.

"Wow. Would you tell Robert about this when we get back?" Janice says and adds, "No, better not. He'll blow a gasket."

NINETEEN

Time is 5:40 in the morning. The boys have finished the morning exercises and are now standing in line, waiting for the flap of the large tent to open for breakfast. Huddled together, moaning, and chatting, one student softly starts reciting, "We want food. We want food." It catches attention, and they all join in, each recitation becoming louder and louder.

The Director opens the flap yelling at them, "Stop that now! I'm sorry guys, but sometime last night, an animal or more got inside and ravaged the kitchen. We have a mess. All we have now are canned items, a few things here and there. I'm sure you'd rather not have pinto beans, relish, or tuna fish for breakfast. So, it'll be awhile."

"Johnathon, Kenneth, I need you two. Get the list of supplies we need from Mr. Chef and get ready to take the drones up to the top."

"Yahoo!" Johnathon screams. He turns to look at his brother. "Sorry, bro, I'm going up, up and away." Jimmy's mouth drops open.

"Once they get to the top," the Director says. "They've got to drive into town, replenish the immediate needs, and come back. The drones can only carry so much. That's another limiting factor. We're talking hours, possibly not until noon or later. Nothing like this has happened before. We were surprised at what we found. Sorry, but we must delay that canoe trip until tomorrow.

"Right now, I need you to come in, and we'll get the area open, and straightened up. Then, if you want, you could play volleyball or go to the archery range." He ties the canvas flap to the pole. They start rolling up the flaps to allow fresh air inside. He directs five of the students to the kitchen area.

Until the End of Time

"Joe," Jimmy says after they've cleaned the area, "come on, you and me on the volleyball court."

On the walk to the court, next to the vertical Canyon wall, Jimmy stops Joseph. He pulls him aside and into the trees. "Joe, there's something fishy going on here," Jimmy quietly says, not wanting any of the other kids to hear his suspicions.

Looking at Jimmy, Joseph asks, "Fishy?"

"Yeah, about the tent and all he said. While you guys were waiting for the tent to open, I walked around to the other side, thinking it might be open. If any animals had gotten inside, you'd think there would have been evidence. You know, something like a pile of dirt, a hole, a rip in the tent, or something. I didn't see anything unusual. The outside was as secure as ever."

"The Director said it was animals. His initial thoughts were possums."

"Possums couldn't do that much, and you'd think there'd be enough noise to wake someone up. Hey, the cameras. That's what'd tell him how and what."

"Yeah, the cameras. But you better leave it alone, Jim," Joseph advises. "I know it's suspicious, but let him handle it."

"No, Joe. It had to be one or more of our guys who did it."

"Who? No way, Jim. Why the hell would one of our guys do it? No, Jim. Drop it. Here they come." They join the other students and counselors discussing the volleyball matches on the way to the court.

Junior says, "Yes, three men teams. It'll be a tent competition."

Youmentis says, "I can't, and John and Kenneth are gone, so let's choose up sides instead, draw straws. There's twelve of you. Four to a side, and we'll have three games."

"Okay by me," Junior answers.

Mohab says, "Junior, the Director has always been against team competition. He'd rather have us in individual competitive events."

"He's not going to be out here, so we can do what we want. We'll do the four-man teams."

Just a Matter of Time

"No," Mohab says. "Individual competition, as he directs us in everything else. We must focus on the individual. The world always divides into groups and tribes . . ."

"Gads, Mohab, we just want to enjoy the day," Junior interrupts.

Mohab continues, "We tend to isolate into groups."

"Let's take a vote on it," Jimmy interjects, looking around the group for agreement.

"Down here, we don't get to vote. That's groupism," Mohab responds.

"Oh, my God," Junior responds again. "All we want to do is have some fun."

Jimmy says, "We vote every two years to choose our representatives, so I guess you consider that as groupism, and you'd be more inclined to have a one-man ruler?"

Joseph speaks up quicker than Mohab can respond, "Yeah, how about team sports? Don't you realize how team sports have contributed to society?"

"Hah," Mohab says, "team sports are divisive when it comes to fans choosing sides. It's the same with political parties. No, we've got to limit ourselves to individual competition."

"Yeah, even then," Jimmy says. "People will choose sides as we did in the sprint races. You counselors were cheering your man."

Junior adds, "Mohab, this is going nowhere. Let's have fun. Forget that stuff."

"You don't understand," Mohab responds. "Or, you don't want to. I'm going in and get the Director." He turns and starts the one-hundred-yard walk to the tent.

Junior joins Mohab. "I'm going with you," He tells the students, "Go, do whatever you want."

Entering the tent, they approach the Director and Mr. Chef sitting together at one of the round tables next to the food counter. "Yes, what can we do for you?" the Director asks.

"We've got a problem," Mohab responds.

Until the End of Time

"Mohab is against the guys enjoying themselves," Junior interjects.

"Hang on there, Junior," Mohab says. "I was explaining to them that individual competition is better than that of choosing teams."

"We were about to draw straws for a four-on-four volleyball when Mohab resisted," Junior exclaims.

"Huh?" the Director responds. "Chef and I are going over the list of supplies we need, and you two come in with a stupid debate over volleyball. Go! Have fun. Enjoy the time away from our planned activities."

"But sir," Mohab says. "Choosing teams is like forming groups instead of promoting self-awareness and individual excellence. And you've always insisted on pushing the individual to do his best."

"Don, I'll be right back," the Director tells the chef. "You two, come with me." Out of the tent, he stops. "How the hell can I trust my counselors to lead this group when you argue with each other about a stupid game? Play the damn game. Have fun for once, and leave all that political shenanigans alone. Now get."

"But sir," Mohab starts.

"Go! Draw straws or whatever. We've got a crisis on our hands. We may not have any food until this evening. One of the drones broke down. Go. Have fun. I'll talk to the students later, and you two also, alone," the Director admonishes, turns and re-enters the tent.

"See what you started," Junior says.

"Junior, in my years of teaching . . ."

"Blah, blah, blah," Junior says.

"We," Mohab starts again. "Yeah, everyone wins when they perform to the best of their ability. In competitive events, everyone gets a medal."

"Blah, blah. It's only a game," Junior states. He looks back at Mohab, "If we see any hatred or the students not being respectful of each other, we'll stop it immediately, but not because the winning team chides the other."

"Uh," Mohab says. "I'm not finished. I know what I'm talking about. But for now, I'll sit and watch."

Just a Matter of Time

They finish three volleyball games. They are now relaxing near the net, joking and gabbing back and forth and wondering about when they'll be able to get something to eat.

"Hey, Junior, what's the last word about lunch?" Albertaldo asks.

"Nothing. One of the drones broke down." Junior answers.

"What? Which one?" Jimmy asks. "They are brand new. Did John make it up safely?"

"Yes, they're okay. A minor mechanical malfunction at the top, Jimmy. You guys want to try your hand at the archery range?"

"Right now, I'd like a bottle of water," Joseph says. "Damn, Jim can't return the serve."

"As tall as you are, and you can't block it," Jimmy replies.

"Al, come with me to get some water," Junior responds. "Mohab, shooting an arrow is individual competition. Take these guys to the range."

On the walk to the range, Jimmy stops and pulls Joseph to the side.

"What if the Director was the one?" Jimmy asks. "Yeah, he and his mate."

"What, they'd do that? That don't make any sense at all."

"This entire system doesn't make sense to me. I'm surprised we're not sleeping on the ground using buffalo fur," Jimmy answers. "We'll be using longbows at the range. The only thing up to date here are those cameras and mikes in the tents watching and listening to us, which, I guess the Director forgot to check."

"Yeah, the cameras," Joseph agrees, looking over Jimmy's brush-cut hair to see Al and Junior leaving the tent and carrying canvas sacks.

"None of this is to get out, Joe. Agreed?" Jimmy admonishes. He gets a high five from Joseph, and they start trotting out of the tree shadows and onto the path to the archery range before those two counselors arrive.

"Hey, guys," Junior announces, as he and albertaldo walk around the corner of pine trees. "We got water, crackers, peanut butter, and jelly. Come and get it."

Youmentis and five students drop the longbows, the arrows and rush over to the log constructed table set near the tree line.

Until the End of Time

Jimmy says, "Crackers? When will the drones be back?"

"They've salvaged quite a bit of the food, so we should have a decent meal for dinner," Junior says.

"The drones?" Jimmy asks.

"Haven't heard any more about them."

TWENTY

"Here it is, Centennial Park," David tells Robert and Janice, pointing to the wide-open area. The car turns into the lot and stops at the gate. David presses the number into the screen, and the gate rises, allowing the car to go to the assigned parking spot.

"DESTINATION REACHED," the dashboard speaker announces, the belts release, and the doors open.

David guides them to the spectator bench reserved for his party of four adults. A high and wide net protects the spectator area from misguided drones.

"This is a speed test," David says. The church has had only three students qualify to compete here. There are practice areas around the city."

They concentrate on following a drone flying through the various targets. As it successfully flies through a target, it blinks green. First is through a square about thirty feet up. It requires a fast-vertical ascent off the runway to maneuver the drone through the square. It takes a quick turn to the right and through a four-foot-diameter circle, a descent to fly through a triangle. The drone turns to the other side of the field to fly through a close-to-the-ground rectangle. The drone flies through a square in the center of the area and makes a full turn to fly through all of those in reverse order and back to the runway.

Robert asks, "Who supervises these races? There's not an adult around anywhere, except here as spectators."

"Sometimes there are, and other times no," David answers. "It's all electronically controlled from the park office. They change the locations of the objects each time a kid does it. He gets three tries."

Until the End of Time

"How do they do that?"

"Computers. Cameras. The kids must pass the practice runs at other places around the city. I've heard the city is proposing a concept for kids to send toy spaceships to a moon facsimile, perhaps a half-mile up. The spaceship would have to land on that moon object, then lift off and come back," David says. "All controlled by a youngster fingering a remote."

Janice says, "If our boys found out about this, they'd think their drone was passé and be in the basement putting together their spaceship."

Robert adds, "Yeah, it'd probably be big enough for one of them to ride inside."

David responds, "Someone in the church is working on that."

"Where have we been for the past twenty years?" Janice says, looking at Robert.

"A small town in the country, thinking everyone's technology was like our rural area," Robert replies.

"Let's get a bite to eat," Ruth says.

"Where would you like to go, Jan?" David asks.

"Someplace where we can relax and catch up on our separate lives," Janice responds.

"With this grandstand here," Robert says. "There must a special time for a major competitive event. Why aren't there more here today?"

"The mornings are usually like this. Come back at four or five, and there may be a dozen or more who've passed the practice sessions, trying their hand at this. The finals will be July fourth. These stands will be full, and after that, fireworks."

Grasping David's arm, Ruth says, "Let's go."

"There's a great spot for omelets up the road a bit."

Inside the car, David speaks to the screen: "The International Restaurant on Jefferson road." The doors close, the belts click, and the car heads out of the park.

"Wait till we tell the boys about this," Robert mentions to Janice.

"Rob, sometimes you seem to think our boys are unaware of what's happening outside our area," Janice says.

"She loves it when I act dumb," Robert jokes.

Just a Matter of Time

"I wish it were an act," Janice responds.

"Here we are, I'm ready for an African omelet," Ruth informs of her choice, as the car parks along the side of the restaurant.

The voice on the screen announces: "Here you are, but before you go, would you like to read your summary, and review your schedule?"

"What was that?" Robert asks David.

"I get that every day at eleven. It was a journal of my activities yesterday. I can read it or press that print button. When I get to the office, it'll be there for me."

"Oh, my. Dave, you signed up for this?" Robert quizzes.

"Yeah, Rob. There's no need for me to make notes." David presses the print button, and the car doors open.

A one-eye robot greets them by name and escorts them to a small room with a chest-height round table in the center with matching chairs. On the walls are mural maps of the various continents. The tabletop is a gloss covered map of the Boulder area.

The robot returns with four menus, and in its monotone voice, "The specialty today is the Honduran Omelet: three scrambled eggs inside a tortilla with refried beans, rice, corn, and sour cream. Hot tea is on the way. Thank you."

Scanning the menu, Janice asks, "That's it? No pancakes, or biscuits and gravy?"

"Rob, see what you're missing. Seriously now," David again urges. "There's so much happening around the area. Please, consider the offer."

Ruth states she's going to have the African omelet.

"What's in it?" Janice asks.

Ruth leans over to point to the spot on the menu, where it lists the ingredients.

Yuck! French fries in an omelet?"

"Oh, it's great, Jan. You'll love it."

A waitress enters the room carrying the tray of four small cups plus a large pitcher of hot tea adorned with a picture of the earth from space.

Until the End of Time

"No coffee?" Robert asks.

She responds, "No coffee, Mr. Amwestson. Tea is best. It's refined from the best leaves of the Mediterranean area. You'll love it."

"I can't get a simple American cup of coffee?" Robert questions.

"Sorry, sir. Not here at the International. Your orders, please. Mrs. Mathish? The same?"

"Yes, the African omelet," Ruth answers.

"Mrs. Amwestson?"

"Gads, I don't . . . Oh well, the North American omelet."

"And Mr. Amwestson, what's your choice today?"

"The Boulder omelet filled with venison sounds good."

"Mr. Mathish? You had the Greek omelet last time, would you like it again?"

"Yes, Thank you," David says, and the waitress walks on to a couple sitting a few tables away.

"Are you sure you must leave tomorrow?" David asks.

Robert answers, "Yes. I gotta be back in the office on Monday. It's been great to get away, but. . ."

"You haven't been to our services yet. Couldn't you call and ask for a few more days? Tell him something happened, and you can't leave yet."

"Dave, nothing is keeping us from returning."

"Think of something," Dave replies. "Jan, how about it? Stay a few more days. You and Ruth could play another round, and Rob and I could, well, look for a house for you."

Ruth interjects, "Yeah, Jan, I need to beat you real good, so stay."

"You heard Rob. We can't."

Robert says, "We got this afternoon and evening. Sorry, there's no way around it."

Dave leans over and whispers in his wife's ear. Ruth nods. "Well, after this late breakfast," David says. "We'll take you to see the church, and to the grounds, we hope to build the new facility on."

Just a Matter of Time

Janice says, "I wish I could stay, but. . ." The waitress interrupts as she brings the meals.

She carefully places the covered meals and removes the lids revealing the aroma coming off the steam. "Enjoy the omelets. Mr. and Mrs. Amwestson, we hope you'll return. Pastor Mathish, your church has blessed me." She reaches for the tray brought over by another. "Now, for being loyal patrons here, we have the dessert special on the house." She slides four dishes of creamed cheese almond cake in front of each. "Thank you."

"Well, thank you," David says, and to comfort her. "Jesus held his pierced hands out to everyone," and then he asks if she'd join them in giving thanks for the food.

"Sure, I'd be delighted," she responds. She reaches for David's and Robert's hand. Feeling her hand grasp his, Robert focuses on the waitress, her facial features, her hairline, the ear and nose rings and the small ring hanging off her chin, and pieces of glass embedded at various points on her tattooed arms. Feeling the firm grip, he looks down, seeing her hand in his, her knuckles, and the gold ring on her fourth finger. They all bow their heads. David ends it. "Thank you, Lord, for this food to bless our bodies, and bless this young lady and all she does, her openness and love."

"Oh, thank you, pastor. Wow! I've got to tell my partner about this," she excitedly says.

Robert intensely watches the girl walk away, wondering about her features, the size of her forearms, and now her use of the word *partner*. Janice recognizes that familiar look. She squeezes his hand as he utters, "Hmm?"

"What's up, Rob? Did I miss something?" David questions.

Janice tightens her grip again, and Robert looks at the plate of food. He responds, "Ah, this looks great," Robert says. "Dave, tell us more about the church."

"You'll be amazed at the technology the elders have implemented," David says. "Your twins, how was it? I mean, how did they get approved for the Canyon Project? They usually resist appointing relatives."

"Jan and I were called in for a roundtable discussion, telling us at first that they couldn't and wouldn't approve brothers, as that was against their policies. They were ready to appoint Johnathon and told us he appeared committed to his work assignments, whereas Jim was more of a jokester."

Robert takes another bite of the omelet. "We sat and listened, and then I brought up the drones that we had recently finalized the purchase. They grew quiet, looking at each other. They asked us to leave the room. We sat in the lobby and decided that we'd pull John's application if they did not approve Jim too. When they called us back in, we were ready to do that. The leader said they would make an exception this year on the condition that the drones would be available for their use. After the summer was over, the boys could have them back. So hey, it worked out fine."

"Wow," David says. "This has been great having you here. Oh, we will miss you guys! Rob, the offer stands. Please, please seriously consider it. We'll go see the church, and show you the land we'll get."

On the way out of the individualized room, Robert takes another look back. In the hallway, he looks at the decor above each door, at the hundreds of national flags draping down from the ceiling. He pauses in his walk to look at the signs and pictures separating the rooms, at the ceiling lighting and the fans slightly moving the flags. His eyes focus on the numerous photos of foreign countries. He purposely steps between the small rainbow-colored arrows on the floor that point to the restrooms. The painting next to the entrance door depicts a serene area of Swiss snow-capped mountains.

"Rob!" Jan reaches back to pull him away from bumping into a couple.

'Oops, sorry," Robert apologizes as he turns to see them frozen in their stance.

"Here it is," David announces, as the car pulls into the driveway leading to the parking lot of the once three-story department store, now converted to Rockin Hillside Church.

David steps on a sign on the sidewalk and the first of three sets of doors open. An elderly lady adorned in a red floor-length dress greets them. "Pastor, it's so nice to see you today, and Ruth, you look great.

Just a Matter of Time

We've been praying for you. So, this is David's sister Janice and her husband Robert from Oregon," Mildred says. "Greetings."

"Yes, Mildred," David says.

Janice reaches to shake her hand when Mildred bends at her waist, lowers her head, and makes the Sign of the Cross. She does the same to Robert, and says, "Merciful God."

"We're going to give them a tour of the church," David instructs. "How's it been this morning?"

"Slow. There was a group from Denver who wanted to see what all the fuss is about. That's the words they used."

"You're a blessing, Mildred, thanks."

David begins to describe the main corridors. "On Sunday mornings, the other two entrances around the perimeter are open. Down this hallway are the restrooms, a café, a lounge, a room for preschool children, and another for second to fifth grade. It's where the scouts hold their meetings. They all need more room. Up the escalator, are the small rooms set aside for group studies, fellowship, and the dining hall — which will open in," he looks at his watch — "twenty minutes. My office is beyond that. Up those stairs is the balcony. Through these doors is the main auditorium where we hold the services. Come on in, but please keep your voices down, as there may be a few at the altar."

As the double doors swing open, the first thing they see is the round platform about ten feet high in the center. Above the stage are four enormous screens for the auditorium circle. Steps lead to the platform at four points, and between the stairs are small altars separated by eight-foot-high partitions. Inside one of the altars, a man has his arm around a woman. In another, a man adorned in a robe has his hand on someone's shoulder.

"David, this is huge," Janice quietly says. "I've got to have pictures of this."

"Sorry, no pictures allowed," David tells her. "The elders are strict about that. They want people to use the facilities, but not adore it. We emphasize the building as only a physical place set aside for spiritual needs and worship."

"Well," Robert says, "I've been doing that, admiring the beauty of its construction, the materials and techniques used."

Until the End of Time

David pulls on Robert's and Janice's arms to lead them out of the auditorium. "Let me show you the video room. He slides his finger across the screen, and the door opens to a stairway.

Ruth announces, "While you're doing that, I'm going to check on how the girls camp is going."

"Here it is," David announces as the electronic door opens at the sight of his face. "Usually, they're here adjusting and checking the controls and preparing the videos for the services. During the warmup time, the videos concentrate on pictures of . . ." he stops, as two guys enter the room. "Here they are."

"Bill and Gerry, this is my sister Janice, and her husband Robert, from Oregon."

"Pastor, we didn't know you had a sister," Bill says. "Glad to meet you,"

"These guys are amazing," David says. "They've got the summer off. They're instructors at the Alpha AIT Technology Academy. Guys, I was beginning to describe the videos you put together. Could you show one to them?"

"Sure, be delighted to," Bill replies.

Gerry says, "We're adding more scenes. You know how people are. Each week must be different in many ways. Otherwise, it becomes the same old, you know, the nothing new–under–the–sun–stuff."

Bill presses a button on the keyboard. He points to a highlighted text. The thirty-six-inch monitor comes alive with a picture of a ball inside a circle of light, moving among the stars. A finger touches the ball, and it grows on the screen. It slowly turns into waters forming clouds that reflect the different areas of seas and land.

It zooms in on the mountains, over open fields, deserts, forests, and into the wonders below the ocean surface, icebergs breaking apart and splashing into the sea. The scene shows rural towns and cities with homes and roads covered with snow, and the same areas in reverse showing the snows melting and waters dripping off leaves. Rains slowly descend. The earth is turning green with focused views of leaves of trees and shrubs extending their branches. Flowers are blooming.

The scenery changes to show birds building nests, and butterflies, bees, and hummingbirds feeding on flowers. It pictures rabbits running, cows and horses in fields, lions chasing deer, and elephants running through the brush. The clouds slowly darken into thunderstorms and flashes of lightning. The clouds move on, and a double rainbow appears, one end touching the tops of the forest and the other descending into a neighborhood.

Gerry interrupts the scenery seen on the monitor, "This is when the drums beat, the horns blast, and words of a song appear. Go ahead, continue."

Now on the monitor screen, they see song lyrics printed below the pictures of a man and woman covered in leaves, their heads down walking away from a beautiful garden. Next, it shows a bearded man touching slouched people, throwing tables in the air, and individually spoon-feeding thousands. The monitor shows a river of blood pouring out of his side. It shows a boulder rolling away from a cave. In blasts of light, Jesus is running through the clouds with his arms outstretched, speaking: *"All of you, come unto me, and I will come unto you, and you'll find your peace."*

"We've got to change much of it every week," Bill says.

Robert says, "Wow! It's an amazing rendition of the bounties of Creation."

"Thanks," Gerry replies. "Let's go on."

The image of Jesus, in a rippling white robe, slowly ascends off the screen and moves onto the ceiling of the church. Lasers project His out stretched arms with streaks of light from His fingers across the auditorium moving back and forth, from the front to the rear, to the sides, to the center sparking the audience.

"We're working on adding more, but that's it so far," Gerry says.

"Very impressive," Janice says.

"Yes," Robert says. "But, why the text scrolling across the bottom?"

"We have to add that to meet the council's approval. And, it also comforts the audience knowing the Civil Rights Council has approved."

"Huh?" Robert utters.

"Yeah, two of them come in every Thursday to inspect and approve the videos," Gerry says. "A few years ago, we had one scene showing Adam taking shape from a pile of dust. They would shut us down if we did not change it."

Until the End of Time

David interjects, "They've been threatened with losing their jobs at the Academy."

"Do they come back later and approve your changes?" Robert asks.

"We gotta show the final one late Saturday afternoon," Bill says.

"If they don't approve the changes, then what?"

"We'll have to use a previous one."

David says, "These guys have done a great job. We don't have live musicians on the stage. We want it to be a spiritual time, not a concert."

"Bill, Gerry, thanks," David says. "They want to see the rest of the church."

"I love to see creative work like this," Robert tells them.

"Great job. Thanks," Janice says, shaking their hands.

The door opens, and David leads them down the stairway. He says. "Let's go to the dining hall for a cup of coffee. Ruth may already be there, and I should spend some time in the office."

"It is impressive, Dave," Robert says. "But the thought just came to me about these presentations. They could become the audience's focus. I imagined myself leaving the service and asking the twins, Well, what'd you think of the videos today?"

*****

On the way to see the vacant property, David explains how the projected sight backs up to their home. The car stops. David announces, "This is the plot of land we'd like to have, all one hundred twenty-five acres. That exit coming off the interstate would pass by our entrance. The wooded area is for the scouts. Along this side, we'll build homeless shelters. Damn it! Oh, if only I had thought of bringing the architects' drawing, you'd love it."

"It's a beautiful site," Robert tells him. "I thought you said the sale has not yet been approved. What are the chances that you'd get it?"

"Sounds good, especially after we added the shelters, possibly room for a thousand. The last word we heard was a faint objection from the EPA after they had surveyed the land. But I'm confident we'll get it and be able to begin construction next spring. So, Rob, please consider the offer. Seriously."

Just a Matter of Time

"It's a beautiful site, Dave," Robert says.

TWENTY-ONE

"Let's sit around the fire-pit," David suggests. He slides open the deck door to allow Janice, Ruth, and Robert to experience the fresh air after the brief, early evening rain.

"Dave. Play some soft music," Robert says, lifting his finger pointing to the camera and mike. David adjusts the recorder to play orchestral music. They stroll away from the house to the center of the backyard, to relax on camp chairs facing the western sky. Robert focuses on the location, at the circle of gravel extending ten feet out. He selects some twigs and pieces of split wood and strikes a match to start the fire.

"Did you arrange this?" Robert asks David.

"No, a couple of guys from church did. It had to be in the center of the yard according to fire regulations. Two guys cane to measure it. They put a red stake saying, "Here.""

The fire blazes. They roast marshmallows and lick the gooey white insides. Ruth starts, "Why, oh, why did I have to miss the camp-out?"

Janice says, "That was so I could finally beat you!"

"You're never going to let me forget it, are you?" Ruth replies. "That forced time in the hospital weakened me. Otherwise, you'd be moaning as usual."

"Okay, let's forget that," Janice says. "It's your turn to visit us. So, how about it?"

"Yeah, Dave," Robert says. "Why not?"

"Haven't thought about a trip for us for a long time," David answers. He looks at Ruth, who's concentrating on the marshmallow over the flames. "The last vacation we took was a short trip to the Black Hills. Ruth, when was that?"

"Hum?" Ruth ponders. "Three years, two months, and five days ago," Ruth answers. "Yes, Dave, let's do it."

"Sounds great. Wow! I could beat you on my turf," Janice says.

"Nah. Forget it, we'll head east somewhere," Ruth answers, and tries to push Janice's marshmallow off the stick into the fire.

"Rob, while we're thinking about that, you be thinking about the offer to be our construction manager. Whatever they're paying you, we'll raise it."

"But Dave, what would I do after it's finished?"

"There's so much construction going on in the area you could easily get a position here. The city has plans, and the state does too. You must have heard that Boulder will host the winter Olympics."

"No kidding, but that's years down the road."

"It was all they were talking about last month."

"I don't watch the news." Robert answers.

"Why?"

Janice says, "I keep him up to *date* on anything important."

Seeing the wink of her eye, Robert says, "Yeah, she sure does. We go on dates every month," he answers, according to their previous agreement on ways they've chosen to respond when questioned on topics they'd rather not discuss. "Well, it started as once a week, but that became a strain, so we changed it to every other week."

"Dates?" Ruth questions.

Robert adds, "Yep, the two of us spending a day or an evening alone together, no kids. We alternate. Jan will plan one, and then I'll plan the next. We added a mystery part to it by keeping what and where a secret."

Janice says, "We put a budget limit on what we could spend. Rob surprised me one time by exceeding, I mean, going way over the budget, and oh, I was upset. I condemned him for it. He showed me a log he had been keeping over the years, saving on previous dates to splurge on an overnight in a log cabin. When the twins were small," Janice continues, "anything spent on a babysitter had to be part of the budget, so it was perhaps a walk, a stroll through the woods, a park, or a lazy cup of coffee somewhere. Rarely ever did we go watch a movie."

"Dave, you're taking me out tomorrow evening," Ruth says.

Janice adds, "another part of our agreement, and I resisted at first, was that if I wanted a new outfit for the evening, it had to come out of the budget. That's how strict it was."

Finishing the toasted marshmallow, Robert says, "Dave, I'm curious about what restrictions you have on your sermons. You said they must be approved by a council committee first."

"Yes, they do. I post it on my tab and send it to; it's called the Civil Rights Council. They look it over and send a yes or no, it must be changed, and they point out what I must delete or change the wording."

"What have they demanded you change?"

"Mostly words. Race is one of the words, even combining it with the word human. Another that is so hard to follow are the words male and female. They sent me sent a list of fifty words I could not use and presented alternatives, such as," David chuckles. "Yeah, I can't say dead, it's now 'living impaired.'"

"You're pulling my leg."

"No, it's on the list."

"Hmm," Robert contemplates. "Well, when we get down to basics, we actually do not die as in forever unconsciously dead as a doorknob. No, it's only this physical body that dies, while our soul continues living in that eternal spiritual realm. So, living impaired could be more of a correct way to refer to our physical death."

"Rob, you're letting them burn up," Janice says.

"Yeah. So?" Robert says. "We're so focused on this present life that's ingrained in us. The media, the academics, atheists, and scientists in effect telling everyone that this is it, folks, this is all there is." He pauses, watching the mallow drip into the fire. "So, relax and enjoy your marshmallow. How does that council consider the words heaven and hell?"

"I can't use 'em as a scare or a reward word. None of that hell-fire damnation stuff. When I bring Adam and Eve into a sermon, I must also say there's no direct evidence."

Just a Matter of Time

"That's ridiculous. How do you manage that?"

"It's difficult. My secretary helps with editing them. One of the theology professors at the seminary counseled me one day when I was so frustrated. That was before the church started to expand. He reminded me of all the scriptures about bridling our tongue. We got to be careful, more mindful of the people listening and their feelings. We do that with each other. Wherever we go individually, we normally watch what we say. Most of us, anyway."

"When Rob goes off on those rants of his, he doesn't," Janice says.

"Yeah," Robert says. "My ribs get sore from your elbow punches."

"Rob," David interjects. "When we were growing up, we knew certain words were off limits, and if an adult heard us, boy, did we get it. The same principles apply to my sermons. There are people in the audience who might feel uncomfortable with certain messages. So yes, I must constrain myself, and keeping a watch over what I say is a way to win them into the church atmosphere where they can freely worship."

Robert ponders that, and says, "Dave, it's not the government's job to bridle what we say, but they're doing it. It's our responsibility, not the government's, and yes, not a council telling you what you can say."

"Yes, Rob. Put a watch on your lips," Janice says.

"I can't watch my lips when you're kissing me."

"Another sermon topic," David says. "Ruthie, remind me."

"Yes," Ruth answers, "and I'll remind you of that vacation we must take, and our date tomorrow."

"You suggested it, so you plan it," David adds. "The budget is five dollars."

"Five bucks? You can't get a quart of milk for five bucks." Ruth sneers. "I'll set the budget on this one, and we'll talk about it. Are you ready for a helicopter ride?"

"See what you started, Rob," David says.

Leaning forward in the camp chair to place another marshmallow on the rod, a flash of light streaking across the horizon grabs Robert's attention. "There went a shooting star!" he says. "Amazing! What a beautiful night," Robert softly says.

Until the End of Time

"There goes another," Janice points to the tail of light, disappearing behind the tall trees. A serene silence overtakes them, as they concentrate on the clear vision of thousands of stars blinking as more of the meteorites streak and disappear.

Robert muses out loud, "Scientists say the center of our Milky Way solar system is 25,000 light years away. How long is a light year? That's too big a number for us to comprehend. When reading these scientists, the distance is always in even numbers. Perhaps it's 24,456 light years away. Do you think Adam or Noah wondered how far away those stars were?"

"Here he goes again," Janice interrupts.

"Yes," Robert answers. "Questions, as I wonder about the majesties of our existence and what happens next. Does one of those stars light a planet where we go after our life on this planet ceases? Do we become one of those aliens, perhaps an angel with the ability, at the snap of fingers, to hang around with relatives still here? Where is heaven? Will we ever have the technology to see into the spiritual realm?"

"Rob," David interjects, "When you get in these moods of yours, do you ever think of the ones listening, that they couldn't care less?"

"No, I suppose I don't," Robert replies. "But why wouldn't it be interesting to think and question things like this? These are all spiritual ruminations. So, as a pastor, aren't you interested at all? These thoughts don't come knocking on your door?"

"No, they don't," David returns. "It's usually about my relationships and how I should present the gospel. I try to concentrate on what people are feeling and wanting to hear. The universe is what it is. But I did like the comment about distances not being specific."

"Think of Noah on that rocking boat with nothing to do but keep the animals quiet, fed, and in clean stalls. Did he dump all that animal waste into the seas? Or, did he have a pile to use later as fertilizer." Robert asks. "Only seeing the waters, Noah must have been wondering when they'd see land again. Come on, its been months. When Father. When?"

Janice interrupts, "Rob, come off that *horse* and rescue that marshmallow."

Robert continues, "Ah, Jan's got a joke about some horse. Anyway, after a bit, the rains ceased. While looking at the stars up there and nothing but water around him, what was Noah thinking? Scientists have measured what's out there, but they still don't realize this amazing earth and how precisely it's where it is. Move this earth a thousand miles away from the sun, and we'd freeze. Move it closer, and we'd be toasted." Robert pauses and adds, "ah, Dave, sorry, but that's me galloping away on that horse. Yessiree, I'm gonna go find Noah when I cross over those pearly gates."

"Ruth," Janice speaks up, "see what I've got to deal with? He goes into these way-out smorgasbord thoughts of his, all the time. He asked me one day if I thought a robin squealed and did she push, and grimace when she dropped her egg into the nest. That's a big egg to come out of her. 'Oooh, that must have hurt,' he said."

"The girl scouts," Ruth interjects between yawns, "sometimes bring up questions like that while we're sitting around a campfire. One girl said she's watched a horse give birth, and all it did was raise its head looking back at the vet pulling."

"Did you tell her that pain is a reminder?" Janice says.

"Rob, tell me more about the work you do?" David asks.

"Simple, coordinating our projects, securing the permits and materials," Robert answers. "Every little detail must be inspected and approved, not by only one, but by several from the same agency checking up on each other as we twiddle our thumbs."

"You make it sound like all you do is sit in the office talking. That can't be all?"

"No, I'm forced to visit our projects and deal with the inspectors. They don't like it when I tell them that, like the cameras installed around our homes, we have cameras and mikes throughout the building site that verify our work. I noticed that there are cameras in the church. Has anyone been upset about being monitored?"

"A few, that's all. For most, it's part of daily life."

"Your staff, the elders? Didn't you say that some of the elders are experienced businessmen? Any have ties to agencies?"

"Oh, yes. One of the elders is an assistant supervisor of the zoning commission, and another sits on the immigration board. We've got one who is the head of the fire department. We are blessed to have them."

"I'm it," Robert interjects. "It's become an obnoxious journey of forms and registrations, inspections, and the waiting time. Now Jan is the expert at finding the right home and making deals for her clients. She is the agent to have."

"But Jan," Ruth asks. "Weren't you more interested in biology?"

"I was at first, started a career in nursing, but the move to Oregon changed all that. Dave, when I cross over, I'm gonna have a chat with Eve. What was she thinking?"

"Hmm?" David ponders. "Oh, how many times someone stated the same to me. All we have is what theologians have written, vague points here and there about their salvation."

"Yes, lengthy essays extrapolated by professors using words they've invented. But surely Adam and Eve will be there," Robert says.

"Extrapolated?" David answers, "You sound like one of them. First Corinthians 15:22 says, *'For as in Adam all die, even so in Christ shall all be made alive.'* That word 'all' is interpreted to mean everyone, yes, everyone ever born shall be made alive because of Christ, just as everyone will physically die. So, on second thought, yes, Adam and Eve will be there."

"All, meaning everyone? Come on. Does that apply to Hitler too? If it does, well, we can do anything we want, and we'll still get there," Robert says. "Dead physically, but alive in the spiritual realm, but it does not necessarily mean satisfied, happy, and forgiven. Those entering hell-fire will be alive in the spirit, but not very happy."

"That's good, Robert," David replies, "but, hell is one of those subjects I'm restricted to speak about."

"That's the point, Dave," Robert adds, wanting to delve deeper into the controversy. "One day, as I was on the way to a work site, signs along the road caught my attention, reminding me of the laws I must follow. Someone made those laws. The city, county, state, or the bums in Washington created them. Laws do not spontaneously happen. They're made for a purpose. The laws of nature, like gravity, was made by The Original Lawmaker." Robert sees them focused on the marshmallows, between yawns, "well, I guess, I'll shut up."

David turns his focus away from the flames rising off the logs, seeing his wife leaned back, her eyes shut, perhaps dozing off. He touches her forearm, "Ruth, do you want to go in?"

"Huh? I better," she reacts and slowly presses against the arms of the chair trying to rise, she sits back down and leans over muttering, "I feel like . . ." Thrusting her head forward, she vomits, gasps, and uncontrollably spits out more. She grabs the tissues offered by Janice, and wipes her lips, around her mouth and under her chin. "Oh my God," Ruth utters. "Dave!"

She leans forward and vomits again. David reaches over to steady her.

"Oh, no," Ruth sputters, "I've pooped. Dave!" she gasps, reaching down. "No, no, no, not again." She pulls hard on the arm of David. "Jan? Oh, my God."

"Yes, I'm here." Janice stands and holds her arm to help her off the chair. Robert pulls the chair away from the pile, so Ruth does not step in the puddle.

"What's going on? I feel like … No! No, it's coming again," Ruth stops, stands tall, squeezing her cheeks together. "Dave? Where are you?"

"I'm right here. We'll get you inside and cleaned up. Jan's got you, too."

Robert walks in front, looks back to see Jan and David supporting Ruth. He reaches for Jan's free hand to help her helping Ruth. Robert slides the door open as David and Janice guide Ruth through the opening.

"What can I do?" Robert asks.

"Pray."

Watching them supporting Ruth through the living room, to the hallway and out of sight, Robert goes back to the campfire, lifting his arms high and begins praying.

TWENTY-TWO

"Good morning, students'. I hope you had a good night's sleep," the Director says. He observes them complaining while devouring the light breakfast of steamed hot dogs with choice of toppings of peanut butter, canned green beans, corn, tuna fish, avocado, and baked beans. "Sorry, guys, but that's all we can manage this morning, as we've got to ration the food until the drones return."

"Before we get started this morning, I wish to clarify a few things brought up yesterday. There was one question I should not have answered as I did. Sorry, but it threw me off balance as that question has never come up in my previous six years. Hopefully, you'll understand when I explain what happened.

"The first was about my name brought up by Jimmy. As I told you, I am known as the Director. That's it, nothing else. My birth name is a secret. It must be that way because of what I do. In an incident from the first year of this project, the Director suspended a student and sent him home. His parents were upset and filed a wrongful dismissal suit against the director and the department for violating the student's rights. The details are not necessarily essential to know. What is important is what happened after the media headlined the story and sent reporters to the Director's home for exclusives. They and many protestors kept badgering him. His safety and the safety of his children were endangered wherever they went. His house was set on fire.

"The judge dismissed the case, as It was the student's word against the directors. But that did not end the rampaging. The protests increased to include department headquarters. When it settled down, the director wanted out, wanted nothing to do with the Canon Project again. His name and his reputation was ruined. The department instituted a new rule that all their people, specifically those responsible for students, would now have their names, their history, and all personal identities kept secret, so their families would not be in harm's way by anyone. We each have a title and, that's it. Officially, I am known as Canyon Director. And Mr. Chef here, that is not his name either. The only other possibility was to disallow suspensions.

"That's it, guys. So, let's go outside and warm up your bodies for the canoe trip."

"Hang on there, Joseph has a question."

"What's keeping the drones from returning?" Joseph asks.

"There's been a few problems on top. They've had trouble securing the food supplies from the vendors in the village. They hope to return sometime today. During that time, a mechanic was repairing the broken drone."

"That's my drone! What happened? It was in perfect condition!" Jimmy exclaims.

"I've not been given the details. We'll learn more as the day progresses. Jimmy. As I said, it did not crash — some minor mechanical malfunction. Johnathon is fine. That's all I know, Jimmy."

"Junior, it's all yours. In twenty minutes, we'll start the canoe trip."

They follow Junior out of the tent to the open field, where they line up for the jumping jacks, push-ups, sit-ups, and running in place.

"Okay, rest a bit," Junior informs, catching his breath. He motions Jimmy to the side. "Jim, if you keep asking these questions, you may be heading for trouble with the Director. I can see it in his expressions. He's getting upset with you."

"What? We can't ask questions?"

"Jim, I say this as a warning. That's all."

"I should have flown the drone to the top. It's mine, not the Directors to use as he sees fit. I've got the title, and the license to use it."

"I understand, but be careful. That's my advice," Junior says. "Your parents signed a paper providing the Director use of the drones as he sees fit when necessary."

"Huh? I would've known about that."

Until the End of Time

"Remember when you first arrived, you went to our tent behind the office. You didn't see your parents going into the office to sign the release papers, did you?"

"It was like . . . Oh, never mind," Jimmy mumbles, throwing his arms up and back down to his side. He puts his forefinger in his ear, turns it around, and brings the finger up to his eyes looking for wax. "Humm, that's why I couldn't hear you correctly," Jimmy mumbles and walks away to join the other students waiting for the Director to come out.

The Director exits the tent. "Okay, guys, I've received an update. One of the drones will be here later this morning with some supplies. I must stick around and be available for more communications from above. So again, I must put off the canoe trip this morning." the Director pauses, and says, "Yes! An older project came to mind, and you can do that. We started it last year but could not finish because of inclement weather. You'll get to use the canoes too. Around the bend downstream a bit, we started to create a replica of an ancient Indian village. It's something the department wanted. It's a reminder to the world of how we have learned from the ancient travelers and tribes who invented their techniques of survival. Junior, it's all yours."

The Director walks back into the tent. "Yeah. Good," Junior responds. "Mohab, get the tools. Okay, guys, the canoes."

Joseph is on the backseat, with Jimmy in front resting the paddle across the bow, as Joseph gives one big push and lets the stream move the canoe.

"Joe rocks ahead on the starboard side. Veer left."

"Starboard?"

"Oh, that's right, you weren't in the navy?"

"And, neither were you. Just point, okay."

"Which way, starboard or port side, stern?"

Joseph dips the paddle in the water and splashes Jimmy. Feeling the waters hitting across his back, Jimmy splashes Joseph.

"You asked for it, Joe, so there." Jimmy slides the paddle a foot deep into the stream and with all the force of his thick muscular shoulders, pushes the eight-inch-wide blade through the water and up toward his partner. Joseph splashes Jimmy on the tee shirt and his Academy shorts.

Just a Matter of Time

"I give," Jimmy exclaims as another splash drenches those shorts. "Thanks a lot, Joe. Don't get too comfortable. Paybacks come at unsuspected times. There may be a frog or a snake in your sleeping bag or inside your boots."

"Ah, you wouldn't dare! Remember, you can't outrun me."

"Port side!" Jimmy instinctively says, raising his voice and then lifts his right arm, pointing away from the large boulders creeping up on them. The river narrows. The front of the canoe dips into the pool as the rear rises over the falls and settles calmly in the swirling waters.

Letting the waters propel the canoes, they soon come to the big bend when Junior shouts, "There it is!"

Jimmy and Joseph follow Junior's lead. The next canoe of Waldo and Darvish, then Mohab and Albertaldo in the last canoe pull into the cove of grasslands. Fir trees border the sloping rocky clay incline to the vertical limestone granite walls. There's an uncovered teepee of tree trunks roped together at the top. Nearby is a stack of limbs. They appear ready for another teepee in one of the six hard clay, weedy, dirt circles.

"Okay, guys, this is it," Junior says. "Over here, we started a shelter they would use during the cold winters and for ceremonial purposes." Junior pauses a moment pondering the abilities of the students. "Jimmy's a stone mason, so he'll work on this. Volunteers? Because of his height, Joseph should be helping with the teepees. Make your choice, guys."

Four students move to stand with Youmentis and Joseph. Jimmy turns and walks toward the foundation where there are hundreds of granite/limestone blocks near the tree line.

"Ah, these stone walls," Jimmy says. "I thought Indians only used teepees."

"Where did you get that idea?" Junior asks.

"School, I guess. Whenever they put the Indian culture before us, they were always in those tents around a bond-fire, where they danced and held their rituals. And, where will we get the buffalo skins used to cover the limbs?"

"Jim, again, you get too inquisitive. Do your job, okay?" Junior admonishes. "Let's get the rocks placed around the edges, so when the mortar is ready, you can build these walls."

Until the End of Time

"Hey, maybe that's the purpose of the archery range so that we can go hunt buffalo."

"Shut up and get to work."

Jimmy softly sings, "Get along little dogie, get along."

Junior tells Waldo and Albertaldo to help Jimmy size and move the rocks closer to the edges of the walls. "Come on, guys, let's get started on the mortar."

Catching up with Jimmy, Albertaldo asks him, "Jim, where do you get these tunes you've been singing."

"Oh, I don't know, I guess it's something to get me out of the boredom of our work here. Aren't you confused or bored?"

"Bored, ha! Try crouching behind brush waiting for hours, possibly the entire day, watching for an animal to come out, so I could take a picture of it. Now that's boredom, After this summer, I could go to Mongolia to spy on bears. Yeah, do that for a day. You've got to remain still and quiet, as the animals can smell and detect the slightest movement."

"Why do you do it? Find another position."

"Hey, the thrill comes when I do get the photos and exhibit them to peers. Then, you want to go back for more boredom."

"So, none of this is driving you up the wall?" Jimmy asks.

"Nope, not at all. I may want to come back as a counselor," Albertaldo says. He grabs Jimmy's arm pulling him toward the pile of rocks. "Come on, let's get this thing built. Perhaps we can sneak girls here. Yeah, in three days, you won't be bored."

"Hmm?" Jimmy ponders. "Hey Al, if we work hard and fast, will that time come quicker?"

"It'll seem like it."

"Well, let's get with it."

Jimmy reaches for one of the rocks and carries it over to the wall and trots back for another. In about an hour, the three of them have separated and placed hundreds of them along the sides of the two-foot high wall. Jimmy takes a brush and starts sweeping away the dust that's gathered on the old stonework.

Albertaldo says, "We're ready for the mortar."

Just a Matter of Time

"Yeah, where's the mortar?" Jimmy asks. "Al, Waldo, go, while I finish the brushing. Hurry, it makes the time go faster." When they start walking to the river, Jimmy shouts, "Faster, faster."

"Hey," Albertaldo says as he approaches Junior near the river. "We need the mortar."

"Over there. Three buckets ready," Junior answers.

"All right, we'll get this process moving." Albertaldo answers. "Grab those two, Waldo, and I'll get this one." He looks inside each bucket and is about to pick the one about three-quarters full."

"No, you don't," Waldo says, grabbing the less full one, and takes a few quick steps to get away.

"Oh, that's the game, is it?" Albertaldo grabs a bucket of water. He catches up to Waldo and dumps the water over his head. Waldo screams, feeling the cool water on his neck. "Oooh, Al, you're going to get it!"

Junior hollers, "Stop it! No time for foolishness! You had better make progress up there."

Waldo and Albertaldo each pick up a bucket by its handle and balance the third one between them and start to walk in step, "Your left, right, left, your left. Come on, run, Jim may be sitting on his butt."

"What took you so long? Oh," Jimmy exclaims. "Wally had to take a dip?"

"Hey, I need a trowel. Didn't we bring any?" Jimmy asks.

"Ah, use your hand, Jim. That's how the Indians did it," Waldo says.

"You think so."

"Must have. There weren't no hardware stores in the area."

"Okay, you start doing the dance and chant, and Al and I will shake our butts. Time will go much faster. We'll have this finished in no time," Jimmy says. Lifting a piece for his buddies to see, Jimmy points to an inscription. "This foundation was not built by settlers. It was a Hollywood movie set!"

"Forget it, Jim, let's get this thing up and, ah . . . Yep, in time for the girls." Albertaldo states while dipping into a bucket for a handful of the tan-colored mud.

Until the End of Time

"Which do you prefer, Waldo, blondes, or redheads?" Jimmy asks.

"It's the eyes, man. All in the eyes." Waldo answers. "Eh, you guys are going too fast, slow down. It's dripping."

Jimmy adds, "Yeah, too much water. Go tell Junior to take it easy on the water."

"You tell him, Jim. You're the stone mason."

"Be glad to." Jimmy starts singing as he starts to skip, "Well, I ain't got nothin but time, I'm foot loose and fancy-free. So, baby, come a walk wit me, cause I ain't got nothin but time."

Listening and watching Jimmy skipping and strolling to the riverbed, Albertaldo looks over to Waldo, who's shaking his head.

"Hey, Junior, take it easy on the water, it's too sloppy," Jimmy tells his tent counselor. "The mortar is dripping over the stones. And, are there any trowels around here? We've been using our hands."

"We've been using them to mix the mortar, Jim. How much less water?"

"Test it, just damp enough throughout. When you pick up a handful, you should be able to roll it into a ball, feeling the moisture between your fingers. You should be able to wipe it smooth. When you place your thumb in the smoothed area, the indented spot should remain. No water dripping out." Jimmy investigates the two buckets that Junior said were ready. He removes a handful and squeezes it, watching the water drip. "See? It's too wet. It needs more clay. The Director would not be happy seeing half the mud hardening over the stones, now would he?" Jimmy says. "But, if that's okay by you . . . So be it. You're the man."

"Jimmy, one of these days . . ."

"One of these days? Yeah, one. . ." Jimmy mumbles, "Cool it, Jim." He reaches for a handful of dirt, sand, more clay, and starts turning and turning the mixture with his bare hands. He sprinkles a bit more on top and begins the walk back to the stone site with two buckets.

"Hey, Al, coming back here. I was thinking. Where are the telescopes the Director said we'd be using?"

TWENTY-THREE

"Is she feeling better," Robert asks Janice, approaching the fire pit.

"No, not much," Janice replies. "She's resting now. David is speaking with the doctor the church uses. Rob, I can't leave while she's suffering like this."

"Jan, we've got to," Robert responds.

"But leaving her like this, I couldn't. You go, but I'm staying."

"Oh, I don't want to leave you. Is she experiencing headaches, any confusion? I didn't see any signs of blood in her vomit."

"No, I didn't either. She does have a headache, a slight fever. But that's expected."

"Let's wait on that decision until Dave's talked to the doctor," Robert says.

"I would fly sometime. Could catch a bus from Portland. Rob, I'll be fine, and worried about you making the trip alone."

"Hon, I can do it. It'd be a lonely three-day trip. But I can do it."

David slides the patio door open, steps off the deck and approaches Janice and Robert at the fire pit.

"How is she?" Robert asks.

Dave leans back in the camp chair, looking up into the sky. "The doctor is on the way."

"He's on the church staff?" Robert asks.

Until the End of Time

"Yes, he's been a real blessing to us. Ruth is resting. Finally got her to calm down. She's worried and upset that you're leaving in the morning."

Janice replies, "I'm staying, but Rob does have to go. I couldn't go and leave her like this, so I'm gonna stay a few days. You don't mind, do you?"

"No, Ruth would love it. Somethings always seems to come up. She's fallen. She gets angry. I don't know what's going on. She'll be great for a week, a month, and then, whamo, her emotions take over."

"I'm sorry I have to leave, but I must," Robert says.

"Jan, go tell Ruthie your plans," David suggests.

"Yes," Janice says.

"You said he's the church's doctor?" Robert asks as Janice walks away.

"We don't fund his practice. It's a retainer, as he does have a private practice. The staff members use him, and he's available to the congregation at reduced rates. He's so generous with his time, to make a home visit this evening."

"That's a pretty good deal for him. How long has he been practicing?"

"Oh, Umm? Like thirty years now."

"What's his focus in that private practice?"

"He's a general practitioner."

"I didn't think states permitted that anymore. Doctors can practice only within their specialty. That's the law. So, what's his? Was it him who put Ruth in the hospital?"

"Rob, what's with these questions?"

"It's clarifying, putting things in perspective, that's all."

"Yeah, well, stop it," David rebukes.

"Sorry, Dave, I didn't think I was prying. Dave, I've always been curious, and like you said, sometimes I cross the line. Sorry, I didn't mean to."

"I was out of line too, Rob. Sorry about that. It's that these occurrences with Ruth get me on edge. We need a drink."

Just a Matter of Time

David strolls away, ignoring Robert's reply, "oh, I don't think so."

Janice softly knocks on the bedroom door, turns the knob, and peeks inside to see if Ruth was sleeping or watching TV. "Ruthie, mind if I come in?"

"You better, or I'll call the police to escort you in here."

"Feeling better?"

"Oh, yes, now that you're here. Don't leave." Ruth leans toward Janice.

"I'm not. Staying until you get this knocked out of you. Rob must leave in the morning, but I'm not. That real estate stuff can wait. Relax, and tomorrow you may feel like getting your hands dirty."

"Oh, Jan, you're a godsend."

"Dave said the doctor will be here soon to look you over."

"Not that same quack the church uses. He's the one who confined me to the hospital. No! Jan, Dave wants to put me away again. Can't stand him."

Surprised, Janice leans back, looking at Ruth flushing, her eyebrows forced together before she slams the pillow against the headboard.

"Ruthie, what's going on?"

"Get me outta here. I wanna go home."

"You're home," Janice says. She reaches for Ruth's hand. "Ruthie, I'm here. Dave is outside with Rob. Can I get you a cup of tea?"

"No, There's nothing here for me. I want to get away, away to Jamil's."

"Jamil?"

Ruth leans back, reaches for Janice's hand and takes a deep breath, sighs, and relaxes. She removes her hand to wipe tears from her cheek. "Jan, I've been seeing someone else."

"Huh?"

Until the End of Time

"Yes, Jan. I don't know how much longer I can put up with David. A guy from church. You met him in the video booth. The tall, dark, handsome guy, working alongside Bill. He goes by the name of Gerry, but that's his middle name."

"Oh, my God, Ruth, what are you saying?"

"Jan, you're my dear friend. I had to let it out, so you know what I've been going through. I've been seeing Jamil. No one knows. Jan, you're the first. Oh, he's so great in bed. Jan, I didn't know what I've been missing with David."

Janice leans back in the cushioned chair, looking into Ruth's eyes. Janice looks down at her own perspiring hands, back up to Ruth smiling tears.

"Ruth, I don't know what to say."

"You don't need to say anything. I'm glad you're here and willing to listen without that condemning look. Jamil is a sweet, loving, smart, and terrific guy. Been part of the church for three years now. We started talking one day, and I was immediately attracted to him. I'd find a way to bump into him somewhere. We would secretly meet in one of the small rooms and chat for hours. He asked me to come to his apartment for one of his South African delights. I did and, yes, ended up in bed. It's been two years now. We meet and talk all the time. Oh, what do I do now?"

"Ruth, I don't know. I'm, ah, well, ah, surprised."

"I'm so envious of you and Rob. You seem so right for each other. You haven't done anything like this, have you?"

"No, I haven't. I can't say I've never looked at another guy. I think that's part of our fallen nature. But I wouldn't let it obsess me. Now Rob did have an affair. It tore me up, but his confession brought us back together. The twins came along, and it's been a wonderful life ever since. Ruth, what are you going to do?"

"I don't know. God, maybe the doctor will put me away for a month. I want to be with Jamil, and I can't put up with David."

"What's wrong with David, besides that inability of his?"

"I know, he's your brother, and you love him, but you don't know him. Yes, I love him, but he drives me crazy too. He's all surface make-believe. He says he loves me but doesn't do anything to prove it. It's all church and no me. His desire is getting the respect of everybody. That's his driving motivation."

"Let's pray about this right now," Janice says. She gets up, locks the door, and comes back and holds Ruth's hand. She lowers her head and begins. "Father God, you've heard the cry, the torment of one of your loved ones." Janice continues to lift up Ruth and David for mercy, forgiveness, and righteousness, to bring them back into a loving relationship together. "Thank you, Lord. Amen."

"Thanks, Jan. You're going to stay a few more days, right?"

"Yes, I am. Perhaps we'll get into the garden." Janice pauses and starts again, "Ruth, I've found something very beneficial. It's what Rob loves to do. I do, too, but alone. Way back in the 17th century, a scientist and philosopher once wrote, *'All of humanity's problems stem from man's inability to sit quietly in a room alone.'* I'll sit in the garden and close my eyes. First, I work at shutting down the noise and all those rambling thoughts. I'll sit there thinking about nature. Sometimes, I wonder how that rainbow affected Noah, or what Eve thought when her belly started to swell."

Janice goes on. "One morning, when I opened my eyes, a big red robin flew to rest, not ten feet away. It was looking at me. It was so fascinating to look at the long thin legs supporting the round body, at its rotating neck, and yellow beak. Oh, it had the most beautiful feathers. It flipped those feathers and looked up at me. The thought came to me that God was looking up at me, offering His comforting feathers to be wrapped around me."

"Oh, that's beautiful. Why have we been separated all these years?" Ruth sighs, breathes in deeply, sighs again, and a bright, joyful, excited look streaks across her face.

"Jan, something's happened. I know it. Wow!" She throws the covers off, swings her legs off the bed, and gets up. She pushes Janice aside, grabs the cotton robe off the bedpost, and unlocks the door.

"Ruth, where you going?" Janice asks as Ruth rushes through the hallway.

"Ruth!" Janice tries to stop her as she enters the kitchen. "You need the rest." Janice tries holding her back, but Ruth breaks free, trotting around the dining room table. She slides the deck door open and runs out to the fire-pit.

"Dave, I'm healed. I'm well. I feel like I did when I walked the aisle into your arms." She kneels in front of him and puts her hands on his knees. "Dave, I've been feeling sorry for myself. I've been so selfish, made it horrible on you these last few years, Ah, forgive me, Dave. I'm sorry for not being there for you. Forgive me, Dave."

"Well . . . Yes. . . I forgive you. What happened."

"You forgive me? Dave, oh, I've messed up. I'm sorry."

"For what, ah . . . but yes."

"Ah, I love you so much!" she stands and starts twirling her arms around in a circle. "Come, let's dance." Ruth starts dancing and singing.

"Jitterbug, Jitterbug, Twist, Jitterbug one.

Move it, move it all.

Jitterbug, Jitterbug, Twist, Jitterbug two.

Move it, move it all."

"Ruth," David admonishes. "The doctor will be here any moment now. You should be resting. You're making me nervous. Here, sit and get your breath again."

"No, come dance with me. Like the old days, and Ruth starts singing again, "Jitterbug, Jitterbug, Twist," throwing her hips back and forth. Raising her arms high, "Oh, Thank You, Lord." She tries to get David to join her, continues twirling in a circle with arms reaching out to David, "Dance, Dave, dance with me!"

"Ruth, stop it now. That's not good for you."

From the deck, the doctor asks, "Am I here for Ruth, or you, David?"

Barely hearing the doctor over Ruth's singing, David sees the doctor standing on the edge of the deck. David looks back at Ruth dancing her heart out and then walks back to greet the doctor.

Janice steps in front of Ruth, "Time out, Ruth. The doctor is here."

"Oh, I feel great. You dance with me."

"The doctor is here," Janice says again.

Just a Matter of Time

"You do look good, Ruth, but, sit down and let me," the doctor instructs. "David called and said you had been vomiting with a bout of diarrhea. Here, put this under your tongue, and let me get a pulse reading. Your forehead feels good." He looks over to David. "How long ago was this?"

"A little over an hour, Doc," David replies. "Janice here is my sister, and her husband, Robert. They came over from Oregon a few days ago."

Robert stretches his hand out. Noticing the plastic gloves, he withdraws his arm. "It's good of you to come to the house on such short notice," Robert says.

"Hmm," the doctor says, removing the thermometer. "Perfect, and your pulse is right too. I watched you dancing about like that, and your pulse is like you'd been sitting. Unusual for your age." He reaches into his case and removes the stethoscope. "Loosen the robe." He inserts the ear buds and holds the end on the left side of her back, and moves it to the right, and then lower down her back. "hmm, Good, and, now on the chest."

"Hmm? What do you think caused you to vomit so much? What have you had to eat today? And yesterday?"

"We went to the International, and I had one of their African Omelets. Ah, that's it. Oh, I also had a slice of the creamed cheese almond cake. Hmm. Yummy. This evening roasted chicken breasts along with mixed veggies. A few marshmallows out here. That's all today, and umm, yesterday we went to the mall and had a Chick-for-me sandwich, fries, and then a pot roast for dinner, and ice cream before bedtime, covered in oh, so delicious, chocolate. Yummy. It was good," Ruth grins.

"Hmm? Pastor, all her external signs are excellent. Her memory is fantastic. But it could be the stomach and intestines. The food at the International has been up to par, meeting all standards, so, the other option is . . ."

"I'm not going to the hospital for more tests," Ruth emphatically says. "I've haven't felt this good for years. No hospital exams for me. I'm fine."

"All right, Ruth, one more, though. But I need you to lie down so that I can feel around your abdomen. Let's go inside."

Until the End of Time

David reaches for Ruth's hand to help her up, when Ruth says, "ah, I . . ." she stops, sighs, and endearingly says, "love you, David."

"Love you too. Come, we'll get this finished."

Robert and Janice watch them walk into the house. Seeing them disappear, he reaches for twigs and small logs for the campfire. Robert leans back in the camp-chair and asks Janice, "What did you do to her?"

"I mostly listened to her and prayed. Her face became alive, bright, and she got up and rushed out here. She's been healed."

"Sure, looks like it, or else she's delusional."

"Now Rob, skepticism will not do," Janice rebukes. "Let's believe she's been miraculously touched." Reaching over for Robert's hand, she adds, "I'll tell you more of what was said later."

The deck door slides open, and Ruth and David come back to join them. "Well, what's the verdict?" Robert asks.

"Like, I said, I'm as well as could be," Ruth declares as she leans back in the comfortable chair gazing into the flames. "Ah, this is so comforting. Thank you, Jan. I'm ready to take you on again. Tomorrow?"

"The doctor did not find anything suspicious," David says. "Ruth is fine. It's over. But, according to the rules, another must confirm his exam."

TWENTY-FOUR

After a breakfast of scrambled eggs, beef sausages, and toast, Robert says, "Well, time to hit the road. Blessings on you guys, and please, Ruth, take care of yourself. Dave, thanks for everything. You've been more than generous." He and Janice get up and head to the Winnie. Inside the camper, Robert and Janice spend a few minutes exchanging words of encouragement with hugs and kisses. "Jan, I'll be fine. When I get home, I'll get another tab and give you a call."

"I'll be waiting. Be careful and watch your tongue while crossing the state lines."

"I will. Now, you take care of Ruth. Love you."

Janice exits the Winnebago and walks back to the front porch into the arms of Ruth. They wave goodbye as Robert waves back. He backs the camper into the cul-de-sac, and waves again.

"He'll be fine, Jan. Come, let's get our hands dirty," Ruth suggests as Janice watches the vehicle disappear.

"Gotta go," David says. "Should be back around four."

Ruth and Janice settle on their knees to pull weeds from the front yard garden of yellow chrysanthemums, alternating with violet blue geraniums. "Is this a poppy," Janice asks, pointing to a bunch of bright lemon-yellow buds.

"Yes, it's a form of Iceland Poppy. Very popular around here and in the foothills," Ruth tells Janice, who's rubbing her fingers across the roots of the weed pulled from beneath the flowering poppy. "Jan, this is great. I'm so glad you're staying." Ruth reaches for Jan's hand, interrupting

Until the End of Time

Janice's grip on the weed. "Jan, you're still thinking about Rob. He's going to be fine. Come on, the faster we pull these weeds, we can go hit the ball."

"Oh, Ruth," Janice says. "On these trips, there's always something that pulls his cord, and he needs me to rein in those rants."

"So, what's his problem?"

"Rules and regulations. Says we can't do a thing without permission. Ah, those inspections at the state lines drive him up the wall. After the one coming into Colorado, he told me this was the last out-of-state trip we'd take. And, after that incident in the motel, he was ready to turn around and go back home."

"Motel? What happened?"

Janice relates what the clerk did and Rob's exit from the manager's office. "Oh, he was mad. We checked out and found a campground."

Janice reaches under the poppy leaves, grabbing a long stem and gently pulls the crabgrass. Before discarding it onto the pile of weeds behind her, she rubs the dirt off the roots. Her eyes focus on the various creamed color roots. She whispers, "God, how did you do this?"

"You say something?"

"Ah, I was thinking," Janice replies. "Have you ever stopped and looked at this system of providing water and nutrients to this stem and leaves?"

"Huh?"

"Yes, look at it. How long the roots are. How thin they get," Janice says. Her left hand supporting the joinery of the stem to the roots, as her right thumb and forefinger gently remove particles of dirt. "It's amazing. A pipeline sending to the stem and leaves what it needs to grow, to leaf out, to make seeds, making new weeds."

"Jan, that's a dumb weed."

"Not dumb. Built within is a designed intelligence beyond anything we can imagine." With a soft sweet voice, she says, "Oh, thank you, Lord. Yes, yes, Rob will be safe."

After a few moments of silence, Janice tells Ruth, "Hey, let's go. I'm ready to whip you again."

"Ha, that's what you think."

Just a Matter of Time

Janice takes the bundle of pulled weeds and pushes them into the burlap sack. They rise and walk to the rear of the house and inside to clean up.

"Here, Jan, I've got bananas to eat on the way. What is it now?" Ruth says as her tab rings. "Yes, Dave, we're heading out the door." She listens, and answers, "Okay, okay!" and slides the tab into her purse.

"What's up?"

"Dave said we needed to talk but did not want to disturb our game. So, we're off."

Ruth presses her finger below the doorknob to open the car. She presses another button, and the trunk opens. Janice carefully places the golf bags and their shoes into the trunk. Relaxed and comfortable in the vehicle, Ruth speaks to the screen: "Indian Peaks Golf Course in Lafayette." The seat belts click, the cord springs back, the car starts, and it backs out of the garage.

"I was told we'd have to join another two-some. That's okay with you?"

"Sure. Ah, male, or two ladies."

"He didn't say, ah . . . I didn't ask. Anyway, you're going to love this course. It opened four years ago. Has great views. Got ponds and streams you can hit into."

Ring, Ring. Ruth grabs her purse and retrieves the pad. "Yes, Dave. We're almost there. Well, we just pulled into the lot. What's up?" Ruth turns the volume control up for Janice to hear.

"You gotta get back here," David says. "The administrator is here to check you out."

"Dave, we're here, got a tee-time at 10:30."

"Sorry, but he . . . needs to confirm the doctor's exam."

"I'm fine. Tell the goofball I'm about to tee off. Haven't felt this good for years. Our doctor signed the report. Isn't that enough?"

"No, it's not, and you know that. Yes, this interrupts your game, but it must be done."

"Well, I'm not going," Ruth emphatically says and closes the tab.

Until the End of Time

"Ruth, we can come back later," Janice suggests.

"No, we're here. Why can't they give me a couple of days' notice? Spring it on me, and I should fall in line, snap my feet together. Oh, thank you, you're so sweet for interrupting my golf."

The tab rings again. Ruth ignores the call. It goes silent, it rings again and again. David provides the doctor with the password, making the call of immediate importance that disables the call ending capability of Ruth's tablet. The doctor is heard saying, "Ruth, this is administrator 2932. I must examine you. It's the law. I'm here now in your office."

Ruth looks at her purse, and up at Janice for acceptance. "Ah, we're about to tee off. Couldn't we arrange another time? My sister-in-law was a nurse, and she's with me." Ruth speaks into the tablet. She exhales loudly.

"I understand, Ruth. I hear it in your voice. But rules are rules, and ah, . . . Ruth, don't go away. I'll be right back."

"Let's get this over with, and then we can come back," Janice says.

"No, we're here, and if we don't hurry, we're going to miss our time." She presses the button to open the trunk.

"Okay, Ruth," the administrator's voice is heard again, "you know what this means. Another doctor must examine you. Your husband has agreed, so I've arranged that, so he'll expect you here at four this afternoon, and you had better be here, or else." He informs and gently adds, "I'm doing you a favor, Ruth. Enjoy your game." The screen turns black.

"Ruth, go in and register, I'll get the bags. Go!"

"My shoes too."

On the way toward the clubhouse, Jan takes the sidewalk to the right, leading toward the empty carts lined up facing the driving range. She leans the bags against the club rack and pulls the office door open as Ruth, from the inside, reached to push the door open. It startles her off balance.

"Jan, did you do that on purpose?" Ruth asks after straightening up.

"Sorry, no, I didn't see you coming out," Jan apologizes.

"We're teamed up with a mother and daughter," Ruth tells her after gaining her composure. "They're waiting for us. Cart forty-six."

"These carts are new, Jan," Ruth informs. She presses a button on the screen installed across the top of the windshield. "Watch this." A slow-motion picture of a golf ball spinning off a tee appears. Then a voice announces, "Greetings, Ruth and Janice. I'll be your caddy today." Words scroll across the screen, "If you want me to keep your score, press 1, if not, press 9." Looking at Janice for acknowledgment, Janice nods her head, and Ruth presses 1. "If you want me to track your shots, press 2, if not press 9."

Janice says, "Sure, why not, let's see what this does."

Ruth presses 2. "If you want me to suggest club, press 3, if not press 9." she presses 3. She presses 4 for sizing up the curvature of the putt. For help on swing techniques, she chooses 9. For pace of play, she wants 9, and for the menu of refreshments, Ruth presses 7.

"Thank you. I'll be watching." The voice ends as the cart maneuvers to the first tee and stops behind cart forty-five.

"Greetings, ladies," Ruth announces as she steps off the cart.

"Hey, you're Mrs. Mathish, the pastor's wife. Right?" the lady says.

"Hmm? Yes, that's me."

"I'm Edith, and this is my daughter Elaine. She's on the school's golf team."

"Mom!" Elaine sneerers.

"She says that puts pressure on her."

Ruth introduces Janice. She then focuses on the daughter. "Well, Elaine, that's what this game is all about. Pressure to keep the ball in play. Hmm? You see the water to your left?" After a pause and a look at Elaine's expressions, Ruth says. "Jan, show 'em what you can do,"

"Sure, watch this make the biggest splash." Janice snickers. She places the ball on the tee, loosens up a bit, rotates her shoulders, takes a few practice swings, positions her feet, and lines up her stance. She lowers the clubhead behind the ball, and slowly starts the backswing, and pow, she knocks the ball 190 yards down the left side of the fairway.

"Nice," Edith says, as Elaine stares open-mouthed at Janice.

*****

Until the End of Time

Having enjoyed the round and interacting with Elaine and her mother, Ruth tells Elaine, "You're good. Keep playing like this, and you'll get that scholarship. You're a natural."

"Thanks."

Shaking Edith's hand, Ruth says, "Keep encouraging her. She'll do well with you as her coach. Hope to run into you at church Sunday. If I didn't have that doctor's appointment, we could stay and fellowship for a while. But, I gotta go, see you Sunday."

"Of course, we'll be there."

"Well, Ruthie, you did it again," Janice says. "You've got your old form back. Good round."

"Thanks, it felt good. And now that doctor will tell me I'm not feeling good." Ruth says, and presses the scrolling words on the bottom of the screen, "Take me to my car."

Inside her car, Ruth informs the screen, "Rockin Hillside Church." Relaxing in their reclined seat positions, they converse about the round of golf, the good shots, and that horrible time on number thirteen. Ruth's ball hit a tree and bounced into a bunker, and her next shot went over the green rolling into the pond.

"Ruth, if it weren't for 13, you might have beat your lowest score."

"Yeah, I suppose that's why golf is a four-letter word."

*****

"Well, here we are, and early too," Ruth says. "Let's satisfy those practitioners because they certainly aren't professionals."

"Good afternoon, Ruth, and Janice, it's nice to see you again," Mildred greets them. "Did you enjoy the game? The pastor is in the office."

"Yes, it was good. Thanks, Mildred."

"Glad you made it back in time," David says as they enter his office. "He called and said he'd be about twenty minutes late. You got time to get something in the cafeteria. He also said he has to do a urine test."

"Great. Can I drink five cups of coffee in twenty minutes? Come on, Jan. To the café."

"Dave, she played great today," Janice says over her shoulder. "Like the old days."

Just a Matter of Time

"Jan," Ruth says. "After this exam, we're going back to the International."

"Sure. But they've got more than omelets, right?"

Carrying their drinks from the self-serve cafeteria, they select a booth overlooking an empty soccer field. "Jan, tell me more about your job. And come on, think how much it'd mean to us if you'd move here."

"I know, Ruthie, but the work involved would be too much. I love my job, and it's financially rewarding too."

"Damn it! Jan, we could have gone home and cleaned up. Stay here. I'm going to the office," Ruth grumbles as she slides to the end of the booth. "At least get out of these," pointing to her golfing shorts.

"Take your coffee. I'll have three more for you when you get back," Janice says, watching Ruth fast walk out the door. Janice brings the cup up to smell the fresh aroma. She breathes it in deep and exhales the fragrance over her golf outfit.

Ruth returns all spruced up. "Well, will this impress the doctor."

"Yes, it's beautiful!" Janice states, admiring the bright red button-down collared shirt, with white trim on the two pockets draped over her breasts, the tails drooping over the black jeans. "Very nice. It's cowboyish," Janice informs. "While you were gone, I got to thinking again."

"Oh, yes, you've changed your mind. You're going to move here, right?"

'No, a scene came back, and when I get home, I'm putting the tablet on a schedule. No more calls interrupting dinner."

"Huh?"

"Yes," Janice says, "it happened several years ago. We were in a restaurant. Rob wanted to catch up on what the boys were up to. We were discussing our plans for the summer when his observation of the boys on their tabs caused him to slap the palm of his hand on the table to get their attention.

He proposed a solution. "All right, you guys, this is it. For the next twenty-four hours, starting right now, you will not watch TV, you will not touch or have anything to do with that tablet. And I want to see a handwritten essay on what you discovered. No less than 100 words. When I get that, you can have 'em back."

"The shocked and upset look on the boys told us all we needed to know. Oh, how they resisted turning the tabs over to him. Now, I'm feeling the same way. I can't even say hi to Rob, and my time of silence is going to be three days. So, when I get home, I'm going to write an opinion piece and send it to the alt2news."

"Jan, I felt the same way in the hospital when they took my tab away from me. Dave could call, but I couldn't," Ruth relates. She turns her head away, looking out the window, watching a few kids running around the track. "I'm not going back there again."

"I'm believing with you," Janice says. "The doctor should be here soon. How much coffee have you had?"

"Not enough." Ruth grabs the plastic cup and drinks, gulping a swallow, another gulp, and another and sets the cup down. She sighs and grabs the second cup. She finishes that, stops, breathes in deeply, sighing an ugh. "What we do to prepare . . ."

"Here comes Dave," Janice says.

"Well?" Ruth asks.

"He's not coming," David announces.

"What? After all this, he's not coming?" Ruth angrily says. "Gads, Dave, what now. We hurry through our golf to get here on time, and he's changed his mind. He doesn't want to see me but will probably send me to that hospital again. Yeah, since he can't keep appointments."

"No, Ruthie, calm down. He's been talked out of it."

"No way."

"Yep. That lady you played with today, is his wife, and she called him. She was excited. So, you're clear."

TWENTY-FIVE

Junior shakes Jimmy's cot. "Hey, get up." Jimmy rolls over and covers his head with the pillow. "Now! Get up. Time to eat. Get the hell up. Now!"

Reluctantly, Jimmy slides out of the sleeping bag, drops his feet to the floor, and raises his arms above his head stretching his stiff joints. Jimmy stands, moves his shoulders left and right. With blinking eyes, he looks toward Junior, and over to Joseph tying his boots.

"Let's go," Junior says. Jimmy looks under the cot for his shorts and shirt.

"Where's Jim?" Albertaldo asks Joseph.

"Still in the tent, I guess."

"I'll go check on him," Albertaldo replies. He walks to the tent. He pushes the flap in and sees Jimmy slumped on the cot. "Jim! Come on, shake it off. Let's go," he says, pushing against Jimmy's shoulders.

"Uh, what?" Jimmy replies.

"Yeah, I'm tired and sore, too. But come on! Get up!"

"Why did we do that?"

Albertaldo grabs a half-empty bottle of water and pours it over Jimmy's head.

"Yaaack!" Jimmy yelps, while shaking his head and wiping the water dripping off his chin. "Al!"

"Let's go! Now!"

Jimmy reaches down to slide into his boots. He runs to the johns.

Until the End of Time

"Mornin," the chef says, opening the flaps, "come get it."

Trotting to the breakfast line, Jimmy picks a tray from the stack. He gets his pancakes and coffee. He joins Albertaldo, Joseph, and Waldo at the round table near the open entrance.

"Jim, I heard you come in. Where were you?" Joeseph softly asks. "Junior was out looking for you." Jimmy gulps the coffee.

Youmentis stands and rings the bell. "Another beautiful day today. The Director is still at the top of the Canyon and will not be back until later today. We'll continue the project we worked on yesterday. As for tomorrow, you know what that is. Okay, guys, let's get ready to finish the village."

On the path to the canoes, Joseph suggests he sits in front, telling Jimmy where to go. "No, Joe, you're too big for the front. Okay, okay, none of the stern stuff."

The village comes into sight, they beach the canoes and stroll around the bend in the path of young juniper trees. Junior stops, his jaw drops, and eyes blink at the sight of the area. "Wow! Oh my God," he declares. He pauses to look back for Jimmy, who's carrying a shovel and burlap sack of supplies.

"This is where you were last night? It's fantastic." The stone walls are up to five feet. There's a beautifully arched stone doorway.

"Does it pass?" Jimmy asks.

"Does it pass?" Junior questions. "Yes, it will pass. You guys did this after dinner last night? I don't know what to say, except – ah, thanks. We should easily be able to finish it up to the roof level."

"I have a suggestion," Jimmy says. "You've all indicated that you wanted this village to look authentic. In the supply area, I saw a stack of extra tent canvas. Why can't we use those? We could make it look like buffalo skins that have been out in the sun a few years.

Albertaldo adds, "Yeah. When I was in Brazil, I watched them do it."

"Yeah, why not? Yes!" Youmentis tells Junior, "Let's go get it."

Junior nods, "We'll stay and make mortar."

Junior pulls Jimmy aside. "Jim, I got to tell you something."

"What's up? What'd I do now?"

Just a Matter of Time

"Last night, as you were here, the Director called. You've been wondering about John, and he wanted you to know what's happening." He pauses. "John was arrested."

"Arrested? For what? Why?"

"The Director said that when he and Kenneth were loading supplies into the truck, John saw, what the Director said looked like a homeless man sitting across the street. John took food from our supplies over to him."

"Good for him. That's John, all right."

"Not only the food but John also gave the guy a Bible verse note card."

'Okay, so?"

"Well, it turned out the guy was a police officer."

"No way!"

"Jim, it's against the law to aid the homeless and proselytize a religion. The officer was disguised for that purpose."

"Baloney, it's not against the law where I live. You're full of it. There's more. What did happen to John?"

"No, Jim, I'm sorry, but John is now locked in the local jail, and he could be transferred to the county jailhouse a hundred miles upstream. I'm sorry. The Director asked me to tell you what happened. That's part of the reason why he's still there. He's in town trying to work things out."

"My dad has got to know about this. Has he been called?"

"The Director said he tried, but the number left at the office was not working."

Raising his voice, Jimmy leans into Junior, stating clearly, "If you're BS-ing me about this, you'll regret it the rest of your life." Jimmy takes off, running toward the river.

Hearing Jimmy's last loud remark, Joseph approaches Junior, "What's going on?"

"Let him go, Joe," Junior says. "His brother's been arrested."

"What? John was arrested?" Joseph sprints hard to catch Jimmy, who's pushing the canoe into the stream.

Until the End of Time

"Jim!" Joseph yells out, "Stop!" He jumps into the shallow water splashing it over the canoe. He grabs it to prevent it from going further.

"Let go," Jimmy shouts, "Joe, I gotta go."

"Jim, hang on."

"I've gotta know . . ."

"I'm going with you. Get up front," Joseph waves his arms at Jimmy. "Push, Jim, push."

"Here we are. Go! I'll beach the canoe."

Rushing into the large tent, Jimmy pauses, looking left to right and heads toward the kitchen. Pushing open the flap, he sees the chef laid back on a cot. "Hey, chef. wake up."

Opening his eyes frowning, the chef raises his head, "Was up, Jim? You posed be at wilage. Somtin wong?"

Kneeling on the floor with his hands on the cot, Jimmy tells the chef what Junior had related to him about Johnathon. "Can I use your tab to call the Director and get the latest."

"Ah, is out ord."

"Please, chef, call him and let me talk to him. About John. I gotta know. Where is it, your tablet? I'll get it for you," Jimmy stands to look for signals, a word or two from the chef, a nod, something. "Is this it?" Jimmy asks as he reaches under the head of the cot and picks up the fourteen-inch square, black, thin box. "Please! Call him."

Holding the tab, the chef presses a side button and waits for the screen to brighten. Jimmy watches as the screen lights to a scene of a covered wagon pulled by a team of four horses through a mountain stream. The chef pushes on a highlighted square at the bottom right of the screen, which makes the sound of a drum beating. A bugle blows, the screen goes blank, and the face of the Director appears.

"Yes, what is it?"

Jimmy leans over to be sure the Director can see him. "Junior told me that John was arrested. Is that so, and what's going to happen? Is he okay?"

Just a Matter of Time

"He's fine, Jimmy. And I may be able to get him released later today or in the morning. I tried calling your dad, but his number is not working. Would you know anything about that?"

"No, it was fine when they left. Dad always has it handy, and he's not the kind to let something like that go unpaid. Will John be transferred to the county?"

"Not if I can arrange his release. Otherwise, well, it's up to them. The jail here is small and can't handle more than three or four at a time."

"Sir, if I could get up there, I could use my tab to call mom's brother in Boulder. That's where they are. Dad and mom would be there, and if they knew, he would pay the fine."

"What's your locker number?"

"It's locked, and I got the key."

"Jim, I'll call back when we get this settled. Don't worry, it's going to turn out okay. The chief of police is aware of this project and supports it, all of us, and what it signifies to the community." The screen goes blank, and the covered wagon reappears.

"Damn it," Jimmy mumbles.

"Sorie," the chef says, and lays the tablet on the cot. "Now, me do lunch. You go work."

Back at the village, Jimmy and Joseph get back to their duties. One stone at a time. Jimmy has been working hard to keep his mind off the uncertainties of his brother's treatment.

Junior yells at them, smoothing mortar between the last few stones. "It's time to go. Dinnertime."

"Okay, A couple to go, and it'll be done," Jimmy says.

Jimmy kneels next to the flowing waters of the stream, washing the mortar off his hands, lower arms and elbows, and splashes water on his face. "Ah . . ." He breathes deeply, enjoying the freshness, leans back resting his buttocks on the heels of the boots. He's hypnotized by the sun sending rays of light through the shadows of the cliffs.

Until the End of Time

"You take the lead, Jim," Junior directs as he watches Jim get his boots wet, taking three steps to the front of the canoe.

As the canoe reaches the bend in the cove, Jimmy's eyebrows lift, his eyes brighten, his mouth drops open, and he starts paddling hard. "Push Joe. Push."

"John!" Jimmy excitedly shouts and jumps out, leaving the canoe swaying as he runs toward his brother calmly standing on the shore. "How are you? What a nightmare?"

The brothers shake hands and do the rehearsed signals of missing the high-fives and knuckle bumps, finally jumping their chests together. "It was a blast, Jim."

"A blast?"

"Yeah."

"Bull, I was told you spent nights in jail. How can that be a blast?"

"Come on, dinner is ready, and I'll tell you all the grizzly details."

"No, stop. Right now! I want to hear it."

"Okay, but just us."

"Over here," Jimmy leads Johnathon away from the path, where they find a few trees to hide behind, "out with-it bro. You didn't get beat or anything, did you?"

"Jim, remember those old movies grandpa had, the westerns, the Andy Griffin types. It was somewhat like that. The sheriff would sit by his desk, strumming his guitar humming country music and entertaining us."

"Oh, bull. Come on, level with me. Was anyone else locked up?"

"Yeah, young kids."

"What'd they do?"

"Something about truancy."

"But why? He told me that you helped a homeless person, and he turned out to be a cop. Is that right? What did Kenny do?"

"We were loading the truck," Johnathon replies. "When I saw this guy sitting on the curb in front of the hardware store. The sight of it struck me. Kenny had gone back into the store, so I grabbed a bunch of stuff and offered it to him. He quickly handcuffed me and pushed me around the corner to the station. Yeah, that scared me. When we entered the station,

Just a Matter of Time

the chief put the cop on another assignment. The chief sat me down and explained what was going on. He said the cop was a rookie, and he had to test his obedience. He said not to worry about it. Said he was testing the Director. Have faith, he said, as the Lord was on his side."

"Testing our Director? John, you know that if a public official is caught praying, he'll be outta there, quick."

"Yeah, but . . . this guy had a way about him that was, well, grandfatherly."

"Baloney! I've heard about these small-town jails before, and they are usually brutal, knowing they can get away with anything."

"I'm not making this up. He thanked me for giving the card to his deputy and prayed with me." Johnathon pauses to get his breath. "When Kenny found out about it and came to the jail, the chief told him there was not much he could do as it was in the hands of the county."

"The Director told me you might be transferred to the county jail if we didn't pay the fine. Said he called dad, but the line was dead. You weren't scared that you might not get back here?" Jimmy asks.

"Not at all. I was relaxed and enjoying it."

"John, this is too much. Too many loopholes. If I didn't know you, I'd be ready to lock you up for lying and making up this entire story. Ahh. Well, I wanna know more. Later okay? Let's go eat," Jimmy says, pushing Johnathon, causing him to stumble.

Reaching the big tent, Johnathon walks in first. The Director blows a whistle, "Everyone, let's welcome Johnathon back. He's safe and sound again."

Johnathon abruptly stops. He raises his arms high to reciprocate the high fives from each of the students. Albertaldo jumps to chest bump his tent mate.

"John," the Director says. "You've been missed by all of us. Thank you for your strong and resolute faithfulness in your time of troubles. This day will go down in the archives of the Canyon Project. Welcome back, John and Kenneth." The Director pauses as the students gather around Johnathon, patting him on the back, handshakes, high fives, fist bumps, thumb presses, and lots of questions.

Until the End of Time

"Now," the Director announces. "Let's enjoy our dinner from the resources you and Kenneth have brought back to us. Thank you. You two deserve to be first in line."

They race to the far end of the tent to grab a tray at the counter.

Jimmy and Joseph join them at the table. Jimmy asks Kenneth, "what were you doing while John was locked up? And what was your reaction when he was not there?"

"Didn't know what to do. I stood there wondering, looking around," Kenneth responds. "I tabbed the Director, and he told me to check the police station. But the chief of police would not let me inside. He came outside to explain."

"What did he tell you?" Jimmy asks.

"That John had given some food to a homeless person, which was against the law."

"What response did you get from the Director?"

Looking around the area, Kenneth leans in, "Serves him right. He shouldn't have done it."

Johnathon says, "hey, let's forget it. We could hash out all the scummy details for hours. Leave it alone and let me enjoy this time. Okay? Now tell me what you've been doing. Jim?"

"The last few days we've about completed rebuilding that Indian village. Now, tomorrow is when we get with the girls."

"Yes, finally. Great timing."

Jimmy adds his suspicions about the timing. "Why was John released today, right before the get-together with the girls, and not yesterday, or the day before? Hmm?" Jimmy says. "And what's this bit about the chief testing the Director?"

TWENTY-SIX

Robert pulls the Winnebago into his driveway two and a half days after leaving Janice. He slides the back of his hand over the front door switch, pulls open the glass door and turns the knob to open the inner door. "Ah." He sighs, scanning the familiar. "Home."

After unloading the Winnebago, Robert starts searching, opening drawers in the kitchen, searching closets, cabinets, side tables in the living room, and along the shelves of the bookcase without books. He continues looking for the Smartphone he kept while everyone else had transitioned to tablets during those early school years.

I wouldn't have thrown that out, would I? Robert thinks as he brews a pot of coffee. He opens the refrigerator looking for a snack, a bite to eat, something. From the freezer, he pulls out a microwavable dinner, turns it over to read the cook time directions. "Okay."

Fork in hand, he finishes the noodles and chicken dinner. He throws the cardboard dish in the shredder under the sink and refills his coffee cup. *It's in the safe. Yeah.* He goes to the office closet and opens the gun safe. On the top shelf next to the permit documents, packed away in its original packaging, is the phone. *Plug this in and give it time to charge. If this works, it'll be a miracle.* Opening the door to the garage, he slides his forefinger and middle finger over the screen, the garage door opens, and the doors to the car open. He fastens the seat belt, the cord releases, and the car starts.

"Where to," the screen asks. Robert answers, "The Tablet Doctor at Depot and First Ave." The car backs out the driveway, and off he goes to buy a new tablet.

*****

Until the End of Time

Meanwhile, back at David's house, Janice and Ruth are fiddling away in the backyard flower patch. "Why do you have to go?" Ruth asks.

"Oh, come on now, we've been over this a dozen times."

"Couldn't you wait until he calls?"

"Oh, he's home, but can't get a new tablet without me. So, he can't call. We arranged the flight, so he knows when to pick me up in Portland, and I'd better be there. He can't even use the tab at work to call."

"Why?"

"Restrictions! Company business only. Employees and contractors. That's it. Oh, Robert screams all the time at the . . . Oops." Janice looks up at the deck monitor.

"But he used David's tab to call his boss."

"Because of David's position, he's exempt from those rules. David told us that. Ruthie, I'd love to stay. It's been great, and I even let you beat me to show how much I've enjoyed our visit."

"You did not let me," Ruth retorts.

Janice chuckles, "ha, I got the scorecard."

"Get busy, and pull those weeds," Ruth tells Janice, flipping grains of dirt toward Janice's hands.

"Yeah, dirt," Janice replies, catching a bit of it in her glove. Focused on the dirt, Janice rubs her fingers together, watching the individual grains of black fall to the ground. "Humm, each grain of dirt, by itself, will not feed the roots. No, it takes a community of dirt to absorb the moisture and sustain the weed and the flowers."

"Huh?"

"Yeah, that golf course was built by a community of workers following the design of the architect, the designer. Without the plans, the workers wouldn't know what to do. If each grain of dirt did their own thing, these flowers, and yes, weeds too, could never beautify your yard. The world is reaching that point by neglecting the spiritual guide. How much longer can a community last without following the plans of the designer?"

"Jan, hush, and pull those weeds."

Just a Matter of Time

"Here's one specifically for you, Ruth. Robert shared this with me. He was sitting on our deck when a squirrel ran around the yard, sniffing and digging for a nut. 'We're like the animals, we've got to work for our food,' he said. He then explained that when we house a dog, a cat, or a parrot in a cage, they don't have to work for food and their comfort, the owner provides it. We're God's pet, Ruthie. He provides our needs. God provided that lady we played golf with, so a doctor would not examine you again."

"Oh, Jan. Thank you. It's beautiful. You're a blessing, but you never used to think like this. We'd be working together, and you'd want to finish and go do something else, like watching me driving the ball fifty yards past yours."

"Yeah, I always envied you and that swing of yours," Janice says. "Then, I'd chuckle when you lost the ball in the creek because all you wanted to do was show me how far you could hit it."

"Well, I still beat you," Ruth retorts, pauses, looking at the pile of weeds and glancing back at her watch. "Come on. Let's get a bite to eat. Lunchtime."

"Yeah, I'm ready for iced tea," Janice answers. She gets off her knees and discards the gloves next to the pile of weeds.

"Iced tea, eh?" Ruth questions.

"I'll get it. You fix whatever," Janice replies, as she reaches for a tall glass. She turns on the water to let it get hot to dissolve the tea. She watches Ruth smear mayonnaise over two slices of white bread, with the packages of sliced turkey and muenster cheese nearby.

*****

Opening the door of the tablet store, Robert picks a number from the display rack and chooses a chair to wait for his turn.

The man sitting in the next chair says, "Hey, you're Robert from Bilko, right?"

Not recognizing the man, Robert says, "Yes, and you are?"

"Lawrance Wilkersen. You interviewed me, oh, about four years ago. And well, I never heard from you again."

Until the End of Time

"Ah, sorry, ah, were you applying for the head carpenters' job?"

"Yes, I was."

"And I didn't reply?"

"Nope. But hey, you did me a favor. Shortly after that, the state appointed me to finish the work on the new hospital. Best thing that ever happened to me. Last month, I got promoted to the inspector general of all construction in the area."

"I remember now. The boss decided to promote one of our guys."

"You know that Bilko was awarded the contract to turn that farmer's runway into housing for refugees. Yep, I'll be seeing you often. Your tablet not working?"

"It was hacked."

"No, kidding. I need an upgrade," Lawrance says. "Robert, it was good to catch up with you, and no doubt, we'll meet again. My number came up."

"I guess so. Take care and be easy on us, okay."

Robert's number flashes. He heads down the hall to room four. "Mr. Amwestson, come in, and what can we do for you this fine day?" the lady behind the desk asks.

"I need a new tablet."

"What happened to yours? Let me see." She types his name onto the screen embedded in her desktop. "Oooh, you met Romesko. Okay. Janice returns from Boulder tomorrow. Come on Monday, and we'll have 'em ready for you."

"What? I can't get one now?" Robert leans forward on the chair.

"No! Monday. And, bring Janice. She's got to sign the release also, and you both need a facial update."

"I need one now! I'll be working Monday, and doubt if I'll be able to get away. Jan will come Monday to sign whatever. But I'll be in the office all day. There's got to be a way around this. I need one now! Can't wait till Monday."

"Mr. Amwestson, sorry, but you know the rules."

"I need a tablet today, like right now. I've got to be able to call Janice, or she may be needing to call me. We can't wait till Monday."

Just a Matter of Time

"I understand, but my hands are tied. You can make that call in the consumer room."

Robert stares at the woman. Resigned, he says, "Well, what do you need from me now to make the Monday process quicker?"

"An O.K. and initials. Yes, and we'll do your scan now, alright?" She slides a tablet across the desk.

Robert looks at the screen seeing his and Janice's name, their address, the ten-digit phone number, bank account number, along with other personal details. He is instructed to initial next to the privacy release, the data collection release, the product safety release, along with checking the box indicating he's read and understands the policies. He sketches his initials. He writes his name with the felt tip on the dotted line, agreeing to the tablet usage fees.

"Thank you. Now, look into the camera. No big smile, just look." The camera clicks several times. "Very good. Now the tablet will be ready by noon on Monday. See the clerk behind the window for available tabs to use."

"Thank you," Robert sighs. In the waiting room, he looks through the window for someone. He waits, thumping his fingertips on the shelf. Waits and thumps. He sees a bunch waiting, others on the tablets. A lady is slowly moving through the aisle, looking at the timers.

"Forget it," Robert mumbles. Noticing the camera over the door, he sticks his tongue out and swipes it across his lips. He pushes the door open and walks toward his car.

Robert's feet and legs tremble, his body shakes, his arms reach out to hold onto something. And just as quick, the shaking stops. "Oh, my," he mumbles.

"Was that an earthquake?" a man asks.

"It sure felt like it," Robert answers.

"Did you feel the one last week?" the stranger asks.

"No. Was out of town," Robert says.

"Yeah, that one was bigger. It tore up the bus station and a church. Well, have a good day," the stranger smiles and walks away.

Until the End of Time

Settled in his car, Robert tells the screen, "Home." The vehicle backs into the open street and slowly moves forward. Seeing fire trucks and police cars rushing to the area, Robert yells at the dashboard, "Go! Go!" but the car maneuvers as programmed.

"Cancel home," Robert soon speaks to the screen and gives it Tom's address.

"Hey, Rob," Tom says, reaching to shake Robert's hand. "What's up? When did you get back?"

"How you doing?" Robert greets Tom.

"Good," Tom answers. "Great, until about twenty minutes ago when the house shook. Another earthquake."

"Any damage here? Hey Linda. How are you?" Robert greets, Tom's wife.

"Jan?" Linda asks.

"She's still in Boulder."

"Did you feel the quake?" Linda asks. Not waiting for a reply, she asks, "Can I get you a cup of coffee?"

"Sure, I'm not disturbing anything, am I?"

"No, Tom was watching a ball game."

"I was downtown when the quake hit. It was enough to shake me off balance," Robert says.

"It was a quickie here," Tom informs. "The news said this area was the tail end. The bulk of the earthquake hit north of Portland near Vancouver, which is in shambles, and the airport received a lot of damage. Tore up the runways."

"No! No!" Robert says. "Jan's flying in from Boulder."

"All flights are canceled. She won't be landing in Portland."

"Oh, my God. My tablet got hacked, and I can't get a new one until Monday. It didn't hit Seattle/Tacoma did it?"

"No, That's where all the flights will go. Hey, let's go out back. I've got the grill warming. Going to smoke ham steaks. Stay and have dinner with us," Tom suggests. He leads Robert through the kitchen, where Linda hands Robert the cup of coffee.

Just a Matter of Time

"Glad you stopped by, Rob," Linda says.

Relaxed on the deck facing the acreage of potato farmland, Robert informs Tom why Janice is still in Boulder.

"Crazy medical stuff," Tom says. "So, how was it when the twins were dropped off at the Canyon?"

"Oh, that Canyon is a marvelous piece of engineering. The boys are enjoying themselves. We had a good time with Jan's brother and his wife, Ruth."

Linda brings out the steaks, the sauce, the seasonings, and places the tray on the picnic table near the smoker. "Rob, how's Jan?"

"She's fine, I guess," Robert answers. He adds more details of the visit. He relates the emergency call to his boss needing to provide him the information the feds want on the project in the Nevada Hills. "That's when my tablet got hacked," Robert says. He delves into his walk on the trail with the teens, and about the boy with the glasses. He shares about the church and its progress. "David is pressuring me to move there and be the construction manager for the new building."

"Are you going to take it?" Tom asks.

"No, Tom, I seriously doubt it. This rural area has been good to us," Robert says. He then relates his feelings about the inspections at state crossings. He summarizes about his suspicions about the entire purpose of the Canyon Project is to pair a boy and a girl together.

"Wow, what a trip," Tom says. "If it's meant to be, it'll work out."

"Yeah, but sometimes I want to scream it all away."

"Go ahead, scream. I want to hear it," Linda says. "Yes! Why not. Let's all scream the host of demons outta here. Let's do it."

"Yeah," Tom agrees. "Ready, Rob? One, two, three, scream!"

"Yaaaaaaaaa," they half-heartedly raise their voices.

"Oh, that almost felt good," Robert states through his grin. He chuckles at the idea, and lets it out again, "OUTTA HERE. YAAAAAAAA!"

Until the End of Time

"That'll wake the neighbors off the couch!" Tom says, looking toward the neighbor's back door. "Have you given any thought to attending the council meeting?"

"No, haven't thought about it."

"I have. I've been discussing this with a few friends, and they're with us. They said they'd support us and be willing to go. It's this week, and Linda says a few gals are ready to go. Right?" Tom says, looking at Linda.

"Yes, they will," Linda says. "They'll make signs expressing our rights to assemble."

Hearing his watch buzz, Tom gets up and opens the lid of the smoker to check the thick, round ham steaks wrapped in bacon. He turns them over, spreads the sauce, closes the smoker, and presses a switch on his watch.

"I'll be picking Jan up Sunday around noon, I guess. And then back to work Monday to see what's new at the office."

TWENTY-SEVEN

"No exercises this morning," the Director tells the students. "You'll need that energy for the trip upriver." Watching the students about to finish the light breakfast, he adds. "But before we go, I'd like to brief you on what to expect during this time of enjoying the fellowship with the best of the girls. They started the project as girls, just as you started as boys. From what I've observed, you're now ready for a ladies and men's banquet. You've proved yourselves to be men over the past month by putting those childish traits away. You've accepted the tasks put before you and performed honorably with courage, integrity, and strength. Coming here as individuals, you've become a unit of one, working together as one. The girls, ah, ladies, have done the same working together as women.

"We expect to arrive in time for a morning warm up period of games, individual table games to start it off, and competitive volleyball before a brief lunch. Need I say more? No. A little mystery is good."

"Any questions?"

Albertaldo restrains Jimmy's hand from rising. With a wink and nod directed at Jimmy, Albertaldo raises his hand.

"Yes, Albert, what's on your mind?"

"We've heard a few things about a paring. What does that mean?"

"A pairing? Hmm? Ah, Yes, two is a pair. You see a bunch of ducks floating on the water, and two of them have separated from the flock. We say watch that pair of ducks. Instead of the word couple, you can use the word "pair." A pair of shoes. Two people playing together, like you'll be doing by playing a game with one of the girls. That's a pair. Right?"

Until the End of Time

"But, do we get to choose, or do you make that choice for us?"

"Someone has to make that decision, or else it might lead to chaos. Every one of the girls may want Joseph in the volleyball game. Or everyone here may want Miss America, the girl in commercials. One of our problems as individuals has always been making haphazard choices that lead to break ups and divorces. Yes, the Director of the girls and I have already paired you with one of the girls for those board games. Back in the third century, the names of available girls were put in a jar. The boys drew out a name, and that was it. There was also the time when parents chose a girl for their sons to carry on the family heritage. Don't worry, I think you'll be delighted."

"If she doesn't like me . . . After the games, then what?"

"Guys, your likes and dislikes have always been subjects of change. What you don't like today many times become what you love tomorrow. It's more of a superficial emotional quality that changes when you get additional information. Looking back into history, the elders of the tribes arranged the unions, and the community prospered. Kings and queens chose who would carry on the family unity. The tranquility of the group transcends petty individual differences, which always leads to disputes and eventually, wars. That's the importance of you ten becoming one unit.

"Okay, we must be on our way. Kenneth will be going with me. Students, you, and your tent mate will be canoeing together in the same order as your tent numbers. You must arrive according to tent numbers. Because of the exhausting canoeing upstream, when we reach the cove, you'll be provided a time to rest a bit."

Junior stands by the canoes, directing the students to the numbered ones. Johnathon and Albertaldo are in the second, and Jimmy and Joseph are fourth in line.

The Director blows his whistle as he and Kenneth paddle out the cove and into the river flowing against the canoe.

During the trip, paddling hard against the waters, there was hardly any talking. Jimmy breaks the silence singing softly, "Cry me a river. With you and me, there'll never be. Oh! Cry me a river. Yeah, this river is crying for me."

The Director finally guides his canoe into a branch where the waters push them downstream.

Just a Matter of Time

"Did those ducks get paired together by their head duck?" Jimmy asks, looking back at Joseph. "A pair of shoes boxed and given as a present. Oh, thank you. I'm so happy." He pauses. "Joe, my right foot is a bit smaller than the left, so sometimes I need to buy two pairs to get a comfortable fit. Could I get two girls? Yeah, that sounds great. Joe, what'll you do if you get attracted to the girl, they've chosen for you?"

"Not likely. How about you? What if you don't like the one picked for you?"

"I don't like the whole idea one bit, from the start," Jimmy answers, as they casually float along. "To think I've got to have somebody else pick a girl for me is, well, outlandish. It's bizarre. They're removing our right to self-determination."

"I'll say one thing about you, Jim. You can tear through the frostings."

"What table game will you choose to play?" Jimmy asks.

"Haven't thought about it."

"I'm gonna choose chess. That ought to get us off to a good start."

They are surprised by ropes suddenly rising out of the waters, which prevent them from proceeding, Startled, Jimmy says, "Huh, what's this?" Looking back, he sees number five experiencing the same barrier. Several minutes later, canoe three turns from the sideways position and moves further downstream, around a bend and out of sight.

"What's going on?" Joseph asks.

"You got me," Jimmy answers, peering ahead for a clue, of sorts. The bend and high shrubs prevent him from seeing what's happening to canoe three. "Oh," Jimmy says, "this is our rest-up time. Well, 'Tweedledum and Tweedledee,'" he starts humming.

"Jim, the rope's going down, get your mind back to now."

"Push us backward, Joe," Jimmy says. "Make 'em wait. Over here to the shore."

"Sure. Why not." Joseph pushes hard on his right side to steer the canoe to the evergreen shrubs. Their hands holding a branch, they wait. Periodically Jimmy looks back to canoe five, a good thirty to forty yards away, still broadside of the protective ropes.

Until the End of Time

"Patience Joe," Jimmy tells his partner, as they sit there wondering. Jimmy leans back to look over the scenery.

Suddenly the waters splash, and Jimmy feels his head and shirt getting soaked. Another splash hits him. "What the . . . Oooh!" He releases his hold on the branch to wipe the waters off his brow, and the canoe starts floating downstream again. Through openings among the branches, Jimmy sees two girls running and yelling, "Gotcha! Gotcha!"

Jimmy takes his paddle and pushes water at the evergreens.

"Damn it, Jim, that was your idea."

As the canoe turns the bend, they see the Director and a middle-aged lady looking and waiting. "Humm," the Director says as they reach the shore.

Two girls, smirking, scramble to stand alongside the lady Director.

Jimmy steps out of the canoe, pulls the front on shore, steadies it as Joseph lays his paddle on the bottom, and steps into the water and onto the sandy beach.

"Howdy, I'm Jimmy, and dis here is Joseph," Jimmy says in a cowboy voice.

The lady Director introduces the girls. "Jimmy, this is Julia Swensen. Joseph, this is Gloria Wombocam. Now shake hands with the girls who threw the water on you. Give 'em a nice warm greeting."

Jimmy shakes Julia's hand and pulls her in tight for a hug so she can feel his wet shirt. He continues holding her to let her polo shirt soak up some water. Julia tries to push away, but Jimmy holds her tight. Over her shoulder, he watches Joseph bow at the waist toward Gloria as he brings her hand up and kisses it. "Whoa there, Joe!" Jimmy mumbles.

Julia pushes hard to release the hold. She looks at her spotty wet shirt, and up to Jimmy, who's giving her the once-over, when she says, "Come, I want to show you something." She grabs his hand and leads him away from the Directors.

Joseph turns and tells the Director, "Thank you." Gloria and Joseph then follow Jimmy.

Pulling Jimmy by the hand, Julia starts running. Gloria and Joseph soon turn onto a different path. Reaching an area surrounded by evergreens, Julia stops and says, "Okay, Jim. Now close your eyes."

Just a Matter of Time

"Huh?"

"Yes, put your hands over them too. There's something I want you to see, but not until we get closer. No peeking." Jimmy puts his hands over his eyes but keeps a gap between his third and fourth fingers. "Jim, no peeking, close those fingers," Julia says, and pushes his fingers together. She takes hold of his elbow and leads him step by step. "This is easy walking. No rocks. No peeking!" She escorts him around a corner and stops about ten feet away from the surprise. She waits, watches Jimmy's fingers, and lets the wonderment build.

"Now, Jim!"

Jimmy opens his eyes and stares in amazement at his drone, sitting on a circle of cement with a painted blue cross.

"My drone!" Jimmy yells, scampering to feel the windshield.

"Julia? How? Bye! I'm going for a ride." He opens the door and begins to slide onto the seat. Julia pulls on his elbow.

"No, you're not going without me."

"We can't. It's a one-person drone."

"Oh, yes, we can. The two of us are under the maximum load capacity. It has been checked and double checked. And," Julia emphasizes, "we've got permission."

"We do?"

"Yes, I sit in the back."

"I'm . . ."

"That's okay, Jim. But first, you must calm down. Take a few deep breaths and get control of yourself."

Jimmy slides onto the seat, his fingers rubbing the directional handle. His foot finds the pedal. His hands caress the lift and speed control handles. Julia watches his movements. Her eyes tear up at his delight.

"Julia, come here. Let me give you a proper hug." She leans into Jimmy, still inside the drone. Releasing the hug, he leans back against the headrest and stares out the windshield at the tall trees and the Canyon walls. "We can do this later. Right now, it'd be better if I let this sink in. Pinch me."

Until the End of Time

Julia's eyes focus on Jimmy as he slides out. She offers her hand, and they slowly walk to the park bench in front of the trees. Jimmy watches Julia sit back. He takes a seat, leaving a gap. He leans against the backrest and stares at his drone. He leans forward and leans back again and folds his arms together.

"What are you thinking?" Julia asks, looking at the transfixed Jimmy.

"Ah, nothing," Jimmy answers.

"Come on, tell me."

"I was thinking of the first time I flew that thing back home. I flew to a local park, and around it several times and landed. I sat on a bench and looked at it, just amazed. A picture came to mind: of the astronaut standing on the moon looking at this earth, and back to the spaceship that took him there. He must have been awestruck. Someone said, "Why not?" and the process started. The technology was imagined, and the parts assembled. The Wright brothers and their first flight excited the world, and here we are. I've got a drone."

Silently, they stare at that flying machine.

"Julia, your last name is Swensen, right? So, you must be of Scandinavian descent."

"Yes, your ancestors are Norwegian Vikings, and you live in a Scandinavian populated area of Oregon."

"Huh? You know things about me, but I don't know beans about you. You've got two minutes, and then I'm going for a ride."

"Two minutes? And how are you going to time me?"

Jimmy presses against the base of his left thumb, press it again and swipes it to the left, and with his right fingernail, he draws the figure 2 on the skin. "There," he says. "It'll start itching when your time is up."

Julia looks at the base of his thumb and leans over, staring into his eyes.

"What?" Jimmy says. "Seconds are ticking away."

She pokes Jimmy and runs off to the drone. Jimmy meanders a few steps and purposely stumbles. He takes another couple of steps, stumbles, and falls face on the ground, and his head turned away from Julia and the drone.

Just a Matter of Time

Julia runs and kneels alongside Jimmy. "What happened? Are you okay? Jimmy!" She tugs on his shoulder to turn him over. "Jim!" she shouts and presses her fingers on the side of his neck for a pulse. She slides the back of her hand across his forehead, feeling for signs of a fever. "Jim! Wake up! Look at me!"

Jimmy grabs Julia, and they roll over. He pulls her head close, and tenderly places his lips against hers.

She pulls back, looks in his eyes, and starts pounding against his chest. "You faker you! How many times have you done that in the past?"

Jimmy rolls to his side, diverting the hits, rolls back to restrict her fists. He pushes her arms out, causing her chest to meet his. Gasping, she lowers her head to Jimmy's right shoulder. Holding her tight, Jimmy rolls to his right, causing her body to follow along to where he's on top of Julia, and he keeps rolling. He stops when they're lying together side-by-side on the grass. Chuckling, Jimmy says, "Gotcha! That's for the water."

Peering into her blue eyes, Jimmy leans forward, looking at her lips, back to her eyes. He releases the hold and begins to rise. Julia raises her head, looking around the area, at the drone, at Jimmy. She leans into Jimmy. She pushes back and says, "Yep, you're a Viking, all right." She grabs his hand and pulls him up, "We're going for a ride."

"Yes," Jimmy agrees, and they run to the copter-shaped drone.

Julia slides in behind the seat sitting with her knees up, her arms holding her legs tight against her body. Jimmy turns the key, presses the button, and the six propellers slowly accelerate the spin. "Sounds great," Jimmy says. The drone slowly rises above the trees. Jimmy steers the drone out toward the river and follows it downstream. "This is our camp." Jimmy circles the site while lowering the elevation to twenty feet above the large tent. He aims the drone at the volleyball court, the archery range, and back to circle the site. "That's my tent," he points to his right. The drone rises and flies downstream, arriving at the village they've worked.

As the drone starts to land, Julia says, "No, go back and fly over my area."

"Sure, we can wave at 'em all, making out," Jimmy says.

Jimmy pulls back on the elevation handle and heads the drone back upriver.

Until the End of Time

"There's the cove area where I threw the water on you," Julia says. She leans forward and points. "Follow that path to your right." After a bit, the trees obstruct his view of the path.

"Keep heading north."

"Wow!" Jimmy says as the area becomes visible. "You've got cabins? We're living in tents, while you're enjoying air conditioning?"

"Yep, but it all ends tomorrow," Julia says.

"What happens then?"

"We're moving in with you guys."

"No way!"

"Yep, part of the program."

Julia starts laughing and tells Jimmy that the area they visited is a tourist area.

Jimmy moves his right arm behind his seat and grabs hold of her ankle. "Your two minutes are up. Going to dump you out. Cabin Two or three?"

"That'll be the day. . ." Julia starts singing.

"This is that day," Jimmy sings back.

"Jimmy, this is like an angel hovering. It's not as noisy as I imagined it would be. What are your plans for it after the project is over?"

"Use it for shopping. Messing around with the guys. Races. Yep, flirting with girls on horses."

"We could make trips with it."

"We?"

"You're so naive. There it is," Julia points out the right window. "This is our area. My tent is the one on your left, right there. Tonight, we'll be at that fire pit."

"Hmm, both areas are about the same." Jimmy lowers the elevation. He points at Johnathon and a girl waving. "That's my brother John." He circles and hovers a dozen few feet above John.

"He's been paired with Sammy," Julia informs. "She's from the Missouri hills area. Gonna be a Vet." She focuses on John. "You guys *are* twins."

Just a Matter of Time

"That guy over there is Joseph, my tent mate. What's he gonna do? He's engaged to a gal back home."

"Gloria will change that," Julia tells him. "We'd better land this and go join the group. You're a great pilot Jim, Thanks. And, you're going to teach me how to fly this thing, aren't you?"

Setting the drone back on the blue cross, Jimmy turns the key and waits for the propellers to stop rotating. He opens the door, steps out, and reaches inside to bring his seat forward to allow Julia room.

"Thanks for the ride. I loved it." She holds his hand as she lowers a foot to the ground, and then pushes Jimmy backward. Giggling and lying together on the ground, she forcefully pulls him close and wraps her lips around his, feeling his warm body against hers.

"The Director was right. You and I belong together," Julia says.

Jimmy sits up straight, looking out toward the bend of the cove. "Julie, you've got to know that . . . Oh, how do I say it? Yes, I like you. You're beautiful and full of life, but ah, . . . There's a part of me that wants to scream, like, ah, why? What is going on?" Jimmy stops and looks at Julia. He bows his head, holding his hands together. He mutters some and looks up to the sky. Julia stands, looking at Jimmy deep in thought.

A moment later, he softly says, "So be it."

"Jim, I think I understand what you're trying to say, what you're feeling. It is like a dream, a fairy tale, something like a movie script written to entice the audience to pay good money to view the make-believe happiness. Actors being paid to play the part well." Julia pauses. "I'm not acting Jim, and I don't think you are, either. Deep inside our hearts, we have each experienced a connection. I first felt my heart tingle when you looked at me after you opened your eyes to see the drone. I knew it then, Jim."

Being still quiet, Jimmy peers into the skies.

"I'm going to say this now, Jim, after being with you for only a few hours. God has performed a miracle. We are meant to be together, and I'm in love with you already. Whatever you've done in the past is history and forgiven."

"Julie, I don't know anything about you. All I know is that, . . . Well, I've enjoyed the morning. But. We've got go slow. Get to know each other's history too. Our trials and, you know, our likes, dislikes, things like that."

"Jim, just a few minutes ago, you said, 'so be it.' Sounded like total agreement with our pairing."

TWENTY-EIGHT

Ring-a-ding, ding. Ring-a-ding, ding, the alarm clock buzzes to wake Robert up this Sunday morning. He turns over in the king size bed to slap the buzzer. "Ah." He lowers his feet to the floor and stomps to the bathroom. After a splash of water on his face and looking in the mirror, he mutters, "Gotta go," and heads to the kitchen to make a pot of coffee. He pours himself a glass of orange juice, peels a banana, and steps out onto the deck, seeing the moon through the branches of the trees.

Ten minutes later, he's situated in the car, the charging cord releases, and he tells the screen, "Seattle-Tacoma Airport." He watches the screen light up to Maps, highlighting the blue dot on his driveway, a red dot on the airport, and a yellow line on the selected highways. Agreeing to the route chosen by the system, Robert says, "Yes, go," and he shortly hears the words, "Arrival time ten thirty-seven." He leans back in the seat, takes a sip of coffee. He lowers the backrest all the way and grabs the pillow to take a nap.

As the car was about to enter the interstate, it pulls to the side and stops. A voice announces, "You do not have permission to leave."

"What?" Robert exclaims looking at the dashboard screen. A line of text appears on the bottom. "Oh!" Robert screams out the window. He reaches forward and starts penning a message on the screen. He pushes send and sits back to wait, and watches other vehicles entering the highway.

Some twenty minutes later, a vehicle stops behind his car. An officer slowly approaches, "Sir, step out, please." Robert opens the door and stands in front of the officer, looking at his tablet, up to the face of Robert, and back to the screen.

Until the End of Time

"Your car needs an update, Mr. Amwestson."

"Yes, I know, I know. I've been out of state the last two weeks," Robert says.

"Yes, I see that. When you get back from the airport, get that done quick, okay?" The officer presses a few buttons on his tablet. "You're free to go now."

"Thanks," Robert says.

Five hours and four minutes later, the car pulls into the airport parking spot reserved for him next to the arrival gate for passengers of OneAir. Robert rushes toward the double door, slides his fingers over the screen. The door opens, and there's Janice, sitting next to her suitcase.

"Why are you so late?" Janice asks. "I've been sitting here wondering."

"Ah, I forgot to get permission to leave. Sorry."

"Rob, well, anyway, you're here and thanks," she says. They embrace and kiss. "I'm worn out Rob, and hungry too."

He picks up the suitcase and holds her hand. "I've got your tea warming in the car. It's a five-hour trip home. You can nap on the way."

"Thanks. But why the switch in airports?" She asks as they exit the building.

"You didn't hear?"

"What? What happened?"

"Earthquake in Portland. It tore up the runways."

"All I heard was the pilot telling us we would arrive at ten fifteen."

Robert presses the key codes on the door to the car. Janice slides onto her seat while Robert puts the suitcase in the trunk and sits next to Janice. He leans forward to tell the screen the destination. The map appears, and Robert says, "Yes, go."

"How's Ruth doing?" Robert asks, reaching for her teacup. "Here."

"Thanks," Janice says. "She's fine. But these three days of not being able to call has got to stop. Rob, we've got to be more careful."

"Tell me about it. Tomorrow we'll get the new ones. I was outside the store when the earthquake hit. It shook me off balance."

Just a Matter of Time

"The house is okay?"

"Yes, it's fine. Go ahead, take a nap."

"That's all I did on the plane. How was the drive home?"

"Just the usual stops. I did stop by the Canyon headquarters to see if there was any way I could talk with the boys. But no, I couldn't. The officer asked me why my phone number was out of date, as the Director tried to call me."

"Why? Anything wrong with the boys?"

"No, they're fine. I'll tell you more later."

"Now, Rob."

"They're fine, Jan. John is back at the camp. There's no problem. It's over."

"What'd you mean back at the camp? What happened? You said it's over. What's over?"

"Okay. John and another guy were sent to get supplies from the village nearby." Robert supplies some details of the arrest. "You know me. Man, was I upset at first hearing that. The guy calmed me down, telling me that If I wanted to know more, I could visit the chief of police and get all the details. So, I did." Robert cracks opens a window for fresh air.

"Jan, they're fine. It's okay. He, Chief Shepall, convinced me of it and prayed that we would be at ease. Besides being the chief of police in that village, he's also the pastor of the one church. We talked for perhaps an hour about the project and the Director. He put me at ease, so everything is going to turn out fine."

"If you say so. But, visualizing John locked up behind bars, well, you know."

"It won't be on his record," Robert says. "He invited us to stay a few days when we pick the boys up, so you'll get to meet him. He also writes about his Indian heritage, how the settlers treated them as strangers, not wanting to assimilate. His newest novel is about the persecution of the church throughout history and what's to become of it in the last days. Ah, Jan, being in a village like that is like being transported into a different world and time." Robert pauses. "You said you were hungry. Travel Stop up here a bit."

Until the End of Time

"Yes!"

Robert leans forward and tells the screen, "Stop there."

Comfortable in a booth, Janice reaches across the table for Robert's hand, "I missed you. Both of my hands did." She reaches for his other hand. "Now Rob, tell me more about this . . ."

"Thanks," he interrupts, and raises his eyes toward the camera microphone, "I'm hungry and can't talk while smelling this delicious burger and fries."

"You're right, it does look fantastic," Janice replies.

"We're gonna plan another trip," Robert tells the waitress after she had swiped his fingers. She posts a discount pass in their name to visit any Travel Stop.

Back in the car with another four hours to go, Robert pulls the chess game out and places it on the pull-down table.

"Before we get started, tell me more of this police chief and your visit," Janice says. You said you were absorbed with him. Why?"

"He's about to retire and has been sent a possible replacement by the county. It's a beautiful little village, of perhaps two hundred people. It depends greatly on the tourists visiting the Canyon. There's a campground nearby, one hotel, one restaurant, a grocery store, and a small hardware store. The one school uses the church built in the late 1800s. You'd love it."

"Sounds idyllic, but about the man himself. What was so interesting about him?"

"Well, he grew up in that village and embraced Christianity as a teen. He's also the pastor of the church even though he's never been to a seminary, nor college. But hey, he seems to understand more about our relationship to God than David does. He said he's 72 years young, has written three novels about Indian life, and is about to finish another one. He gives them away for any donation. Jan, this guy is like someone invented by an author or by Hollywood."

"But Rob, how was John treated?"

"He said John reminded him of one of his sons who's gone on to become a doctor. He inferred that John knows what he wants to do, is deeply committed to living life to its fullest. Jan, we've got nothing to be concerned about John, nor Jimmy."

"Yeah, except for this pairing scenario the boys are experiencing. I was thinking about that during the flight. Wondering how I would have reacted, knowing that the government had assigned us to be together. What would I have done? How would I have reacted?"

"Yes, I've thought about it too. It's so far out of our thinking process. Then, I got the thought that God, who knows everything, brought us together through that fence."

"Oh, Rob, thank you." Janice reaches for his hands and leans in to embrace and kiss. She then focuses on the board, "Now, I'm going to put you in check-mate faster than you can sneeze."

"Ha, You think so."

"Yep," Janice replies, moving her Pawn to take his Knight.

An hour later, the game has progressed where Robert is down to six players protecting his King. Janice has nine.

"You're in check again," Janice announces as she slides a Bishop diagonally, removing one of his Rooks.

"Oooh! I should have seen that!" Robert answers. He moves his Knight and takes her Bishop off the board, "that's it, Jan." He leans back and smiles, watching her think.

"Jan, before we go to the house, let's stop and pick up the tablets," Robert says and leans forward to inform the controls when Janice interrupts.

"Rob, it's Sunday. Stop somewhere, and we'll take something home."

He leans toward the screen to change their destination to the drive-through at Chick-for-me.

*****

"Come on out with me," Robert tells Janice after he places her suitcase on the foot of the bed. She freshens herself at the make-up table. He grabs her hand and leads her to the kitchen, where he prepares two glasses of red wine to sip as they eat the sandwiches and fries on the deck.

Until the End of Time

"Peter has okayed you're leaving again, right?"

"Tentatively. I'm not looking forward to getting back to the office in the morning. Peter has agreed to another State renovation project here in town." Robert describes the comments of the man at the tablet office. "As I was leaving, he said that he'd never again agree to do another one of those, and now he has."

"I don't want to go back to the office, either. I'm still thinking about Ruth and David."

Anyway, tomorrow, we'll get the tablet and be back to normal."

"Normal?"

TWENTY-NINE

After a long silence of looking over the area next to the drone, at the trees, the sun shining off the walls of the canyon walls, Jimmy turns his head to look directly into the eyes of Julia.

"Sorry, Julie," Jimmy says. "But I'm still skeptical about this entire pairing fiasco. You know, two people in authority getting together and choosing who should or shouldn't be paired as one. And, since that seems to be the agenda, shouldn't we forget the learning part? Is that the plan for tonight, waiting in line and then we get fifteen minutes in the tent? This whole thing is wacko. I like making my own choices, the freedom of it, and if I make a mistake, well, there's always consequences: some good and some bad. It's how we learn, from the time we fall off the bike and hit our head as a five-year-old to the time we choose well, someone to live with."

"Jim, you can still refuse to do this. You can go home after it's over and forgot about the great time we had, forget about me, and this entire program. You can endure these two days together and say goodbye. Make up your mind, Jim. I'm going in. See ya." Julia starts to get up.

"No, don't go. Stay," Jimmy says, reaching for her elbow.

"Why? You're obviously against it all. And me, too."

"No, no, I'm not against you. If I saw you in a crowd, somehow, I'd try to get in your way."

"Yeah, stumble and fall," Julia says, leaning forward, her left elbow on the ground, her right hand on his shoulder. She looks deep into his eyes.

Until the End of Time

"Okay. My name is Julia Swensen. I'm nineteen years old. I'm from a small town in Nebraska, near Omaha. I did acrobatic training for the Olympics. But I loved the study of biology and vegetation more. Dad's a farmer with six-hundred acres. Got cows, horses, a few pigs, and chickens. Grows corn. I've got two brothers, one three years older, and the other two years younger. And two sisters too, one twelve and the other ten. Jacob, my older brother, was selected for this project two years ago and came home with Reba. They're expecting a son in September. He got the job as one of the associates of a corn processing plant. Besides being a mother to three or four kids, I would like to be able to work an acre or so and sell the produce in one of those farmer's markets. I love to travel, too. I'm not too bad of a cook. There, that's me, Julia." She sits up straight, her arms around her knees, looking out at the horizon.

Jimmy rises. "That was your two-minutes." He puts his arm around her shoulder, pulling her close, feeling her warmth and the strength of her shoulders. He softly says, "Julia, I accept you."

She relaxes and rests her head on his shoulder. She breathes relief and slowly sighs as they sit silently, gazing at the beauty of the Canyon.

Breaking the long silence, Jimmy says, "Let's go in. I'd like to see what's going on with my brother."

Jimmy and Julia, entering the large tent, stop to look at all the couples playing games. The lady Director approaches them, "Well, that took longer than expected. You've only got an hour before lunch, so get with it."

"We're going to play chess," Jimmy says, looking to Julia for a reaction.

"Chess! Yeah," Julia says. "Ah, you're one of those, are you? Yeah, thinking girls can't play that game of analytics and deep concentration. Ha, this is going to be fun." She looks at the Director. "We may forgo lunch."

"I'll bring the game over," The Director tells them. "There's coffee or tea at the cafeteria line."

"Go, have a seat," Julia says. "I'll bring you three cups of coffee, as you'll need it."

Jimmy takes the few steps to Johnathon's table, "How ya doing?"

Just a Matter of Time

"Jim, this is Sammy. She's from Missouri. How's it going with Julia? Hey, you went for a ride. Why? How come you got permission, and I didn't?"

"Ask the director, John. Sammy, nice to meet you. Julie told me a bit about you." Jimmy responds. "We'll have more time to talk later, but, well, I've got to beat Julie, or I'll never hear the end of it." As Jimmy turns, Johnathon winks and smiles.

Watching Julia arranging her white pieces on the board, Jimmy says, "Thanks for the coffee. You can go first."

Julia moves her Pawn one space in front of her Knight. Jimmy makes a similar move on his side of the board.

A bit over an hour passes, and the Director blows her whistle, "All right, everyone, stop. It's time for a quick lunch. We had planned on enjoying volleyball before lunch, but time has passed. So, come and get your sandwiches. You can leave your games as they are, as you may want to get back to them later." The students meander over to the cafeteria line and select a choice of ham and cheese, peanut butter and jelly, grilled cheese, or tuna fish with mustard, and they also take a large iced tea.

"Julie, I . . ." Jimmy begins.

"Don't you dare!" Julia exclaims.

"What?"

"Yeah, I saw you. You were about to move your Queen as you passed the table."

'No, I wasn't," Jimmy rebukes her.

He feels her elbow in his side, "kidding."

He pushes her off balance, causing her to reach back to grab him.

On the way out of the tent carrying their bags of sandwiches, Jimmy and Julie catch up with Joseph and Gloria. The two girls scamper ahead of the boys.

Jimmy says, "Hey Joe, with you and Gloria, we ought to win this easy."

Joseph answers, "We'll take the net, and you two in back. Looks like you're having a good time Jim."

Until the End of Time

"Yes, it's okay," Jimmy says.

"Just okay, huh. Yeah, right."

"Same to you, Joe. But what about Maria?"

"Ah, Man, I don't know. Gloria's something else. That's all I can say. We're here, and let's, ah, what do they say? Go with the flow."

"Whatever will be, will be," Jimmy softly sings.

"All right," The director announces. "At net one, it'll be tents one from both sides playing tent two. The second net will be tents three against four. Tents five will play the winner of the first, and the winner of that game will face off against the winner of tent three and four. We'll not be playing twenty-five points to win. No, to make it quicker, the first team with twelve points wins. The boy's Director will officiate one, and I'll do the other."

Tent two wins over tent one.

"Well, ah, nah," Jimmy starts to say something after he, Joseph, Gloria, and Julia easily beat Harold and Henry and the two girls twelve to three. "Never mind. Leave it be, leave it be Jim."

"Huh?" Julia says. "I know what you're thinking.

Now it's tent five. Waldo and Darvish and their two girls up against Johnathon, Sammy, Albertaldo, and Marsha. Closely watching how his twin reacts with Sammy, Jimmy tells Julia, "It looks like their enjoying each other."

"Yes, sweet, isn't it? And when you get to know Sammy, you'll know why."

Jim, your name reminds me of Jimmy Dean. I love it," she pauses. "But when are you going to sing to me?"

"Oh, I'll sing to you all right," Jimmy responds. "You'll be running away, and I'll start singing with joy." He gets another stomach punch. She reaches for a handful of sand and throws it at him. Jimmy responds with two handfuls of sand, one at her stomach and the other down the back of her neck, and soon they're joyfully lying flat on the ground. Jimmy starts softly singing, "Take me home, take me, I wanna go home."

He gets another punch as Julia rolls away and sits up straight, "Yeah, I'm gonna send you home," she says, pulling and shaking her tee-shirt to get rid of the sand.

Just a Matter of Time

"Julie," Jimmy says. "Why are the names and moves as they are in Chess? Kings can only move one step at a time when Queens can move about anywhere? Huh? Why is that? Shouldn't Queens be restricted, and Kings do what they want?"

"Ah, ha," Julia says, "You want queens restricted to the kitchen. Perhaps the inventor of Chess was a queen."

THIRTY

"Rob, do you have a minute?" Peter asks over the office intercom.

"Yeah, sure, be there shortly," Robert speaks back.

Monday was a recovery day for Robert at Bilko Construction. Tuesday was better. So far this morning, Robert has returned from a visit to the construction site of tearing up a farmer's runway for a refugee settlement. Then a casual luncheon with the State Inspector.

He focuses his eyes on the screen and tells Dale, the onsite foreman, that he's got his permission to let the worker go. "All the paperwork, the pictures, the recordings you sent us is enough. That should do it. Dale, I gotta go."

"Where's Sandy? I couldn't get through to her," Dale asks.

"She's off this afternoon. If he resists in any way, send him to me," Robert replies, closes the tab, and secures it in the sack.

"Come in," Peter responds to the knock on his door.

Entering the office, Robert sees the back of a gentleman's head, and his body squeezed between the arms of one of the chairs in front of Peter's littered desk.

"Rob, I think you might remember Ralph Carmichael," Peter says.

"Sure," Robert answers, reaching to shake the man's hand. "You're the legal counsel for the department, right?"

"I was, but not anymore," Ralph answers.

"Rob, I've hired Ralph as our legal counsel."

Just a Matter of Time

"Huh?" Robert replies.

"Yes, Rob, I have. The department suspended him. He was impressed by your ability to break ideas apart and get to the core issues. He thought he'd like to work alongside you. You were on vacation, Rob. I couldn't confer with you on this because your tab got hacked. His legal mind is top notch, and he knows the security measures, too."

"But Peter, our security here has been more than enough. It's protected us all along. Why now? You could have waited a couple of weeks. Sorry, Ralph."

"I understand where you're coming from, but the timing was imperative. Anyway, I made a decision. Ralph will be working for us as an undercover attorney agent. I understand you're about to fire one of our men. That's under review. Ralph will be handling the personnel and our legal issues from now on. That will be taking a lot off your shoulders. His office is secure, in an undisclosed location. Rob, this is to remain within the walls of this office. No one is to know of this besides us. No one!"

Robert's mouth drops open, and his forehead wrinkles.

"You and I will refer to him as Mr. Leah-cim-rac." Peter slowly pronounces the name. "It's got to be that way because of his previous inside connections. He brings with him thirty years of experience working for the department. He will advise us on all matters related to complying with the rules and regulations. His name and identity are now confidential. No one is to know his former identity. No one, not even Sandy. Not your wife or anyone else. Now, Rob, to secure this information is between you and me, and that it remains that way, Ralph has advised me to rewrite your contract. To summarize the changes, it says that if you violate this agreement in any way, you will be handcuffed by him and relocated to an isolated location."

"What? You're joking!"

"Yes, I am. I said that to emphasize how important it is to keep this within this office. I believe you can imagine what might happen to him or me if his work for us was discovered. Rob, over the years, you have proved yourself trustworthy, and I have appreciated that faithfulness, so this contract raises your salary."

Robert reaches for the paper to read the fine print and signs it. "Thank you. But . . . I don't need that to stay."

Until the End of Time

"It's appreciation. Mr. Leahcimrac will now accompany you to your office and help you secure everything and provide you with whatever he thinks necessary."

They exit the office, and Robert leads him down the hallway. "Ooh," Robert exclaims as they pass the men's room. "Please make yourself at home in my office, but I need to use the restroom, really quick. Go on in. I'll be there soon."

Robert opens the door to the restroom. He looks back and observes Ralph entering his office. Robert opens the door to Peter's office and softly says, "Peter, do you really trust this guy? He could be here to spy on us. I've been your security for all these years, and now when I'm gone, you hire someone who's been investigating us. Didn't that cross your mind? This doesn't make sense. Why?"

"Rob, I've checked him out. You don't think I'd do this without a thorough check?"

"It's still suspicious. Why now? Do you think that after thirty years, that they'd let him go? That's not the way Washington works. Sorry, Peter, but I'll be watching him. I'd take it slow and give him time to prove himself. Right now, there are things I'm gonna keep private. I told him I had to use the restroom. He's in my office now, so I should go." Robert leaves and proceeds to his office.

"Sorry about that. Must have been something I ate." Robert tells Ralph. "And, sorry about the fuss I made in there, but the surprise has kicked my butt. Well, anyway, what do you need?"

"I understand. What I would like is, well, mainly access to your files. But first, I must check your security apparatus and make sure it is doubly secure. It's so easy for hackers and dubious characters to penetrate even the most secure folders nowadays. That will not take long. I'll need a list of all workers, and an up to date on the project currently working on. And all previous contracts. I'll provide you with my net address, so you'll be able to access files and contact me with any questions."

"Can I ask you a few questions?" Robert says,

"Yes, of course, Rob. We're working on the same team now."

"What happened in the department? After thirty years, I would've thought your position was as safe as any. You're about ready for retirement, right?"

Just a Matter of Time

"I thought so too, but when the new top–dog administrator took over everything changed. I wasn't the only one let go. I did get a retirement fund out of the deal. I could go to Hawaii and enjoy myself. But, I like a daily routine rather than having to look for something to do. Yeah, and this rural area is intriguing."

"I know what you mean there," Robert says. "I try to keep up with the latest technology and all those under-the-table regulations that eventually filter down to this level. I'm sure Peter is looking for ways to circumvent those rules thrown at us. You should be helpful in that area."

"I hope so, Rob. I should get this done here, and then I can set up my office equipment. Memorize this, Rob. It's my alt3net account where you'll post my requests." Ralph hands Robert a card with a scribbled https address. "You and Peter are the only ones with that information. I see that you are up to date on security. Very efficient, Robert. We shouldn't have any problems there. I did make one change, though, to catch the latest. It's hard to keep up to date as these techniques are advancing so fast.. Not too long ago, someone breached my home security, and that could have resulted in the department investigating me. We've got to be very careful in all our communications."

"Can I get you a cup of coffee? Tea?" Robert asks.

"Sure. Coffee, black."

"All right, be right back," Robert excuses himself, closes the door and heads back to see Peter. Bursting into Peter's office, Robert says, "He's asking for the personal data of all employees. He wants all my files. I don't want to give him access to any of that. I wouldn't trust him with a pocketknife. Get rid of him before he gets everything. And dang it, he's already done something to my security measures."

"Rob, leave it be."

"No, I can't. Come on, wake up, Pete. His name? That was his suggestion, right? That's his name backwards. A five-year-old could figure that out in less than a minute. End this now before he destroys us. Ah, I must get back. Told him I'd get him coffee."

Until the End of Time

"Here you go, Ralph, made a fresh pot." Robert hands him a cup with the company name inscribed in black over the pale blue ceramic cup. "The secretary's out this afternoon."

"Okay, your files, I've relocated them on this portable disk. You'll still be able to access them through that alt3net address I gave you."

"You're telling me that all my files, everything is no longer on this tab?"

"Yes, that's the way it's got to be."

"Why?"

"Security risks. It's easy for the department to access. We've been doing it."

"No, you haven't. I'm aware of how these things work and have installed the best programs: my own. Sorry, but I can't agree with your methods."

"Hah! You will."

"Huh? You'll force me?" Robert exclaims. He peers into his eyes. "Get out of here. Now!" Robert grabs the small disk out of Ralph's hand. "Get out!" Robert screams so loud so that Peter comes running to see what the commotion is.

"Peter, get him out of here. He's removed all my files. I . . ." Robert freezes. Looking at the owner of the company that he helped build from a struggling beginning over the past twenty-two years, he emphatically says, "Peter, it's either him or me!"

Silence, as Peter's eyes dart to Ralph and back to Robert.

"Peter, I will not work under these conditions. Choose him or me!" Robert puts the disk in his pocket, picks up his office work tablet, and rushes out of the office, leaving Peter dumbfounded.

On the way home, his mind wanders back and forth, reviewing the events, the conversations, his possible loss of employment. Robert starts humming, "How great thou art, then sings my soul. . ."

Just a Matter of Time

"Rob, what are you doing home so early?" Janice asks, as Robert abruptly enters the kitchen carrying his office tablet.

"Had it out with Peter."

"Huh, again?"

"Yeah, only this time may be the last," Robert sighs, breathes in deep, letting out an extended wisping sigh. He focuses on Janice. "This may be it for me. While we were on vacation, Peter started the hiring process of a guy who investigated us in the past. Supposedly, he will be working for us as an undercover agent to provide Peter with legal advice as we deal with the feds. I'm not supposed to reveal his identity to anyone. He took all my files and transferred them to his private account. When I walked out, I grabbed the transfer disk, my tab and told Peter it was either him or me. And, yeah, Peter even had the gall to bribe me with a raise."

"Oh, my God. What are you gonna do?"

"Don't know. If he calls, I'm not answering. I've had it."

"Dale, does he know? How about Sandy?"

Robert's eyes brighten. He screams, "Yah!" Robert grabs Janice and throws her around. "I'll call them at home. They'll agree, I'm sure of it. Then Peter and that guy can have at it. Yahooooo! Robert hugs her, twisting and singing more joy. Robert grabs his tablet. "Sandy's off, I'll call her now."

THIRTY-ONE

"We're ready to go, Jan. Everything is loaded. Let's lock up and get on the road." Robert announces. He grabs the snack sack from the kitchen counter. Robert slides his hand across the security box outside the door. He takes a few steps, looks back for one last safety check at the blinking camera.

He slides into the driver's seat of the Winnie and carefully places the sack on the floor within reach. "Thank you, Lord, for our safe travels." He turns the key, and the sound of the rotors become familiar again. Janice, holding the tablet on her lap, brings up her contact list. "I'm letting Tom and Linda know we're leaving."

"I did that last night," Robert says.

"Well, now they'll know the time," she says, pressing the send button.

"Rob, this tablet can do anything. It's amazing." She thumbs and puts her forefinger on a symbol, and the view of her sitting there comes into focus. She waves at the screen seeing herself waving back. She slides her finger downward, and the screen shows the top of Winnebago as it backs out of the driveway. She slides her thumb and forefinger slightly together, and the neighborhood is visible with a blue dot placed on top of the camper. She watches it turn the corner and enter the four-lane road.

"We're being followed," she says.

"Yes," Robert answers, "and probably listened to also. Jan, it's just a matter of time, when—hmmm? They'll smell us too in these end times."

"We'll get there, ah, Thursday, right?"

"That's the plan. What else fascinates you about the tab?" Robert asks as he turns the vehicle into the southbound interstate mingling with private cars and a delivery truck. "Hey, yes. Find the Grand Canyon on there and see if you can zoom in on the campground. If it can see us moving in real time, perhaps it'll show the kids."

"Oh, wow!" Janice says and starts sliding and pressing against the screen.

"Yes, here it is," Janice excitedly says. "I see a group of boys walking near the river." She zooms in on the group. "Ah, their faces are blurred, but that sure looks like Jimmy and the way he walks."

"Can you hear them."

"No, it's muffled," Janice says after sliding the volume key up to eighty.

"So," Robert begins. "We're being watched. I suppose the ones in the offices can see our faces and hear us talking. But, Jan," Robert continues, "there are too many people in the world to watch everyone continually. There must be one or more, or a dozen triggers that would bring one scene into their immediate attention. A word said, or a certain type of act done. We have to be careful with what is said."

"Oh, my. How useful this would be to a disgruntled wife watching her husband and his every move."

"Hmm? You're right. Yes, like everything else, it has its good points as well as the invasive ones, and that's how they get these things accepted. Now, if they'd inform us what those words are, it'd, well, alert us, and most of us would refrain from saying it."

"Rob, are you sure, positive that they can't hear us talking?"

"In this, yes, I am. Outside, well, they probably can."

Janice looks back onto the tablet screen and sees the group of boys split into two groups, one heading across the river, the other toward the walls of the Canyon. She watches the boys climb a ladder and disappear into a cave. She focuses on the other group who are on their knees removing dirt around a partially exposed wagon wheel.

"Try David and Ruth. See if it'll zoom inside the house," Robert suggests.

"I don't want to mess with this anymore. "What do they say? The spy in the sky."

Until the End of Time

"Now, it's the drone in the sky, but just wait, it'll soon be flies."

"Flies?"

"I'm sure you've noticed how big the eyes of flies are. Technology is forming new ones a bit larger than the real things. Only these are spies. Their eyes watch your every move. They can land on your hair, or sit on your shoulder, and you wouldn't notice, but they'd be sending your movements, your words back to the offices. The eyes of the, it's called the ed-fly, can see 360 degrees, telegraphing to those watching fifty screens. They know where you are, who you're talking to, and hearing what's said, and it's all recorded. If you ever see one, let me know. I got a special spray that'll fog their sight, and they'll crash into something."

He pauses to rub his chin. "What if we the people had thousands of those ed-flies spying for us on the people in Congress and the bureaucrats in their closed-door offices making the laws that govern us?"

"Rob," Janice says. "There's one sitting on your shoulder."

Stunned, he looks at his right shoulder. "Oooh, you're going to get it. Read that romance novel you downloaded, and perhaps you'll learn something. And, refill my coffee."

"Nope. I'm going to peek in on the kids again. I wonder how that pairing went with them?"

"We'll find out soon enough. Too bad, we did not have that tab when the twins were getting together with the girls." He pauses and asks, "My coffee?"

"Oh? Did you ask for coffee?"

He reaches over to pinch her ticklish zone.

"Well, that wasn't too bad," Robert says as he drives the Winnie out of the Oregon-Idaho border crossing station, and back into the traffic. "Up here a bit, we'll get a bite."

Janice says, "you'd think the states would put a restaurant at these crossings, so as we wait, we could use the time to grab something."

"Tell that to them at Colorado."

They stop at the Travel stop for a quick snack, and to use the one-half-off coupon to refresh Robert's coffee pot with dark roasted Jamaican blend, and Janice's Constant Brazil tea.

Just a Matter of Time

"Thank you, Mr. and Mrs. Amwestson. We hope you'll stop again on your return trip from the Grand Canyon," Susan, the clerk says, after watching Robert's face light up as he touches the screen with his two fingers. "Safe travels."

"Thanks, Susan," Janice tells the clerk, as she and Robert leave the counter, hearing the beep-beep as they exit. "Jan, the more I think about it, I'd sure like to make it to Salt Lake City tonight," Robert tells her as she makes herself comfortable.

"Whatever. Go," Janice replies as she inserts a Beethoven disk. "That's okay?"

"Sure."

They make it through Salt Lake City, and Robert steers the camper into an open spot in the RV area on the eastern outskirts of the metropolitan area. He locks the door, pulls the blinds, and tries not to disturb Janice when he slides into bed next to her. "Ah, Thank You, Lord." He turns the pillow sideways and pulls the cover over his shoulders.

"Wake up, Rob," Janice says as she sits on the side of the bed, rubbing Robert's elbow.

"Huh?" Robert says, seeing Janice's face, and the sun shining through the blinds. "What time is it?"

"Eight-thirty."

"No! Why didn't you wake me earlier?"

"You looked so comfortable. I couldn't. Here, coffee. What time did we get here?"

"About eleven," Robert answers. He inhales the aroma and takes a slow swallow of the medium warm coffee. "Thanks, ah, that's good. How long have you been up?"

"Two hours. Come on, get up. Breakfast is ready," Janice informs. She gets off the bed and leaves him, putting the coffee cup to his lips. "Get up," she says again. "We could make it this afternoon if we get going."

Until the End of Time

"Thank you," Robert says as he rubs her shoulder and bends over, placing a soft kiss on her forehead. "Looks good, thanks," he says, seeing the scrambled eggs, two sausage patties, and a glass of orange juice.

"Rob, an earthquake ripped up Vancouver Island in British Columbia yesterday," Janice says. "Another one hit off-shore sending tsunami waves toward Astoria, Washington. Another one erupted in downtown Los Angeles. And, listen to this, a volcano rose and closed off that Gulf of California. An earthquake off the coast of Brazil, and another south of India." Janice pauses. "And if you don't eat your breakfast, I'm gonna erupt on you. Rob!"

"What?"

"Eat, we gotta get going."

Thinking they're about an hour away, Robert looks over to Janice, "Hey, Jan, find that village I told you about, the campground, and see if there's an opening for us."

"Hang on a minute. Let me finish this chapter," Janice replies. Five minutes later, she slides her finger across the screen of the tablet, taking her away from the novel. She touches the symbol and the blue dot on the map. Another symbol and another, and the campground appears, showing three empty spots. "Yes, we're clear." She presses the alpha/numeric box and reserves number thirty-six.

"Arrival time three-twenty-seven," the tablet announces.

"Great, we'll park this thing and hitch a ride to town, so you can meet Chief Shepall."

"Hitch a ride?"

"Yeah, on that tab, there's a symbol that looks like a trailer hitch. Press that to arrange a ride. And yeah, check the police station and let Shepall know we would like to visit. Oh, about four something."

Janice looks at Robert, "You want this thing to poke you out of a daze? It's doing everything else."

"There's a symbol for that too," Robert smirks.

*****

Just a Matter of Time

"So, what'd you think about the Chief?" Robert asks as they're finishing dinner in the Winnebago. "What impressed me," Robert adds."Is how he mixed his native Indian spiritual culture with our Christian beliefs without tearing either one apart."

"What I liked," Janice says. "Was his openness and what he said about John: that he has his feet on solid ground."

"He was praising you, Jan."

"I'm looking forward to reading his novels. Wow! I got a real book to hold in my hands. Yeah, I can turn pages, and could write notes if I had a ball-point pen."

"He couldn't get away with that anywhere else," Robert says. "Don't let any of the inspectors see it."

In the morning, they eat a leisure breakfast, take a stroll around the area, sit for a bit alongside the creek before driving over to pick up the twins.

"Here we are, Jan," Robert holds her hand as they exit the Winnebago to greet the officer in front of the Canyon Project headquarters.

"Good morning," the officer says.

"Morning," Robert greets him.

"Here's the menu. You're the first to arrive. We won't get started till about four or five this afternoon. The kids are making their way up here as we speak. When they arrive, they'll shower and rest a bit."

"Gads, I wish we knew that earlier. We could have slept a few more hours, watched a movie, or visited a museum for five hours."

"You did not get the details posted in your account?"

"No, we did not."

"Sorry about that. Must have been a glitch. Let's check." He pulls a tablet out and starts fingering here and there on the screen. "Okay, Mr.

Until the End of Time

Amwestson, here's the data we have on you. Look, and if you see anything's not right, we'll correct it."

"Lot of good that'll do me now," Robert mutters as he looks at the information. He sees a blank line where his contact number should be. "There's no phone number. How did that happen?"

"I'll take care of that now and send you the information."

"Whoopie doopie. We're here, or do you want us to leave and go back home to read the information," Janice jerks her hand inside Robert's elbow. But he continues, "huh? Then we can follow the guidelines properly to arrive at the suggested time, as it says right here in the menu."

"Rob!" Janice rebukes him, and to the officer, she says, "Sorry, sir, it's been a long ride. He's tired."

"No, I'm not tired. . ." Robert retorts. He breathes deeply and sighs. "Sorry, we learned that the Director tried to call, but the number was unattainable when my tab got hacked." He looks at the officer, "Ah, well, guess we'll see ya later." He and Janice walk back to the camper.

"I'm gonna get back to the novel," Janice says. "Take a nap, Rob or go run down the trail and greet the boys."

*****

At 5:30, the ceremony is about ready to start. "Okay, everyone," the loudspeakers announce. "Please take your seats in the auditorium, and we'll get started shortly.

As before, an officer escorts the families to their seating arrangements. Robert and Janice join a family of two young girls, a teen boy, an older boy, and his pregnant wife. "Ah, you must be the Amwestsons. Robert and Janice, right? We're the Swensens, Monica, and Daniel from Nebraska."

Robert and Janice greet the family.

"My son here," Daniel turns and points to a young man a few paces away, "Matthew participated in this program two years ago, and we'll be grandparents soon. Jackob, here," pointing to the teen, "is sixteen, and we hope they will select him for the program a few years from now. But, if it's not this one, it could be one closer to home. Their creating these programs all over the country now. That one in the Appalachians is terrific."

Just a Matter of Time

Pointing to her daughter, Monica says, "Our daughter Julia is up there. The fourth column from the left. She's in front of your son Jimmy."

Robert and Janice look up to the columns and see Jimmy standing behind the girl. "Yes, that's Jimmy," Janice says. "His twin, John, is two columns to his left."

A man sitting in front of Robert and Janice turns around, "That's Sammy, our daughter, with your son John. We're Walter and Samatha Octomson. We're from a small town in central Missouri. Good to meet you."

"It's a pleasure," Robert replies. "We made the trip from Eastern Oregon."

"Let's give these students a loud reception," the male Director yells as he and the lady Director run onto the stage. The audience goes wild, cheering and waving their arms at the kids standing tall at the columns.

"Thank you. Please take your seats," the Director says. He waits for the crowd to grow quiet.

"Ten weeks ago, your child stood up there, not knowing what to expect. Now, I am proud to say that they've all performed admirably with determination, courage, and respect. Yes, respect for each other, for the environment, for the wildlife, but mostly respect for themselves. They've worked honorably. So, let's bring each pair to the front. During the opening ceremony, I asked you to hold your applause until they were all introduced. Now, let it rip as they come forward. Show them your excitement that their achievement is something to celebrate."

"Ready students?" The two Directors shout together. "Come on down!"

This time they run down the steps reaching out to high five, waving and shouting to their parents and relatives. Sitting seven spaces away from the aisle, Robert and Janice could only wave and yell at the twins as they ran down the center aisle. Reaching the front of the stage, the twenty students scamper up the steep steps and disappear behind the curtain.

The audience quiets, and the Director starts speaking again. "Yes, you saw their excitement, their happy faces, and then they disappeared. Isn't that the way life is? As proud parents, you've watched them grow,

Until the End of Time

learn, and saw their excitement at each completed phase of their lives. And then they disappear doing their own thing as adults. These twenty students disappeared for ten weeks. No way to contact them. No pats on the back. No corrections. No loving embraces. No, they disappeared from your view. They left you wondering."

A noise thunders from above as ten small planes fly over the stage and circle the auditorium, each pulling a banner flag. The audience follows the planes while concentrating on the names on the long white flags.

Janice points Robert to one banner displaying the words: "Johnathon and Sammy."

"And so, this year's project comes to a close," The Director says. "No, I will not spend time telling you what they accomplished over the summer, what enjoyments they had, what discoveries they unearthed, what new friends they made, nor what they learned about themselves. That would take hours to summarize. This is it. Each of them has already received their diploma of achievement. We will not waste time calling each pair forward. Congratulations to all of these twenty adults." With a raised voice, the Director shouts, "Come on out!"

The curtain splits, and all twenty graduates', holding hands with their partner, step to the front of the stage and bow down to the audience. The crowd stands to cheer, to wave, and to applaud as two airplanes drop loads of confetti over them. The students scamper off the stage and up the steps out of the auditorium, following the confetti drop, and out of sight.

"Now hold on there," the Director shouts into the microphone, raising his arms to deter the sudden rush of parents assuming the ceremony is over.

"Whoa, there, folks, not yet. There's more."

The Director of the girl's program speaks up. "The students are now preparing a spot for you, a lovely area where relaxation is easy. There are ten areas set up behind the offices where you'll enjoy dinner, beverages, and time of fellowshipping together with your son or daughter and their partner, along with their families. You may already have met your son or your daughter's partner's parents as we tried to seat you together. That removed part of the mystery. As we lead you to those areas, you'll have the opportunity to learn more about these relationships. I can testify as to the girls. They've done an admirably excellent job of adjusting to the hardships our early settlers had to endure. These girls are now able to do that which those settlers learned the hard way by trial and error. There's no room for trial and error in our culture.

"Now, to end this brief ceremony," the lady continues, "we will take you to those areas. Now, remember that these pairings are of the student's acceptance. Sometimes it's difficult for parents to accept the choices their child has made. Think back, you were in the same kind of situation when you announced to your parents that you were moving on in your life, or, perhaps you spontaneously left, leaving the parents devastated, if they cared at all. They may have been happy that you left. They may have been sad. That is history. This is now. Thank you for allowing your son or daughter to participate in this program."

The Director of the boy's program takes over the microphone. "Thank you, Mannia. We will now proceed. As I call your names, please stand, and we'll direct you to your son or daughter and their partner. Thank you." The two Directors walk off to stand at the steps that lead up and out of the Coliseum.

THIRTY-TWO

Guides lead the ten groups to their special sites. Robert and Janice, along with Walter and Samatha, Daniel and Monica, their son Matthew and daughter-in-law Reba, their son Jacob, and the two young girls. All eleven of them following the guide on the five-minute walk through the brush.

The twins and the girls look up and see the excitement of their parents and relatives. Julia and Sammy rush to greet their parents. Sammy, her mom, and dad embrace. Julia's large family exchange hugs in a circle shouting their glee at reuniting with their excited daughter.

"Oh, you guys look great," Janice says as she pulls the twins in for a hug. "Missed you." Robert embraces the boys, and they do the usual hand maneuvers.

Robert introduces the twins to Sammy's and Julia's parents, brothers, and sisters.

Jimmy grabs Julia's arm. "Mom, Dad, this is Julia. She's that one-in-a-million, except she can't play chess."

"Ah, it's so good to meet you finally," Julia embraces Janice, and leans into Robert. "Jim told me all the horrible things you've done," Julia says.

"Julia!" her mother rebukes.

"Ah, mom, they've got to know right away, I can diss it out."

Looking at Julia and back to Jimmy, Janice says, "horrible things? Jimmy!"

"Mom, she breaks right through the surface. Dad, no mikes here."

"Hmm? So, you like to diss it out, eh. I'm hungry, so *dish* it out." Robert tells her.

Johnathon introduces Sammy, adding, "she's gonna be a vet."

"Oh, it's so great to meet you Mr. and Mrs. Amwestson. John told me about the surprise of the drones. He'll get that land."

"Well, someone around here has manners," Robert says, his eyes rolling toward Julia. "Nice to meet you, Sammy. Now give us a proper hug."

"Well, boys, what can I say? You've made it, and, got more, it seems." Robert tells the twins.

"Hey, folks," Daniel announces. "Let's sit and get acquainted."

They meander to the two end-to-end six-feet long picnic tables. Seeing the name tags, Robert says, "Like everything else, the seating is arranged."

Sammy responds, "Yep. You're all mixed up."

Julia adds, "There'll be none of that mom and pop only talk at this table."

Seated next to Robert, Walter says, "I've never heard of twins appointed into the same program. It's quite unusual."

"The offer of the drones did it," Robert answers.

On the table, the kids have placed two large bowls of Noodles and bar-be-que hash, along with glasses of wine for everyone.

Robert rises to address the group. "Now, if you don't mind, I'd like to ask blessings over this event that'll go down in our history books. Let's all stand, hold hands, and pray." Robert reaches for Monica's and Walter's hands. "Oh, Lord," he says. "Sometimes, it's hard to submit, and this is one of those times, so help us. Help me. I'm asking Lord, that you'd bless us and all our conversations. Direct this gathering, our boys, these girls, and their families. Thank You for this opportunity. We accept this food in the name of Jesus. Thank You, Lord."

Julia and Sammy grab a bowl of noodles, and with a forked spoon, they place a portion on everyone's plate. They then pick up a bowl of hash. When Julia gets to Robert, she says, "See. Now I'm *dishing* it out."

Until the End of Time

Robert leans back and tells Julia, "I like the seating arrangements. Was this your idea?"

"We both did."

"Thank You. Now I can get to know more about you directly from your mother, and I'm sure she has some horrible things to say about you." He looks at Monica, "kidding, *dissing* it back to your daughter."

Julia moves on, spooning hash over the noodles on Walter's plate. She places the chopped meat, onions, green peppers, tomatoe sauce, and spices on her plate and skips Jimmy to spoon it on the plate of her ten-year-old sister. She finishes the round with her dad. Julia sets the large bowl in the center of the table and sits next to Jimmy, who's changed plates. She looks at her plate of only noodles and over to Jimmy's.

Chewing, Jimmy says, "Hmm, this is good."

"Hey, Matthew, hand me that bowl," Julia asks her older brother.

"Why? Did you forget someone?" He answers. "Forget it, sis. You made your way, now enjoy it."

"Hey, you too," their mother, Monica says.

Watching the commotion, Daniel stands, reaches in for the bowl and gives Julia a spoon full. He leans in close to Julia, whispering something.

"Okay, okay!" Julia says.

The group of fifteen get to know more about each other. Robert asks Walter and Monica about what they understood about the project. "There was nothing whatsoever about this pairing fiasco in any of the literature we saw," Roberts tells them. "I only saw the word pair once, and then it was easily interpreted as two to a tent."

Janice, in talking with Sammy's mother, and Julia's father learn more about the girl's high school years and whatever details Janice desired to know. They ask about the twins, their work assignments, and the years at the Academy. "I don't know," Janice says, "to think that a government agency chose a, well, possibly a marriage partner for my sons. My head is spinning."

"Janice, two years ago, Monica and I felt the same way as Matthew was assigned to Reba. But, my oh my, they appear to be great together, and now we're going to be grandparents in a month or so."

Just a Matter of Time

Samatha, Sammy's mother, says, "Janice, it seems to be working fine. It started in Europe, and they're claiming the divorce rate has diminished greatly. Watching Johnathon interact with Sammy, warms my heart. I see it. They're in love already."

The girls' Director approaches the table, "Well folks, how's it going? I hate to say this, but closing time is approaching. Thank you. It's been a blessing to see the comradery and cohesiveness of your families. If you would, please, on our site is a page where you can take our survey and leave comments. The Department would appreciate it. Your students have already done that on the secure site reserved for them. We've expanded next year's project to twenty boys and girls. If you hear of someone who'd like to take part, information and applications are available on the site. Thank you. Safe travels."

Robert stands. "Well, what do we do now? Is this it? Now we all split up and go our separate ways? What's next? Jim and John start working at the museum in three weeks. I've already taken all my vacation time this year, so I can't leave. And I'm sure you've all got your schedules, too? And they certainly can't date and get to know each other when we all live so far apart."

Daniel says, "Two years ago, Matthew went and stayed with Reba for three days, and then they flew in to stay with us for three days."

Johnathon looks at Jimmy, giving him a thumbs up. Jimmy stands and begins speaking. "Dad, to relieve your concerns, we've had five days. The first two days turned into three. We returned to our respective camps for two weeks. We got together again for two more days. Another return to camp, and now today." Jimmy pauses looking at his dad and mom, sitting at opposite ends of the table.

Jimmy continues. "Who makes these decisions and when? You told us about how you proposed to mom without asking your parent's permission, nor did you approach mom's parents first. That was your decision, mom agreed, and here we are. This will be our decision, not yours, and when we're ready, we'll do it. If not, you'll hear about that too. We're no longer five-year-old's needing your say-so in everything we do. So, here we are today, and this is John's and my time to make a decision." Jimmy winks and nods at Johnathon, who rolls his eyes toward Sammy.

Together the twins kneel on the ground to face their girlfriend. The girl's mouths drop open. Jacob snaps pictures. Walter takes pictures. The twins reach into their pocket for a piece of string. The twins start wrapping the string around the girls' ring finger. Tablets are out capturing the scene. The twins recite the words together: "I don't have a ring yet." They continue tying the string and leave inch-long rabbit ears above the finger. "Will you marry me and be my wife forever and ever?"

Daniel grabs his tablet to take pictures of Julia's tears of joy, streaking her cheeks.

Julia excitedly agrees and joyfully throws her arms around Jimmy, and they passionately kiss. Jimmy pulls Julia off the seat into a tight embrace, forcing her onto the ground, and they roll over together. Johnathon and Sammy skip toward the fire-pit and happily embrace. Samatha stands and claps her hands. All eleven join in with gleeful shouts of excitement and surprise. Robert's face changes to enlightenment. Janice is rubbing her cheeks.

The next five minutes are congratulations and questions.

"We've got to discuss what happens next," Walter says.

The male Director, standing with his crossed arms, looks at the group, "Sorry, but it's time."

"Hey, buddy," Robert says, looking at the Director. "You don't put a time limit on this kind of a thing,"

"We're on a schedule here, and we must keep it," the Director replies.

"All right, we're going," Daniel replies, and tells the group, "outside the gate, there's a spot where we can pull over."

Sammy and Julia join Robert and Janice in the camper for the short ride outside the Canyon Project headquarters. The twins have the drones warming up, getting ready to join the group in the open area. All fifteen of them wonder and think about what's next. They gather around and discuss what the next step should be. Sammy and Julia finally propose a solution, to which everyone agrees to as the best for them all.

The girls will go home with Robert and Janice for the first of three ceremonies, the second at Julia's home in Nebraska, and then on to Missouri to Sammy's. While Julia and Sammy gather their items together and say good-byes to their families, Jimmy and Johnathon share their idea inside the Winnebago with Robert and Janice.

"Mom, dad," Jimmy says, "that is what we plan to do when we get home."

"But . . ." Robert answers.

"No butts about it," Johnathon rebukes. "We've discussed it, and we'll make the arrangements. This is our time, so please, go along and help us. It's also a surprise, so don't say anything to the girls on the way home."

THIRTY-THREE

"Well, girls, this is home," Janice tells Sammy and Julia.

"It's beautiful," Julia says.

"Come on, we'll give you a quick tour," Robert says. "When the boys get here, we're going out for dinner." The girls carry their suitcases and follow Robert into the house, through the kitchen, and down the hallway to the spare bedroom.

"That is actually two twins," Janice says. "We'll separate them later."

"I'm gonna call home and let them know we made it safely," Julia announces after placing her suitcase next to the bed.

Sammy is already on the phone. "Hi, mom, yes, we made it. It's a beautiful area." Listening to her mother for a minute, she hangs up and says, "they won't be home until tomorrow, and then they'll make the arrangements. She'll let me know later."

"Rob, let's have a drink outside. Relax from the ride," Janice suggests.

Stepping onto the deck, Robert glances up at his hidden safety camera, and a quick peek at the other camera. He takes another look. He sets the wine and glasses on the picnic table, throws his arms up, and announces to the air: "Oh, what a beautiful day."

Understanding Robert's comment, Janice watches him walk back into the house, as she and the girls relax in the cushioned chairs.

"Oh, I love it. Oh, my, I've dreamed of a garden like this," Julia says.

Just a Matter of Time

"Ahh, this reminds me of our backyard, except we don't have a garden because of the dogs," Sammy says. She then briefly describes her home in the rolling forested hills of central Missouri.

"Tomorrow, girls, you can help me pull weeds," Janice says.

In the basement, Robert opens a closet door, pulls the light cord, and removes the plastic box of Christmas ornaments. He pulls the black screen away from the wall. He presses the on button to view the video. He slides his finger across the screen and watches the small boxes of the dated views. One of them catches his eye, and there it is. Two men with yellow straps across their shoulders stepping onto the deck. They remove the old camera and replace it with a new one. They place another camera at the corner of the backyard fence and one on top of the greenhouse. Robert replaces the screen and the box of ornaments. Sitting at the table, Robert nods his head at Janice rolling his eyes toward the corner of the canopy.

Clinking the glasses together, Robert says, "To your happiness." He sips the California Red and looks into the overcast sky.

Julia informs them her family made it in last night. "Dad said he's sorry for not being able to make it here."

"Anything we could do?" Janice asks.

"Nah, it's his work," Julia answers. "Is the land we'll get anywhere near here?"

"It's about ten miles southeast of here in the agricultural area," Robert answers. He leans forward, taking a posture to focus on the girls. "Julia and Sammy, I want to thank you for openly sharing with us so much of your life on our trip back. You are a delight. I mean it. And, well, I probably said things earlier I shouldn't have. I'm sorry if I offended you in any way. Forgive me. We're blessed to have you join our family, and we're going to make this ceremony the best there could be."

Julia replies, "Thank you. I didn't believe a word about those horrible things Jimmy said about you."

Robert says, "I guess I did some of that too. But, ah, you're the one who started it."

"I'm reserving some for Jim."

Until the End of Time

Janice begins to say something when the sound of rotors spinning louder and louder interrupts. The two drones come into view over the treetops. "They're here!" Julia screams. They watch the drones landing in tandem. Slowly the rotors stop, and the twins open the doors, step away, and into the arms of their girlfriends.

Janice tears up watching the boys hugging, kissing, and twirling the girls. "Oh, my," she whispers.

Hand in hand, Jimmy and Julia step onto the deck, followed by Sammy and Johnathon. Janice stands to hug her twins.

"How was the ride back?" Jimmy asks.

"Come here." Robert shakes their hand and whispers in their ears about the new spy cameras.

"Yeah, we saw that," Jimmy whispers back.

Released from the hug, Johnathon says, "we were making final arrangements and looking at the tracks of land we'll be getting. Ah, Sam, you're gonna love it."

"Take me there now."

"Tomorrow, we're going out for dinner," Johnathon replies.

"Come on, I haven't been in one yet," Sammy grabs his elbow, pulling him toward the drone.

"Jim!" Julia pulls on Jim's arm.

Watching the two drones rise, hover a bit, and then angle out of the yard and over the trees, Robert leans into Janice and softly asks, "do you think the girls are aware? Did you mention it in the Winnie?"

"Almost," Janice answers. "But Rob, if we did anything like this, we'd been chastised big time by our parents."

"Yeah, but we know what's happening," Robert pauses, sighs relief, and asks, "Over the past two days, talking with the girls, what are your thoughts now?"

"They're terrific Rob. Oh, Julia, my gosh, she's a mirror image of Jim. In the restroom, I could hear her singing. Sammy's more reserved, like John. She loves to write. She has put some essays on the altnet, and she's working on a novel." Janice's hand caresses up and down Robert's arm and slides her fingers between his. She focuses on Robert, looks up to the sky and back to him, leaning against the headrest. After a period of silence, Janice wipes a lone tear away and says, "Over the past years, I've often wondered how twins could turn out so different."

"Here they come," Robert announces. The sound of the two drones gets louder as they fly over the house. Over the deck, they hover side by side for a bit and slowly descend to the two landing crosses. "

Approaching the deck, hand in hand with Johnathon. "Wow!" Sammy says. "That was great. He's gonna teach me how to operate it."

"Dad, Mom," Jimmy says. "Let's go to the restaurant in that lodge near Cove."

"Good idea," Robert says.

"Do you girls need to freshen up a bit before we go?" Janice asks.

"Nope," Julia answers.

Sammy says, "yeah, I do." Janice gets up to follow Sammy and Julia.

"We'll take the Winnie," Robert announces.

"Good evening, folks. Welcome to our lodge," the middle age gentleman says. "We've got a special room for you." He leads them down a hallway, past two doors, and opens the next oak stained door. He stands aside to admit Janice, followed by Julia and Jimmy, Sammy holding Johnathon's hand, as Robert brings up the rear to hand the gentleman a note.

"Oh," Sammy says. "This is beautiful."

Holding Jim's arm, Julia whispers, "Oh, my!" Her hand rises to rub a falling tear.

The room has a big half-circle table next to the picture window facing the forest. Ten cedar framed paintings of historical representations of forest life decorate the walls, three on each side wall, and four along the corridor wall. A six-sided candlelit chandelier hangs over the table. In one corner, three tuxedoed men softly play the violin, a cello, and a clarinet.

"You may be surprised at the view," The waiter announces. "A deer or two may come and feed at the trough. There's a bird feeder off to the

Until the End of Time

right." He pulls a chair out for Janice and Sammy next to Janice and Julia next to Robert.

"Let's have a drink first," Johnathon says.

The door opens, and two wine stewards dressed in black with white towels draped over their forearms enter with glasses, and a bottle of wine. They pour wine into each glass as the musicians continue.

"Jim and John stand, gazing at their girlfriends. Together they raise their glasses. "To you, we toast this evening." They all sip the wine, as waiters bring the pre-ordered meals of grilled steak filets, fried potatoes, and steamed mushrooms.

The conversations continue along the line of the three upcoming ceremonies — their hopes and dreams for the future. The twins share their trip back in their drones, their ability to chat back and forth on the ride, the stops to re-charge. "The weather was perfect," Johnathon summarizes. "No stops at the border, dad. No curves, straight line flying. We had enough time to finalize this."

John leans in and whispers in Sammy's ear. She goes ecstatic and throws her arms around his neck. Julia reacts joyfully after hearing Jim's whisper. "Yes, yes, let's do it!"

"Are you sure?" Jimmy asks Julia. "The first of four."

"Yes, Jim, I'm ready," Julia excitedly answers, rubbing her cheeks,

Jimmy raises his arm and snaps his finger.

A short, gray bearded elderly man enters the room and takes a spot next to the wall. Janice pushes her chair out and leads Sammy to the opposite wall. Julia takes Robert's arm. The musicians begin softly playing a concerto increasing in volume as the four of them slowly approach the twins and the gentleman. The music softens as only the violin continues to play.

The gentleman nods. He takes Julia's and Sammy's hands and places them together. He pulls a red scarf from around his neck and lays it over the hands of the two girls. "If either of you wishes, you can remove your hand from under this scarf, and we will not continue." He looks at the girls. They look at each other and tighten their grip. "Good." He removes the scarf and wraps it back around his neck. Holding hands, the four of them lower to a kneeling position.

Just a Matter of Time

He starts reciting the vows, "Do you, Julia and Sammy, voluntarily and wholeheartedly give yourselves to these young men? Sammy to Johnathon. Julia to Jimmy, for as long as you shall live?"

"I do," the girls say together.

"And, do you, Jimmy and Johnathon, of your own free will, give your life, your support, and love to these women as long as you shall live? Jimmy to Julia, and Johnathon to Sammy."

The boys turn to face the girls. Together, they recite: "With this ring as a symbol of my love, I do." They slide gold rings onto the girl's ring finger to meet the rabbit ear strings. They stand facing their partner.

"By the authority provided to me by the state of Oregon, I now pronounce you husbands and wives. Now," he continues. "One more step to pledge in front of these witnesses, and to each other. Since this is one of four ceremonies, do each of you pledge to reserve yourselves from that scared union till after the fourth ceremony?"

"Yes, we do," the four of them answer.

The musicians change to lively dance music.

"Oh, Rob," Janice softly says, pushing her hair back and dabbing her wet cheeks, watching the twins dancing with the girls. "It's a fairy tale. Come dance with me." The joyful evening continues as couples dance and change partners. Finally, the six of them dance together, arm in arm circling to the lively music.

A waiter enters the room, carrying a double-layer white cake decorated with six burning candles on the lower level and two crosses on top. The tempo of the violin, cello, and clarinet slows to mellowing. They stop dancing to exhaustive sighs and approach the table to view the frosted cake.

Robert stands and toasts his sons, daughters-in-law, and their future endeavors as couples. "Lord, we are thankful for your bountiful blessings on them. Guide them in all they do, and Lord, may these next three ceremonies be an eternal sign to them that they'll treasure throughout their lives."

"Let's see," Janice says, "normally the bride cuts the cake, but since there's two of you, I will cut the cake." Janice holds the knife with both

Until the End of Time

hands. She cuts the four-inch high circle into six parts, a candle on each, and places them upright on the plates.

Watching the way Janice cuts the cake, Robert says. "Imagine with me the symbolic nature of this cake. It's formed as a circle, it's complete, a unit of one. Jan cut it into six pieces. Each of us is one slice. As individuals, as ingredients, we came together to form this one unit. Julia and Sammy, you are now a slice of this family of one. The only way one piece could go missing is by an outside force cutting and slicing it away, which leaves a gap, an empty spot."

The waiters present framed pictures of the wedding cake to Julia and Sammy.

Robert continues: "This is our present to you. So, place this picture in a prominent spot in your consciousness, on the wall of your home, and every time you look at it, think of what it means. We do not want to see an empty slot. Ever!"

"Oh, my gosh," Julia says, looking at Jimmy, "You should have thought of recording this so that I could show it to mom."

"We did. Yes, we did," Jimmy says.

"Your parents are now watching," Robert tells the girls. "The ceremony has been streamed to your families, from the very beginning as you walked into this room. Yes, Julia, even when you told Jim to shut up and dance, or there'd be no dessert. Look up, right above the window, and wave at your family."

They wave at the camera. "Hi, ah, I'm blown off my feet, mom," Sammy speaks toward the camera. "We'll see you soon."

Likewise, Julia waves, comments, and adds, "I miss you all. Oh, you gotta come."

Robert starts talking to the camera. "As the boys were flying home, they were able to make these arrangements over the air. We appreciate you for the work you're doing to make your ceremonies the best. Thank you. Because of their participation in the Canyon Project, we already have the permits. Not only here, but there too. Janice and I wish we could attend each of your ceremonies. Jim and John will bring the equipment to record and stream those back to us. Thank you. These girls are a continual joy. We are blessed. Anytime you wish to visit with your daughter; we'd be glad to see you again. We have an extra room."

"God bless you all," Robert concludes his comments.

Just a Matter of Time

Janice says to the camera, "The agency has arranged the flights, and you'll see them soon."

Julia and Sammy, wiping their cheeks, look to the camera, "Love you all."

THIRTY-FOUR

"No, we don't know how many are going to be able to make it?" Janice informs the girls sitting on the living room floor. They're looking through pictures on their tablets. Sammy focuses on wedding scenes in outdoor settings. Julia is finding ideas on table settings, cakes, and flowers.

"If it were on a Saturday or Sunday, yeah, we'd have a crowd," Janice says.

"Mom said she's already received over a hundred replies," Julia replies.

"How about you, Sammy?" Janice asks.

"They're still working on it, but I suspect that the entire town will be there. All my sorority sisters. Dad knows the mayor, who could have the police escort our arrival, and when the party's over, escort us all out of town."

"Have you decided where you'll go for the honeymoon?" Janice asks.

"I heard John say, Branson," Sammy answers, getting a nod from Julia.

"Watching you two, I had an idea," Janice says. "But first, I gotta say this. Marrying off my two sons at the same time is, well, we never thought it'd happen like this. And four different settings. Girls, you're making history. So, here's my idea. . ." Janice pauses, noticing the girls appear concentrated on the tablets, she raises her voice, "Are you listening?"

"Yeah, go on," Julia replies.

Just a Matter of Time

Janice details the idea of having all four recorded ceremonies spliced together.

Julia interrupts her. "Jim and John have already made those arrangements. The Directors of the Canyon Project had contacted them about that possibility. They would use it as a recruitment tool. They're sending a reporter here for Friday, and he'll be recording and documenting it all. The next two also. And, they want interviews and to record parts of the honeymoon."

Stunned, Janice leans back. "Well," Janice softly says, "I'm only a spectator to my sons' weddings."

*****

"Come on, let's play pool before dad gets home," Johnathon says, as he and Jimmy enter the house. Johnathon reaches for Sammy's hand. "You and I against Julia and all thumbs Jim."

"Ah ha, bro, tell her how our last game ended," Jimmy replies.

Nodding and winking at Sammy, Julia says, "Wait a moment, hang on there, this is gonna be us against you two. Two women, beating up on two boys. Janice, join us as we whip them to tears."

"Nah, go ahead, have fun," Janice says.

An hour later, Janice is sitting alone on the deck.

Robert approaches Janice. "Whatcha thinking?" He asks.

"Rob, I'm just a spectator. That's it. They've arranged everything."

"Where are they now?"

"In the basement."

"I know we've discussed this some, but have you thought any more about a wedding present?" Robert asks.

"I was thinking of providing them with the down payment for the land."

"Nothing to wrap up, like ah, put a pair of socks in a box, and watch their mouths drop open."

Until the End of Time

"Ha, funny," Janice replies. Her eyes brighten, "Yeah, I love it. Put that inside the socks."

Dark clouds blow over the house. Sirens start blowing, and they rush inside.

"Hey, a storm is coming," Robert hollers down the basement. "Stay there. It's a big one!" The sound of thunder, a bolt, and another steak of lightning flashes through the windows. The town's emergency whistle crescendos, with interrupting horn blasts.

The basement lights blink and shut down. Pitch-black darkness envelopes them, and Sammy yells, "John!" Feeling his hand, she throws her arms around his neck.

"Julie, say something, and I'll find you." Jimmy waves his arms in front of him, feeling for a solid, familiar touch. His fingers find the pool table. Gently touching the wooden frame, he inches closer to the sound of Julia's mumbled humming.

"Thank you," Julia responds to his fingers on her.

The skies rumble, and another blast flashes the room. And another. And another. A flashlight illuminates the basement stairs, as Janice leads Robert down the stairs.

"This may last awhile," Robert says. He sets the flashlight on the pool table, its light pointing at the ceiling. "Hmm? Who was winning?"

Jimmy opens the door to the closet and brings out two lanterns, a small flashlight, and a box of matches. Kneeling on the floor and holding the light between his lips, he turns the knob and strikes a match. The wick ignites and slowly brightens the floor. He lights the other lantern and places them at strategic spots around the room. Boom! Another blast of thunder.

"Okay," Jimmy says. "Julie, I think it's your turn. Dad, you moved a few balls with the flashlight."

"Well, excuse me," Robert answers. "Turn the lights off, and we'll start over."

Boom!

"One-one-thousand, two-one-thousand, . . ." Janice counts. At her count of six, another booming thunder. "One-one-thousand . . . When she reaches six, lightning flashes, another massive boom, and another count by Janice. The vibration of each strike shakes the two light fixtures over the table.

Just a Matter of Time

"Woah, there, horsie!" Robert blurts out. He joins Janice, now sitting on the floor in a corner with her arms crossed over her knees, softly praying, *"thy kingdom come, thy will be done. . ."* Robert wraps his arm around her shoulders. A bolt rattles the two small windows. Hail pelts the windowsills. Soon sirens overpower the noise of the pelting rain. The sound of thunderclaps slowly fades. Boom, another swift lightning strike.

"That sounded like an Amen," Janice says.

"It could be over. I'm gonna peek outside," Robert says.

"Be careful!"

Two minutes later, Robert shouts down the basement, "All clear. Jim, John, we've got work to do."

The boys rush up the stairs and see Robert standing on the front steps. "The garage door is blocked." Robert enters the house and into the garage. He swipes his fingers across a screen. The garage door starts to swing out, but stops, leaving a two-foot opening.

Jimmy opens a closet door. He hits the switch for the emergency light and raises the lid of the cabinet. He finds three sets of gloves, unhooks the cord from the chainsaw, and hands it to his brother.

"Dad," Johnathon says. "I'll do it."

They slide under the partially open double car garage door. Johnathon pushes the choke button and pulls the cord. On the third pull, the blade starts rotating around the oval guide bar. He starts cutting the limbs leaning against the door. Jimmy tosses them on the grass.

An hour later, the twins have cleared away enough of the tree, allowing the door to open all the way.

"Thanks," Robert tells the boys. "Take a break. From what I see, the soffit and roof are okay."

Robert walks to the street to get a clear view of the neighborhood, "hey guys, since Charlie and Arlene are out of town, bring those limbs over here."

"How's the backyard look?" Robert asks Janice watching from the steps.

"It's fine, one small branch over the deck. The girls are taking care of small branches and leaves in the back yard," Janice says. "Rob, I

Until the End of Time

checked the news. The power company said it might be tomorrow or the next day before we get our power back. The regional news broke in saying it was triggered by an EMP attack, and we may not get power restored for a month or more."

"EMP? No way, if it were that, your tablet wouldn't work."

"It was centered over Anchorage. Everything there has shut down."

"Anchorage? That's what? Eighteen-hundred miles as the crow flies. Let me see," Robert says, reaching for the tablet.

Robert presses an icon to bring up a national weather site, as Janice watches. A message scrolls across the bottom, *"that site is not available, three-six,"* and a picture of a horned man flashes across the screen. "Huh," Robert mumbles. He looks at another news icon, scans the headlines, softly presses the highlighted tab, and begins to read national news. "Yep, Anchorage." Robert continues to read more.

"Oh, boy!" he mumbles. "Come on, let's go inside. This is serious."

"All right," Robert says after filling his coffee cup. He calls the girls in. "We've got news. Let's have a seat in the living room." The two girls and the twins anxiously sit looking and seeing Janice's wrinkled forehead and the demeanor of Robert leaning forward in his recliner.

"Jan thought she'd get a weather update as we were clearing the driveway. They interrupted the local station to say that an EMP triggered the storm and described the horrific conditions in Anchorage. I read it too, and it didn't look good. Now, this is what the news has been saying about the storm." Robert starts to explain. "They say our storm was triggered by one of those nuclear atmospheric electromagnetic pulse attacks, yes attacks over Anchorage earlier this morning. Another hit the east coast, and one in New Orleans. Yeah, they're suspecting China, Russia, North Korea. They're not sure who or how yet, but the military is being activated."

"Activated?" Johnathon interrupts.

"Yes, John. Anchorage, and as far south as Vancouver, and parts of Seattle have had all electricity disabled." Robert summarizes what he read on the alt2news site. "The Military is preparing for possible war."

"We could be called up," Johnathon states.

"Yes, that's right."

Just a Matter of Time

"No, no," the girls scream. Julia grabs Jimmy's hand.

A siren blows loud and sustained, and a voice beams throughout the neighborhood. "This has been a test. This is a test! Tune into WBCN2 for the update." It keeps repeating the message.

Robert points the tablet at the TV screen. He focuses on the on/off button. The red light blinks. He closes his eyes and blinks twice into the tablet. The TV screen lights up. He gazes and blinks twice at the station symbol. A suited gentleman is talking, as a series of words scroll across the bottom of the screen, '**Disregard, this was a test.**'

"Halleluiah," Janice sighs. They quietly listen to the reporter explaining what happened as the girls sigh deep breaths of relief.

"Why?" Jimmy asks. "Scare us to death for half an hour and then tell us it's a joke? Whoever it was should be hanged."

"I think we all know the why," Robert answers. "Yeah, and, if the one responsible walked in here now, he'd be begging for mercy."

"I'm gonna get us something to drink," Janice informs.

"Make it a double," Robert tells her.

"Surely, the station knows who has the power to interrupt, to broadcast over them," Jimmy says.

"You saw the explanation on there," Robert says. "Will we ever be provided an honest answer? No, I doubt it. It's part of the program to keep us tuned in, to obey, and fall in line."

Ring, ring. Julia's tab vibrates. "Hi, mom," she answers. "Yeah, sure, we're fine. No problem here, it was all a mistake, some kind of a test." She listens. "Thanks, yes, the ceremony is in the works for Friday. Yes, we'll see you on the fourteenth. Love you too."

"So," Robert says, "they heard about it in Omaha?"

"Yes, they did. Mom said the program they were watching was interrupted."

Janice approaches with glasses and a picture of iced tea. "Rob, it must be from the very top to have the entire country notified. It's got to be."

Until the End of Time

"As I was saying," Robert resumes. "Years ago, little ole North Korea indicated they had the power. They showed the world what they could do. Well, it was more to inspire and unite their people than to scare us. My feelings are that we've got enough threats within the country that are and have been slowly destroying our freedoms more than any threat from without."

Sammy presses a button on her tablet to call home. "They heard about it wiping out Anchorage," Sammy interrupts, "but didn't think we had been affected. They're excited and have everything ready to go. And, Mr. Amwestson, that analogy you made about the cake. They thought it was so amazing that they presented it to our pastor, and he's going to use it in our ceremony."

"Thanks," Robert answers. "Jan, how'd it go with Ruth?"

"They're somewhat like us, Rob," Janice replies. "Ruth did not know anything about it. She's well. No more health problems, but Dave is still working on a way to entice you to accept that job offer."

"You gonna move to Boulder?" Jimmy asks.

Janice quells the question. "No! We're not moving."

"End of story," Robert says. Smiling, "we're gonna wait until you have babies and want us to babysit. That'd be a good time to move, right, Jan?"

"Julie wants eight, so you'd sure come in handy," Jimmy says.

"Oh, you're gonna get it," Julia replies. "Four sets of twins, all girls."

"Good, we got that settled. Babysitting is all you want from us," Robert says. "Now, back to what triggered all these rumblings. The socialists had been set back in previous elections. The candidates and ousted politicians fueled the fire with screams of every kind of ism they imagined against the existing regime. The media added to the noise. There were riots, shootings, massive parades, smoke bombs, and attacks against the families of officials. Bad news gets our attention like it did today. Those were triggers, and here we are.

"To summarize all this, let me say, there are two kinds of noise, natural and manufactured. It's the loud, consistent rumblings on the airwaves that gets our attention. It's a horn beep or a loud crash that causes us to look. The media and what we hear on the tube, see on videos, hear on the shows, from Hollywood, from Washington, and locally, is manufactured noise that has the effect of dividing us in fear and hostility, as that EMP raised the fears of war.

"Second, there is the noise of nature. We experienced it today, thunder and lightning, volcanoes, earthquakes, hurricanes, tsunamis, the roar of a lion or bear, the growls of a rabid dog, the hissing of a snake. We run to take cover. We huddle together. We reach out for a solid, safe hand to hold onto. It's the natural noise that draws us together in the fear of God like we did tonight."

"You should be a teacher," Julia says. "Or a pastor."

THIRTY-FIVE

It's now two weeks after the three-day honeymoon in Branson. The newlyweds have settled in their small portable homes on their acreage on the outskirts of town. Jimmy and Johnathon have begun their assigned work at the new museum on the outskirts of town. Sammy has secured a position as a Veterinarian intern. Julia is working part-time at the local tree farm.

"Whatcha doing?" Robert asks Janice, sitting in the living room, rubbing her fingers together.

"Good morning," Janice greets him.

Clinging to his coffee cup, Robert sits in his easy chair next to Janice. "You look deep in thought."

"Ah, thinking. Honey, here we are in our fifties, and time is passing like a whirlwind. I get up on Saturday, and before I know it, it's Saturday again. I looked at the basket this morning, thinking I just did it."

"Hmm? Yes, I get the same feeling now and then." Robert says. "Wanna take a trip somewhere? Plan for a Florida get-away?"

"No, I don't want to go anywhere. Was thinking about the boys. Was I asleep for the last four years? I had to stop myself from yelling down the basement: 'It's time for school.'"

"Come over here." Reaching for Janice's hand, he pulls her onto his lap, wrapping his arms around her. Janice slides her forehead next to his ear and kisses his neck. His hands continue caressing her arms as she softly sobs.

Janice finally tells him, "You should be heading to the office. How's it going, now that Peter's gone?"

Just a Matter of Time

"Good. Hey, invite the kids over Saturday. It's time for a cook-out, a campfire."

"This is Saturday," Janice says. "Got three couples to show around today." Janice slides off his lap and plants a kiss, "Thanks, Rob. Go. I'm fine."

"Knock it out of the park today," Robert tells her. "I'll be home around six."

"Good morning, Sandy," Robert says, entering her office.

"Dale called."

"Has Peter called?"

"Yes, to say hello from Hawaii."

"That's it?"

"Yep. Rob, you got a message you must read first."

"Thanks. Lawrance Wilkersen is coming over at nine, so send him in when he gets here."

Sitting at his desk, Robert reads the message from Ralph Carmichael, the Ag lawyer Peter was about to hire. He slowly rereads it to absorb the legal terms. He starts to make comments on the screen when the message disappears, and the screen goes blank, except for the white text at the bottom '*You cannot add to or delete any part of this document.*'

"Ah," Robert slaps his hand against the desk.

"Okay, Dale. What's up? Sandy said something about missing parts." Robert asks, looking at Dale's face on the tablet.

"Yeah. The shipment we got Thursday did not include the elbows for the sewer lines."

Looking at the shipping manifest, Robert says, "I'll pick 'em up at Ace. Everything else on schedule?"

"No problem. Whatever you said to the inspector, ah, he's been checking, well, like his eyes are closed. There's no interference from him at all."

"Good, keep the donuts handy. He's coming here this morning."

"Donuts?"

Robert's tablet rings once, and Janice's face appears before him. "Hi, Jan. How you doing? Peter made it to Hawaii."

"Rob, I'm scared. I'm sitting in the restroom now."

"Huh? What's going on?"

"I've been talking with these two guys. They're in the office now. I had to excuse myself to call. Rob, these two want our house. They're scary. He has a legal document showing that he is the owner of our house. It looks real. And," breathing hard and fast, Janice softly asks, "what have you heard about barcode implants?"

"Jan, what's your boss say about it? You say they've got the tattoo?"

"Yes. Steven read it and shrugged his shoulders, like, ah, there was nothing he could do. I am not going to let them in our house. But what'll I do?"

"Leave. Excuse yourself. Go home and lock the door. If they come, tell 'em we've had possession of the property for the last twenty-two years. Ah, if you need it, our deed is in the gun safe on the top shelf."

"Can't you come? You're better at this."

"Jan, I couldn't get there until after lunch. Got a meeting this morning, and then I need to take supplies to the worksite. Jan, it's going to be okay."

"But Rob!"

Hearing her heavy breathing, he says. "Call me if they show up, and I'll talk to them. Relax, Jan. They cannot force it upon us."

"Yeah, I'll call and let you do it."

"I'll be glad to stick it in their face. Bye, I love you." Janice's image disappears.

"Rob, I'm forwarding another message," Sandy tells him over the intercom. "Same sender as the earlier one. Mr. Wilkersen is here."

"Lawrance, how you doing? Have a seat. Coffee? Donut? No, ah, have a cinnamon roll. Jan made 'em."

Just a Matter of Time

"Sure, thanks," Lawrance replies.

Robert hands him a cup of coffee and places the fragrant roll on a paper plate on the desk. Robert sits back in his chair and bites another piece of his half-eaten roll, "Hmm? What is it about these things? I always feel better after having coffee and a roll this time of the morning."

"I hear you. My grandmother used to make these, and I'd be sure to beat my brother to the kitchen so that I could sneak one in my sack for school. Anyway, Rob, the project is progressing well. Dale has been so cooperative. I feel like I'm not doing my job. Dale is seeing things that need correcting and points them out to me. It's my job to find errors and short-cuts, but I'm not."

"Hmm? Sorry about that. You know that Peter is gone now, so I've made a few changes. Dale is spending all his time supervising. Before, he physically had to do some of the work. Hey, one call to Dale, and I'll tell him to let a few things slide so that you could report us."

"No, don't do be ridiculous. I'll handle it."

"If you say so, but I'd be glad to help in any way I can. We're there to satisfy the needs of the renters. You guys are paying us to do that." Robert slides his tablet off to the side.

"How's that new tab working out for you?" Lawrance asks.

"Oh, it's something else. The technology is well – hard to keep up. I thought the Earth map was something. We were on the road to the Canyon and needed a spot to park my camper, so Jan zoomed in, seeing there were some empty spots. The program allowed her to reserve a spot next to a creek that she liked. It blows my mind with what it can do. She also focused on the boys at the bottom of the Canyon."

"Dad gave me an iPhone when I was seven, and I thought that was great," Lawrance says.

"Now, on this tablet, the Real Earth Program is well . . . Frightening. Where is this technology taking us?"

"I don't know, Rob. There's talk that a hovering drone will do my job, and robots doing the construction. I could sit in the office using an app on my tab, controlling the drone to see through cement to check sewer joints."

Until the End of Time

"Hmm, sounds like we'll be sitting at home being entertained and watching the world go around. But, oh man, would I get fat."

"No, Rob. You're robotic servant would provide your food according to your bodily needs, and my app would let me watch you eat your sandwich."

"Huh?" Changing the subject as Sandy recommended, Robert says, "I enjoy getting out in the woods, waiting for a deer to bring home. Is that going to be done by robots too?"

"Could be to get rid of our guns. I got my license and permit already. A buddy and I plan on going north to the Umatilla National Forest later this fall."

"Oh, I love that area. I got an elk up there last year."

"Hey, why don't you come along with us?" Lawrance suggests.

"I'm not sure that's a good idea. You're inspecting my work. Your supervisors would, ah, possibly think you're cooperating rather than overseeing."

"Forget about them. What I do on my time is none of their business."

"Nah, I better not. But, oh, It's tempting. But, Lawrance, they could be watching us together."

"I've got a way to fog our faces. Think about it. I'd have no problem with it."

"What's your friend do?"

"He runs the lodge over by Cove, so he's very familiar with the area."

"No?" Robert exclaims. "My sons were married in that lodge."

"Those were yours? He told me about a very unusual wedding about a month ago. Rob, you gotta go with us now."

"I'll think about it, but if I suspect you'll get into trouble, I couldn't," Robert says as he stands. "I need to get going. Thanks for coming over this morning. I'll think about it and let you know. You're welcome here anytime." Robert looks down at his tab and says, "Right now, the screen shows me that your toenails need to be trimmed."

"Very funny."

Just a Matter of Time

"Did it help?" Sandy asks Robert entering her office.

"How did you do it?"

"You'd be surprised. The first time you went hunting was with a bow and arrow outside Boulder when you were twelve. You got a rabbit and felt like you got a bear."

"Huh? How'd you know that? I told you!"

"No, you didn't."

"I must have. That kind of information is not available online."

"Ha! Don't ask."

"Okay, smarty pants. Look up this name and tell me what you find." Robert writes the man's name on a notepad. He leaves Sandy's office to go to the restroom, and then back to his office to call Dale.

"Rob," Sandy says, entering his office. "Be careful with these two. One is from the IRS, and the other is with the FBI."

"Bull. Give it to me straight."

"Gads, you're hard. Can't get a thing past you, can I?"

'No, and when you were thirteen, you and . . ."

"Oh, hush," Sandy interrupts. "All right, one of them is a grandson of the old man who sold you the house. He died a few years ago, leaving his grandson several rental homes in the area. The grandson recently found the deed to your house. He believes it's still good, so he came to take possession. The guy Janice is talking to is my cousin. We haven't been in contact with each other for years."

"We bought your great uncle's house?"

"Yes, you did," Sandy says. "Last time I saw him was when I was eight. But now, his grandson is one of those supporting chipping and barcoding. I posted a picture of him to your tab if you do see him."

Thanking her, Robert tells her to send the picture to Jan and add a note explaining it all. "I gotta go. Be at the site."

Until the End of Time

"Dale, they're in the trunk," Robert says as he enters the portable office.

"Thanks, Rob, but I could've got 'em," Dale replies, looking up from the large screen on the table displaying the details of the new buildings that replace the old run-down airstrip. "The blocks are shipped, right?"

"They said they'd be here Thursday, and the first load of lumber is also on the way."

"Great. Peter, how's he doing?"

"Sandy said he called this morning to say hi from Hawaii."

"So, Peter has officially retired, and that gives you the permission of ownership."

Robert raises his voice, "Yes, it does, so, get to work, or I'll find someone else to do it."

"Yeah, now you sound like Peter," Dale retorts.

Robert opens his tab to show Dale a picture. "Dale, have you ever seen or heard of this guy?" His wide-brimmed hat shadows his eyes and the barely discernible tattoo between his streaks of hair falling over his forehead.

"Let's see," Dale mutters, leaning in closer to see the name on his Forest Ranger Uniform.

"Ah, yes, last year, he guided my scout troop on a tour of the Hells Canyon Recreation Area. Why do you ask?"

"He's Sandy's cousin. She lost contact with him years ago."

"So?"

"Curious, that's all. He supports the bar coding of us."

"How was the meeting with Lawrance?" Dale asks.

"No problem. I told him you'd leave a few things for him to find. Dale, I gotta go. Need to check with a friend about attending the city council meeting this afternoon."

"Let 'em have it," Dale says.

Robert signals the company van. He speaks to the screen, "Home." He slides his finger across the tablet, and the face of Tom appears. "Tom, I can get to the meeting today. Could you make it?"

Just a Matter of Time

"Yeah, sure. See you there. Starts at three?"

"Jan, I'm here," Robert hollers.

"Thank you, thank you," Janice rushes into his arms. "What a day!"

"Did you get the message from Sandy?"

"Yes. Showed it to 'em. Our deed too. They mumbled about coming back and took off." Janice breathes a sigh of relief. "I was about to go back to the office when you drove up."

"Go then," Robert says, "I need to clean-up a bit. Tom and I are going to the city council meeting."

"Good," Janice replies. "You'll be home by six, right?"

"Should be. If you don't mind, I'll ask Tom and Linda to join us."

"Yes, that's fine," Janice says. "Did a search on this next couple, and they look legit. Could be a big sale today," she then tells Robert that the kids would be here in time for dinner. Janice plants a kiss on his lips. "Love you."

"Are you ready?" Tom asks Robert as they meet in the parking lot of City Hall.

"Where are the girls?" Robert asks. "I thought they were coming with signs."

"I texted them after you called, but they expected the meeting to be on Tuesday."

"Oh, well. Hey," Robert asks, "Why don't you and Linda come over this evening? Having a barbeque, and the newlyweds will be there. Then possibly a campfire."

"Ah, what time?"

"Sixish."

Until the End of Time

"I'll check with Linda," Tom replies. "Rob, that wedding was fantastic. The performance the girls put on was, well, Linda wants a video of it to give our granddaughters."

"It was their idea. Turned out well, didn't it?"

"I'm sure Linda will be excited, but I'll let you know for sure."

"Good. Now let's let 'em have it," Robert says. They approach the double sliding doors. A beeper goes off when they enter the first set of doors. Through a small window, a police officer tells them, "No electronic devices allowed in the building. Return them to your vehicle, please."

Robert turns to leave the tablet and his watch in the car.

"Okay, how's this?" Robert raises his arms in front of the officer, and the second set of doors open. At the desk outside the chambers, Tom and Robert slide their fingers over the screen, and the chamber doors open.

"I don't see your names on the list," the lady at the desk replies to Robert's question. "You did not request permission to speak. That must be submitted ten days before the meeting."

"Huh?" Robert asks. "Ten days!"

"I did not see that on the city web," Tom says.

"Yes, sir, it's there. Been doing it this way for years," she replies.

"Are we allowed to stay and watch? Or do we, oops!" Robert cuts himself off from his thought of needing a permit to watch.

"Sure. Go on in."

They slowly pace their steps looking at the small attendance, several police officers, two firemen, half-dozen ladies in hijabs, a few farmers, and some others. Several men in shirts with BB Giants emblazed across the back are chatting with three of the council members in their blue suits.

"Looks like a college classroom," Robert whispers to Tom, as they select seats in the second row, two steps up on the left side of the main aisle.

Two gavel knocks are heard from the long counter, "Come to order, please. Let's all stand and recite the city banner of allegiance."

Just a Matter of Time

"Oh my," Robert says as he and Tom stroll to their cars after the two-hour meeting. "I don't know what I expected, but this stuff the city has implemented, and planning is, well, gads, I wanna move. We're now required to post our work hours inside the package box?"

Tom replies, "Well, at least they said something about holding back on the drone surveillance. And changing the limits on home meetings."

"Yeah, right," Robert says. "Come on down and get permission, be inspected, and if they feel like it, they'll issue the permit to be displayed in front of the house a week before the meeting. The drones? Yeah, we can get a part-time job watching what the drones are seeing. Sounds like fun. I could watch you and Linda."

"That UN order about the bar codes," Tom says softly as a couple walk past. "I heard rumblings about it being done overseas and in our big cities, but here? So soon?"

"Well, we already can't buy anything without our fingerprints," Robert says. He exhales deeply as they near their cars. "Tom, let's shake the dust off our shoes and go home. Time to relax. You're coming tonight, right?"

THIRTY-SIX

Janice stands on the deck, looking at Linda on the tablet, "No, you don't need to bring anything."

Linda replies, "I've had plenty of time to make apple pies, so we're bringing 'em, like it or not. See ya."

Janice lays the tablet on the table and pushes the ignition button to warm the grill. The sound of the drones breaks through the breeze. She steps to the edge of the deck, watching Jimmy's drone land on the cross painted on the grass. Johnathon guides his drone to land at the other mark. The whirling rotors slowly stop. The boys open the doors, step out, and pull their seats forward to let their wives slide out.

"You guys are early," Janice yells.

"Beat you again, bro," Jimmy chides, as the girls trot to greet Janice.

"Thank you," Julia says, handing a sack to Janice, "an apple pie."

Sammy rushes into Janice's arms. "Thanks for the video. My parents love it." She hands Janice a red rose petal tied to a bottle of wine. "The coach suggested it."

"Did you see us flying like a roller coaster?" Julia asks.

"Roller coaster? No!" Janice replies. "And probably better that I didn't. Guys! Please! Don't get reckless. It's not a toy!"

"Okay, mom. But . . ." Jimmy says.

"No buts. Now, I need two more chairs, and the table leaves up from the basement."

"Sure," Jimmy says. He pulls Julia's hand, "Come on, play you a game." Jimmy, Johnathon, Sammy, and Julia rush to the basement. They get their favorite sticks, chalk the tips, and set the balls up.

Just a Matter of Time

"Eight-ball, we got the solids," Johnathon says.

"Girls first!" Julia exclaims.

"Hey, guys, the chairs and leaves!" Janice calls from the top of the stairs.

"John!" Jimmy says, pushing him off balance.

"Oh, you're going to get it," Johnathon replies. He opens the closet door and removes two twelve-inch leaves. He slides them over Jimmy's foot. "I got these. You get the chairs."

In the dining room, they finally push the table tops together.

"Okay?" Jimmy asks.

"Thanks. Leave the door open," Janice tells them, as they head back down the stairs.

"Your turn, Jim," Sammy says, as the boys reach the bottom steps.

Jimmy takes his cue stick, lines up, aims the white ball at the eight-ball. He changes his aim to get the nine-ball next to it. He pulls the stick back and pushes forward, watching the nine go into the corner pocket after it bounced off another.

With two large spoons, Janice is tossing the salad when the doorbell rings. "Arlene, come on in, door's open," Janice hollers, after seeing the face of her neighbor on the monitor.

"Hello, Jan," Arlene says, entering the kitchen.

"When you get back?" Janice asks.

"Last night. You're expecting company?" Arlene says.

"Linda," Janice answers. "How's the trip? The newlyweds are in the basement."

"Newlyweds? The boys got married?"

"Yes, they did. Four ceremonies."

"Huh?"

"Yeah. I'll brief you on it later. How'd you like Alaska?"

Until the End of Time

"Oh, Jan, that Yukon River appeared to have turned red after that blast. But, oh, it's great to be home and feel safe again. I see you're busy. So ah, perhaps we could have lunch sometime soon."

"Yes, let's do it. Monday?"

"Good, I'm free. Text me in the morning." Arlene leaves.

"Hey, guys," Robert shouts down the basement, "your mother needs some help."

"Never mind," Janice yells loud enough to cancel Robert's demand. "I'm fine, Rob," Janice replies. "I made an apple pie. Linda is bringing two, and Julia gave me another. Think that's enough?"

"Arlene and Charlie got home last night," Janice tells him. "Said they experienced that blast in Alaska. I'll get more details over lunch on Monday. But it sounded like it was a real black-out."

"You didn't invite them over, did you?"

"No. Why do you ask?"

"Oh, it's that stupid limit of seven. Anyway, Tom will be dropping Linda off. But he still wants to pop in for a few minutes and say hi to the kids, while Linda sits in the car. What can I do?" Robert asks.

"The grill is ready. The ribs are ready."

"Have the kids said anything about those marriage coach visits?"

Janice avoids the question as she reaches for the pan of ribs.

"Well, did they? Jim said something the other day. Anything new?"

"Leave it be. Please! Let's relax and enjoy the evening."

Robert removes the lid. His finger swipes a rib. "Umm–good." He takes the pan to the deck, sets it alongside the smoker, and forks the ribs onto the grill. The flames rise as the juices drip onto the burner. He breathes in the sweet aroma.

"Here you are," Linda says, as she opens the door to the deck.

"Linda," Janice rushes to embrace her good friend. "How are ya?"

"Good. I see that the boys are enjoying themselves."

Just a Matter of Time

"Ah, yes, they are. Coffee?" Janice asks.

"Yes, thanks. Is there any way I could get a copy of those wedding videos?" Linda asks. "I want to give it to our granddaughters."

"Sure, of course. I'll zip it to you."

"From what I observed of the girls. I suspect they went all out."

"Oh, yes," Janice says. "At Sammy's, the girls rode horses through the streets. The entire town of 250 lined the streets and attended the ceremony in the local park."

"No! How did they get permission for all that?"

"Because of their attendance at that Canyon Project," Robert says. "The Directors were recording it all. They wanted to show the administrators how successful the project turned out this year."

"The kids can tell you more over dinner," Janice says. "Come, help me get everything ready." Janice gets up and leads Linda back into the house.

Robert raises the hood and turns the ribs.

"That looks good," Jimmy says, as he and Johnathon join him on the deck.

"So, how's the work at the museum going?" Robert asks. "And what's this deal about marriage coaches?"

"Go ahead, Jim, you discovered it," Johnathon says.

Jimmy raises his thumb, pointing it at the camera over the deck. They move to the fire pit. Gathering twigs and some split logs, they make it look like they're getting ready to start the fire. "Dad," Jimmy softly says. "I was assigned to straighten and rake up the area around the site. I was raking everything down the slope toward the stream when the rake hit something solid. I stopped. There was this metal covering. I pulled on it, and it opened to a tunnel. I peered into the darkness. But I didn't have a light, so I replaced the lid, covered it back up, and told John about it."

"Dad," Johnathon says. "There are thousands of those paper books in there. It's like those pictures we've seen."

"Does anyone else know what you found?" Robert asks.

267

Until the End of Time

Jimmy answers, "Julia and Sammy."

"What do you think you should do?"

"Keep it between us. I don't feel good about informing the supervisor."

"I agree," Robert says. "What kind of books?"

"Hardcovers. Paperbacks. History books. Names I've never heard of before, like Aristotle, Durant, and Huxley, and oh, thousands more. I brought one home by C.S. Lewis."

"Jim, you know what they'll do if they find that book in your possession. But I'd sure like to explore that cave with you. Do you think that all this might be part of the Museum's plan?"

"Nothing's been said along those lines."

"Guys, unless it's made public by the Directors, there's a reason why it's kept secret all these years. Again, let's keep this to ourselves, and somehow let's find the time for me to explore it with you. Ah, dinner may be ready. We'll have a campfire later and possibly play a game. And I want to hear more about these marriage coaches."

"We've got a meeting next week with the State counselors," Johnathon says.

During the meal, Linda kept asking about the Canyon Project, what their daily chores were, what it felt like when the boys first met the girls. "It's unbelievable, this technology now," Linda says. "The government knows everything about everyone, all our likes, and dislikes, our personal preferences, the clothes we like, the food we eat, and the desserts that we fancy. It's all recorded on every purchase we make."

"Hey, enough of that," Janice says. "Let's sit around the campfire and enjoy the evening. Rob, you and the boys, get the fire going. We'll bring the pies and the games out."

Linda says, "Tom is outside. He wants to come in for a bit, so I must go. Thanks for a wonderful meal and chat. Girls, take care, and God's blessings on you all." She pulls each of them in for a hug. "See you all again soon."

"Linda, come over tomorrow afternoon and give me a hand in the garden," Janice says.

"Sure. Love to."

Just a Matter of Time

Linda leaves through the front door. Janice leads Tom to the fire-pit. For ten minutes or so, Tom and the girls trade stories over slices of apple pie, and finally, he asks the twins. "How soon will you start construction on your houses?"

"We've received the licenses and permits," Johnathon answers, "so possibly next week sometime, if dad can get the crew ready."

"You're the crew," Robert says. "The backhoe will be there next Saturday."

"Great," Julia says. "That was part of my training at the Earth Academy."

"You can operate a backhoe?" Tom asks.

"Sure, press the dig button, the lift button, turn button, and dump. Easy."

Tom says, "Well, I better go. It's been great. Linda's waiting. Thanks."

As Tom disappears around the side of the house, Jimmy says, "I think we all like the challenges of chess. Dad, you and mom can play a game, and we'll be right next to you. Julia and I against John and Sammy."

Jim goes in to get a couple of lanterns to light the table.

Looking at Robert, Julia says, "yeah, I can lean over and give you advice."

An hour or so later, Janice takes her eyes off the chess board after moving her Queen into position. "You want a refill, Rob?" She asks.

"Sure, thanks. Nice move, Jan."

"It's your move," Robert says, leaning back, taking sips of coffee.

Janice pushes her hair back over her ears, considering the next move. She moves a Pawn two-spaces forward, putting the pressure back on Robert.

Suddenly, everything shakes. The chess boards rumble. The tables move, causing the lanterns and pieces of the game to fall to the ground. They all reach out to grab hold. The sky turns to pitch dark. No moon, no stars. It's darker than an indoor closet.

"What?" Robert exclaims. He raises his hands to check his eyes, his forehead feeling for something that might have suddenly shut down his ability to see. "Jan, you okay?"

In the blink of an eye, the entire sky from the eastern horizon to the west, emits rainbow-colored lightning from the northern clouds across the midnight sky to a volcanic ball of fire in the southern sky, while the ground continuously rumbles.

Two lovely eye-shaped spots turn the sky brilliant white, illuminating the atmosphere, magnifying the transparent sky. Ear shattering joyful shouts, followed by a single long blast of a trumpet, penetrate the atmosphere. Pebbles of light rise from the ground. Thousands of those lights streak up to meet the eyes. Streaks of lighting move from the ground up, splitting the sky open to a trailblazing path of reflecting diamonds, rubies, and arched golden candles lighting the narrow path to an open book in the hands of Jesus.

"Welcome Home!"

Just a Matter of Time

Robert and Janice delightfully skip along an emerald path singing songs of praise.

"Hey, Noah."

"Welcome, Robert. Yes, and no! I knew it'd be just a matter of time."

Janice continues dancing toward the beginning.

"Janice Amwestson," Eve says. "Perhaps, if you had walked in my footsteps, you would have done the same."

Until the End of Time

The End of Time.

About the Author.

Arnold Kropp

Back in the days when Arnold was a kid growing up in south Chicago, he freely roamed around the neighborhood after school. Arnold learned to be a writer in Germany, where the Army transferred him after Morse Code training. The Army transformed Arnold's life, as did embracing Christianity. It stimulated his need to write and create new worlds, as he did in his anthology "Rummagings," and his creative non-fiction work, "The School Bus Then and Now." Arnold also has three previously self-published novels. Mr. Kropp's works can be found on Amazon, in both hard copy and eBook.

Until the End of Time